Advance Praise for *THE HOLLYWOOD FIX*

"*The Hollywood Fix* is a dazzling romp replete with intrigue and glamour set in Hollywood's Golden Age. Richard Kirshenbaum's signature wit and style is on display in this masterful telling of the PR man in charge of the reputations of the studio bosses and stars. At turns suspenseful, emotional, and compelling. Get ready for the glitz, and all that's behind the shimmer. No one writes about show business like Kirshenbaum—buckle up!"

—Adriana Trigiani, *New York Times* bestselling author of *The View from Lake Como*

"Not since *What Makes Sammy Run* and *The Day of The Locust* has there been such a revealing and intriguing novel about Hollywood's golden age. A page turner so sexy and spellbinding it's sure to make a great series."

—Jim Wiatt, former CEO of The William Morris Agency

"I couldn't put down *The Hollywood Fix,* the best insider novel about Hollywood since *What Makes Sammy Run*. Cinematic in scope and storytelling, it will be a hit in any format."

—Bill Gerber, Academy Award nominated-producer for *A Star Is Born*

"A dazzling, razor-sharp portrait of Hollywood's glittering façade—and the ruthless machinery grinding beneath it. *The Hollywood Fix* crackles with wit, intrigue, and unflinching honesty. Kirshenbaum lifts the velvet curtain on the Golden Age of show business and its modern echoes, delivering a page-turner that is equal parts glamorous, suspenseful, and deeply human. A must-read for anyone who's ever wondered what really happens behind the flashbulbs."

—Bill Robinson, president
of James Patterson Entertainment

Also by Richard Kirshenbaum

North Bay Road
Rouge

The Hollywood Fix

THE DIRTY BUSINESS
OF KEEPING THE STARS
SHINY AND CLEAN.

RICHARD KIRSHENBAUM

A POST HILL PRESS BOOK
ISBN: 979-8-89565-284-8
ISBN (eBook): 979-8-89565-285-5

Cover design by Chris Cereda

This book, as well as any other Post Hill Press publications, may be purchased in bulk quantities at a special discounted rate. Contact orders@posthillpress.com for more information.

Post Hill Press
New York • Nashville
posthillpress.com

Published in the United States of America
1 2 3 4 5 6 7 8 9 10

To my stars; Dana, Georgia, Talia and Lucas.
May you always continue to shine.

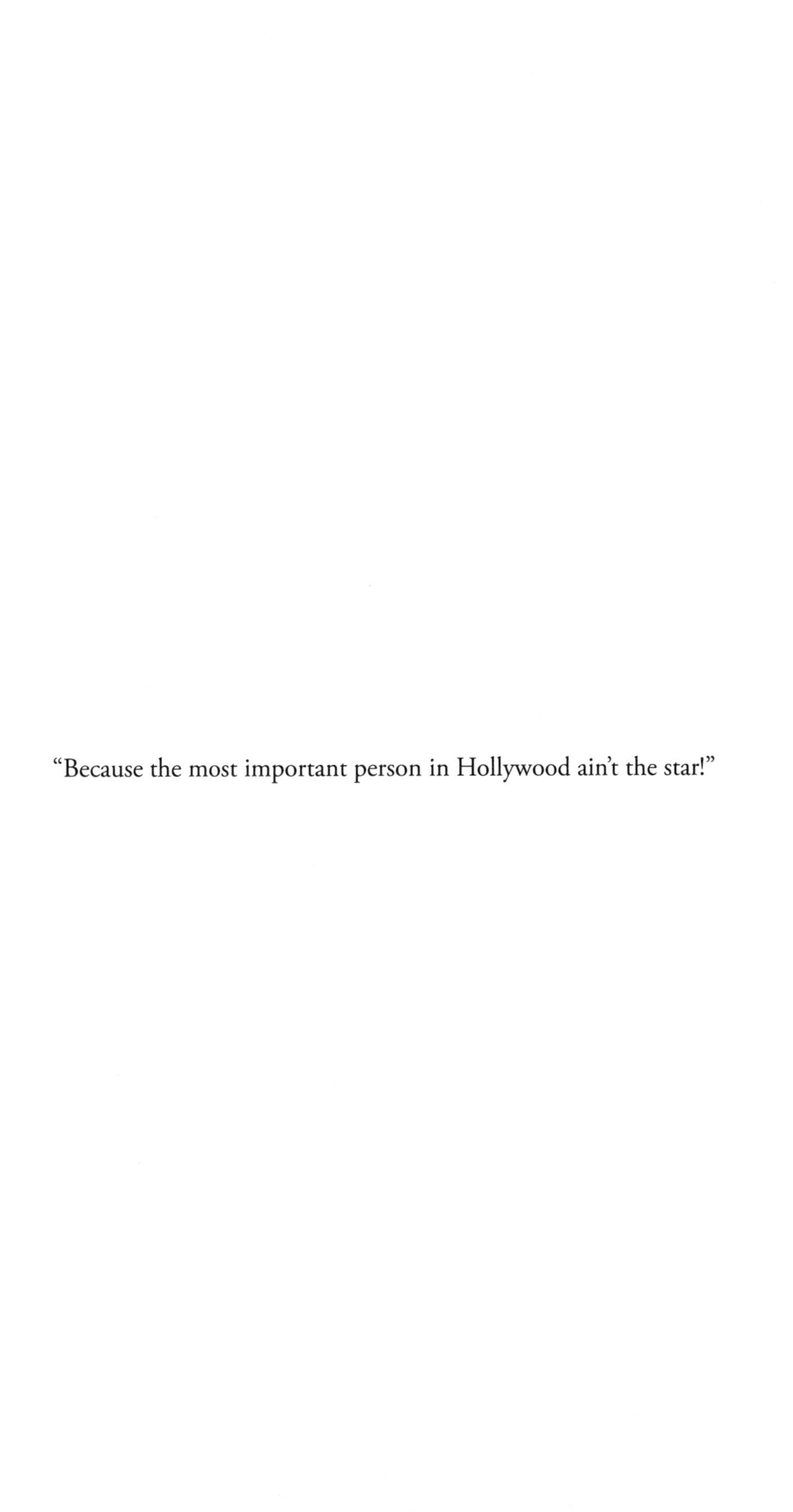

"Because the most important person in Hollywood ain't the star!"

Prologue

Barston Maddox
Los Angeles
1983

I remember the indelible evening as if it were merely yesterday—even though, in reality, it was more than thirty years ago. It does not appear in my mind in flashbacks but as celluloid that I can rewind and fast forward.

Rewind.

The white hot carnival lights of Hollywood Boulevard beckoned for the 1955 Oscars, turning the wide avenue into a veritable street arcade replete with attractions—only tonight, a stuffed animal, goldfish, and overzealous carnies would not do. Despite the odds, equivalent to a ring toss, the evening had special meaning for me. It was a culmination of a bumpy if not buoyant career and the ingenious manipulations I had come to call "the studio fix."

At the time, I was still in the thick of it, but detached enough to view the proceedings slightly from afar; the trick was to be *in it* and to be *out of it* at the same time and to see it all through the lens the way in which the public did. If there was an award for what I did, I would have been nominated too, but I wasn't the one up for a statuette that evening; my client was. And that was for "Best Actor."

I am what they call in polite circles a Hollywood press agent, or I was. That term, however, is an oversimplification of a complex series of daily decisions, outrageous ideas, and, most importantly, artful deceptions to achieve a perfect result—a virginal dream, if you will. What I have seen and done in my career is akin to any great spy novel, now all locked away in the vault of my brain, and, after all these years, finally seeing daylight. And it's not just the myriad marketing campaigns I gave birth to, to sell a picture or set up an *at-home* magazine spread to launch a starlet's new career or current film. It's what I had to do to *kill things*—to keep stories under wraps in the press to keep Hollywood dreams sparkling and pearly white. The truth, however, was a seedy gray or, to quote another great star, Tallulah Bankhead, "I'm as pure as the driven slush."

Getting back to that auspicious night, I recall the humid air crackled with invisible electricity, strung like festival lights at an Italian bakery as the gleaming cars pulled into view depositing the town's brightest stars. Here was Bing Crosby, the sylph-like Audrey Hepburn, and the magnificent Grace Kelly, who would, in an upset, take home the prize for "Best Actress" over Judy Garland in *A Star is Born.* Lacquered heads craned to take in another stunning sight: Dorothy Dandridge, the first African American actress to be nominated in that category for *Carmen Jones.*

Finally, after checking my trusty Hamilton a few times with slight anxiety, I breathed a sigh of relief as the familiar chauffeur-driven Rolls Royce Silver Dawn came into view, seamlessly gliding into line. He had always had a Rolls and a driver; it was stipulated in his contract, and from the earliest days the studio was happy to pay for it as it was part of his fulfilling my PR strategy: the Aristocratic Brit and his Rolls.

The car idled purposely, bringing arguably the world's most famous couple directly in front of RKO's Pantages Theatre. The onyx block letters from above the art deco marquis boldly proclaimed "The 27th Academy Awards." I had been there hours earlier, readying myself and the handlers for this exact moment and for *him.* Not bad for a small-town kid from South Dakota to be in charge of the details large and small!

The burly chauffeur attired in livery opened the car door to help the buxom sex symbol exit the car in a halo of white mink, sequins and diamonds. I had arranged months earlier for the studio designer, Jean Claude, to create the masterpiece of design for her, and he triumphed by creating a nude gown with an intricate girdle, overlaid with flesh toned chiffon, emblazoned with thousands of tiny platinum rhinestones to make it appear as though she were wearing *nothing*, yet everything. The gown created a false sense of modesty only through the placement of the infinitesimal stones. As the sparkling apparition appeared, a migrating roar rippled in a wave crashing to shore. She knew her voluptuous body well enough that she pretended to lean down in order to avoid contact with the ceiling of the car, and with her vanilla hair and her spangle-encased décolletage, she thrust her luminous chest forward, rising onto the red carpet. It was an artform, *chest first.*

The crowd went wild as she turned and extended a satin gloved hand for *him,* as I had planned for dramatic effect. After all, it was the 1950s, and a lady waiting for *the man* was newsworthy. Her stack of diamond bracelets, which he had gifted her at my suggestion, sparkled under the heat and glare of the klieg lights. The roar went up again as the man of the hour, Duke Drake, emerged bracing for the pop of the attending paparazzi's artillery. He beamed his famous, dazzling smile, highlighting his canyon-like cleft chin, then smoothing the form-fitting tux that had been poured onto his legendary, mannequin-like six-foot-four frame.

It was said of Duke that "every woman wanted to be *with* him, and every man wanted to *be* him." I had coined *that* phrase myself for his hit movie *She Man* opposite Mae West when he was a supporting actor, the handsome younger foil for aging female stars. Duke took his wife's gloved hand, and they artfully started their procession and made their way through the throng of celebrities, studio brass, and press, accepting congratulations from the reigning players, the producers, agents, managers, and directors. Before entering the press line, I handed him a white silk pocket square should he need to dab his glistening forehead under the harsh lights. Advanced thinking was a signature of my work.

He was met with a chorus of "Congrats Duke!" and "You're going to win tonight!" It was all anyone could hear as he had the favored odds. I was on hand in a rented tuxedo and directed him to have a photo taken with our boss, the legendary Solomon Myers: the most important studio head in town and his steely wife, Freyda. It was said that Freyda was the *president of the president* which by default, made her the most powerful person in Hollywood. Myers seemed unusually relaxed that evening, swimming in his ill-fitting tux despite his ever-present nervous energy and gleefully clapped his asset, Duke, on his back as they took their photos and interviews with archrival columnists Hedda Hopper and Louella Parsons, the leaders of the press corps.

"Congratulations, Solly. You have the knack for picking a winner." Hedda acknowledged the man who had discovered and created this British phenomenon.

"You're a shoo-in, Duke." Hedda lifted the black net veil of her signature couture hat and bestowed a regal kiss. "Remember our exclusive if you win." She staked her territory like a predator. "And we must have *both* Drakes on the radio show."

"Of course, Hedda, how could I *ever* forget?" Duke nodded amiably, an old hand at buttering up the press.

"I'll call you to set it up, Hedda." I inserted myself in the dance as if he had already won. That was my job, to parse out the interviews, the payback, the trading of stars. It was all in a night's work. I had to hand it to Duke; I had met him when he first arrived in Hollywood, and his smile was his mask—always his greatest defense—but tonight, it was brilliant and highlighted his looks, which had only burnished with age. He was now acknowledged as *the* bona fide leading man in town, and that had been no small feat for him…and for yours truly.

After the madness of the press corps and the thundering fans, it was time for the nominees and the audience to take their seats and face the outcome. To nurse the cruelty of the loss or relish the ecstasy of the win. The famous and the fallen, the newly anointed, and those on a downward spiral, the bedecked and bejeweled players all made their way to the plush seats in professional order. The Drakes were given the front row, reserved for the nominees and Hollywood royalty. I had arranged it with the Academy to place Duke on the outer left center aisle—with no one to his left—should he win and need a clear path to the stage.

"You look magnificent, my dear." Duke observed his famous wife as he led her into the front row by the gloved elbow.

"Thanks." She cracked her gum in plebian yet distinctive fashion, part of her charm and allure. "I'll never be nominated or win an Oscar in this damn town, that's for sure." The platinum blonde shrugged, her monumental cleavage jiggling. "But my panty girdle should win…for best *uplift*!" She checked her décolletage. "Oh, Duke, did ya ever think?"

She turned and admired her handsome husband. Theirs had been a wonderful, successful union, and they both knew it; the perfect match as industry wags commented on the powerhouse duo. "I know that Duke Jr. is going to be so proud, too. I told Maria he is allowed to stay up and watch the telecast." She smiled at the thought of their adorable platinum haired three-year-old boy in his footie pajamas, sitting in front of the black-and-white TV set, the nanny adjusting the antenna.

She opened up her gold woven minaudière, retrieving a 14K lipstick case and viewing herself in the bag's interior oblong mirror as she applied a fresh coat. Then, she adjusted her hairstyle, which needed no adjusting—after all, it was Duke's night and, as Mrs. Duke Drake, she knew all eyes would be upon them. At forty, Duke smoothed his glossy hair, the encroaching streaks of gray at the temples rendering him formidable. His film, *Robber of the Riviera*, had leapt from the screen and instantly became a Hollywood classic. Duke played the continental jewel thief who fleeces continental heiress Mirielle Montaigne, all shot in technicolor in the glamour of Monte Carlo. Their on-screen chemistry and sophisticated banter was so rare that I had planted a story with Louella, suggesting that they might have had an affair since they'd been spotted in a sports car exiting a hotel on the Corniche. The role had been written for Duke and few were surprised by the nomination.

After many lesser awards, Bette Davis emerged, her frenetic energy commanding the stage in a jeweled turban, and announced the nominees and the winner with her distinctive delivery. Bette may not have been a typical beauty, but she had already won the top award and had also been nominated for her role as Margo Channing in *All About Eve.* Her presentation of the award among actors was akin to the Queen's Knighthood ceremony.

"And this year's best actor award goes to…" She purposely paused and opened the envelope, drawing it out dramatically as only Bette could. "My very good friend, Duke…" She smiled wryly. "Duke Drake!"

I could see he was experiencing *it.* I was told it was a feeling unlike any other from those who had won, and there weren't many. I could see the realization setting in, the deafening applause, the trancelike walk to the podium, kissing Bette, receiving and holding up the gold statuette, which he later told me was heavier than he anticipated. He knew his life would change forever now that he was officially part of Hollywood's firmament. He held the statue in victory as he dutifully thanked Myers and SGM Studios. When he thanked yours truly, I must admit had a tear in my eye. And then, in a touching tribute to his wife and three-year-old-son, Duke Jr., "who needs to go to bed *now,*" he wagged his finger at the cameras with laughter in classic Duke Drake charm. America was enthralled by the grainy, black-and-white telecast; Duke represented the masculine ideal: the perfect combination of man's man, family man, all with the underlying cache of the world's most urbane ladies' man.

I distinctly recall later an evening of dancing, dining, and celebrating at Romanoff's where I nearly spilled a drink on Grace Kelly's aqua evening gown. After making the rounds, I summoned the car in advance to make our way back to Drake Manor. Theirs was a palatial Tudor pile nestled high on a crest in tony Bel-Air, and I accompanied them by sitting on the jump seat, helping them relish the win while executing a few menial tasks which were not above me. Mrs. Drake reached over and examined the iconic statuette lifted against her cleavage.

"I never thought I'd see one of these firsthand. Can we use it as a doorstop?" Duke laughed out loud at the thought and her comic delivery.

"I'm going to put that on my stationery. *Mrs. Academy Award!*" She giggled in her breathy tone. "Duke, I'm so proud of you." He reached over and kissed her.

"Except," she groaned, "for these damn heels. I can't wait to get out of this girdle."

"Well, you looked more beautiful than humanly possible. I know you have close-ups tomorrow." His eyes sparkled at her.

"They shaved another half hour off my call time now that I turned thirty-nine," she sighed, wistfully looking out the window. "The *end* is near." She blinked a jaundiced eye.

"You're at the top of your game, and you know it." He whistled.

"You are both number one and two box office stars. Anyone in this town would take those odds," I offered glibly from the opposing seat. "And now with the Oscar win…"

Once the driver navigated the ornate gates and impressive drive, pulling into the capacious car park, both exited the Rolls and walked inside Drake Manor as I followed, carrying her mink stole. There were times I was a PR whiz and times I was also a glorified errand boy, but I didn't mind. The staff lined the entry hall with an ovation, which he accepted graciously, especially from old Mary, the cook; he signed her autograph book with flourish. He was more than happy to do so, always the English gentleman.

He took his wife's hand and they walked up the grand, carved staircase together to their boy's room. She had taken off her glittering pumps and left them stranded in the foyer for the help to pick up. She had always been lazy and threw her things everywhere in a haphazard manner, which the staff scooped up and silently put back into place. Things meant everything and nothing to her.

I waited in the hallway and peered in as they entered the little boy's room and saw their towheaded son sleeping on a child-sized bed, having only recently graduated from a crib. Duke lightly kissed him on the crown of his head so as not to wake him. I remember being touched to be close enough to see this lovely domestic sight on such an auspicious evening.

"He was so proud of his daddy," Maria, the nanny, said, beaming. They held hands as they gazed at their beautiful boy. Back in their bedroom suite, Duke motioned from behind, eventually placing the Oscar on the carved fireplace mantel.

"I want to keep it there…or maybe here," he said, deciding on the spot. "So I can see it the moment I wake up in the morning."

"Perfect," I said out loud.

"Would you help me out of this contraption?" Mrs. Drake turned to me as I started unhooking the gown and the underlying bodice.

Duke kissed her neck while I struggled with her hook and eyes of the fitted gown from behind.

"You are divine," he added, smiling.

She turned to me, and I was close enough to smell the distinctive Fracas Eau de Parfum. "Drop him off for me?" She turned sideways, covering her voluminous breasts with her hands and crook in her arm. I knew I was lucky, but I had seen it all before.

"I'll have the car take you home afterward," Duke offered. "You're part of this!" He held up the statuette. "And us."

"Dinner tomorrow at Chasen's?" he offered to his wife.

"Perfect," she replied, nodding.

"I'll make the reservation." I made a mental note. "Okay for Hedda to send a photographer?"

"Sure, why not?" They both agreed.

"My winner!" She walked up to him and played with his lapel suggestively, and he kissed her one last time before he bounded out of the room with nervous energy.

Duke enthusiastically led the way down the grand staircase of the English revival style castle, passing an original suit of armor, and walking out of the mansion into the waiting car. I followed as his liquid shadow.

"Sit there." Duke offered me the seat next to him. "You, my friend, are a gem. I want you to know how much I—we—appreciate all of it." His eyes misted. "All of it!"

"That means a lot," I replied. He pumped my hand and saw the glistening tear. That he was appreciative meant the world to yours truly; after all, much of my career had gone into crafting his perfect image, all the crazy "fixes" that had gone into making Duke Drake…Duke Drake. The Rolls Royce made its way down Sunset to a different part of town…to Los Feliz. It was a little less tony, a bit grittier, and yet, the mansions in the hills were still imposing though from an earlier era.

The car hummed as it climbed up as it did most evenings, and the looming Mediterranean mansion was a familiar sight entering the iron gates and into the car park.

The house was eerily dark, and Duke looked a bit surprised.

I had, of course, been privy to all and carried his evening coat and white silk scarf behind him as he strode through the double mahogany doors. He seemed perplexed as he entered the darkened entrance gallery.

"Anyone home?" he called out in his distinctive accent. Just then, the lights flew on with cries of surprise and the flash of glitter, streamers, and jazzy music. A sea parted, and a handsome older man emerged from the center of the room and beamed his signature smile, embracing Duke in the folds of his silk robe before the long and smoldering kiss to raucous applause. It was an incredible sight for sure.

Then, as things came into focus, I saw that the party he planned was what I imagined; everyone was naked or nearly so, the waiters all holding silver trays of Champagne flutes in their bow ties and athletic supporters. The boys—smooth surfers and hairy, barrel-chested bodybuilders—all crowded around Duke, congratulating him. Gorge Lamont motioned me over and clapped me on the shoulder, and anyone who saw him would have taken him for his own screen image of the all-American football player, a bit older and more distinguished, his blonde silky locks now shot with grey.

"Stay for a drink?" He winked. The festivities were just beginning, and naked men, actors, ex-Marines, and Army types who worked in town as valets were starting other types of festivities on couches and on the oriental rugs; moans started to build.

"I think I'll get back." I took a sip of Champagne so as not to offend, and we all clinked glasses before I headed out. I knew my place, and it wasn't here.

That said, it was my job as Duke's press agent to know everything and keep it all private. And when there was a leak or a problem, I was called in to clean it up as the fix. The studio fix. But the real job, the real work, was making sure things never hit the press in the first place. They just had to vanish and, like the evening at hand, perhaps never to have existed. Other times, it may have been a matter of image, of box office, and not to mention, in some cases I will tell you…a matter of life and death itself.

As for yours truly, I never would have imagined that my ultimate studio fix would be so utterly complex and intricate that in the end, it would actually end up saving my client, but also…*me.*

Part One

Chapter One

Cora-Lee McCoy
Los Angeles
1933

Cheap perfume masked the mild desperation and perspiration that clung to Cora-Lee McCoy like a viscous cloud or suntan lotion that left a residue after toweling off. She would only last a month at Schwab's Pharmacy making a three-dollar-a-week salary, not that she minded making chocolate malteds at the soda counter or putting a pretty red cherry on top of an ice cream sundae, but Cora-Lee knew a thing or two when opportunity knocked. It didn't happen very often, and when it did, she was savvy enough to make sure she was home to answer the door.

She had arrived in LA four months earlier, having fled Spokane, happy to put it behind her. Her seventeen years had already been marked by a lifetime of neglect, a nubile body, her damnation, and her only ticket out after having been routinely dumped in a series of foster homes when her mother's nervous breakdowns forced her into the local asylum.

Cora-Lee would stay with her alcoholic aunt and uncle when they had work and could afford another mouth to feed, and when they couldn't, she was sent to a foster family for a few weeks for pay. It would always start the same way: her trying to be a good girl, helping around the house to the worn mother's delight. Then, like clockwork, in the late gloom of the night, the grizzled father or visiting uncle would sneak into her room, put his hand over her mouth to silence her as he unzipped his trousers, and force her to do unspeakable things.

When she was fifteen, Cora-Lee finally found a family she was comfortable with and, at first, she thought she had glimpsed Heaven. She helped the kindly mother with her chores, and she and the shy sixteen-year-old brother talked about movies and sports. She read to the younger sister at night and would lovingly tuck her in, wishing she had always seen such stability. She knew the family was getting paid to house and feed her, but they seemed better than most. One Sunday night when she heard her room's door hinges squeak, she felt her body go cold as an ice pop on a sweltering day. She looked up and saw the son. She knew not to make a sound when he roughly grabbed her breasts. He threw his body weight on her as he unzipped his trousers and then forced himself into her. Afterward, as she lay crying, he turned to her scornfully.

"Stop your cryin'. My daddy said you wouldn't mind, that you're the kind of girl that would like it." The father arrived that night, and each night thereafter, it was either the father or the son—sometimes both. She knew it was her fault; it was always her fault with her damn tits; they led her into a room like a waiter's serving tray. She knew she had an unremarkable face and mousy brown hair, but she had the body of a "sinner," as one of the foster mothers had told her while slapping and beating her with a belt strap after she found her husband exiting her room and zipping up his fly.

It was always the same and always her fault. After two months in that home, she realized she was pregnant, and she did what she could: she stole some money from the mother's purse and went downtown for an illegal abortion—where all the girls like her knew where to go. After the procedure, she hid at her aunt's house pretending she had a stomach virus, glad when the bleeding stopped two days later. She knew she was lucky that time.

When she healed, she set out to visit her mother, who was receiving a new form of shock treatment in the home and found her looking off into space in the courtyard not even realizing it was her. There was no conversation, yet she seemed more vacant than usual as Cora-Lee tried to cheer her mother up with bubbly chit chat. As she was leaving, her eye caught a flier on the community board about a local bathing beauty contest sponsored by the newspaper, *The Spokesman Review*. The grand prize was tempting: a photo in the entertainment column of the paper and fifty dollars. *What did she have to lose?* she thought in desperation. The only thing going for her was her body anyway. The only problem was she couldn't afford a new bathing suit and had to borrow one from a girlfriend—who was two sizes smaller—which she struggled to get into the day of the competition. Plus, her borrowed pumps were a half a size too big. When she emerged on stage in the skin-tight one piece, the crowd of mostly men went crazy whistling and hollering for her. When she tripped in her oversized high heels, there was silence and then spontaneous applause as she stood up, brushed herself off, patted her ass, and laughed at herself. The crowd ate it up, and she naturally took home first prize and the purse. Best of all, though, she felt like she finally had some power, having felt entirely powerless for so long. She quietly kept the prize money in safekeeping wrapped in tissue paper in her brassiere and had learned an important first public lesson; size, presentation, and first impressions matter.

A month later, after her mother had hung herself in the home and was buried in a potter's field, Cora-Lee decided to leave her aunt's house for good, and her uncle's response was to put his hand on her ass. She swatted it away and promptly packed her sad, half-empty satchel and two copies of her photo in the newspaper and promptly bought a bus ticket to LA. She left five dollars and a note that said, "I'm going to Los Angeles." No forwarding address. She had just turned seventeen.

Los Angeles. "City of angels…and devils," she would soon say and laugh to herself. A job sweeping hair in a beauty salon led to a waitressing job in a greasy spoon. She and four other girls shared one room in a boarding house, and when one girl got knocked up and needed an abortion, Cora-Lee showed up for her shift at Schwab's, not that anyone noticed the difference. They said starlets were often "discovered" there, but another type of discovery was in order for her that afternoon.

A handsome, gray-haired lady sitting at the bar ordered a vanilla milkshake, reading her elegant paperback volume and subtly looking her up and down. What she would not tell Cora-Lee was that she routinely scouted places like Schwab's soda counter and other diners to see the new wannabe actresses right off the bus and would eye the ones she thought had potential. Maude Ryan sat silently with a book at the counter—*The Great Gatsby,* which she never read—to look more cosmopolitan and respectable. She surveyed the young, nubile, brown-haired girl in front of her like she was eyeing ripe peaches at a farmstand. She could see past the ratty brown hair and bad makeup; the girl was pretty and well-endowed, her young, full breasts straining the apron.

"I'll have another napkin, dear." Maude struck up a conversation as she usually did, with restraint at first. It was never good to appear overly interested.

"Here you go." Cora-Lee handed her a linen napkin and observed the well-dressed matron.

"That's very kind of you." Maude fingered the napkin and placed it on her lap in ladylike fashion. "Are you new here? Haven't seen you around before."

"Filling in for a friend," Cora-Lee said, washing a glass ice cream dish in the metal sink.

"I see. I always come here for lunch or a malted." Maude peered at her over her novel. "Thought you were new."

"Everyone knows Schwab's," Cora-Lee said with flair.

"Yeah, lots of actresses come through this place. How much do they pay girls like you here, doll?" she asked, knowing full well the answer.

"Three dollars a week, plus tips." Cora-Lee peered at the paperback. The woman didn't look like anyone she'd ever met: streamlined and smart.

"Really?" She paused at the notion. "Not sure how you young things survive on three dollars a week." Maude whistled, which seemed out of character.

"Well, if you have any better ideas…" Cora-Lee smiled, shrugging with resignation.

"Actually, I do, but you probably wouldn't be interested." Maude rolled her eyes and yawned on cue.

"Depends on how much." Cora-Lee Lee smiled sweetly.

"Oh, just fifty dollars a week." She shrugged.

"*Just* fifty dollars a week? You're kidding, right?" She stopped in her tracks.

"As if!" Maude looked at her with steely confidence. Cora-Lee raised a slightly arched eyebrow. She had heard all this before.

"I dunno, you look kinda…*scary*," Cora-Lee heard herself say. What was this silver-haired lady offering her money for? The men had all wanted her, but ladies? No way.

Maude burst out laughing. "I never heard that one."

"I don't go in for that kinda stuff," Cora-Lee added, looking her up and down.

"What stuff?" Maude asked.

"I like boys. Men." Cora-Lee stood her ground and chewed on her lip.

"Oh, so *that's* what you thought. Honey, I like men too." Maude laughed.

"So, what do I have to do to earn fifty dollars? Certainly not sweep the floor. Want more malted?" Cora-Lee lifted up the large metal cup from the mixer, sensing an opportunity.

"No, thank you." Maude put down her book. "Well, I own a social club, and if you want to, you get to meet the most powerful men in this town. All you need to do is meet them."

"In what way?"

"My girls earn fifty dollars a week…just for *mingling*." She smiled and lifted her glass so Cora-Lee could see her deco diamond bracelet.

"Mingling? That's all?" She stopped wiping the counter.

"You don't have to do anything you don't want to do. You get fifty dollars a week for mingling, and then if you find a gentleman you like, and you want to entertain him, and he pays you, you get to keep half. Fifty-fifty. Some of the girls at Maude's make a hundred dollars a week. *Cashola*."

"Hey, is this on the up and up?" Cora-Lee asked without offense. She did not add that weeks before, she had been already supplementing her income by posing nude for men's calendars. She had had a few sessions with a greasy photographer who had directed her to lie naked on a red satin sheet in lewd poses. She didn't think many people would see them and had rent and sundries to pay. She figured if she turned her head sideways, people might not recognize her.

"Look, you wanna be an actress." Maude surveyed her and stated rather than asked her. She could smell it a mile away as she had been one of these girls herself.

"Yeah, sure. That's why I moved here; I won a bathing beauty contest," Cora-Lee said proudly. "In the top newspaper in Spokane."

"Like every small-town girl who takes a bus here. Listen, when I was seventeen, I was just like you, cute and perky, won a beauty contest in Akron, myself. I came out here and for the first five years, I had quite a time in the silent reels with Keaton and Chaplin. That said, I never was going to be Pola Negri or Mary Pickford, and as I got older, I had to work on my back to get anything, even extra work," she said in a low knowing voice. "You know what I'm getting at. And do you know what?"

"No. What?"

"I was on my back for seven out of the eight roles. Lousy little roles too, mean little crowd scenes. That's this town, darlin'! Then one day, I decided I'd had enough givin' it away and was going to do things Maude's way. And there's nothing better than being *flush,* I can tell ya that." She let the thought linger. "And best thing about Maude's is no one will ever know it's you."

"How's that?"

"I dress my girls in costumes to make 'em look like famous movie stars; wigs, makeup, the works. I even had one or two now famous stars start at Maude's. Can't tell you who, but you've seen 'em on the big screen. Best is most girls use the day off to go to the beach or auditions since the hours of the social club are only at night."

"Wow, that sounds...well, swell." Cora-Lee was taking the bait.

"And you'll make real money; I can tell ya that." She put the book down and leaned in.

"And why's that?"

"'Cause Maude spotted you, and Maude *knows.*" She sipped her coffee.

"What does Maude know?" Cora-Lee came back to hear the answer after filling another customer's chipped ceramic mug of coffee at the far end of the bar. She placed her hand on her hip and bit her lip. Maude knew she had an eager one and went for it. She had nothing to lose with this one.

"Maude knows you ain't no virgin from the way you walk and men look at you, and Maude will take a bet you know how to...*fuck*."

"Well, Maude knows more than she should." Cora Lee winced at the words but knew it was the truth. Was it that obvious? She gulped.

"You do the math." Maude placed the book down on the counter. "Look," she added in a sympathetic tone, "I know you've had it rough; I can tell. I also know it's the same with these men, and you hate that; we all do. But in the back of your mind, you know you have power over them, and if you know how to play it, and it's your game, then it's exciting." She smiled. "So, what do you think about what I just said?" She handed her a simple white card that had the words *Maude's* engraved in black script with a phone number. The card looked as professional, discreet, and expensive as her gold and diamond bee brooch.

"A hundred dollars a week just for mingling in costume?" Cora-Lee chewed on her lip.

"Yes. Makeup, wigs, the whole shebang. You could be Gloria Swanson, herself, and no one will ever recognize you."

"Listen, I'm a good girl," Cora Lee protested.

"Didn't say you weren't, but are you a *smart girl*?"

"I hope to be."

"So, whaddya say? I have to get back to the club." Maude put down ten dollars as Cora-Lee's eyes widened at three weeks' worth of work for one malted. She went over to the fridge, took out a banana, put it into a fancy glass dish, and put two scoops of vanilla ice cream at the base to have it resemble a penis. She brought it over to Maude and, with a long silver spoon, took a bite out of the banana.

"For a hundred dollars a week, I have no problem eating the real thing." She laughed in a saucy fashion. Her delivery was high, breathy, and incredibly funny and unexpected.

And Maude laughed so hard, milk came out of her nose.

Chapter Two

Norman Slough
Stoke-on-Trent, England
1929

Norman Slough lay beaten and bloodied, tossed about like an unwanted homemade rag doll at the bottom of an attic trunk, at the back door of the theater. He was kicked for good measure in the stomach, which had him doubled over in excruciating pain as the gang of local hooligans who had chased him there cursed him, spit on him, and urinated on his pant leg. They also laughed in unison as they called him a pansy, a queer, and a pervert. Unfortunately for the sensitive fifteen year old, the beatings and the derision were almost a daily occurrence wherever he went. There was no hiding in the working-class mining town like this depressing English backwater. He tried to tune out the usual taunts and laughter as he brought his body into a protective ball.

"Stop this instant! You there!" The figure of a large man in a sweeping charcoal cape emerged from the back theater door like a bat expanding his wingspan and causing immediate panic as the door eerily slammed shut behind him as if on cue. He furiously tapped an elegant black lacquer cane with an ominous carved sterling falcon handle onto the cobblestone, the sound echoing in a ghoulish salute.

"Leave the lad alone this instant, or I will call the police." He raised his voice against the herd, and they stopped in their tracks, turning at the deep, resonant voice which flooded the back alley.

"Old queer," a cockney shouted.

Augustus Drake pulled himself up to his full height of six feet, two inches. "You!" He pointed to the pockmarked, unruly youth who had shouted the slur and was hovering over the boy with a knee at the ready. He moved forward fearlessly, raising the ominous cane in a threatening manner. The small mob cowered as he rose, the cane now above his head twirling in the air like a propeller. The boys looked petrified as the looming figure swept closer, the cape creating a more menacing look.

"What's it to ya?" The lone voice questioned the approaching ghoul.

"When I fabricated this cane," he said in a low sonorous voice, "I had them drill a lead rod in the center, for heft. Imagine how it would feel against your *jaw*." He smiled his best theatrical evil smile and saw how they cowered and shivered as they did in the audience. The big shot in the group slunk back more than the rest. He knew that the man's evil grin had power, and they were not immune as they shielded themselves in fear.

"When I was your age, I gave a command performance for the Queen. *You*..." he pointed to the boy, the lone voice in the crowd. "You'll be dead by the time you're twenty from black lung," he hissed. "Now, you touch this boy again, you'll all be sent to reformatory school, I can assure you of that. The chief of police in this Godforsaken town is a fan of mine. Off with you. Touch him again, you'll have *Augustus Drake* to contend with, and don't you forget it!" he commanded as they ran off.

Augustus turned from the departing gang who ran with shouts of "Old Queer!" and turned his attention to the young boy in pain sprawled like pancake batter that had dripped on a kitchen floor. He had spotted him in the theater the day before between the sets with the sweepers and had commented on his fine features: his elegant, honed profile and long dark lashes.

"Now there's a leading man in ten years when he grows his hairs." He had turned to his leading lady, Colleen.

He leaned down to assess the damage and lent a hand lifting him up. He was skin and bones, hardly weighing as much as a bag of potatoes. "Not too bad?"

"Thank you, sir," Norman said in a high pitched, tremulous voice.

"How long has this been going on?" Augustus asked in a low voice as Norman brushed himself off and winced at the pain on his side.

"Since…forever." The young boy looked down in shame.

"You will *use it*, I promise you, when you play Romeo or Hamlet or later, Othello. One day, you will tap into the pain and it will make you a better actor," he commanded.

"How did you know I wanted to be an actor?" Norman looked up at his savior with awe.

Augustus smiled as he was bolstered by his thick arm.

"With your profile, it's not whether you want to become an actor but that an actor wants to become *you*." He assessed the young boy's languid, beautiful features framed by the longest, most luxurious lashes he had ever encountered. They were almost obscene in their movie reel femininity.

"You might have to play a young girl in Shakespeare first. Would you mind skirts?" Augustus probed.

"No."

"I thought not. Do you have any family to speak of?"

"My mother died of the flu in a mental hospital. I live with me aunt," he whimpered. "She can't afford me, so I left school and came yesterday lookin' for work."

"Well, you seem to have found it; follow me, boy." He deftly took out a tarnished nickel skeleton key from his deep coat pocket and reopened the door to the theater. They both walked silently into the backstage area and then toward his dressing room. "You'll join me as my personal valet."

"Really?"

"Don't be so excited; one has to be ready to perform. Are you ready…to perform?" He squinted at his young prey.

"On the stage?"

Augustus laid his hands on Norman's bony shoulders. "And *off*!"

Norman looked into his kindly eyes, now lustful with a lascivious intent. The older man reached out and touched Norman's face and then reached between his legs and roughly grabbed his crotch. Norman wasn't shocked and just looked down.

"Yes," he whispered.

"Good. Now let's get you out of this forsaken town. By the way, what's your name?"

"Norman. Norman Slough."

Augustus let out a good laugh.

"My dear boy, that is your old name. We'll invent you a new one."

"When?" Norman searched eagerly.

"After your audition."

Chapter Three

Barston Maddox
Sioux Falls, South Dakota
1929

The three mile walk to and from school each day barely tired the energetic Bartie, but with each step, his feet rubbed and blistered more. He walked slowly to try to avoid the dark pebbles and omnipresent grime that seemed to seep into his thin, tattered socks through the worn shoe soles. At fifteen years old, he was growing so quickly that no sooner did he seem to get a new secondhand shirt, pants, or shoes, his body seemed to suddenly expand—much to his mother's despair.

"Like a weed," she would mutter with a combination of pride and resignation. The Great Depression was all anyone could talk about, and a layer of fear and anxiety had settled onto the lined and dour faces of the average men and women they met at the boarding house like the overflowing grease in the leftover kitchen pans. While they had always been poor, his mother had somehow managed to provide a warm place to sleep and put some grub on the table, and he knew he was luckier than most. Her job at the diner may have kept her away due to the long hours and the daily grind, but they found moments of connection whenever they could. They would sit together and count the small tips she got each week: a handful of pennies, nickels, and dimes that they counted out together on the faded, quilted bedspread. It wasn't much, but it paid their way for basics, and while she was mostly always behind with her rent, the gray-haired old woman who ran the place, Elsie, always seemed to pat Bartie's head and give him an occasional piece of penny candy she kept in her apron pocket. He made sure he was sweet to her too, bringing her wild daisies he picked in the fields in hopes she would be sweet to them when down on their luck, and she was.

That was before his mother lost her job at the diner. Eight weeks after the market crash, the owner made a plain and stoic announcement that not many people could afford to eat out anymore, and he couldn't keep the diner going with little to no customers. He just hung a sign on the door that said "Closed for business." That was that; resignation without a fight or remorse at all after nineteen years in business. It was a bleak time, and he gave Bartie's mother and the others a day's pay, which she thanked him for.

That night, Bartie saw the look of fear on his mother's pretty face for the first time when she told him the news. Her eyes suddenly had a red rim, and he hugged her and told her he would take care of her, which seemed to make her happy even though they both knew it was a fantasy.

Two months had passed without work, and now, things had changed. Bartie knew he needed to come home late from school and walked slower, trying to take a different route so he would avoid what had happened the week before. He tried to push the memory of it from his mind, but it still haunted him.

It was a Monday he would never forget. Bartie had gotten an "A" in English—his favorite subject—and had wanted to show his mother the paper and the impressive grade and ran home, taking the quickest route. Mrs. Frawley, his teacher, had also taken him aside and told him he had talent, a keen and quick mind, and that he had the makings of a writer. He bounded up the stairs of the boarding house to their room and opened the door without knocking to tell his momma the news. It was a very confusing sight as he saw a large, hairy man, apparently a traveling salesman, on top of his mother and under the covers. He seemed to be swallowing her up, and he was groaning; was he hurting her? Bartie did the only thing he could think of and ran over and pummeled the man's wide back with his fists.

"Stop! Stop!" he heard himself shout.

"What the...?" The man turned over and he saw his mother's flushed face and then the shame.

"It's my boy," his mother said calmly. "It's okay, Bartie, he's a friend. Just go for now," his mother added sweetly, pulling the covers up to her neck.

"Here, kid." The man sat up in bed, reached over, and retrieved a Liberty silver dollar from his pants pocket, which hung on the cracked bedpost. As he had reached into his pants pocket, Bartie saw his big belly, encased in a yellowed T-shirt covered in perspiration and a field of fur.

"Go get some ice cream. You're a good kid to care about your mom so much," the man said in a kind way.

His mother looked down in shame but told him to be back before dinner and not to worry. Bartie turned and walked quickly toward the door.

"Take the paper too!" the man called after him. Bartie turned around and looked down to scoop up the folded newspaper, *The Argus Leader*, and walked out of the room before running as fast as he could. He pocketed the silver but knew better than to spend it on foolishness. Once he found his way to his favorite sitting rock in the park across from the town square, he plunked down to look at the newspaper, trying to get the image of the fat man on top of his mother out of his mind.

He looked at the front page and saw a crisp black-and-white photo and story about a pretty blonde girl about his age getting out of a chauffeur-driven car in New York City. She was wearing a white fur jacket and a matching fur hat as she walked up the courthouse steps with her Aunt. The headline blazed:

WHO WILL GET POOR LITTLE RICH GIRL? CHILD'S AUNT SUES "ABSENTEE" MOTHER TO CONTROL FORTUNE!

He looked at the grainy photo of her sad face and suddenly felt a kindred spirit. Even though the press called her "the poor little rich girl," she seemed rich but sad, just like him. Then he noticed her name... Grace Greystone...fancy pants! He thought term "the poor little rich girl" was so interesting and clever. *Who came up with that?* He read the story with avid interest. He'd never heard a name like that before. Grace, daughter of the late Grey Greystone. *Grey Greystone*...he mulled it over.

Sounds like money, he thought. Yet with all that money, he could tell she was unhappy too, and it made him feel a little better knowing that. He looked at the fur and the limousine and the woman in jewels holding the girl's hand on the courthouse steps. It was a world he couldn't fathom or imagine as he leaned down and picked up a dirty pebble and threw it. All he knew was that when he got older, he would never get married and have kids. He would never want to have his mother's burden, and he would never mention the man again or any of the others. He would just say he found the silver dollar in the street and hand it back to her, and that's what he did, and he saw his mother's shy smile.

The next day, he had the new pair of shoes he so desperately needed.

Chapter Four

Baroness Irene Von Mendelssohn
Vienna
1933

It took an entire half-day for the staff to individually place and light the beeswax candles in the golden, baroque chandeliers of the *palais*. Although electric lights had been added in the '20s, the baron liked to entertain the way in which his grandfather did: by candlelight and with violinists and an operatic performance on the screened-in Juliet balcony. The French Renaissance *hôtel particulier* outwardly glowed on the *Heugasse* and was something of a talisman for the local passersby, and when the Von Mendelssohns were entertaining, things were well in the world. The monumental and gilded ballrooms and salons with the works by Titian and Tiepolo was as luminous as an ancient moonstone and beckoned the guests who would arrive by chauffeur-driven motor cars in tails, top hats, with wives in ermine and silver foxes, helped off running boards into the grand courtyard by liveried staff in velveteen breeches and scarlet embroidered coats.

It was an unusually chilly night as the formidable staff of thirty set up the formal dinner in honor of the president of Austria and, despite the June evening, the understaff were called in to stoke the fireplaces in the entertaining and dining halls to banish the chill.

He seemed not to notice the synchronized staff; the distinguished, silver-haired Baron Karl Frederich stridently paced his famed, three-story library after reading the news from the *Neue Freie Presse* and shook his head, his pomaded steel gray temples refracting off the soft wall sconces. He passed the invaluable collection of first editions and revered Medieval religious leather-bound manuscripts that lined the paneled walls and peeked out of the tall French window onto the avenue catching the purple fading sunlight. He put the newspaper down quietly and sighed at the news; Hitler had been made chancellor of Germany by President Paul Von Hindenburg. It was less-than-favorable news, and he thought what was once impossible was now reality. Hooligans and brown shirts were officially in office, and rhetoric to annex Austria was growing at a fever pitch. The politics were one thing, but the madness and the manners one now had to deal with were another thing entirely. The baron had been raised in an era of gentility, where one always stood for a lady, kissed a gloved hand, pulled out her chair, and always took "differing issues" to the men's library over cigars and brandy—never in public. If a dissenting opinion was proposed, voices were modulated and shouting was considered a vulgarity. One always presented an image of worldliness and of compassion for those less fortunate, not these awful actions and vociferous slogans and speeches at a fevered pitch. Even after the Great War, while the terms negotiated were onerous for Germany and Austria, the treaty meetings themselves were done with manners and respect—even if the outcome itself was devastating.

The baron had been born in this very palais, one of the grandest in the city and only eclipsed by the numerous Rothschild palais that seemed to outdo everyone, including the royals themselves. Karl Frederich Von Mendelssohn was a distant relative of the famous composer Felix Mendelssohn Bartholdy, and his grandfather, the renowned Jewish philosopher Moses Mendelssohn. His great grandfather had founded Mendelssohn et Cie, the venerable Viennese bank, and his late wife, Margherita, had been chosen carefully: a wan, chic beauty from the cultured and aristocratic Italian Jewish Montefiore clan. As a young newlywed, she had turned the palais into one of the grandest and liveliest salons in Europe where "everyone stopped at her doorstep," and her alluring and now-famous gold-and-aqua portrait by Klimt attracted international admirers. Her brooding, gold-dusted and heavy-lidded eyes and elusive smile along with her famed diamond and sapphire choker captivated the guests. They came to view and visit her portrait even more so since her early departure.

Since Margherita's death the previous year due to a weakened heart from early rheumatic fever, their only daughter, Irene, was now in charge of a certain amount of her own mothering toward her dear, beloved father, taking time away from her studies and her beloved chemistry projects. Tonight, Baron Karl Frederich would be leaning on his lovely sixteen-year-old daughter Irene to be his hostess, and while he knew she was officially too young to be trusted with such a task, the lithe and elegant brunette had grace and elan far beyond her years and had proved to be an asset on the social and political circuit. She was much admired for the stunning beauty and intellect her mother's genes had gracefully bestowed upon her. In addition to her intelligence, riches, and sophistication, Irene was widely known as the most beautiful young woman in Austria. Her heart-shaped face, small, upturned perfect nose, and emerald eyes were commonly acknowledged to be almost supernatural gifts.

"Of course, Papa," she said with her usual deference. He knew she could rise to the occasion and host the president of Austria, Wilhem Miklas, head of the Christian Socialist Party as her dinner companion at her left and the Italian Ambassador to her right deftly. His own mistress, the redheaded actress and seductress, Madame Rigaud, a divorcée of low birth, would not be on the premises despite her convincing whining—her table manners alone were enough to ban her from the evening's events. Her prodigious milky bust, however, was noteworthy among the denizens of the Austrian and German elite who had seen her perform on stage wearing only an array of colored chiffon scarves in the scandalous production of *Scheherazade.* A few had sampled her wares, but most could not afford the services of the renowned courtesan except for those with multiple palais and country estates.

Additionally, Baron Frederich wanted to see if his lovely daughter could pick the president's brain on his feelings about the seemingly popular proposed Anschluss. It seemed that Hitler's movement to unite Germany and Austria, while outlawed by the Treaty of Versailles after the First World War, was gaining immense popularity and traction;

some journalists suggested up to 80 percent of the public was already pro-Anschluss. If Austria was indeed to be annexed with the full support of the president, perhaps other plans needed to be made for the baron's beloved daughter, given the rise of anti-Jewish acts brewing in Germany.

He, of course, like most of his ilk, had always considered himself somewhat immune and Austrian first. While increasingly anxious about the news, he comforted himself that he was a leading aristocrat, a worldly and well-respected businessman, celebrated philanthropist, and decorated war hero. While he would never, ever consider leaving his beloved palais, the painful words and searing anti-Semitic rhetoric were extremely disturbing and becoming more unsettling by the day.

Baron Frederich often thought about his now-famous distant relative, Felix Mendelssohn, who, while a fervent Christian convert, had always been subjected to anti-Semitic rants from jealous rivals like Wagner, and it seemed that the old disease was never without roots, blossoming again. His only thought was that if Germany sought to annex Austria, he would discourage young Irene from a certain Viennese suitor, whose proposal seemed imminent. Perhaps a year in Paris at the mansion of Princess Bonaparte, his late wife's childhood friend, on the Île Saint-Louis would do the trick, and his own famed vineyard, Chateau Von Mendelssohn, in Bordeaux would also offer up a favorable weekend solution and retreat.

Irene, though sweet, was also like her late mother: soft on the outside but headstrong, and she seemed taken by her enigmatic and inappropriate suitor, who had been her chemistry partner at school. The baron knew her head had been turned by the canny and handsome Hans, whose father was a bourgeois saloon keeper and whose own uncle was a virulently anti-Semitic Catholic priest. Despite their differences, they had spent a great deal of time holding hands and stealing kisses in the solarium.

Hans, an older, charming, and popular scholarship student at the same lycée as Irene's, had courted and squired her around for almost a year. His own razor sharp, aquiline nose and platinum blonde hair plastered flat to his forehead seemed to irk the baron. He spent many evenings at the palais overwhelmed by the grandeur, seemingly mentally cataloging the master paintings while declaring his undying love for the young and stunning heiress. Only being shy of her seventeenth birthday saved her from a serious marriage proposal.

As she stripped her chemistry smock stained with phosphorus stains from the school lab, she bathed and then dressed for the state dinner. After an hour of her *toilette* and review of a few formal gowns from Poiret and Worth, Irene made her selection and then surveyed herself in the long silver-flecked mirror. Her lady's maid, Magda, provided the silk slip and hook and eyed her into a proper black silk beaded gown that highlighted her long, slender figure and celery-stalk-thin waist. It was offset by long, white satin gloves and a fresh aromatic lily on her wrist. Only her mother's long old mine diamond earrings and her grandmother's intricate diamond diadem seemed to elevate her position, despite her age. It was so finely crafted it was called the "lace" tiara as it appeared to be woven of the finest diamonds and appeared to be as delicate as lace or silk. It had been a wedding gift from the first baron to his wife, Irene's great-grandmother, the baroness, and one of the great Mendelssohn jewels kept in a scarlet silken and tooled leather box in the safe and only taken out for special occasions.

As the distinguished guests arrived and Irene descended the grand, carved marble staircase on her father's arm, they were greeted by "oohs and aahs" and genteel applause, her beauty a wonder to behold. She was the perfect hostess, refined, deferential, and raised with the most exquisite manners all delivered in upper-class French. After drinks and Champagne in the picture gallery, once seated at the beautifully set table, she executed her hostess abilities perfectly as her elegant mother had taught her, speaking first to President Micklas on her left through the fish and soup course and then to the Italian ambassador to her right during the main meat course.

Despite navigating the difficult political landscape, as the dinner came to an end, as an amusement, Irene was also called upon during the dessert course and then led the group into the baroque ballroom where she sang an aria in the role of Elsa from Wagner's *Lohengrin* for her guests. Accompanied by the renowned left-handed pianist Paul Wittgenstein, whose other hand had been amputated in the first World

War, this performance proved a most moving sight. The combination of her great beauty, lovely dramatic soprano, and the sight of the wounded war hero was astonishing. Eyes teared for the past, present, and seemingly darkened future. Irene shone that evening like a night star, and the question arose of how one person could be bestowed with so many gifts.

That, however, was soon to change. After the successful dinner, the musical performance in the ballroom, and the departure of the esteemed guests, Irene retreated to her father's library, where she kicked off her low satin heels and collapsed on the brocade sofa while her father puffed at his cigar in a nearby armchair. Indeed, she confirmed what he already thought: while Wilhelm Micklas was unpopular with the Nazis, he was facing extreme pressure due to their popularity, the existing economic woes of record unemployment, and inflation due to the terrible terms of the Versailles treaty. The idea of the Fatherland Party was growing, and whether it was Germany or Mussolini in Italy, closer ties with Austria were imminent.

The very next day, Hans, Irene's suitor, arrived in haste looking pale and solemn and asked to speak to her privately. In some ways, Irene thought he might propose to her father's consternation. They entered the glass-enclosed greenhouse pavilion off the courtyard, and he looked intently at the array of tropical flowers and orchids—but not at his intended. The words that emanated seemed completely foreign to her as was the tone of his high-pitched voice verging on the hysterical. "The world is changing quickly," he thundered. His family would never attend a wedding to a Jewess, no matter how rich and powerful. It wasn't a question of her conversion, which he would never ask, since she would never be, in their minds, pure blooded. He was throwing his support behind the Anschluss movement to reunite Germany and Austria as one Germanic nation and the Nazi party if Austria was to once again thrive. As much as he loved her, or thought he loved her, Hans loved the Fatherland more. Irene sat down on a carved stone bench in shock.

"Hans, why won't you look at me?" she asked and begged. "Just look at me! This isn't you."

He turned for a moment.

"I can't look at you. You're too beautiful, and if I do..." His voice cracked. "I'm lost," he sobbed. "It's a curse." Suddenly, he turned on his heels and gave the Nazi "Heil Hitler" salute before fleeing the palais. At first, Irene sat quietly in the greenhouse after he left and then she walked in a flood of tears back to the main part of the mansion. Her lady's maid, Magda, had been on hand discreetly listening behind the double glass doors. Once she saw Irene's tear-streaked face, she immediately dispatched the butler to summon the baron that something was amiss.

Irene retired to her room and collapsed on her bed, overwrought with both sadness and anxiety. She had only recently survived the death of her mother and now Hans was gone—for reasons that were beyond her comprehension. She dramatically threatened suicide and would not rise from her bed for three days, rejecting all sorts of soup and food.

Baron Frederich, distraught at the sight of his beautiful and once vivacious daughter becoming a shell of her former self, paid a visit to Berggasse 19 on the recommendation of his dearest friend and Irene's godmother, Princess Bonaparte, and presented his handwritten introduction. After an intense consultation with the eminent Dr. Sigmund Freud, the bearded psychoanalyst advised that the Irene should have a rest at his colleague Breiner's sanitarium in Switzerland. The calm and beauty, with a dose of psychoanalysis, would be an antidote to her nervous condition, not to mention the emerging disturbing political climate in Vienna. Later that week, after plans and calls were made, the staff bundled Irene's thin body in mink blankets and placed her in the back of the ancient Daimler. The baron and his trusty chauffeur drove her on the long trip to the clinic on Lake Geneva. At first, he thought his daughter might oppose being left in the clinic, but Irene remained too besieged by emotional turbulence to have a considerable reaction at all.

The baron, himself, was somewhat shocked but loath to admit it to anyone now, not even his daughter, that he would now have to completely rethink things. Times had indeed changed when a poor, lower-middle-class boy would reject a Von Mendelssohn! Especially such a young man so overtly impressed by their material possessions.

Once they arrived, the imposing former mansion on the lake, which had been converted into a sanatorium, seemed like a perfect solution. Dr. Breiner, a friend and colleague of Freud's, personally greeted them and appeared warm and fatherly. "The fresh air and sunshine would do Irene a world of good," he said in a comforting tone. The baron, after admitting Irene, tearfully left Breiner's and had his driver make another important stop in Geneva, this time to the Moritz Bank of Switzerland, where he opened a numbered account in both his and Irene's name. The managing director, Mr. Rudolf Scheid, bowed and scraped as he was astonished that the founder's grandson of Von Mendelssohn et Cie was opening an account with their bank. Within the private world of Swiss banking, there might be whispers, but no outright discussion would ever occur, and the baron knew this and gave no reason for their business transaction. Within days, he had transferred millions to the bank account. With each visit to see Irene, he would bring pieces of his late wife Margherita's renowned jewelry collection to be held in multiple safety deposit boxes. He sighed to himself as he thought of the current state of things. Despite his esteemed position and title, he was smart enough to be one step ahead as his father, the second baron, had always been.

Chapter Five

Norman Slough
Stoke-on-Trent, England
1929

Within a mere few days, Augustus Drake had proved to be all things to young Norman: part teacher, father, actor, and lover, yet most importantly, his liberator. A week after their first encounter in the alley and then the darkened recesses of the dressing room, the very elegant, erudite, and well-known Augustus Drake paid Norman's haggard and dour Aunt Trudy a visit in her depressed sliver of a row house. He had brought along his leading lady, Madame Colleen Drummond, for support. She had plucked her best aqua satin dress with her faded robin's egg blue velvet and mangy brown fur-collared coat for the occasion. She had searched her extensive wardrobe trunk to find the right frock and coat, and while it had a slightly old-fashioned Victorian flair, it was meant to intimidate and impress. Aunt Trudy's knees literally buckled when the two well-known actors arrived unannounced, and she self-consciously curtsied as if they were visiting royalty, smoothed her rumpled and tattered cotton housedress, and rushed to put on a kettle of tea, taking out the three mismatched and chipped flowered China cups—her best—from the dingy cupboard.

"Dear me, Norman. You should have told me your fancy theater friends were stopping by. I would have made me-self presentable," she scolded him, patting her unkempt hair, resembling an old nest long abandoned by its residents, into place.

After a few awkward pleasantries while Norman was banished to the tiny yard, Augustus prevailed on Aunt Trudy's common sense that Stoke-on-Trent was not the place for a refined and delicate young lad like Norman, and they both wanted to hire him as a traveling valet.

"The bruises inflicted from the mob of ruffians are reason alone, Madame!" he intoned sonorously, replete with theatrical hand motions she was only now seeing on the silent reels.

Aunt Trudy misted over on cue, and nodded. She knew Norman was subjected to ongoing beatings from the neighborhood gang. "But isn't that part of becoming a man?" she queried.

"No man should be subjected to ongoing *abuse.* Why, dear Aunt Trudy, he was almost *murdered* in the street. I saw so with my very own eyes." Augustus played his best performance to date.

"Murdered? Dear me, my sweet Norman? Why, he never said a word," she proclaimed.

"Why would he want to trouble his dear Aunt Trudy, who he is so grateful to?" Colleen offered in a tremulous, theatrical voice.

"Yes, that's my Norman, longsuffering." She sniffled as she took stock of Colleen's finery. "It runs in the family, I'll have you know."

Augustus then went on to explain Norman was being offered a job as his personal valet. Life in the theater may look a bit unconventional, he noted, but wasn't it better than a dead-end factory job in ceramics—or worse, a coal or chalk mine and the dreaded black lung? All talk of his becoming an actor was left out.

"A theatre valet is not what his dear, departed mum would have wanted, but I guess I might be able to see my way to the idea," she sniffed. "If it…*adds up.*" She sensed a negotiation at hand.

"He's a fine boy," Colleen said. "A valet is *very* respectable, I can assure you, and I promise to look after him. Sort of a mum on the road. 'Tis the opportunity of a lifetime." She drank her tea with her pinkie out, scrunching up her nose, and taking in the dismal, squalid surroundings and ancient peeling wallpaper, like a princess comforting the needy.

"And his meals will be included," she said proudly, thinking of the somewhat malnourished boy who clearly wasn't getting a full portion of lard and biscuits from Aunt Trudy's bare cupboards.

"We leave in a week, as we have had a limited run in Stoke-on-Trent. Not many are interested in Shakespeare here, just the pub," Augustus shrugged. "But I, myself, had a command performance with the queen when I was not much older than Norman." He puffed out his chest.

"*Hamlet.*" Colleen shook her high, russet curls and confided proudly.

"Really, the queen?" Aunt Trudy gasped.

"Yes, my dear. You see, life in the *t-h-e-a-t-e-r* has perks, you know. You'll be doing your nephew a great favor, I can assure you. I predict *greatness*!" Colleen said with a dramatic gesture, her hand in a mini royal half wave.

"Greatness…as a valet?" Trudy screwed up her eyes at the overdone compliment.

"One should always strive to be the best at whatever they endeavor, my dear woman." Augustus gave Colleen a withering look. "I shall drop off the paperwork this week after my agent prepares it," he added, pausing for effect. "And the *money,* of course." He let the word linger, offering it in such an offhand way, it became a verbal aphrodisiac.

"*Money*?" Aunt Trudy salivated at the word.

"Yes, six months upfront for your troubles. We want everything to be on the up and up. Do know we are not only offering Norman an opportunity—but a real job. I never want to be accused of, well, you know, coercing a boy to work on the road. It must all be signed, sealed, and delivered by his guardians. So sad my other valet's mum died and a fine position opened up and doesn't come along often, not to mention the stipend, a percentage, of course…" He paused with theatrical intent. "For his dear Aunt Trudy, who he is so fond of." He gestured grandly.

"Stipend?" She perked up. "And how much would that be?" Her yellow-tinged eyes widened at the thought.

"If you agree, you will get ten percent of young Norman's salary until he is eighteen. That would be four pounds a week. His salary is two-hundred and eight pounds a year. That would be over twenty pounds for the first year for you; we'll round it out to twenty-one pounds. Ten pounds upfront when all the paperwork is signed and legal."

"Well, I should think so." She tried to calm her enthusiasm with a sip of weak tea, having used only one tea infusion for all the guests. "After all, Reggie and I will have to get someone in to do the cleaning and sweeping now that Norman will be *taken*—I mean, on the road." She paused. "I do believe that will do, though. Ten pounds you said... up front?" She smacked her lips this time. "And twenty-one pounds per year, you say?" She was mentally packing his squalid belongings at the mention of the fee.

"Yes, as long as Norman keeps his job with the company."

"He'll do a fine job, my Norman. Won't you, Norman?" she barked. "Although I shall miss him so. He's become so dear to me," she said for effect—though she couldn't wait for him to leave with his growing appetite and her bare pantry.

"And how did you two meet anyway?" She knew she had to ask in order to appear somewhat maternal.

"He was on the ground...looking for work and immediately made himself helpful, picking up the broom, bringing tea for Madame Colleen, helping in the costume department. And he did so without a word or complaint."

"Your Norman is quite special," Colleen added. "He even picked me daisies. Quite a womanizer he'll be one day, I dare say." She beamed.

"My Norman?" she queried, wide-eyed.

"Yes. So, what do you say, Mrs. O'Shea?"

"Well, I hate to see my beloved Norman go, but if he promises to visit his old aunt and uncle every now and again and the...the payments are *on time*..." She licked her dry lips against her green, cracked teeth. "I think it should be fine."

"A deal then?" He extended his hand.

"A deal." They shook on it as he recoiled at her papery skin.

"Do you need your husband's approval?" Augustus asked.

"Oh, no. O'Shea is me third husband. I am Norman's only blood guardian, my dear sister gone with the flu in the asylum." She paused, knowing her unemployed, no-good husband was dead drunk in the upstairs bedroom after yet another night at the pub.

"But he'll sign when I say so, and we see…the money. Norman!" she called in a shrill voice. "Bring our guests their coats and thank them for being so generous and offering you this fine opportunity."

"Once in a lifetime, I can assure you." Colleen sniffed.

"And Mrs. Drummond…" Aunt Trudy said rising, her spindly purple-veined legs somewhat obscene in contrast to the well-dressed actors.

"Yes?"

"I have to confess, I did see you many years ago on the stage when you were just a young lass. You played Juliet and oh, I did swoon. I never thought the likes of me and Norman would be having *Colleen Drummond* over for tea. Well, it's certainly an honor after *all* these years. Why, it must have been over—"

"Oh, I remember," Colleen replied, cutting her off. "It wasn't *that* long ago." She fussed with her dyed coiffeur. "Yes, my Juliet had rave reviews, if I do recall."

"Yes, it did."

"Colleen will look after him like a mother, I can assure you," Augustus proclaimed in a most convincing manner, although he left out the fact that the aging Colleen Drummond was a notorious nymphomaniac and alcoholic, picking up anyone backstage and strays in bars on the road, two or three at a time.

"Just promise this old woman one thing." Aunt Trudy saw them out.

"Yes, anything." Augustus raised a hand to his ear thinking of Norman's willing disposition.

"Protect him from…the *wolves on the road*," she whispered.

Chapter Six

Cora-Lee McCoy
Beverly Hills
1935

Like Goya's naked maja, Cora-Lee lay in repose on the sumptuous, red satin bed to great effect, rubbing Marty Lester's thick, swollen, and purple-veined feet with peaks of her white beauty creme from the jar, as luxurious as errant snow drifts. While he was one of her favorite regulars and proclaimed to be seventy-five, she knew he had to be in his mid- to late-eighties or even older, yet she was thankful for Marty because he was generous, a real gentleman, and she didn't have to sleep with him, suck his cock, or whip him like all the others. He just showed up punctually every Thursday night after playing nine holes of golf and dinner at Hillcrest. It was their standing date, the same each week, and she actually found it quite pleasant at first, and then after a month or two, looked forward to it. First, he would whistle under his breath and tell her how beautiful and sexy she was and how much she looked like the real Jean Harlow in her ingenious costume.

"You're a dead ringer for her," he marveled, and he knew since he had produced Harlow in her last movie right before she died. He lovingly pinched her cheek in a grandfatherly way.

"What a *punim*!" he exclaimed. Then, holding hands, they made their way into the ornate lounge where they listened to a chanteuse perform a set in the bar and downed a few cocktails. He always requested the lovely African-American vocalist sing Fanny Brice's signature "My Man," and Enrique, the Latin bartender, always had a dry martini, straight up with olives, chilled and at the ready, exactly the way he liked it. The only time Cora-Lee ever saw Marty Lester get frazzled was when they ran out of his favorite mixed nuts in the bar, as he was a creature of habit. Marty was a great storyteller, and with his kindly, pale turquoise blue eyes and grandfatherly demeanor, he regaled her with anecdotes about the stars and pictures he had produced. Of course, most were silent films with old timers like Valentino, Rod La Rocque, and Vilma Bánky, but it was entertaining enough, and she prompted him to tell a few of his favorite stories over and over, like a child who wanted her father to reread a worn, yet favorite children's book.

Afterward, they retired to his bedroom of choice, the extravagant scarlet and gold room where he kept a silken robe and satin slippers in the closet. After he undressed, they lay in bed nude together, and she gave him a nice massage and foot rub as he moaned in delight. He loved admiring and playing with her high, full breasts, and sometimes he would spring into action given how sexy she was. But best of all, Marty was generous and always gave her a fifty-dollar bill, which would cover her for a week or two. Her eyes sparkled, dressed as Jean Harlow, while hearing his stories of the ill-fated star who was one of the town's top box office draws. Marty had retired as a producer, but he still had sway in Hollywood circles, and it was said he spent more time and money at Maude's than he did at Hillcrest Country Club with his cronies.

"You know, you do a convincing Harlow, and you give a great foot rub, *shayna punim!*" He smiled at her.

"Shay-na—what?" Cora-Lee screwed up her eyes.

"*Shayna p-u-n-i-m.* Means pretty face. If you're gonna succeed in this town, you gotta know some Yiddish, baby."

"No, I just gotta know *you*, Marty." She kissed his foot as he laughed out loud at her breathy delivery.

"You're a nice girl—and funny too." He appraised her like he was taking in an impressionist painting he had seen at Frances Taylor's gallery in The Beverly Hills Hotel. "Listen, take this the right way. You look like Harlow, but lemme see what you look like under that wig. I know it's a wig; I'm in the movie business."

"Maude says never to take off the costume. I could get *fired*, Marty!" Cora-Lee looked around in a guilty fashion, as if someone were there in the room with them.

"Listen, I fuckin' built Maude's house here with all the money I shelled out over the years. After my wife Sadie died, I've come every week like clockwork." He shrugged in a good-natured way, his wizened, sun-spotted hand punctuating the thought.

"Okay." She looked in the mirror and slowly removed her wig, shaking out her wavy brown hair.

"Come over here," he ordered. She did as she was told, and he took her face gently in his hands as he rotated it.

"You *almost* have it, kid." He shook his head in a knowing fashion.

"Have what?"

"Star quality," he stated.

"Almost doesn't count." She looked forlorn at the thought, and then her eyes turned downcast. It registered with Marty that he may have hurt her feelings, and he regretted his words.

"What's your real name, anyway? I know it's not Jean," he said in a fatherly voice.

"Cora-Lee McCoy."

"Boy, that's almost as bad as Moishe Levinsky." He laughed out loud, before adding, "That was my real name before I changed it to Marty Lester. Look, here's what I'm gonna do for you 'cause I like you, kid, you know that. I just plain think you're a nice girl and funny too. I'm gonna send you to the family doctor, the one that fixed my granddaughter's schnoz. He'll take that bump you have out for me, and I'll put it on my tab. Then, you go to my studio makeup artist, Marnie. She's the best in the biz. You gotta be blonde in this town, and she'll peroxide you up. Next, we need a new name." He appraised her. "Cora-Lee.... It's like you're straight off the fuckin' farm." He shrugged his narrow, bird-like shoulders, spindly and pale.

"I have it!" he bellowed. "No more of this Cora-Lee business...I like Carol. It's kinda like Cora-Lee, but better. I'm never wrong. I made more silent stars in this town than Chaplin." His eyes sparkled.

"Are you sure, Marty? You'd do all that for me?" She nestled into him.

"I told you, I like you, and you're a good girl, and you make me laugh, which no one else does these days—especially my children. Now, we need a last name for you. Any ideas?" He propped himself up against the red pillows, excited by the thought and suddenly looking decades younger.

"I really like Carroll, but can it be with two Rs and two Ls? That feels like class, and I want to be classy and...*expensive*," she said in an animated, childlike fashion.

"Well, you already are classy and expensive. Costs me a fortune here."

"No, I meant my last name." She looked at the three twenty-dollar bills he had slipped her. "Hey, who's the president on the highest bill?" Her eyes lit up at the thought.

He gave it real thought. "Well, I once had a $5,000 bill. I got it as a bonus after *Ben-Hur* was number one at the box office. Carl Laemmle gave it to me, himself."

"Who's Carl *Lemons*?"

"No. Laemmle. He founded Universal, honey."

"This Carl, he wasn't on the bill, was he?"

"No, not him. I think it was James Madison. They only made a few of them."

"Oh, Marty, I like that! Carroll with two Ls and two Rs Madison. That's it!" Her eyes danced at the thought. "Carroll...Carroll Madison. That will be my new name."

"Carroll Madison." He looked her over and smiled. "Doll, I think we're in...*business*."

"Business?" She kissed Marty happily on the lips, and her eyes lit up like a child opening a present under the tree on Christmas Day. "But Marty, I thought you were retired," she asked.

"I am...but you, *Carroll Madison*," he wagged his aged, crooked finger, "*you* are going to be my *last* Hollywood project."

Chapter Seven

Duke Drake
London
1933

Norman and Colleen huddled by the four-poster bed, draped in faded scarlet brocade in the tiny studio walk-up off Mayfair. The air was thick with illness and sickly sweat, and Colleen dabbed her eyes with her wilted and yellowed lace hankie, but also covered her nose with it at times to mask the stench. There was nothing pleasant or alluring when the human body was in the death throes of decay, and Augustus Drake was dying as Colleen and Norman stood vigil. Augustus had horrible coughing fits due to lung cancer, which depleted him greatly, and then he would fall into a stupor and nap. In his lucid moments, he would weakly squeeze Colleen's wrinkled and spotted hand, not at all worried that her stage makeup, which covered her spots, was getting on his dressing gown. She was still vain in her late sixties, and they both knew and ignored it. Norman looked at the two with an ache in his heart when Augustus woke briefly and spoke.

"You know I have loved you both in different ways," he began, interrupted by his hacking cough.

"I want you to know I have divided my estate equally between the two of you," he continued. "Ep-*stein*, the rascal, came last week, and when I asked him if he had any roles for me," he laughed bitterly, "it was clear the agent had none for a *consumptive.* John Keats would be too young for me at this stage, although I am loath to admit it...." He gingerly took the gold crucifix off of his neck and handed it to Colleen, who, when she understood the gesture, moaned and cried a real sob, followed by a stage cry with a corresponding lavish hand motion.

"Here, Colleen. You'll be needing this for protection. 'Twas given to me when I was performing in Ireland by a Catholic nobleman who shared—shall we say—similar interests...and he wanted me to repent, each and every time he buggered me. Well, needless to say, I never did, but I accepted the gift and a rosary. And now, my dear, it's yours, and we all know you'll need it..." He rolled his eyes to great effect, before erupting into a fit of coughing. He continued, "...after each pint and shag!" He snorted.

"Oh, my darling, it's *glorious*," she cried. "So much *gold* content." She felt the weight of the necklace, her cupped hand receiving it like a venerable jeweler's scale on the Ponte Vecchio.

"The apartment, we all know, is small but well situated and will command a pretty penny. Sell it and split the profits, my dears, when I depart. You know I was right to buy in Mayfair. Once, my old lover, Johnny Devine, said it was only a 'good address with a bedroom attached,' but I was right, and he was wrong," Augustus entertained.

"It is all too generous!" Colleen cried again, indicating that the young Norman should fasten the necklace around her sagging neck.

"I will truly treasure it and think of you, darling."

"With every drink and fuck," he teased.

"You're naughty! And the property? Why, Augustus, I couldn't!" she cried.

"Fine, I'll give it all to young Norman, then!"

"*No*, I didn't say that. I think it's quite generous, don't you, Norman?"

"I am overwhelmed." Norman lowered his handsome, well-formed head in tears.

"And now for my young Norman," Augustus touched his hand tenderly, "my handsome, wonderful Norman...*Slough*. You do know that if we were both *normal* and in a respectable profession, Colleen here and I would have married and had a son, and I must say, that despite... *things*...you do know that you are the son we never had."

"It is *true*," Colleen cried. "Norman *is* our son!" She looked at his handsome face. "He looks like me when I was an ingénue," she said proudly.

"No, me," Augustus argued, then spat up some phlegm. "Look at the photo on my desk and feast your eyes. They said I was the prettiest man they had ever seen…and I paid a heavy price for it!" He laughed ruefully.

"You are both me parents I never did have," Norman cried.

"No more of this *me parents*—cockney shit. Only the King's English will get you where you want to go," Augustus lectured.

"Yes, sir."

"Well, I have one final surprise for you, my dear Norman. One that Colleen has known about and fully approves of. I have legally adopted you; just sign the papers over there."

"What?" Norman shook his head. He was now bawling.

"No more of this Slough nonsense. You are now officially a Drake. Now you can legally have my name, money and carry on the profession, and I will have the immortality I have always desired!" His hand gesture had Shakespearean perfection.

Norman caught sight of himself in the pretentious, gilded, oversized mirror hung over the dresser.

"It is true. Augustus said from the moment he laid eyes on you, you would be a star. Why, look at the profile," Colleen marveled. "It's Barrymore perfection. If I weren't your mum, and in my early days, you would have fallen for dear old Colleen, I can assure you!"

"Hands off, doll, he's all *mine.* And I want you to know that I have never seen a face, a profile, or a body to match. You will put Barrymore to shame, Norman."

"Why, thank you…*Father.*" Norman looked down.

"You see, he always knows exactly what to say, even in the gravest moments." Augustus coughed.

Norman had, in the past two years, indeed grown into one of the handsomest men anyone had ever seen, and they both marveled with pride at his long, lean, muscled, aristocratic body and face and his cobalt blue eyes under lustrous lashes and wavy onyx hair. His unique cleft chin was set into a square jaw under razor sharp cheekbones, which seemed to set everyone—women and men alike—aflame. They often congratulated themselves that they had, indeed, picked a winner. Norman had recently been cast under the name Norman Kent, to wonderful reviews, as the young lover of aging star Gertrude Burns in the West End production of *Giddy Up*. A casting agent had spotted him at an opening night party and offered him the part of the young cad after inviting him to his office to test him out—in more ways than one.

"I always said the young lad had the bearing of a count or a duke," Colleen said. "He will take your name to new heights, Augustus."

Suddenly, Augustus stood straight up in the bed, to their surprise, as he was animated, with great energy.

"That is it, Colleen!" he called out at the top of his lungs. "You have it! That will be his stage name. *Duke Drake*!"

Norman looked toward the mirror once more and saw a handsome young man staring back. He smiled and wiped a tear from his eye at the same time he understood the regal name, Duke Drake. It made him stand a few inches taller and the crown of his head leapt skyward. Before anyone could comment, Augustus gave a huge dramatic groan and collapsed as Colleen let out a theatrical and piercing scream. And as Augustus Drake lay dying…Duke Drake was *born*.

CHAPTER EIGHT

Bartie Maddox
Sioux Falls, South Dakota
1933

Bartie ran and ran, this time with a different sense of urgency than on the track field. His eyes were watering at the words old Elsie had uttered in her rocking chair. "Your momma's in the hospital—go now, dear child, before it's too late," she urged with misty eyes and a dirty hankie, wiping a true yet invisible tear. He knew his mother was sick but had been hopeful. He now processed the bleak news. It was awful and apparent that old Elsie was close to eighty, and yet *his* mother was the one that had been taken away.

He ran and ran and was out of breath, doubling over with a stabbing pain when he got to the old crumbling hospital ward. When they finally told him where she was, he knew it was bad—really bad. She was in a vast room with the other dying patients, row after row of the dismal chipped and dirty white metal beds and rough, gray woolen blankets alongside a heavy cloud of resignation and despair. He saw his mother's eyes perk up from a distance when she saw him across the room, and while she was now gray and painfully thin, he could still see the prettiness of her features—a shell of what she had once been. He approached the bed slowly, tentatively, knowing she had already resigned herself to never getting out of there. With his head down, he walked over to her, a lump already in his throat, and then kissed his momma gently on the forehead and took her tiny hand in his. He felt the softness of her skin he had always loved, yet now it was thin and crepey.

"Visiting hours are only 'til six. Son, you have only ten minutes," the older, masculine nurse said, shaking her head at the sight of the poor boy and his dying mum. She knew she would give the young man more time, but she needed to say it.

"They gave me something for the pain," his mother said in a low voice.

"I'm glad, Momma," he gulped, holding back the tears.

"They say it's uremic poisoning. Not good," she whispered, her parched lips moving slowly as if in a bad dream. "Sit. Two things I wanted you to know."

"Yes, Momma."

"Now you don't say nothin', you hear? Come close." He felt her sour, hot breath against her ear.

"In the room, in the dresser, look under my slips and brassieres. I hid a small box for you."

"Yes?"

"You'll find a gold watch on a chain. I need to ask forgiveness. I took it for you a few years back from a man I knew. It wasn't right what I did, but you take it and sell it. I've been holding it for you ever since," she said firmly.

"Yes, Momma." He was crying now.

"You buy those eyeglasses you need and a train ticket with the money, and you go," she said. "I was happy they wouldn't let you enlist. I know you wanted to, but with your eyesight, it's a sign, a blessing. Now I know you'll be fine." He offered her a small glass of water. "I never told you something," she said, looking off.

"What, Momma?" Bartie tried to hold back the tears.

"When I was your age and won the talent contest, they gave me a train ticket to Los Angeles, and I went and didn't tell anybody. Only your daddy came looking for me out there and took me back. Said I was underage and that we were married, and there was nothin' I could do about it. I was also in the family way with you and didn't know it," she shrugged.

"I'm sorry, Momma. You were so beautiful. I have the photo clipping," he said proudly.

"You go. You look like me, and you can write real well, and you can get a job there. There's nothin' for you here and, most important, I want you to be in the sunshine. That's what I remember most." She lay back and reflected. "The sunshine and the oranges! They had the most delicious oranges. They said I was the prettiest girl they had ever seen with my golden hair and big blue eyes, and I was happy. And then your daddy came, and…well, that's what happened."

"I'm so sorry, Momma."

"Just promise me you'll go, and I can be happy again."

"I promise I'll go."

"And don't get tied down with the first girl that comes along and have a brat."

"I promise."

"That said, if you find someone or something that makes you happy, you grab it, you hear? If only for a moment's happiness."

"Yes, Momma." He started weeping. "You know…you are…," he cried, his nose running and eyes in freefall, "the *best momma anyone could ever have*."

"Really?" She seemed happy at his proclamation. "I'm so glad. Be free, Bartie." She seemed to be floating. "Go…and be…" She paused before finishing, "happy."

Days later, after a tearful and wrenching burial in a potter's field cemetery, Bartie covered her grave with wildflowers and bid Elsie goodbye with kisses and hugs. She wept that he was leaving and gave him five silver dollars wrapped in a kerchief. He had another ten dollars, paid to him in full by the kind jeweler who bought the gold pocket watch and questioned the inscription on the inside: "To Marcus on his twenty-first birthday—Love, Mom and Dad." He had known and liked Bartie's mother and missed seeing her at the local diner. He shook his head, knowing the watch was suspect and had heard the sad rumors of his mother. Yet, he knew he was doing a kind thing for the boy, and Bartie had been quick on his feet.

"Whose watch is this anyway? Who is Marcus?" the jeweler had asked.

"My mother's brother. She had a twin. Her name was Milly, and his name was Marcus, and when he came through town, he left it for her."

"And why would he do that?"

"He was a traveling salesman, and he knew my mother lost her job, so he gave her the watch. Said he was named for Saint Mark. Patron Saint of Venice," Bartie said firmly and in a believable tone. He had made it up on the spot and almost believed it himself.

"You either have a generous uncle, or you can spin quite a yarn, young man, but I believe you, so here's ten dollars. I would have given you eight, but the story is so good, I'm giving you an extra two dollars for the entertainment." He winked.

Bartie had no idea how he thought of Saint Mark in the moment, but remembered that he had read that tidbit in a travel guide a guest in the boarding house had left behind. He had always been quick on his feet in school and as head of the small debate club, where he had excelled at extemporaneous speaking. With the fifteen dollars hidden in his shoes, Bartie bought a one-way train ticket to Los Angeles. He would ration his money, eating only one meal a day, and had one change of clothes in a brown paper bag. He cried for his mother and his lost childhood as the train chugged out of the station, but he knew he was on his way to the sunshine she had loved. As he sat back and saw country farms and towns fly by, he felt so grown up, all at sixteen years old.

Chapter Nine

Baroness Irene Von Mendelssohn
Geneva
1933

The baron stood immobile, like a proud painted metal toy soldier at attention in front of the imposing French windows of the villa as he stared at the tranquil view. The mist had dissipated over the placid lake, and he saw the sun break through the gray fog in a slight whisper. It was hopefully going to be a lovely afternoon, yet he knew the outcome of the report had nothing to do with the weather; it would only be lovely if he received a positive news about Irene.

He heard the soft padding of footsteps on the worn oriental carpets and turned in the well-appointed room to see Dr. Breiner enter. He was a thin, sprightly man with a peppered goatee. Why was it that he resembled Dr. Freud so much? Was there a particular look or style associated with the new psychoanalysis? Clearly there must be, just like his accountants who all looked the same.

"Baron Karl, so good to see you." Dr. Breiner walked over and extended his hand. He smelled like a combination of tweed, mothballs, and pipes—slightly offensive yet oddly comforting.

"How are things in Vienna? I hear the political mood is quite disturbing." The doctor took a seat behind his sprawling desk, which was stacked high with papers.

"To say the least."

"Please have a seat," Dr. Breiner insisted.

"The lake looks so peaceful, a word that I never thought I would long for when I was younger." The baron removed and snapped open his engraved golden cigarette case and motioned to the doctor. Dr. Breiner nodded vigorously, indicating that he was not inclined.

"No, thank you. I don't indulge," he punctuated.

"Smart. It's a nasty habit," Baron Karl said.

Dr. Breiner opened the manila file on his desk.

"Well, I have good news for you." He leaned over and peered into the folder. "Our beautiful Irene can be released this weekend, and I feel she has made wonderful progress."

"I'm delighted, Doctor." Baron Karl exhaled relief. "She does seem vastly improved since the last visit," he added, nodding.

"Yes, I think the peace and quiet of Breiner's has done her a world of good as well as the therapy. She has quite an anxiety disorder, which was only exacerbated by her mother's death and her breakup with the young man, Hans. She will need to keep this under control, and I believe that she now has the tools to do so. She also seems happier, having made a good friend here."

"Oh, yes, she mentioned the American girl. I believe I have met the uncle, Reggie McClean, from the shipping lines family." The baron nodded.

"Yes. Grace Greystone. She entered the program around the same time as Irene due to her mother's suicide, and I actually thought it was a stroke of luck for both girls. Grace had the public case years back where her aunt and uncle sued her mother for control of her fortune. They won, which is why she was raised in London."

"Poor thing." The baron inhaled deeply.

"Yes, quite. I do think part of the reason both girls have done so well is that they have each other." He paused. "I have been giving this a great deal of thought and would suggest, if possible, it might be a wonderful idea if they roomed together once they leave here. Both indicated they have an interest in studying in Paris and, given the political climate in Austria and not having to see the young man in Vienna, I greatly approve of this idea." The doctor's clear blue eyes blinked firmly at the thought.

"Why, I think that's a marvelous idea," Baron Karl exhaled. "I've been conflicted about taking Irene back to Vienna anyway. We also have the vineyard in Bordeaux, and they can relax there on weekends. That reminds me." He made a notation in his wallet. "I am going to send you a case of wine."

"That's not necessary, Baron."

"Of course it is. The twenty-eight is a very good year."

"Why, thank you. I do adore a good Bordeaux now and again."

"And you said this Grace is interested in this idea as well?" The baron seemed happy at having a plan.

"Yes, indeed. I hope you don't mind. I have already taken the liberty of speaking to her uncle about it, and he agrees that it makes sense for his niece as well. There was quite a bit of scandal in the press in London when Grace's mother killed herself, and he thinks the French will be more forgiving on such matters. He said he would reach out to you after we spoke. I hope you don't mind that I told him I would make the recommendation to you."

"Not at all. In fact, I think it's a perfect idea. After Margherita died, I also know Irene has missed female companionship. Two girls without mothers—at least they have found each other! I will start looking for a suitable *maison* for them. I'm in Paris next week on business, anyway."

They both looked through the window at a nurse in a white uniform walking a middle-aged woman down the path to the lake. *What was she in for?* the baron wondered.

"I only wish you could also cure the political climate the way you can cure your patients," the baron said with a forlorn look. "It appears the world is going quite mad."

"I couldn't agree more." Dr. Breiner sighed at the observation. "And you, Baron Karl Frederich, do you plan on staying in Vienna?"

"Funny you should mention that. A year or two ago, it would have been inconceivable for me to leave Vienna or my family home, but now…" He shrugged.

"I'm seeing a great many of the best families who have moved or are moving to Switzerland, Baron. I treat many of them due to depression."

"Well, I may become a client myself one day." The baron forced the hint of a fake smile in an offhand way.

"I'm always here for you and Irene," he offered.

"Thank you kindly, Doctor, for taking such good care of her, and I do think your plan makes a great deal of sense."

"Well, then I think Paris it is for Irene and Grace," he said, shaking the baron's hand. Both stood and looked at a large, ominous cloud overtaking the sun.

"*Voila*! Gay Paris it is." The baron turned as the cloud suddenly eclipsed the sun.

Part Two

1934–1940

Chapter Ten

Bartie Maddox
Los Angeles
1934

"Here, take these." Declan Mooney, the caustic yet efficient head valet at The Beverly Hills Hotel threw the jangling car keys for the sturdy black Nash at Bartie. "You've just been promoted from bellboy to valet. That asshole Sweeney is late or drunk or drunk and late again. He's finished. You don't drink? Do ya, boy?" The older Mooney barked and surveyed him as if he were inspecting vegetable produce in the market and then realizing vegetables weren't on the menu.

"Never touch the stuff," Bartie said in a low voice.

"Good, just park it straight in the lot. No fancy moves."

Bartie had never driven a car before, but he knew this was an opportunity of a lifetime and got behind the wheel of the Nash pretending to know what he was doing. He felt like he was moving in slow motion as he figured out how to put the gleaming automobile into drive. He'd been around the car park adjoining the pink palace long enough, loading and unloading the luggage, to observe and mimic what he saw the valets do. The car lurched forward, but he quickly got the hang of it.

Within days, the tan, lean, and handsome Bartie was part of the team that parked everyone's cars from Mr. Goldwyn, when he was driving himself rather than being deposited by his limo, to the glittering Joan Crawford. The tips alone got him out of the flea-bitten dump and into a safe and clean rooming house near the Hollywood Biltmore. At seventeen, he looked nineteen, kept to himself, and worked a six-day shift. He knew his all-American good looks and can-do attitude had created certain openings and that his studious eyeglasses gave him an intellectual look like an Ivy college boy on spring break. Most days he felt lonely, but lucky.

When he first arrived at the train station in LA, he was terrified despite the optimistic sunshine. Those early days were the hardest; now everything was looking up and a bit easier after he had ended up in an awful rooming house that had no locks on the doors. Once in the middle of the night, an older hobo had tried rob him. Bartie, used to sleeping with one eye open, bolted up in bed and punched the ghoul in the face, picked him up by the collar, and literally threw him out the door.

In the hallway, a kindly neighbor coming home from his night shift helped chase the menace away. His name was Sidney Torcelli, a friendly ex-stockbroker who had lost all his money in the crash and was living with his mother on the same floor. His sweet Italian mother always pinched his cheek when she saw him and would deliver half a cannoli wrapped in wax paper when she could, saying she was trying to "fatten him up" in broken English. Sidney felt sorry for the motherless Bartie and tipped him off that the greasy spoon off La Cienega, where he worked as a waiter, had an opening for a busboy position. That was the way it was with Bartie; there always seemed to be sunshine at the end of the storm. The next day after getting the job, Bartie looked upward and thanked his dearly departed mother, who he felt was looking down on him.

The lowly position only paid fifty cents a day, but the fact that he had found a paying job made Bartie feel like a prince. One thing led to another and two months later, he heard there was a higher-paying busboy job at the tony Cocoanut Grove nightclub where the stars and movie executives gathered. He put on his one secondhand white button-down shirt, tan slacks, and showed up. The manager gave him the job thinking he was a college boy and would be a better look than the regular applicants. A bellboy position at the Beverly Hills Hotel was soon offered when he helped another busboy with a school paper since he was so good in English. The college student mumbled something about "the tips alone could make you rich." That wasn't exactly the case, but now with his lucky break as a valet, Bartie had a room with a lock on his door and could afford three square meals a day. He also met other young men who were from better families studying at university or earning spending money on the side while they earned their degrees. The contacts were improving and so were the social opportunities. Bartie saw the young, nubile actresses on the arms of the older producers give him the once over as he opened the car doors and helped them out.

"She has the hots for you, that tramp!" the other bellboys would laugh. "I bet you she would throw you a free one." They would sum up the Hollywood whores and the dime-a-dozen contract actresses who frequented the bar and posh hotel pool looking for an upgrade. One starlet even slipped Bartie her phone number, but he just kept the slip of paper in his pocket. He knew that he couldn't afford to mix business with pleasure, and since he had no back up, he was at work earlier and left later than his contemporaries, often volunteering for two or three shifts including the night shift. He would often receive extra tips from stars like Cesar Romero and the glamorous and lovely Carole Lombard, who would fish through her evening bag to give him a five-dollar bill when he brought around her cream-colored Cadillac convertible.

"You remind me of a Midwestern Thalberg," she joked as she took in his good, lean, sandy-blonde looks and professorial eyeglasses.

The staff also got to know the comings and goings of the stars and the studio execs—who was dating or sleeping with whom and who arrived and left with someone else. The guests in the bungalows also provided a steady stream of visitors and gossip. Bartie mentally filed everything away and got to know the lay of the land.

It was 1:45 a.m. on an uncommonly humid Tuesday night, and the old black 1929 Ford swerved into the drive as wavily as the billowing palm trees. Mooney opened the door and helped the drunken guest out onto the pavement. He was handsome, with fine features, blonde slicked-back hair and although forty, looked fifty.

"Bartie, get over here and help Mister Fitzgerald out. Maybe you can help him to his bungalow."

"Of course, Mister Mooney." Bartie always spoke to his elders using their last name, which was why he was a favored valet. Fitzgerald looked up, his eyes red and pleading as Bartie lifted him under a damp, sweat-stained armpit, which had bled through his expensive linen blazer. He smelled like a brewery.

"Thank you, my good man." He croaked in a clipped upper-class accent.

F. Scott Fitzgerald, the legendary writer, was a local celebrity who, at times, checked into one of the smaller bungalows when he was trying to finish a script or put the finishing touches on a novel. It was said that his wife, Zelda, was in a sanitarium in North Carolina and that he lived with the movie columnist, Sheilah Graham. Word was the well-known writer was eager to finish a novel based on none other than Irving Thalberg himself, the youthful head of production at Metro. He had come out to Hollywood to work for the studio and was paid well for it, but with his erratic, drunken behavior, those days were numbered. It was common knowledge that once the studio's got their paws into you, if you didn't produce, you were done, and Francis didn't exactly understand deadlines. Bartie steadied Fitzgerald and walked him through the plush lobby outside to the well-manicured, tropical grounds to the rear Mediterranean bungalows when they arrived at one of the smaller back ones.

"Damn Johnny," he said.

"Johnny who?" Bartie asked.

"Walker. You know he's pleasant at first," he groaned. "And then he becomes troublesome when you get to know him better."

"I'll get you some water when we are inside."

"You helped me once before, I think." He looked up at him with his unfocused eyes.

"Yes, Mister Fitzgerald, the other night? The name is Bartie, sir."

"Spending too much time with Johnnies and Barties, it seems. Never will finish this damn novel."

Bartie opened the door with his room key as F. Scott entered and collapsed on the couch. Bartie walked over and picked up a high-ball glass that had obviously contained gin and washed it out in the bathroom sink before bringing it to F. Scott with some fresh water and some aspirin he found on the shelf.

"Here. My mother always said aspirin and water will cure just about everything."

"Your mother was right, but clearly *a bore*," Fitzgerald groaned looking bleary-eyed, but he took the pills and the water and grimaced as he downed them.

"Well, I'm just joking, you know…your mother is a smart lady."

"Was."

"Oh, sorry. Listen, good old Bartie." He paused and surveyed him, taking in his innate intelligence. "You look like you're a strapping college student. Have any friends who can type? I'm well behind in my novel and need a bit of an assistant. I can pay a dollar twenty-five a week," he groaned. "Extra!"

"Well, um. That would be something…I could help you with." Bartie's eyes glistened. "I would just need a typewriter," he said, not knowing if he could do it but feeling a lust for the keyboard nevertheless.

"I have an extra one at the bottom of the closet. Go over there. You'll find the Wanderer at the bottom, like me, the wandering non-Jew, in this town." He laughed a bit bitterly.

Bartie laughed too, walking over to the closet. He saw the typewriter in the weathered carrying case stashed in the back of the closet with the words "Wanderer Typewriter" in faded gold letters.

"That one was with me in the South of France. It's seen better days, but you'll find it still works. Help me to my feet, and I'll give you the yellow pad. It's near my bath; I write in the bathtub."

Bartie ran and helped him to his feet. He looked far older than he was, but he was still handsome.

"Don't worry. I'm not going to ask you to help me into the bath. I'll leave that to Ramon Novarro or Gorge Lamont, who you might have met as well." He chuckled.

Bartie walked him into the well-appointed bathroom and saw the writing tablet.

"Try to make out my scribbles. We can fix it when you have the meat of it down."

"Of course, Mister Fitzgerald."

"Fuck the Mister Fitzgerald thing. I'm not your father. Call me Scott or Francis. Was named for Francis Scott Key, all that rot."

Bartie took the pad out of his hand and looked at ink-stained paper filled with cursive writing.

"What am I typing?"

"A new novel. I'm toying with the name. Tell me, either…*Last Loves of the Last Tycoon*…or *The Last Tycoon*, based on good ole Thalberg, himself. Which do you like, kid? I'm just calling you Kid from now on."

"I like the first."

"Me too." He reached into his pocket and took out a few bills. "Here, a down payment." He gave him five dollars. "Now get to work while I get to bed."

"Thank you, Mister…I mean, Francis."

"Kid, fuck off, and come back when you have my novel typed."

Chapter Eleven

Duke Drake
New York City
1934

London had proven a delightful appetizer, but New York was the scrumptious main course on the menu. Duke looked out of the window of his hotel room, high above Times Square, and saw the Camel Cigarette advertising sign blinking beyond the blackened soot that had settled at the window's peeling sill. He should have been enthralled, yet he winced in pain at the dull ache of his jaw. He'd only been in New York for two days, but the tooth ache had started on the McClean line and throbbed terribly, the pain increasing by the hour. At first, he tried to numb it with shipboard brandy, and then graduated to whiskey, but it was clear he needed a real dentist, and he had never been to one before. He always prided himself on his set of glorious, perfectly arranged white teeth but knew deep down something was terribly wrong. Wincing in pain, he fingered the small piece of purple lined paper his co-star Gertrude's dresser had given him.

He had arrived at the grand Selwyn Theatre for the first day of rehearsals for *Giddy Up*. The play and reviews had done so well on the West End in London that the producers decided to open it in New York, and he was thrilled to take on the new world with his new reviews and new name. Yet, despite his initial denial, he was now in grave pain and needed to have his back tooth fixed immediately before the New York opening. Sally, the kind and matronly dresser, took stock of the situation the way a mother does at an ill-dressed child before a snowstorm. With a warm maternal shake of the head and wag of the finger, she ordered Duke to go to the dentist as she scanned her address book for the phone number. She happily proclaimed he was the dentist that handled all the New York actors and actresses and show people on Broadway. Duke looked down at the name on the crumpled paper. Dr. Jerome Stein. Well, he would have to give in to his anxiety and pay the little old Jewish dentist a visit, the ethnic name giving him some comfort if only he was brave enough. After a night of tossing and turning, he finally caved and called to make the appointment with the greatest apprehension.

It was a freezing cold November that penetrated his thin winter coat, which wasn't up to the task of warming well. The taxi took him to a residential area in Murray Hill and, after approaching the looming townhouse, Duke saw the oval brass engraved sign next to the front door for a street-level office. "Dr. Jerome Stein" written in a grand engraved script seemed out of character. The dark, pitted oak paneling, frosty receptionist, and streamlined deco furniture did nothing to inspire his confidence but only raised more questions. What little old Jewish dentist had tony gray velvet deco chairs and a silvered coffee table? After a half hour of dawdling in the waiting room, picking up and nervously putting down a copy of the *Daily News* and *Photoplay* magazine, Duke was shown in by the nurse to a gleaming, antiseptic white office with the strange-looking dentist chair boasting leather restraints and odd contraptions. His feeling of dread was growing by the minute as he took in the sterile and gleaming cruel-looking sharp steel objects. He almost gave into his feelings of dread and ran out, but his nerves were only slightly dimmed by the shots of whiskey he had imbibed right before he came. Suddenly, the door flew open and a strange apparition of a tall, muscular, ginger-haired man in his thirties breezed in. He had light green eyes and a square jaw and looked nothing like the little Jewish dentist Duke had conjured in his mind. They were both taken aback at each other's good looks.

"Well, hello. You must be Duke?" Dr. Stein extended a firm hand and smiled brightly. He had a nice white smile and high cheekbones with just the right amount of stubble. "Jerry Stein."

"I wasn't expecting *you*. I mean I thought you would be older and… I'm sorry." Duke just smiled.

"That's what they all say; I'm used to it." He smiled and nodded again. "However, on the other hand, you look exactly like a *Duke Drake*. Now, tell me what the problem is…?" His demeanor immediately calmed his nervous patient.

After Duke explained his issue and the imminent opening night of the show, Dr. Stein suggested a gold crown for what appeared to be a fractured back molar. He said that he would start with some anesthesia called cyclopropane. Duke lay back in the odd chair and tried to calm himself as Dr. Stein prepped for what seemed like a great deal of work. The only thing that put him at ease was how good-looking, kind, and calm the doctor was, and the warmth of his fingers on his jaw.… He kept glancing at his impressive physique as he slipped on his own gown, gloves, and mask.

"Ready?" Dr. Stein asked as Duke nodded, his eyes ablaze with fear.

Dr. Stein gently affixed a plastic mask to Duke's face, and Duke instantly fell into slumber. When he awoke, he felt pain and tingling in the back of his mouth and yet also an odd sensation in his crotch. When he came to, he was shocked to find Dr. Jerome Stein on his knees with his mouth on his penis sucking him to orgasm. The room spun into focus.

"Do you do that to all your patients?" Duke said in a groggy voice, as he surveyed the sexy doctor and tried to make sense of things.

"Only the very handsome ones. I couldn't help myself, and now your tooth is fixed, and so are you." Dr. Stein spit into a napkin, wiped his mouth in a natural and nonchalant manner, and then smiled at Duke.

"Why would you assume you could do that?" Duke looked at him sideways, unsure of how to proceed.

"I can tell *our* kind." Jerome smiled.

"Is it that obvious?" Duke had always tried to affect a more masculine image to conceal his natural desires, which could have had a less-than-favorable effect on his career.

"When you looked at my zipper in the first five minutes, yes. Would you care to reciprocate?" The dentist smiled knowingly.

"When my mouth feels better, I might." Duke reached up and grabbed a handful of the doctor's crotch. "Very nice."

"And?"

"I just wanted to see what I was getting into. Nice equipment, Doctor," he joked.

"Dinner?" Jerome asked softly, putting the metal tools into the sink.

"Not tonight. I have a cast dinner with the director. But tomorrow?"

"Fine, I have plans, but I'll cancel. I would rather have dinner with my new client, the handsome Duke Drake. When did you get into town?" He smoothed his white smock.

"Thursday."

"Fine. I'll show you the ropes," Jerome said, his eyes taking in his handsome conquest.

"That would be nice. I'm not tied up here," Duke laughed.

"Not yet anyway." Jerry smiled again, teasing him. "I'll bring the rope—just kidding, but Duke, everyone here has to be careful. In New York and LA, the police are pretty aggressive, and there's a network here I can introduce you to. Especially since you are in the public eye. You don't want to end your career before it begins."

"Why did you mention LA?"

"I can tell with your looks, you'll be out there soon enough. And it's best to be in the right hands, you know, birds of a feather. We all introduce...*friends*." He shrugged.

"I think I'm going to like New York, Doctor Stein." Duke smiled gratefully.

"Call me Jerry." He leaned down and kissed him fully on the lips. "Welcome to New York, Duke Drake. I know exactly where I'm going to take you for dinner."

"Where?" Duke looked up wide-eyed.

"Ever had a kosher hot dog?" Jerry Stein laughed.

Chapter Twelve

Baroness Irene Von Mendelssohn, Grace Greystone
Paris
1935

"I absolutely want nothing to do with him! Are you insane, or should I check you back into Breiner's?" Grace Greystone shook her lovely golden brown head at Irene as she affixed a pair of deco platinum and diamond clips to her silver-gray spangled Lelong evening gown.

"He's the biggest ladies' man in Paris and, from what I hear, a total social climber," Grace added. The two new roommates reveled in their newly-decorated boudoir in their grand maison and their sense of freedom and sudden adulthood. Irene felt so grown up as she sat at her dressing table, the round mirror lit by a lamp of a striking elongated silver naked woman holding a frosted ball of light with two outstretched hands. The large globe glowed like a large moonstone above the circular mirror of the dressing table, illuminating her satin skin.

"One cannot climb, *Grace*, when one is already at the top of the ladder," Irene remarked with a seriousness, as if she were lecturing a grade school class on etiquette. "I've known Louis for years and while a total cad, is *très charmant*...and it's just a dinner at Maxim's. You'll actually be doing me the favor. He wants to introduce me to Fritz Langenheim, and you must come as a double date as I cannot be seen out with two men at the same time." Irene gave her a pleading look with her exquisite emerald, slanted eyes. "Please? It's the new year. Time for a fresh start," she laughed.

"You mean Fritz Langenheim, the famous young composer?" Grace nodded in questioning approval.

"Yes, Louis went to boarding school with him at Le Rosey before he went off to the conservatory. He said, 'He's brilliant, Viennese... and Jewish, like you.' And I think it's rather sweet he's thinking of me." She applied a powder puff to her rouged cheeks, the powder creating a misty, sparkling cloud. Irene's mother's deep green emerald ring seemed a tad too big for a young woman her age, but it also created a striking contrast. As Aunt Rose McClean often said, the older a woman gets, the larger her stones for distraction. Grace and Irene had no sense of this, and the two heiresses' jewels were often so large as to be comical in their extravagance at such a young age.

"Yes, but I can also assure you he's thinking of the Greystone fortune. That's what I meant...he's dated every rich girl in Paris." Grace shook her head against the idea.

"You're thinking too much. Remember what the doctor at Breiner's advised: 'Live in the moment!' Just come to dinner. He's the most handsome, eligible marquis in Paris."

"There is absolutely no way I'm going to dinner." Grace shook her head, now a gorgeous halo. "He has a new girl every week, and each one is richer and uglier than the next. My reputation is already slightly tarnished, and this might put me over the top."

Irene knew that Grace wasn't often very serious, but when she was, it was like hitting a brick wall. In the last year, their Île Saint-Louis mansion the baron had rented had become known as one of Paris's great salons. Grace, the American heiress and the beautiful young baroness threw extravagant and madcap evenings; fountains spouting Dom Perignon, costume balls that devolved into midnight swims in the indoor pool, jazz-age style, gin-soaked soirees that attracted European intellectuals, royalty, and visiting celebrities. The salonists would comically cry "Chez Von-Greystone," and café society would arrive on a Thursday or Saturday night to an open-door policy. Even starving artists were allowed entry as the girls felt it was their responsibility to offer a free buffet and bubbly to the brilliant...and the *broke.*

Grace, while pretty with lovely violet eyes and brown-blonde hair, was even seen as a great beauty with the couture, jewels, and accouterments creating the haze of real money glamour. Irene, a bit more serious, though still creating a stir with her beauty, worked a few days at *La Surrealism de la Revolution,* André Breton's literary magazine, which always added interesting guests to their list like Max Ernst and Peggy Guggenheim. One thing was for sure, the two roommates had *tout la Paris* at their well-shod feet.

"Ladies," their maid said as she entered the room with fresh hand towels.

"Yes, Magda?" Irene looked up.

"The gentlemen are in the library," she announced.

"What!?" Grace cried. "You invited them *here* first?"

"*Chouchou*, Louis has been to many parties here. You know that."

"Yes, when he's been among the throngs. And even then, I wouldn't deign to look at him. Peggy Guggenheim told me if you look into his eyes, all you see is…dollar signs."

"Mademoiselles…" Louis knocked on the door and peeked his well-formed head in. "I hope you're talking about us and are in various states of undress while doing so." His eyes sparkled in a playful puppy dog way. "Fritz, this is the great beauty, Irene, Baroness Von Mendelssohn I've been telling you about."

"*Enchante.*" Fritz entered the room, following Louis's lead without regard for propriety. He was tall and slim with a head of refined, auburn curls and both cut dashing figures in tails and silken top hats. As he viewed her, he stifled a gasp at her sheer beauty.

"Actually, although we are both very much dressed…don't you think it a little forward of you to barge in on us like this?" Grace sniffed, flashing a frozen smile. "My Uncle Reggie would have your heads for entering a woman's boudoir unannounced."

"Yes, but we are neither respectable nor impressive." Louis's charming smirk disarmed the situation.

"We've been waiting forty-five minutes, and we just didn't know if you were ever coming down or not, so we decided to take matters into our own hands." Fritz laughed, bowing at the waist and displaying a snow-capped smile. Irene broke the ice by walking across the room to the men and extending her now-gloved hand as Fritz bowed and kissed it in a formal European gesture.

"Fritz, it's lovely to make your acquaintance. I am a huge fan of your last opera, *Die Liebesgeschichte und Die Herzensbrecher*. My father and I saw it in Vienna in the spring to stellar reviews."

"A lady after my own heart. You are exactly as Louis described, beyond description, a legendary beauty and a heartbreaker in the flesh." He bowed and kissed her gloved hand. "And this, may I ask, is the famous Grace Greystone?" He walked over and kissed her extended hand as well.

"Famous," she bristled. "Unlike you, sir, I prefer being out of the press, I can assure you." She shook her luxurious waves at both young men.

"We've come to collect you for oysters at Maxim's—our chariot awaits."

"I'm afraid I already have...plans," Grace sniffed, turning back to her dressing mirror.

Louis walked over, dropped to one knee, and produced a bouquet of long-stem roses he had hidden behind his back. Inside was a card. Grace shrugged and read the card.

"Grace, how sweet of Louis," Irene pleaded. "*Et ma fleurs*?" She gave a theatrical raised eyebrow.

Fritz also dropped to one knee and produced a bunch of violets.

"Oh, Fritz, violets are my favorite!" Irene's eyes twinkled. "Grace, come for dinner, please?"

Grace handed Irene the card and walked over and threw a Russian sable stole over one shoulder.

"*Peut-etre est-ce dans les cartes*." Grace handed Irene the card from the flowers. Irene saw the script.

> Dear Grace,
>
> Roses are red. Violets are blue. You're an American beauty.
> *Et J'taime chouchou. Louis*

She hadn't wanted to, but she broke into a broad smile.

"You'll come, then?" Louis gave a mirroring smile, lighting up the room.

"*Peut etre*. Just for an oyster or two, monsieur." Grace smiled at the athletic and handsome marquis. "Or three."

Chapter Thirteen

Bartie Maddox
Los Angeles
1935

Bartie's pulse quickened with sexual excitement as he entered the imposing gates to the SGM studio lot for the first time. The sun-bleached yellow of the Mediterranean stucco buildings seemed more vibrant, the bougainvillea more reminiscent of the intoxicating pink of upturned breasts he had seen in illicit nudie magazines. It was as if he had walked into a Kodachrome studio and had to adjust his eyes to a new electric tableau. He'd never experienced such a vibrant energy: fast motion, interlocking machine parts, each one rotating in unison, and it was exhilarating and intimidating all at the same time. Bartie knew deep down from the moment that the sole of his secondhand, weathered brown Oxford landed on the lot pavement, he was *home.* He would have to get this assistant job that Francis had told him about. He was being rewarded for his quick typing skills and helping F. Scott get out of his myriad drunken scrapes—his typing ahead of schedule and his quick hangover remedies at the ready.

He peered at the numbers on the lot buildings and found the one scribbled on the notepad. He breathed in deeply, opposing his shallow breath as he approached the small building resembling a small Tudor cottage at the back lot. The secretary in her late twenties looked him up and down as he walked up to her desk. She was all hard, illuminated edges: a cheap peroxided blonde with dark roots, bright red lipstick, and streaks of rouge she hadn't quite rubbed in. Her pendulous breasts were straining a thin white blouse and sweater set. Her immediate salivating gaze had him blushing as he felt like a piece of chopped meat at a steak restaurant. Was she actually looking at his loins? She quickly noticed he noticed and looked up, unabashed.

"So, yer here for the assistant position?" She stated the obvious. Bartie could tell she was a few years older than him but friendly *and* suggestive.

"Yeah," he gulped. "This would be exciting."

"Well, it sure is interesting, I can tell ya that." She snapped her wad of gum. "Hi, I'm Mavis, by the way." She stood with a friendly gesture, extending her hand. "I didn't think you would be well…*you*, when you set up the appointment. Never met a Bartie before." She smiled in a congenial way and patted her upswept dyed blonde curls.

"It's short for Barston." He smiled at her through his eyeglasses, his eyes fixated on her large, alluring breasts that seemed to be waving hello. She wasn't exactly beautiful, but Mavis sure was sexy.

"By the way," she offered in a low voice, "his bark is louder than his bite. Just say yes to everything, and I bet you get it." She laughed in a good-natured way as she talked about her boss. The phone rang, and she picked up the receiver. Bartie heard a bit of commotion on the other end.

"Yes, Mister Menowitz, he's here, and I'll send him in."

"He's ready for you now." She pointed to the office door. "Good luck…Bartie." She bit her lip as he saw her look him up and down once more with a lascivious grin taking in his lean, muscular physique and chiseled jawline.

"Thanks," he nodded as he saw her bite her lip again.

He walked down a short hallway and then glanced up at the door and read "Mr. Isidore Menowitz, Head of Studio Publicity," which was stenciled on the door in matte, flaked gold lettering on the frosted glass. As Bartie entered the office, he spied a heap of nervous energy. While only in his forties, Izzy Menowitz looked ten years older. He was a gangly, scrawny man in an unseasonably bold Prince of Wales black-and-white checked blazer with overly large shoulder pads. He gave him a shrewd one-second once-over.

"You're not a dame," he blurted out as he tapped his cigarette in the large crystal cut ashtray and sighed.

"I hope not." Bartie gave a wry smile.

"I thought you were going to be some looker recommended by F. Scott. Can't keep his hands to himself with the ladies." He sighed again, disappointed by the presence of the male species, peering over tortoise shell frames, which strangely highlighted his gleaming bald pate and searing, auburn eyes.

"That's why he needed a male typist to keep him working and sober, which I did," Bartie explained and shrugged.

"Well done," he said in a snarky tone. "Maybe he'll finally publish a novel or a script…in a few *years*." He emitted a laugh. "You have his letter of recommendation on you?" He tapped the Camel cigarette carton against his wood desk briskly.

Bartie slid the manila folder with the letter F. Scott had written for him over the desk. "Here, sir."

Menowitz looked down at the sheet and gave a nod as he saw the letter only had one line and his signature. It simply read, "Hire him. He's good. F. Scott Fitzgerald."

"Francis usually doesn't say nice things about people. In fact, he's known to shit in everyone's hat, so this is impressive. You're not a queer, are you?" He looked him up and down. "I mean, I couldn't care less what hole you fuck, but Mister Myers hates *queers.* One of my biggest jobs here is getting all the fairies married."

"Married?" Bartie looked up in confusion.

"So the public doesn't know. Don't be naive. Most of them are cornholing it with someone." He took a drag on a cigarette. "My mother doesn't know what I do, ya know? I tell her I get press for movies. That's five percent of the job. The rest is arranging for abortions for knocked-up starlets, covering up drunken auto accidents by paying off the injured, and getting the fairy stars married—called a lavender marriage." He paused and scrutinized Bartie, surveying his all-American looks. "You look like a good kid. Why don't you run for the hills before you get…corrupted?" he sneered.

"Why, I find this all very exciting, Mister Menowitz." Bartie looked up wide-eyed.

"So is walking on hot coals. Look, you have morals, scruples?" he sighed.

"I think so."

"You religious, church on Sunday, that sort of thing?"

"Sometimes?"

"I'm telling you right now, this job is not for you. Trust me. Look, kid, just go away. I can tell you don't have it in you." He waved a hand capped by a glittering navy star sapphire in his platinum pinky ring.

"What don't I have?" Bartie asked eagerly.

"I can see it. You're too *good.* You're squeaky clean, have Brylcreem in your hair and wear fresh underwear. You most likely don't drink and screw around." He paused. "This job is for someone else."

"So why are *you* good at it?" Bartie confronted his gaze.

"Because I'm a conniving piece of shit," he grinned, revealing a new set of oversized caps.

"Maybe I can learn," Bartie said enthusiastically.

At that, Izzy Menowitz let out one of the great belly laughs of his career. In fact, he was so wracked with laughter, he started coughing and called for Mavis to bring in the seltzer siphon and bicarbonate of soda.

"Are you okay, Mister Menowitz? I never heard you like this before." Mavis fluttered like a desperate moth around a door light.

"Like what?" He screwed up his dark eyes at her.

"Laughing," she gulped. "Didn't know you had it in you." She smiled at Bartie and licked her lips. She was a trashy piece for sure.

"So, you've met Mavis…my *sex*-retary…" He laughed again.

"Very funny. Missus M called. She said, 'Don't be late for dinner… or else.'" She had a hand on her hip.

"Or else what?"

"I wouldn't want to tangle with Missus M, but that's up to you, boss."

"Yeah, in the doghouse for sure. Anyway, Mavis, say hello to our new junior publicist. *Bartie!* Congrats, you just got the job." He pumped his hand as Bartie looked up, stunned.

"Bartie, just sit there while I go take a piss." Menowitz coughed again and bolted to the men's room. Bartie sat in a chair as he observed Mavis and her voluptuous figure and nervous sexual energy, which seemed to bounce off her.

"I don't know what you did, but I have *never* seen that before. Congrats." She cracked her gum. "And welcome to the lot." Mavis toyed with the button on her blouse. "That's very impressive. The only time he hires that quickly is if a girl has the numbers."

"Numbers?"

"Yeah." She cracked her gum. "Thirty-six, twenty-four, thirty-six."

"So why do you think I got the job?"

"Look." She leaned against the deco desk before her boss reentered the room. "You got a recco from F. Scott. But you done something no one has ever done before."

"What's that?

"Made the mean bastard laugh." Mavis licked her lips. "I think you're going to do just fine here Bartie…?"

"Maddox."

"Bartie Maddox." She smiled. "And lean on me if you need anything." She licked her ruby lips again. "I mean, anything."

"Anything?" Bartie coughed, himself.

"Anything."

"I think this is my lucky day." Bartie smiled.

Menowitz broke back in as if in a freak storm reading a telegram and barked, "Get me Wattenberg on the phone. I'm going to break that motherfucker's legs, myself, and then fix them up."

"What happened, boss?" Mavis asked, nonplussed.

"Gregory Lancaster just got into another drunken car crash on Sunset. Was getting a blow job in the front seat by this contract girl. All her teeth are knocked out, and his dick needs stitches. Maddox, first assignment. Call the hospital and arrange for a private room. Tell him Mister Phil Smith is coming back for an appointment."

"Phil Smith?"

"His alias, you dumb fuck. Just do it. Mavis, call his unit and alert them we're in code red."

"Unit?" Bartie looked up in confusion.

"Greg Lancaster is such a fucking drunk, the studio assigned him his own special unit, a bodyguard, and an ambulance with two doctors to attend to his drunken fights, car crashes, and whatever other messes he makes. They show up weekly to just clean up the mess. America's most *respected dad* is a dead drunk, a degenerate hole chaser, and it's a full-time job cleaning up his escapades and paying off the whores and the injured. You'll get used to it."

"Of course." Bartie could not believe what he was hearing. Greg Lancaster's image was as pure as Ivory soap and a Norman Rockwell painting.

"Mavis, post the bodyguards we always use on the floor. No press, no nothing. Call Louella on the phone and tell her to bury it. She'll know, and say I'll trade her…what's his name?" He thought. "Um… that kid, Grant Bellows. Tell her his contract ain't gettin' renewed since he's a fag and sucking off every fairy director on the lot. Mister Myers wanted him to marry Nita Eriksonn, but he won't. From what I hear, he gives bad head anyway. Throw that damn fairy under the bus for Lancaster's raggedy ass."

Bartie looked on, wide-eyed. He had read in Hedda Hopper's column that Grant Bellows was the newest heartthrob on the lot—a teen idol they were saying was the next Mickey Rooney. The news actually shook him to his core, although he tried to remain cool and calm. It was almost too much information to process at once.

"Welcome to SGM, Bartie." Mavis shrugged as she sashayed out the door to her desk to help set up the latest studio fix.

Chapter Fourteen

Baron Karl Von Mendelssohn
Bordeaux, France
1936

Euphoria perfumed the air with young love, nightly soirees, and stolen, heated embraces. Thoughts of work and higher education were suddenly on the back burner as Irene and Grace were officially being courted by Fritz and Louis, respectively, and everywhere they went, the foursome created an uproar. *Tout-Paris* embraced their youth, looks, fame, and money, and the press swirled around them documenting every move and furtive kiss.

While the two heiresses played coy, the young men mounted an offensive that was as serious as a Napoleonic military campaign as they spent a great deal of time visiting the cavernous Louvre and the Musée de l'Orangerie as well as spending languorous afternoons at Café-Flor and Brasserie Lipp. Fritz and Irene and their love of music took in the grand sights and sounds of the Paris opera. Theirs was an intellectual rather than physical attraction, on Irene's part. However, she was captivated by Fritz's genius, and nights at the L'Opera with the charismatic prodigy did much to inflame her passion. Grace, however, despite her initial objections, was swept away like a nocturnal wave under an opaque full moon. Louis's constant and ardent campaign to win her affections finally wore her down and subsequently washed over her, sending her tumbling headlong into a romantic surf.

Louis possessed an inner light that was magical, elfin, refreshing, and always unusual. He'd persisted for months and had seemingly worked overtime to woo her, deploying every tactic, realizing the element of surprise and throwing her off kilter was the key to penetrating her hardened shell. He possessed an innate sense of timing and seduction, and the flowery French poetry and candlelit dinners eventually softened Grace's stance as much as his tall, blonde looks, ancient title, and elegant physique did. The campaign to win Irene's hand was also in full swing with Fritz taking a more intellectual approach and keeping it lively. Both couples often double dated for a late dinner at Maxim's, and the men's opposite personalities provided an amusing counterbalance for both young women. Of the two, interestingly, Grace fell quicker, while Irene was more guarded and strategic in her approach; after all, she had the baron to contend with. Perhaps it would have been easier if there had been a French marquis in the wings like Louis de La Faucigny with a grand title, but despite the European acclaim for Fritz Langenheim's talent, her father let it be known he wasn't exactly keen on the match. It had none of the flourish or allure of French aristocracy or heir to a great fortune, though he did try to control his disappointment seeing how happy Irene was.

It was a sparkling Seurat-style afternoon at the Chateau Von Mendelssohn in Bordeaux where an al fresco lunch was taken on the rambling lawn next to the artfully trimmed boxwoods under the rustling, cool breeze of an ancient oak tree. The seventeenth-century chateau cast its long-armed shadow over the capacious terrace, and rows of festooned and faded turquoise shutters seemed to exhale in languid sighs, suggesting a casualness not usually attributed to such formality.

The distinguished baron alternated seats between courses, first on his wicker chair and then reclining on his chaise, under a chic straw boater with a whimsical aqua silk band, which brought out the Cap-Ferrat blue in his eyes against his trimmed, peppered, gray beard. The staff, per his doctor's orders, had set up the chaise next to the table as he was recuperating from a mild heart attack; the doctors recommended a rest in the country at his vineyard and away from stressful Vienna politics. The incredible stress had indeed caught up with him, and he began by sitting upright and then lounging between courses to regain his strength.

Irene and Grace sat at the beautifully set table and sighed at the exquisite afternoon and recent turn of events. The previous week, Louis had taken Grace to the top of the Eiffel Tower and proposed on one knee with his grandmother's venerable Cartier diamond ring. It was now complemented by the stack of slim deco diamond bracelets, a traffic jam of diamonds in platinum set with cabochon rubies red for love. The Greystone/de La Faucigny match was widely viewed as a glamorous merger by the baron and the press, yet had cloudy thoughts as it applied to his own daughter's burgeoning romance with the "musician" as he called him.

"Well done, Grace." He raised a sparkling water glass in her direction. "However, I'm just not as sure about Irene's beau," the baron sighed over a bottle of their famous Bordeaux, which had been decanted in a shaded area of the table. He looked skyward once it was poured into a goblet and swirled the ruby red liquid.

"Daddy, that is so *mean*," Irene uttered with a low moan, which made her look even more like a silent screen star in a complex, dramatic scene.

"Fritz is accomplished and Jewish," the baron surmised out loud, "but there is something about this match that I am just not quite *sure* of." He swayed as he often did when considering an important subject. "I'd like your thoughts on the subject, Grace, as you seem to know him better and have spent more time with 'the musician' than I." He widened his eyes to show his seriousness on the matter.

"But Daddy, we already have one famous composer in the family." Irene's emerald eyes pleaded as she shot a look at Grace for support. They had gone by train to Chateau Von Mendelssohn for a long weekend for a bit of rest and relaxation and to visit Daddy, who was feeling better, but the attack had seriously scared her.

"Yes, but Felix was a Von Mendelssohn. The Bartholdy was added for vanity's sake and religious reasons. It seems times haven't changed all that much." He sighed, thinking of the mounting storm clouds gathering in Europe.

"He's brilliant, handsome, and *Juden*. What more could you ask for?" Irene offered.

"A Sassoon or a Rothschild would do quite well," he sniffed.

"Oh, you're such a snob, Daddy." Her arms encircled his thin arms, her own diamond and sapphire bracelets sparkling in the sunlight as she kissed his now gaunt cheek.

"And Grace, what do you think of the illustrious Monsieur Langenheim?" the baron asked.

"I just *adore* Fritz, Baron Karl. He is *très charmant* and quite brilliant. The sun also rises and sets on Irene." She smiled as she tossed her sun-streaked hair.

"As it should, for both you girls," he added.

"Daddy, I just want you to know that a proposal may be imminent as it was for Grace." She paused. "Doesn't his brilliance and acclaim make up for the lack of breeding?"

"*Au contraire.* My issue with Fritz isn't a lack of breeding or title as much as it...well..." A racking cough took over, and he paused to find the right words.

"Daddy, please don't upset yourself." Irene surveyed his ashen complexion as he hesitated. "Of course, go on," she said with the deepest respect.

"Darling Irene, it's not that I don't *like* Fritz. I quite like him. I just *loathe* certain aspects of his personality. He's just a bit of a know-it-all. In fact, I have never met anyone who seems to know as much and about more things. If he were just an authority on music, I could forgive him, but it seems he also knows more about running a vineyard and Raphael and Titian than I do, which is a bit maddening since I am the one who owns them all."

"Daddy, Fritz is just...*passionate*," Irene pleaded.

"So is Mussolini." He groaned slightly.

"Daddy, that is a terrible comparison." Irene laughed into her hand.

"I just don't want to see you under autocratic rule. Grace, can you enlighten our Irene here? I am sorry to bring up the subject, but we are among dear friends."

"I'm not so sure." Grace defended Fritz and Irene in a respectful way as she was taught to do. "I think Fritz is kind and brilliant," Grace said, her bracelets casually clinking against her wine goblet. "Personally, I find him and his talent enthralling."

"Well, there it is, young love for you both. Don't say I didn't tell you, though," he wagged a finger at Irene, "...when you come crying to me." The baron had a gray and torpid cast.

"Daddy, you know I love you more than anything, but you have all these antiquated rules." She looked at Grace and said aloud, "I was offered a starring role after I sang *La Traviata*'s aria at one of our state dinners by Kurt Weill, himself, and father said it 'wasn't appropriate for someone of *my station* to be on the stage.' Princess Marie organized a summer job in Madame Curie's laboratory. No, no, and all no. Then, he abhorred my last boyfriend—although, I must say he was maddeningly right...and now it's Fritz?" Irene threw her lovely hands skyward, her ruby polished fingernails grazing the sky. "I'm not sure anyone or anything would do."

The baron eyed his daughter, took a deep breath, and smiled.

"Yes, *liebschen*. I do suppose the world is changing, and my rules may be old-fashioned...and that you are too good for anyone," he sighed.

"Now, Daddy, don't upset yourself. You are recovering, and Grace and I are here to nurse you back a bit and also drink some of your very good wine while Louis and Fritz are off riding. The doctor said no stress. You don't want to have another attack, now do you?" Irene reached over, kissed him on his cheek, and took his slightly trembling hand.

"I do, however, want to officially congratulate you, Grace, on your engagement to Louis." Baron Frederich raised his goblet. "His father and I are old friends, and he certainly hails from one of the most important families and titles in France. How does your uncle feel about the match?" He coughed again, which shook Irene. "I'm sure he must be pleased."

"Honestly, I think my uncle is more *relieved* than happy," Grace said, looking very American, with her lanky and tan figure looking toned and athletic in the newest rage, navy Chanel trousers. "According to the pundits in Newport and London, I am still, as always, something of a scandal magnet. I think my Aunt Rose and Uncle Reggie are hoping *that* current title will be replaced with the Marquise de La Faucigny sooner rather than later. I think Aunt Rose was worried no man in London would want me except for the money. Uncle Reggie had a very lengthy interview with Louis and his father and insisted on a longer engagement but was very positive on the match. Although I do feel Louis's father was not as happy about the marriage due my mother's 'issue,' as he called it. I should think he is a bit scandalized by it all."

"Grace, you are a beautiful and smart young woman. Louis is lucky *il est très chanceux*! I cannot think of two more desirable young women in all of Europe." The baron looked at his daughter with love. "And when the time comes, I would be happy to walk you…*both* down the aisle." He reached out and took Irene's hand and smiled at her.

"Really?" Irene asked, wide-eyed.

"Really," he nodded, looking at the electric smile on his gorgeous daughter's face.

Irene jumped up and hugged her father and then ran to Grace and as they hugged, they laughed.

"Oh, Daddy, I am so happy. I didn't want to say, but Fritz also proposed!" She and Grace gave each other conspiratorial looks. "I didn't want anything to upset you, and I said I would talk with you this weekend."

"That was kind of you to wait." The baron tried to stifle a slight grimace with a false smile.

"So, you give your permission and blessing? Really?" Despite her summer dress, Irene walked over and knelt and put her beautiful head into her father's lap, like a little girl. "I didn't want Fritz to ask for my hand if you wouldn't say yes."

"How could I deny you one more thing to make you happy?" he said softly. "I wish you and Fritz only the very best."

He kissed her head like he used to after he had read her a bedtime story. "However, he must come and formally ask for your hand."

"Yes, Daddy. He was planning on it. I love you so." Irene's eyes sparkled like Colombian emeralds.

"*Mazel tov*," he whispered under his breath as the uniformed servants cleared the soup tureen and brought out the roti de boeuf and mushroom risotto under polished silver domes reflecting the approaching storm clouds in the distance.

Chapter Fifteen

Gorge Lamont
Los Angeles
1937

The casting couch was his regular booth at the Brown Derby, and the seat was always occupied and warm on Thursdays with new, fresh trade and the worst kept secret in LA. Gorge Lamont strode through the landmark and whimsical hat-shaped restaurant at 3377 Wilshire Boulevard and flashed his trademark, high-wattage platinum smile beneath his framed, stylized caricature on the wall. He double-checked to see it and was happy his framed likeness still occupied prime real estate between Fairbanks, Pickford, and Swanson. He was looking tan and successful to his usual fanfare, turning heads amid a sea of waves to industry cronies. In the '20s, Gorge Lamont had been dubbed by the studio PR department as "the handsomest man in the universe," and "every schoolgirl's crush," and although that was ten years earlier, he knew he still lived up to the title. He nodded and waved to columnists Hedda Hopper and her rival, Louella Parsons, who politely waved back and sat at opposing tables. They were powerful columnists who'd long controlled Hollywood images in the press and the stars in its firmament.

Gorge Lamont didn't walk so much as stride as his longer than usual limbs created a larger-than-life impression. Perhaps it had been his Midwest corn-fed genes, but everything about Gorge was on a bigger scale. His shoulders were broader, his teeth were bigger and whiter, and his silky blonde hair wasn't just blonde, but the color of summer wheat. It fell effortlessly over his famed eyes…the robin's egg blue that put every other shade to shame. His lanky torso was the perfect mannequin for his fashionable, high-waisted and pleated cream-colored slacks, the hard crease cascading down the middle of the trouser and breaking subtly on his tan and white spectator shoes. His shoulders were so naturally broad and his waist such a perfect V, he needed less shoulder padding than the average actor on the lot, and studio tailors worked overtime to remove the stuffing, remarking on his perfect proportions; not many could sport a natural shoulder and still look sufficiently padded. His fame only added to his glow for the average, visiting tourist hoping to spot a star or snag an autograph with a top celebrity.

He nodded to a few studio execs doing deals over juicy burgers, and the actresses who were confidantes; a few like Joan Crawford, whom he stopped to kiss and kibitz with. Although he hadn't been in a movie in the last six years, he was still considered a major star in Hollywood; number one at the box office in '29 as his houseman, Akito, would be the first to tell you. In 1931, he had been in his one and only "talkie," which was now a legendary and scandalous affair, and although he knew deep down his time as an actor was up, the one thing the studio couldn't take away from him was his looks. At thirty-four, he was a magnificent blonde Adonis, and his mere presence in the room set both women and men aflame. He stopped and graciously signed two or three leather bound autograph books for tourists and fans then made his way to his table awaiting what he called "his second meal."

Gorge Lamont, and every single industry person in the room, knew that he would be dining that afternoon with a handsome younger man. Whether that man would be a one-night trick or the next new star depended on how expertly that man sucked cock and whether Gorge felt he had *it*. The endless supply of "trade" was sent to him by a variety of sources, one being his dentist in New York—Jerry Stein, who was known among his set as "the driller." Jerry was a discreet member of "the circuit," and when he came across talent, he made the introduction by sending Gorge a coded telegram about a new young actor visiting the West Coast he thought had "potential." Gorge returned the favor when one of his tricks was en route to New York for the stage or needed capped teeth. He knew that Jerry had good taste and saw up and coming theater actors, but he also knew he had been wrong as much as he had been right about their acting ability, and Gorge took the lunch with minimal expectations. Jerry never sent anyone who wasn't, at the very least, good-looking, and more often than not, it was a quick BJ in the back of the car before he headed back to his Santa Monica beach house.

That was the thing about Gorge: he was handsome, successful, and rich enough not to care and had been one of the only actors in Hollywood system *not* to play by the studio rules. Since he had always been above it all, with an avalanche of fan mail and even a despondent female fan who had committed suicide over him, his nonchalance and superiority kept him afloat. But the flaunting of his sexuality had torpedoed his once-thriving career and had him at odds with the most powerful man in Hollywood, his studio boss, Solomon Isadore Myers.

What everyone in town also knew was that there was nothing more that old Solly hated than what he called "a leading-man fag." In his conservative, conventional mind, this category of fag made him more rabid than a director-fag or costume-designer fag because, in his mind, if the public ever found out, it could possibly ruin his investment, his asset, and cause a major scandal for the studio. Solly hated, but could tolerate, a costume-designer fag because they were *all f*ags, but a he-man like Lamont? It was inconceivable. He also simply could not fathom what two men would see in each other when there was so much beautiful pussy to fuck. He became nauseous at the thought of what they did to each other, trying not to imagine every depraved act. Yet, Solly Myers had to work with plenty of "fairies": producers, writers, directors, and actors. The "dykes" bothered him less, but he still bristled at having to tolerate, in his mind, degenerate behavior. Most of the actors on the lot were chastened by Solly Myers and understood the need to keep their sexual activities and hijinks under the radar if they wanted to succeed with SGM and their moral clauses.

His long-term studio publicist and fixer, Izzy Menowitz, also hated fags, yet had arranged more lavender marriages than one could count on a hand. But no one had flaunted their "flaming fag behavior" in his face more than Gorge Lamont. The years 1927 to 1929 ushered in Gorge Lamont as SGM's biggest silent film star and heartthrob, and the situation drove Solly Myers to drink. He screamed, he yelled, he became beet-faced trying to explain to Gorge that young "*goils* across America needed their heroes to be real men! Not *cock-suckahs*!" The studio had also spent a substantial amount of hush money when Gorge Lamont was busted in various raids by the vice squad. Keeping the matter out of the press was a full-time job for Izzy Menowitz, who had a standing Bromo Seltzer dissolving in water on his desk. No matter what he was accused of, the constant rants and raves and lectures, Gorge Lamont just sat there and shrugged, flashing his high-wattage smile. He just seemed to not give a rat's ass, and that alone ate at Solomon Myers *kishkas* daily—so much so that when his public relations fixer, Izzy, worked overtime for a studio fix and Gorge turned it down, he went into a punitive rage.

"Is he out of his fucking *fag* mind?" Solly kicked and screamed. "We are giving him platinum pussy on a silver-plated platter," Solly had cried in one of his so-called rants. Myers was street-smart but never had more than a high school education, if that, and was noted for his malapropisms, traded around dinner parties called *Myerisms.* These were greedily collected and passed around Hollywood golf clubs and steam rooms to great laughter. The last one and proposed studio fix: an arranged romance and marriage between Gorge and Nita Eriksonn, one of the most beautiful and elusive Swedish stars in the world. It would have yielded great press as she also happened to be a lesbian. The fact that Gorge refused to play ball when they were already great friends, spent time together socially, and could have had separate entrances in a huge mansion, solving all their problems, so enraged Solly that he eventually set out to destroy his biggest star.

In 1928 and '29, Gorge Lamont was the number one silent film star on the lot and SGM's biggest moneymaker. With the advent of talkies, the public was eager to not only see their favorite stars, but also to hear them. After one particularly heated exchange with Lamont after Menowitz, and the studio had gotten him off on vice charges yet again for giving a gas station attendant a blow job by the pump—in broad daylight no less—Myers insisted on the Eriksonn union. Lamont demurred and, in a rage, Myers demanded the marriage or ruin. Lamont, in turn, threatened to go public about Myers's many affairs and his own casting couch with young female stars calling him out as a hypocrite.

Enraged at the audacity and never one to not have the upper hand, Myers came to the conclusion in his paneled library over a whiskey neat that night that Gorge Lamont had gotten too big for his Hollywood britches. He knew he had to do something, but what? He tossed. He turned. He schemed. He plotted. He planned. And then it came to him in a semi-conscious dream state in his Bel Air bedroom; he knew exactly what he needed to do. There was a new army of sound technicians at the studio, and one night, he summoned the head of the division to pay a clandestine, nocturnal visit, and he was paid handsomely to take the bass out of Lamont's voice in secrecy after hours. And when Lamont's first talkie, *Jazz Age Jingo* debuted in New York and LA theaters, audiences broke into spontaneous laughter at Lamont's tinny, high-pitched voice and seemingly overdramatic acting.

While effectively killing his greatest cash cow and star's career, Solly knew it served a higher purpose for SGM. He gleefully let the urban legend spread, neither confirming nor denying what he had done to Gorge Lamont, but the overall message was crystal clear: Mr. Solomon Myers could make you, but if you crossed him, he could also break you. For months, Gorge went into hiding at his Los Feliz mansion with a cadre of young men, hoping for a comeback. That was not to be, as Myers did what no other studio head could; he kept Gorge paid under his contract, paying him his minimum but not giving him a new film, so he was locked up and out of the public eye—equivalent to cinematic purgatory. Distraught, Lamont took out a full-page ad in the Hollywood trades that said, "I am under contact by SGM, neither allowed to work on any film or at any other studio." It was the final death knell of his career.

That said, Gorge Lamont was still impossibly handsome, rich, and had a great eye, and his passion for interior design allowed him to decorate the home of many of his friends, many of Hollywood's top female stars. Despite being banished on film sets, he kept busy sprucing up cavernous Tudors and furnishing newly built center hall colonials. Word spread about his chic and glamorous taste, and he soon emerged as one of the most talented LA-based interior designers, a career which would keep him busy and in the social swing for years to come. Decades later, when they were both too old to care, Solly Myers would actually hire Gorge to decorate his Palm Springs home to great fanfare. The hatchet would finally be buried in his eighties as Myers latest, youngest wife pined for Gorge's chic design skills.

The year 1937 saw Gorge Lamont turning thirty-five years old. He had looked in the mirror that very morning and saw a few emerging crow's feet, and for the first time, he panicked. The death of "baby," his great friend and film star, Jean Harlow, had all of Hollywood reeling and dealing with mortality, and Gorge saw the fine lines as a portentous sign. All of which to say, when he saw the tailored and elegant twenty-year-old Duke Drake stride into the Brown Derby, he sensed an inner soulmate and also a lifeline reflecting his own life force. All eyes were on the stunning actor as he made his way to Gorge Lamont's table. His cinematic face was so ravishing, a young girl actually gasped at his beauty.

"Mister Lamont." Duke extended his hand in a firm, manly shake. "It is a great honor and pleasure to meet you. I have always been a huge fan. You are bigger than life!" He gave his own high-wattage smile, the cleft in his chin glistening.

"In more ways than one." Gorge raised an eyebrow to see if he would take the bait.

"That's what Jerry Stein said, so I was even more eager to make your acquaintance," Duke quipped in his clipped and honed British accent. "He said I would be in, and I quote, 'the best hands in Hollywood.'" He flashed his devastating smile again for good measure.

Gorge Lamont was stunned and breathless—actually taken aback. He often had to beat around the bush with much lesser talent, but here was someone as good-looking as he was, which was one in a million, and he was meeting him on his own terms and as blunt about his sexuality.

"Yes, Jerry is my East Coast dentist, talent scout, and has earned his nickname 'the driller.' I send him lots of business, if you get my drift. Would you also care for a Cobb salad, Mister Drake?" Gorge indicated to the waitress that Duke would have one as well. After all, the finely chopped salad and recipe had been invented on the premises.

Tongues wagged as Gorge did not stay for dessert as he usually did, for he and Duke made a hasty exit. Within hours, Gorge had taken young Duke back to his beach house in Santa Monica. The level of passion and desire was something neither of them had ever experienced—as if they were the mirror images of one another. Since they had such a high opinion of themselves, they feasted on each other as if they were making love to themselves. When Gorge kissed Duke, he couldn't get enough, as if he had turned into a sexual vampire. When he pinned Duke down, he fucked him from behind with such force, he broke the bedframe. Most men had a hard time accommodating his huge member, but when Duke yelled, "Give it to me harder!" Gorge knew he had finally met his match. Within days, Duke moved into Gorge's Santa Monica house and Los Feliz mansion, and Hollywood's newest couple was the talk of the town. In fact, everyone wanted a glimpse of the handsomest man to arrive in Hollywood since, well…Gorge Lamont. Everyone, including Lamont's agent, Virgil Lindstrom, who handled—almost exclusively—the up-and-coming gay stars and was happy to add Duke to his roster at Gorge's request.

It seemed that everyone in LA was watching, not to mention, one Mr. Solomon Myers.

Chapter Sixteen

Bartie Maddox
Los Angeles
1937

Bartie knew better than to get in the way of Izzy Menowitz first thing in the morning—before his boss had his strong black coffee or a screaming call from Myers, both of which would have him yelling and inhaling Bromo Seltzer. Each afternoon, though, was rarely different, and he often emerged from his office as if smoke were pouring out of his ears.

"Get in here. It's fucking Sterling Dumont…again!" he shouted, his voice laced with weary vitriol about the tough character actor who was trouble when drunk, which seemed to be a daily occurrence.

"What happened now?" Bartie asked in a low voice.

"He ended up brawling in a bar fight and beat the living crap out of a guy who called him a 'has been.' Now the guy is in a coma. Bartie, remind me to get Wattenberg in the finance department on the phone. I'm going to need to have him get a cash advance to pay off the family and the press. Sit, sit, *sit*! Let's first brainstorm. Now," he began as he paced, "how do we get out of this one with a good…*fix*?" He paused, Bartie hearing the term again, which was now seared into his brain.

"Sterling's in the same hospital wing with a bruised jaw and a broken wrist. Any ideas, Kid?" He swigged from his coffee mug. A temp was filling in for Mavis, and he yelled at the young woman who put the coffee mug on the wrong side of the desk.

"Fa Chrissakes…can't ya see the ring from the coffee cup is on the other side of the desk?" He grumbled as she looked at him like he had two heads. "So, the press has spotted him in the hospital?" Bartie asked.

"What are you, a member of the *Moron* Tabernacle Choir? I just said he's at Mount Sinai." Izzy shook his head in disgust.

Bartie was always best under pressure, and Izzy knew it. The more he insulted him, the better he was, and in the first few weeks, he always seemed to rise to the occasion like a john's erection at Maude's—the Hollywood brothel—when a sultry Lana or Rita would appear.

"I think," he paused, "I have it." Bartie thought back to when his own mother was in the hospital and the nurse scolded him about visiting hours.

"Okay, genius, *cough it up*. Myers will be calling in exactly ten minutes, and we'd better have a plan."

"Okay." Bartie stood up and paced the office, blocking out his idea with his hands as he thought aloud. "The guy's seriously injured, in a coma, and Sterling is in the same wing, right?"

"Is being a parrot what they're famous for in Sioux Falls?"

"So…you first pay off the family," Bartie replied, ignoring his taunts, and continued.

"I said that already…and?" Izzy shook his head at his process.

"Here's the rub." Bartie offered the idea up like a perfectly wrapped present at Christmas. "We send a studio makeup artist for the jaw, put the broken arm under an overcoat, and the photographer then takes some shots of ole Sterling sitting at the guy's hospital bed—whereas Sterling Dumont is visiting his old army buddy who had a heart attack. We take a negative and turn it into a positive. Dumont Sterling is the tough guy who is just a big softie, not to mention his service to our country!" Bartie said with a wry smile.

Izzy Menowitz sat back in awe; the kid was dense at times, but when he got it, he got it.

"Good!" He nodded his head. "Now listen, I wanna let you know I have a new *piece* starting on Monday, so hands off. You can dog her all you want after I'm through with her, but remember, they all turn into pains in the ass, which is why I have to rotate 'em." Izzy glared at Bartie, who was taking notes.

"You hired a new secretary? What happened to Mavis?" Bartie had a lump in his throat at the news.

"Again with the repeating. Don't think I don't know you were bangin' Mavis, which is all the more reason I sent her to work in the commissary. She started blabbing that she had a thing for you. I was pissed, but at least Myers knows you're not a *fairy,* which would have been worse. But hands off the new piece, Darlene. She's mine until I get bored of her, *capiche*?"

"Yes, of course, Mister Menowitz. As far as Mavis goes, I...I apologize." He looked down, red in the face.

"Save your sob story, sister! I don't wanna hear it, but if I ever find a used rubber in the garbage pail again, you're toast, do you hear me?" He said it in a more kindly way than he had thought he might. "By the way, I did you a big favor with Mavis; she's banged half the guys on the lot before she got to you; believe you me, she's just waitin' to get knocked up, so she can have somebody's brat and be paid fer. Be glad it ain't you." He lit up a ciggie.

"Yes, sir." Bartie hung his head down in shame at being caught thinking he had been so careful.

Two weeks into the job, the Thursday night they were working late after Menowitz had left, Mavis had walked up behind him and looked over his shoulder.

"Relax," she whispered from behind. "Let me give you a massage," she crooned before she started kneading his shoulder blades. "This job is stressful...I know." He collapsed under her firm touch. Then, before he knew what was happening, she unbuttoned her blouse and, quicker than he thought possible, placed her nubile breasts in his face. The next thing he knew, they were fumbling with buttons and zippers and rolling around on the carpet, and he started dry humping her. He remembered to pull out the condom he kept in his wallet that the other valets had given him, just in case, which he never thought he was going to ever get to use. Clearly Mavis knew what she wanted and was on his johnson before he could say the Marx

Brothers's A Day at the Races. *He was shy and tentative at first, but she was a horny piece and ground her thick hips into him.*

"Give it to me. I've wanted you since the first day you walked in here. Now I see what you got, and it's more than I expected." She leered and hungrily grabbed his package before greedily guiding it to her. He quickly gained his footing as he felt her hot breath as she moaned and bit his neck. And then it all happened: he fucked her in the front office, and the next day on the couch. He fucked her from behind by the window and then again on the kitchen floor. The more he gave, the more she took, and it was as if that fact opened up a whole world for him that a woman actually liked it, which was hard for him to conceive. Afterward, he did not admit that he had been a virgin, so skillful were her deft hands and ruby red mouth, which seemed to have better suction than a bicycle pump. The second time, he felt immense guilt at having had his way with her on Menowitz's desk, but all she said was, "I've been on it before, so who cares? Listen, I also have scars from the carpet burns." It was as if Bartie were led into a candy store and had never had candy before, and now wanted it after every meal.

"Now get to work and find your own *trim*." Izzy was reading his mind. "If I hear you lay one hand on Darlene, you'll be slinging hash in the commissary with Mavis, ya hear?" He wagged a long and bony finger at him.

"Yes, Mister Menowitz."

"Now, go fix the Sterling sitch. I have bigger fish to fry with coming up with a plan for this new fag Myer's wants to sign."

"Who's that?"

"His name is…um…" He looked down at the report in front of him. "Duke. Duke friggin' Drake. And word is every studio wants him."

Chapter Seventeen

Marty Lester
Beverly Hills
1937

The hunter green card room at Hillcrest had more comics than a headlining vaudeville act that day, the borscht notwithstanding. Of Burns, Berle, and the Marx Brothers, three out of the five of them were out in full force; Harpo Marx was sitting at a corner table talking to the visiting New York wit, his great friend Alexander Woollcott. At the prime center table sat the power players in a dome of ghostly cigar smoke. The poker stakes were high—a hundred dollars a hand—and Solly Myers was grinning, which meant he was on a winning streak. He didn't usually, and thus he was in a chipper and magnanimous mood as opposed to Marty Lester, who was losing big time.

"Fa Chrissakes, Solly, you're cleaning me out of house and home." Marty shrugged, stamping his cigar into the overflowing cut glass ashtray as he noshed on dyed red shelled pistachio nuts.

"When are you going to retire from poker, Marty?" Myers joked. "It's like taking candy from a baby." Myers shook his head. "I actually feel bad fleecing ya." Myers swept the mound of green bills toward himself and looked at Marty with a cool eye.

"Maybe I should leave early for Maude's," he shrugged, his star sapphire platinum and diamond pinkie ring glittering in the swirling smoke.

"Any good new talent there?" Myers asked.

"Yeah, there's a few new ones..." Marty nodded. "The Rita Hayworth ain't bad. And Tallulah looks just like her." He offered the information to his cronies at the table.

"Knowing her, maybe she's actually moonlighting there. In fact, wouldn't be surprised in the least. She makes some of those girls over there look tame with her antics," Myers agreed.

Marty sipped his martini and said sideways, "Listen, Solly, I want to know who I can get a girl to...at the studio, I mean. I have been out of the game awhile, and she needs an *intro*."

"Intro? Who's the broad?" Myers looked at him in surprise.

"She's my girlfriend," he said sheepishly.

"Girlfriend?" They all stopped in their tracks, wide-eyed. "If she's at Maude's, she's everyone's girlfriend," Groucho Marx said, laying down his hand with his signature delivery.

"No...no...she's not at Maude's," he stammered. "She's been *living* with me," he said proudly.

The table came to a screeching halt.

"Marty, at your age, you have a girlfriend living in the house? I don't believe it." Myers looked at him in shock.

"Well, believe it."

"Who is she? Sadie's sister, Gussie?" Sol winked.

"Very funny. No, she's a great gal, beautiful and funny to boot."

"I didn't know you still had it in ya, Marty. You're nearing a hundred and can still get it up for a broad? What are you taking?"

"I keep telling you *schmoes*...Schnapps every night and wheatgrass or spinach juice in the morning, daily massage, and yoga, but no one listens to me." He wagged his finger and spoke with a seriousness that could not be discounted. "And red meat only once a month."

"You're a kook, Marty, but we love ya. And how do your kids feel about this...new girlfriend of yours?"

"Ach, I've already handed over most of the dough to them. They know it's making me happy, but I mean, they won't have anything to do with her, but who cares. You know my old saying...'family first, pussy second.'"

"What's her name, and where did you meet her?" George Mackay, the director, asked.

"Carroll Madison. I met her when she was working at…" He paused. "Schwab's."

"He went in for a vanilla malted and came out with a blonde!" Groucho raised his famous bushy eyebrow skyward. "Every guy's wet dream."

"Oh, so she's a counter girl. Carroll Madison…hmm." Myers repeated it. "I like the name too. Not bad. Has a ring to it."

"Yeah, I remember the first time I had sex too. I also kept the receipt," Groucho quipped, puffing on his signature cigar.

"Look, she's a sexy and funny gal, a good kid. I want to help her career." Marty neglected to tell his friends that he had met her at Maude's, had paid for her nose job and blonde makeover—clothes and all—and no one was the wiser.

"She's a good kid," he said again.

"Okay, okay." Myers blew smoke into the air. "Have her call Mick McDonough, my head of production. I'll tell him to give her a standard contract, sight unseen. And then have her see Menowitz, my head of PR, and he'll think of a gimmick for her. If this old dinosaur can still get it up for a broad, she must have…*something!*"

"Thanks, Solly, I really appreciate that—and so will Carroll. That was worth losing my *do-re-mi* for today."

"What are friends for?" Myers lifted his frosted martini glass and toasted Marty. He patted him on his back and had a tear in his eye.

"Do you know this man, Marty Lester here, gave me my first production job when I came out from New York back in 1920?" Myers reached out and pinched Marty's cheek with great affection. "I would do anything for this man. That's loyalty; that's friendship." He beamed at his own largesse.

"I have to hand it to you, Marty," Groucho said as he shook his distinctive head, "I'm impressed, fellas. Marty's smarter than all of us put together—he discovered the fountain of youth."

"How's that, Groucho?" Mackay asked.

"Well, a man's only as old…" he paused and highlighted the punchline, "as the woman *he feels.*"

He puffed and shrugged to the laughter at the table. After all, there was truth in comedy.

Chapter Eighteen

La Marquise de La Faucigny
Paris
1937

The impressionistic May light, so stippled and incandescent, seemed to give reason for optimistic expression. However, across town, a certain solemnity dampened the exuberance.

"Damn *La Presse*!" Le Marquis Louis de La Faucigny subtly frowned and peeked out the tremulous windowpane, sighing deeply, hoping this was not the way it was always going to be. Always the press men hovering about them like so many yellow bees scattered and congregating on silken, woven Napoleonic tapestries, buzzing, omnipresent and unrelenting. He sighed as he pulled back the sheers of the towering, louvered windows of his Le Vésinet mansion, seeing a group of international photographers gathering outside the gates, smoking their Gitanes, shrugging and crushing them underfoot on the gravel when finished and waiting. Waiting for *them*. Always waiting. At first, the attention had stroked his ego. Then, like swarms of bees, it was something he had tried to get used to or swat away. It was also a sore subject he knew his father was angered by and did not approve of. When he saw an article or photo of Grace or the glamorous new couple in a newspaper, the old and stately marquis would roll his pale, flecked, red-rimmed eyes and mutter, "Ah, *l'Americain*," under his breath and shrug with his ramrod posture in that oh-so-proper French way indicating his dismay, disapproval, and ultimate consternation. Louis had at first been seduced by the glamour of Grace's social firmament and, most importantly, her bank account and enjoyed the sea of crackling flashbulbs. Then, over time, it grew and became tiresome. Then, the constant attention became unbearable. The news photos of him and the madcap heiress suddenly seemed endless; dinner at Maxim's or Lipp as were their social triumphs as the Sun King and Marie Antoinette at the Baron Etienne de Beaumont's Bal Masque. It was always the same; the young marquis and the lovely heiress looking divine, arriving here or departing there, seemingly without a care in the world as the news outlets put them on a pedestal and documented their every move. As the engagement was announced, the press corps became more intrusive, and they went from being friendly to a nuisance and now with no privacy, a heavy burden.

Louis carefully adjusted the thick silken cravat in the Louis Seize gilt mirror and had his aged dresser help him on with his dove-gray morning suit, the older man silently yet dutifully helping him into it and smoothing the shoulders, then brushing it with a horsehair wooden and metal whisk.

Today was the day he had long been planning: his marriage to the famous American heiress, Grace Greystone. However, as he studied his image in the mirror, he winced at the lingering hangover, fractured pieces of the prior evening returning in shards of explosive memory. His two best childhood friends, Egon and Francois, respectively a German count and baron, had blindfolded him and had taken him in the back of a limousine to Le Sphinx, Paris's most extravagant and well-known *bordello*. After a few rounds of drinks and listening to the chanteuse Édith Piaf perform her stirring "Non, je ne regrette rien" in the bar, they retired to a bedroom and ordered up Louis two lovely and nubile American girls at the same time, one White and one Black, as his friends cheered him on, watched, and applauded. He overdid it with the tangle of arms and legs and stray body parts that seemed disassembled, collapsing together in a sensual heap. In the morning, he moaned at the nausea from the mix of gin and absinthe and then noticed a creeping of purple and black under his eyelids as he emerged from the duvet and checked himself in the bathroom mirror. How had he gotten home? He couldn't remember. Of course, the three musketeers! They had realized their responsibilities as best men and had stripped, deposited, and thrown him into the down covers. In the steel light of the morning, the splash of freezing water in the antique white porcelain basin brought him into stark reality. He groaned, but he knew that he would rest after the ceremony and reception and asked his valet for an espresso, tomato juice, and aspirin, which would fix him up.

The night before at dinner, his friends had toasted and roasted him over their steak frites on his successful campaign to win over his American *parvenu* and her Croesus-like bank account. While he liked, adored, and even publicly professed his love for Grace, he knew despite the joking that this match was the best thing he was ever going to do for his name and family. He had staged a monumental campaign to win her, and he had won. Even his father had to admit that the Greystone heiress was a *très bon choix*, given his own acres of disintegrating chateau roofing and primitive metal pails to catch the rainwater and antiquated plumbing at their family seat in the Loire Valley. It was now a given in ancient drawing rooms in France that old aristocratic names needed new American heiresses, with their loud mannerisms, thick legs, and robust and unlimited funds these days, and a merger with the Greystone rail and shipping fortune was not to be underestimated—although somewhat tolerated *avec* the slightest roll of an eye. It had been a common theme among European royals: a great title and a dissipated fortune and vast estates that needed romantic and expensive upkeep as Consuelo Vanderbilt had set the trend eighty years earlier when she married the indebted Duke of Marlborough, becoming the chatelaine of the vast and gilded Blenheim Palace in exchange for a grand title. Other nobles soon followed suit to protect their glorious yet diminished patrimony.

The ceremony had the formality of a true royal wedding; a horse-drawn enclosed carriage dating back to the seventeenth century housed in a barn was now dusted off; nobles were congregating from all over Europe in a sea of opulent millinery; and the tycoons from the United States lining the cathedral with hundreds of well-wishers waited in the street to catch a glimpse of the happy couple. The press, of course, blared "The World's Poor little rich girl weds Royally." Even Grace's great aunt, the imperious and portly Dowager Rose McClean, who had arrived from Newport, seemed unusually happy as she emerged onto the steps of L'église de la Madeleine with her towering, glittering tiara and Rhode Island contingent, her son Reggie and his own English countess in tow. They were both suitably pleased that Grace was now settled within an aristocratic cocoon, hopefully away from the harsh glare of scandal and her late mother's suicide—never again to be mentioned in polite circles. France had been a wonderful antidote.

The next day, much would be made of the bride's nine-foot Chantilly lace train and old mine antique diamond-and-pearl necklace, which had belonged to Comtesse du Barry, the last *maîtress-en-titre* of Louis XV, commissioned right before the revolution from the court jewelers, Boehmer and Bassenge. It was whispered among the older set, who knew such things about provenance, that the famous necklace had a curse on it, the heads of those who had worn it, including du Barry's—sliced in a guillotine during the reign of terror. Grace had bought it at auction and had never looked into the legend or provenance—as Americans often don't—although it would portend things to come. The crowds gasped as the famed beauty, Baroness Irene Von Mendelssohn, her maid of honor, emerged from the Rolls-Royce Corniche in gray silk and pearls and attended to the lengthy train, trying hard not to steal the moment from the bride, which was *très difficile* given her surreal beauty. Uncle Reggie proudly walked his niece down the monumental aisle to the *oohs* and *ahhs* of the attending crowds. Indeed, this was the way a Greystone and McClean should have been married in the first place! Aunt Rose dabbed her eye in the front row, her twenty-seven-carat round diamond blinding those around her as she manipulated her lace hankie to great effect. At the tented reception, the elegant Baron Von Mendelssohn gave the toast, highlighting Grace's many fine attributes and dabbed his own eye as he related that he had come to think of Grace as one of his own, her lovely attention to his illness a shining example of a new generation. "An angel," he declared to the nodding crowd "and Louis, the luckiest man in Europe."

Louis combed his hands through his hair, the color of freshly-churned country butter, and smiled. It had all gone according to plan.

Later that evening, after the exhausting service and extravagant festivities, Louis visited his young bride in her suite in his mansion by climbing the vast staircase. Grace was nervously awaiting her husband in a conservative white lace nightgown, looking beautiful and fresh in the candlelight. He walked in and gave a formal bow before kissing her neck and stroking her hair, admiring her lovely and languid ivory hands.

"Ah, the newest Marquise de La Faucigny! My darling, you were magnificent today." He kissed her cool hand. "A triumph! I am the happiest and luckiest man in Paris. I think even your Aunt Rose was suitably impressed." He smiled brightly, removing his signet ring and putting it into the Limoges ashtray next to the bed, clinking against the delicate porcelain.

"Oh, yes, she was in Heaven with her Newport friends. I think I finally achieved something she is proud of, thanks to you."

"Come here my dear." Louis approached her tenderly. "Are you nervous?"

"Yes," was all she said and hoped he would be gentle as he kissed her passionately, and she sighed. Then, he stood and disrobed, and Grace marveled at his perfectly sculpted and lean physique. He had a sinewy, muscular body without an ounce of fat, with broad shoulders and long, aristocratic limbs. She was aroused at the sight.

He slowly undressed her and kissed her lovely white, upturned breasts and pink nipples. Before mounting and entering her, he suddenly and unexpectedly dove between her legs to her great surprise, kissing and licking her.

"You know we call it a *baiser francais* for a reason." He looked up and joked, his eyes sparkling in the flickering candlelight at Grace's laughter.

After the discomfort of her first time, their passion emerged, and for over an hour, he took her. He was pleased with her lovely body, and while, truth be told, her legs were a bit heavyset for his tastes, he knew that he had gotten a wonderful package in Grace.

As he lay on the bed, she wanted to please him, and she could see he was still erect.

"Would you like me to…" she asked sweetly, "…again?" She nuzzled into him as she basked in the afterglow.

"You are *parfait, ma cherie,*" he said, rising and kissing her softly. "I will meet you for breakfast tomorrow before we leave for Cap-Ferrat."

He smiled as he rose suddenly from the bed, his muscular posterior glistening with a sheen of perspiration.

"But where are you going?" Grace looked up in surprise as her new husband seemed to have other plans.

"Oh, I am a nocturnal creature. I know you like your sleep, my dear, and don't want to keep you up."

"Yes, but it is our wedding night." She was quite surprised, though tried not to nag.

"All the more reason for you to get some rest as we will be up early for our trip down south to the Cap." He gave her his most brilliant smile.

"Yes, I suppose." Grace stretched and yawned like a cat. "Just tell me where you are going, so I won't worry."

"Many nights it is my habit to meet Egon and or Francois for a celebratory drink at the Ritz for a nightcap," he declared.

"Oh, I see. Well, of course, if that is your regimen. Having a wife shouldn't interfere with…your friends." She smiled, yet remained a bit crestfallen.

"Thank you, darling—yes, a bit of harmless conversation and gossip. I shall see the newest marquise in the morning." He kissed her tenderly on the lips.

"That was so lovely." Grace smiled at their lovemaking, which had been tender. She also loved his lingering scent of aftershave and how handsome he was.

"This was the happiest day of my life, *chouchou*." She reached out and kissed him again, tousling his buttery, silken hair.

"*Moi aussi*," Louis said. He looked into her eyes and touched her nose with his finger. "Until tomorrow, my dear wife."

"Tomorrow." Her eyelids fluttered faintly. When he entered his separate bedroom quarters down the hall, Louis pulled a suit from his armoire and dressed quickly, slipping his wallet and keys into his pocket, combed his hair for effect in the armoire mirror, and then quickly made his way down the darkened staircase to the waiting car. The driver nodded knowingly, first congratulating him as they drove silently to the Left Bank.

From the interior of the ancient Daimler, he could see the starry lights of Paris against the broad avenue of the Seine. Then, over a small *pont* to the charming Left Bank. The car motored along crooked cobblestone streets, deserted except for a drunken reveler who seemed to be having a dialogue with the moon. As they took a sharp right down the Rue Jacob, he sighted at the familiar smoky limestone facade with great arched oak doors. He exited the car and removed a skeleton key with a sense of habit and ease and then rode the caged elevator to the third floor where his mistress, the young and incredibly sexy actress, Ghislaine Garriaux, was waiting for him. He was as silent as was she. He found her waiting, as usual, naked on her oblong satin bed, propped up on all fours, a magnificent sight to behold. Without saying as much as a *bonsoir,* he removed his trousers in a singular motion, walked over to the bed, and took her from behind with guttural force, grunting in ecstasy before breaking into a sweat, and a wry smile appeared on his aristocratic face.

It had been a most magical day, he thought, and an even better *nuit* now that he had it all.

Chapter Nineteen

Gorge Lamont
Santa Monica
1938

The *brrrng, brrrrng, brrrng* of the phone call came just as Gorge Lamont emerged from his morning ocean swim, wading through the glistening, blue green surf of the Santa Monica Bay. The foam on the sand and the scorching lemon sun highlighted his rippling muscles as he emerged from the surf. He saw a couple pointing in his direction, which was a common occurrence. He was used to the stares and often flexed to give the onlookers a bit of a show. He always felt lighter in the water and more burdened with each step as he walked to shore in his soaking Hawaiian print bathing suit, finally resigned to never working another day on a studio lot—unlike his younger paramour.

Duke had slipped out of their bed at 5:30 a.m., trying not to fully wake him, kissing Gorge gently on the forehead before leaving for the studio. He had been cast in a new film at Warner Bros. when another young actor dropped out due to a death in the family and was quickly making a name for himself around town. Gorge's agent, Virgil Lindstrom, had taken him on and sensed enthusiasm from the studios for the new, handsome, and cultivated Brit in town and had negotiated a loan-out price for his services at $650 a week with the standard six-week minimum guarantee. A full-time contract from a studio seemed imminent now that he was on his second film and building buzz among actors, directors, and press agents.

Gorge awoke at his touch, swallowed his pride, pulled Duke close, and French kissed him full on the mouth before he left for the studio. He whispered in his groggy, gravelly morning voice how proud he was of him, yet he missed puttering around the house with Duke in the morning, their coffee, and the easy camaraderie of their beach walks and spontaneous sex, but he knew it would only be two weeks of shooting and wanted to be supportive of Duke's burgeoning career. He vowed to himself never to become a nag like some of the older queens he had once known who had pushed away their younger lovers with their own possessiveness and insecurity. In some ways, his own forced retirement actually felt as imminent as Duke's new career, yet he also felt a lingering sadness.

Gorge wiped the stinging sea water off his eyelids as he saw Akito, his diminutive Japanese houseman, appear on the verandah indicating there was an important phone call. He assumed it would be news that the pair of Queen Anne loveseats for his friend, the actress Joan Blondell, would be ready for his latest interior job. He slowly walked to the house, knowing that there could also likely be some problem with the trades; a late fabric delivery for the drapes or a question for the sheers, and he walked even slower at having to deal with ordinary problems. He loved the creativity of the design process, his ability to envision beautiful and chic environments for his friends' homes, but he bristled at the realities of the mundane billing payments and measurements. He had become so busy, he knew he was at the stage of needing to hire a real design assistant, but he also realized that once he did that, word would get out, and his acting career would officially be over.

Maybe it's Duke on the phone taking a break, he thought happily. He often touched base after filming a scene; it was so fresh and exciting for him and, while also a bit jealous, he knew to be supportive knowing Duke made quite an impression everywhere he went with his abundant optimism, gorgeous face, sophisticated accent, spectacular physique, and dewy young skin—as he once had done. He had secured a second role in a Hal Roach comedy called *The Weary Widow*, where Duke would once again play the young cad against an older female star, Norma Shearer. Not many younger actors had the looks, bearing, and humor to pull off the believable heir-about-town, yet, with Duke, it was innate. Gorge knew he was on the verge of stardom, and while he wanted to protect him, shield him, or even hide him away, he knew his fame was as inevitable as his own had been. Duke had *it*, and they both knew it was a one-in-a-million gift. He was a bit depressed at the thought, but was trying to both enjoy having this young man in his bed and also navigate his own journey as he tracked the golden sand on his tanned feet onto the veranda of his Santa Monica beach house. He knew the moment his thin veneer cracked, it would be the end of the relationship, and he needed to play a new role: the part of the beneficent older star.

"Damn it." He bristled at the idea. He hated the thought of "older" but also knew it turned Duke on, most likely given his lack of a father figure.

Akito handed him the phone and, once he answered it, he was truly shocked as it wasn't Duke and certainly not the upholsterers calling. He took the call and calmly accepted the appointment at hand but was also sad he had to now decline the luncheon invitation and attending antics down the beach at Marion Davies, Hearst's mistress's one-hundred-room manse he had built for her. Fifty-five bathrooms were just part of the lure, and the white Georgian revival pile was often compared to the western Buckingham Palace or the Santa Monica White House! It was always a rollicking afternoon, and now Gorge had Akito telephone and send his regrets.

After the phone call, he carefully dressed for the occasion, choosing a light beige linen blazer and white shirt and pants, which brought out the sun streaks in his blonde hair. He knew he looked healthy and tan, and that would give him some of the confidence he needed as he took the roadster out of the garage and made his way across town.

It was like a strange time warp as his car rounded the familiar turn and approached the famous yellow and white Mediterranean facade of SGM Studio. Old Jonny at the front gate tipped his hat as he peered in.

"Nice to have you back, Mister Lamont. Right this way." He opened the gate, and Gorge drove his bright yellow Duesenberg roadster up to the main office building. Today, he would once again be seeing his archnemesis, Mr. Solomon Myers. He had no idea why his archenemy had urgently requested a meeting, but he wasn't going to play coy and turn it down.

"Why, Mister Lamont, so nice to see you again after all this time," Edna, Sol's assistant said, raising a steely eyebrow in a smirk. The woman never seemed to age as she had been born seemingly at fifty-five.

"You can go in. Coffee?" she said without any enthusiasm.

"Yes, black please. Nice to see you too, Edna. You haven't changed a bit, yourself. Still look like a prison warden!" he said with his best dazzling smile.

"Flattery will get you everywhere." She shook her head.

Gorge walked slowly into Solly Myer's office and took a deep inhale. The familiar and distinctive odor came back to him at once: coffee, cigarettes, cigars, and pungent sweat mixed with English cologne. It was a man's office for sure, and to Gorge, it was an aphrodisiac. Not much had changed in the intervening years, except that the long walk to Solly's desk—*the walk to Myers*—now seemed even longer. The device had been conceived by Myers, himself, as well as the studio set designers to intimidate anyone knowing they would have to enter and walk what seemed like an interminable half mile to get to the famous oval, white deco desk—and the man himself. Whether it was a star who needed to be chastened or a visiting head of state, the *walk to Myers* was legendary and made everyone, no matter how big their ego, feel smaller.

Solomon I. Myers had seemed to have shrunk a bit to Gorge, making him look elfin with his shiny bald pate and large protruding ears, his hands reclining against the Cadillac of a desk, like one of Disney's seven dwarves.

"Well, well, if it isn't the *late* Gorge Lamont." Sol Myers leaned against its front panel, waiting, his arms now folded against his oversized peaked lapels in victory, a smirk securely on his laconic face.

"Solomon Myers, it's so very *interesting* to see you," Gorge answered, smiling.

"You're looking well, as usual. All that time off, and you seem to have the perfect tan that goes with *not working*! Have a seat." Myers smiled as if he were greeting an old friend. Edna silently brought in the usual coffee setup on a silver tray, the click of her sturdy, sensible shoes loudly echoing.

"Okay, SM. And you look…older, thinner, and *shorter*. So, let's get on with this charade. I don't suppose you are here to tell me you are letting me out of my contract or lending me to another studio. Every offer has been turned down." Gorge shook his perfectly-formed head in dismay.

"You get paid. You cash your checks." Sol looked at him intently with a blank stare.

"Yes, I do. It's been my one consolation, especially when I use it to pay for a nice, long…*blow job at the gas station*," Gorge said plainly. "So, why the call? Why am I here? What's so urgent after all these years of ruining my career?" he glowered.

"Ruining *your* career? You're the one who ruined your own career and put *my* studio at risk!" Solly paced angrily. "However, I am prepared to overlook that now. I do finally have a deal for you," he said with sinister intent.

"It's already 'no deal,' but I am just interested to hear what that scheming mind of yours has concocted. Go ahead." Gorge sipped his coffee as Edna silently busied herself by straightening magazines on the coffee tables at the far end of the office as she clearly wanted to hear as well.

"Look, I'll get straight to the point. There's a new star in town, or so people say. His name is Duke Drake, and I hear he just so happens to be your…close friend." He said this to confirm the hearsay.

"He's my lover, and no dice. Not in a million years. Hell could freeze over," Gorge glared.

"I know Warners and Twentieth are getting ready to offer him a contract. I want him. He's got the look, whatcha call sophisticated and English. We need to fill that slot for our comedies."

"So am I?" Gorge said in a British accent, yet he lost his power as he pitched himself.

"You're ten years too late," Solly laughed. Yet, despite his win, Solly Myers knew he had a hard nut to crack and decided to take a different approach than the usual insults. Gorge Lamont was finished, and they both knew it. He turned and picked up something from his desk and then walked over and threw a thick white script at him.

"This is yer comeback role. It's called *Grand Voyage*. It's about a good-lookin', *middle-aged* Midwestern doctor—*you*—who loses the love of his life, his wife, to some *farkakte* disease. He can't save her, and thinkin' it was his damn fault, goes on an ocean liner to Europe to forget, where he falls for this Nazi spy. We're thinkin' Dietrich or someone like her for the spy. It's the perfect comeback role…for a *mature star in yer middle age.* All you need to do is convince Duke Drake to join the SGM family, and it's yers. Gable and Spencer Tracy are dyin' to do it…so whaddya think?" Sol clipped his cigar and lit it with a solid-gold lighter.

Gorge sat in the brown nubby armchair thinking about the offer and what it meant. He took his time in reacting, which, to Solly Myers, meant he was interested.

"Let me read the script first and see if the role is meaty enough." Gorge flashed a devastating smile.

"That's the one thing I still like about you, Gorge. You're as much of a whore as I am."

"Problem is you just didn't like who I was sleeping with. One other question…if you had a problem with me liking men, why would you not have a problem with my *lover*, Duke Drake?" He played up the word lover to shock.

"Word is Duke Drake plays ball with the studio PR people and fixers. He may be living with you in 'Pansy Hall' as we all call it, but word is he's happy to go to the Troc or the Cocoanut Grove with some dame actress and act like he's interested, something ya never did! At least *he* pretends. That's because…he's a *real* actor!" Solly Myers squashed the cigar after a few puffs and then opened up a gold engraved cigarette case and offered one. Gorge waved his hand away.

"And also, a little birdie told me," Solly continued, now gleefully going in for the kill. "Word also has it that he goes both ways." Myers lobbed this one to a shocked Gorge. "I heard he banged Bankhead. She loves a good screw and her queers, and word around town is he gave it to her but good in her dressing room last week. May be the wrong hole, but she still has tits!" he gloated.

"He can sleep with whomever he likes as long as he comes home to me." Gorge gulped at the news, trying to maintain his cool.

"That's the problem with you, Gorge. You just weren't flexible. Ya don't think it killed me you wouldn't bang a broad, a co-star, or get married, or at the very least pretend? I tried, I really did, but ya forced me to..." His voice went up an extra octave and cracked. "Ya forced me to!"

"At least I'm true to myself," Gorge said, defensively.

"Yeah, and look where it got yas!" Myers paced with nervous energy. "You spend your days picking out wallpaper and haven't been on the screen in eight years. Is that how you want to go out? A fag *dreck*-orator? Look, I'll give it to ya, you still look damn good, Gorge, always did... but time marches on for all of us. This role is the best thing that's ever going to happen to ya—*if* you deliver Duke. You'll be able to clear your name. You still have hair, and you can do it all while you can still carry off close-ups without the Vaseline on the lens. Five years from now? No dice; you'll be the older handsome guy who just has to pay for it on Sunset Boulevard. So, time is money, and you heard it here first!"

"You're really something, Solomon Myers." Lamont looked down.

"So are you. Don't think ya weren't a handful. Menowitz saved your ass a hundred times from being in the press on all fours. You're just ungrateful. That said, just get this deal done. I can see you're itching to get back in front of the camera, and I would be too if I looked like you, and the reason you're gonna do it is you absolutely *love* yourself. And do you know what? I won't even bother you anymore about your... *condition.*"

"Condition?" Gorge looked surprised and laughed.

"You know, I have a few new cocksuckers on payroll I'll even send over to your dressing room. On me."

"So now you're a pimp?" He shook his handsome head.

"SGM has the biggest group of stars in the galaxy, and I'll do anything to keep it that way. You know that, Gorge."

"Anything?"

"Anything! Now go read yer script and get back to me. You have twenty-four hours. Shooting close-ups starts next week."

"If I do agree to it and make it happen, there is only one thing I want." Gorge brightened at the thought.

"What's his name?" Solly glowered back.

"Solly Myers."

"You're kidding me, right?"

"In a way," Gorge said softly. "I want you to take me to lunch at Hillcrest or the Derby. I want everyone in this town to know you and I are back in business again, and I want Hedda and Louella to see it with their own eyes."

"Deal!" Myers smiled, revealing new white caps and his rapprochement with Lamont. Neither thought this was a genuine thawing between them but *business,* and to Myers, putting the show into business was everything.

Chapter Twenty

Madame Fritz Langenheim
Vienna
1938

"Irene, you must listen to me. Your husband is a very talented… *moron.*" Baron Von Mendelssohn lay failing in his cavernous and darkened bedroom suite, the frolicking white and gold rosy-cheeked cherubs on the ceiling fresco of the palais peering down like mischievous childhood friends, beckoning him to a loftier world. The electric lights and candles in the bedroom flickered like his own life force. He had spent the morning and more energy than he had a right to muster trying to convince his stubborn son-in-law to take Irene and move to Switzerland, Paris, or New York to no avail. With the horrendous anti-Jewish laws and reported persecutions in Germany, advancing news of the impending Anschluss and Hitler's aggressive expansionist plans in Europe, it was clear there was no stopping the madman's endless, voracious appetite. Certainly not within arm's reach of Vienna.

"Fritz…is an idiot and a *moron*—more off than on!" the baron lamented out loud to no one in particular since Irene was accustomed to his outbursts. For those in the know, Hitler's recent hosting of Mussolini in Munich had centered on creating an alliance where Austria, the small country sandwiched between them, would be gobbled up under the guise of German reunification. It also did not escape the baron that Hitler had been born in Austria and would try to use this as an excuse to achieve his nefarious, expansionist goals.

"Father, please don't upset yourself." Irene tried to smile and, in her despair, looked even more beautiful, if that was possible.

"Excuse me, Baron Von Mendelssohn." Gunter, his personal valet, knocked softly and then announced with little emotion, "The Princess Bonaparte is waiting outside to see you both, sir." He bowed.

"If Fritz won't listen to reason, at least listen to Princess Marie, who was your mother's very best friend and has been more than an aunt to you," he reminded her.

Princess Marie Bonaparte, Princess George of Greece and Denmark swept majestically into the room. Upon seeing her beloved friend Baron Karl Frederich so close to death, silent tears streamed from her large and soulful eyes as she gathered Irene in a maternal embrace.

"Karl, my dearest, how are you feeling?" She mustered her remaining shreds of optimism, giving him a kiss on his alabaster forehead. "You are looking *so* much better." She smiled kindly and with a dose of forced optimism in her lie.

"You know I look like death warmed over, but you are too gracious and elegant to say so. Marie, will you please talk some sense into my ill-informed daughter. She must make plans to leave Vienna immediately, and that husband of hers just wants to spend his days composing in the music room of the palais. He keeps repeating that Schuschnigg said everything was going to be fine. The young fool has strudel on the brain. Please tell her to make alternate plans, so I can depart in peace knowing she will be safe," he lamented.

Princess Marie shook her head, trying to stop her tears and put on her best face. She took Irene's hand in her own satin-gloved one and started slowly.

"Irene, you know your mother and I were the closest of friends, and your father has been nothing short of a miracle for me. He is as smart as Doctor Freud, and I owe him so much, having been the beneficiary of his wonderful mind and advice all these years. I also have seen you grow into the most beautiful and talented young woman, and I do hope you know I am also very fond of and admire your Fritz." She paused. "However, I must say," she pulled on her long rope of luminous pearls, "the world, our world, the old world has gone mad. What your father says is quite true; my friends in Munich have taken Hitler and Mussolini at their word that they will force the Anschluss, and they will start the anti-Semitic legislation already in place in Germany. Even the Rothschild German cousins are not immune and are fleeing or imprisoned for ransom, their grand palaces immediately taken over and looted. They have also thrown the intellectuals, artists, homosexuals, and Jews into camps. I must agree with your father, and while we all love our beloved Vienna, I think it's best you go to England or the United States, dear Irene." She looked down. "And you know I am also urging Doctor Freud and his family to go as well," she said kindly.

"Fritz won't leave," Irene said nervously. "His librettist is here, and he says he is on the verge of his greatest masterpiece. He adores the palais and says it has unleashed his creativity. How can I force him to go? He says he is protected by his friendship with Chancellor Schuschnigg and that nothing is going to happen to us. He's sure of it."

"Schuschnigg is a noble, paper tiger. Rome is burning, and all Fritz wants to do is finish his damned opera, which is clearly more important than protecting my daughter, my jewel." The baron's eyes burned brightly on the issue.

"Creative people can be quite obstinate," Marie shrugged in a knowing way.

"You see, I wasn't being a snob, Marie, when I opposed the match. He loves living in the palais and fancies himself lord of the manor, as I am on the brink of the afterlife and all I have is the smell of his Bourgeoisie background on him like three-day old fish wrapped in newsprint. If she had married someone in our circle, they wouldn't be so impressed and would know when to take the paintings off the walls and *leave.* Irene, we're a nomadic people for a reason. That's why in the Bible it says we live in tents. We have always had to uproot ourselves over the centuries…that is our fate. And this fool you are married to…." He shook his gaunt head.

"Your father is right. From what I hear, Schusschnigg's days as chancellor are numbered," the princess agreed.

"They'll throw him into a camp too, mark my words. Irene, I think the best thing, given his obstinate disposition, is to tell the *artiste,* given my illness, you are taking over the management of the vineyard and need an apartment in Paris. Grace is there with her new husband and can help you set it up. The plan once you left Doctor Breiner's was for you to stay in Paris. Moving back to Vienna because of Fritz was not in the cards, and I never should have allowed it. This way, if the Anschluss happens, and it *will*, you have a place to go, and of course, we will open a bank account in Paris and will send funds there. I already gave you the bank information in Switzerland, and you have the numbered accounts in my leather diary and your bank book. Do not tell your moron husband."

"Listen to your father. There is no smarter man," Princess Bonaparte pleaded. "Half his friends would be in penury if not for his sage advice."

"Yes, Father, and thank you, Aunt Marie." She paused. "I will go. It will be hard for him to argue about the vineyard with you no longer there, Father, and certainly having a Paris apartment is a good idea. I can also spend more time with Grace and Louis. It *has* been lonely here with Fritz always wiling away his days in the music rooms."

"I also want to ship some of the masterpieces to Paris. The Rembrandts and the Raphaels and more. I have made copies over the last three years. The originals will be sent to Paris."

"Father, you think of everything," she whispered, tearing up.

"He's much more forward-thinking than Freud. I am having a very hard time convincing him to go to London, but my plan is in place, and I am trying to get his library out as well. I must say, even Mussolini told his long-term Jewish mistress, Margherita Sarfatti, and her family to go to South America until the war is over, and no one held more sway over him than Margherita. She told me, herself, that she is moving to Argentina and Uruguay. You know these are dark times." The princess held Irene's hand tightly.

Irene started to weep.

"I don't know what I will do without you, Father."

"You will do just fine. You are a Von Mendelssohn, and we always think ahead. You have to make me one promise though."

"What's that?"

"If Fritz won't leave Vienna for Paris, I want you to promise me you will leave. Promise me! He is risking your life and future."

"Yes, Father, I promise...." Her voice cracked. "I have seen he can be quite stubborn."

"An understatement!" he thundered. "Marie, you know the plan. Next week, Enzo, our driver, will drive you straight to Paris. Irene, Princess Bonaparte has agreed to accompany you since she has a Christian passport. It's a sad day when the 'J' stamped in your passport would do you harm, but they won't stop Princess Marie at the border and you as her niece. I also advise you to go to Geneva and access the accounts—that's where the bulk of the money is and all of your mother and grandmother's most important jewels are in the safety deposit boxes."

"I am here for you both. Next week it is..." Marie started. "I know it is *très difficile*, dear, but you must start packing, and I am happy you are listening to your father and I...and reason."

The baron reached out with his withered hand and touched his daughter's young and ivory one.

"You have made me very happy today," he said in a low voice. "Now, I can go in peace."

"No, Father. Please," Irene sobbed.

"One last thing, Irene." His voice cracked.

"Yes, anything."

"If they invade Austria—and they will—they will eventually try and invade France and then England. Promise me you will find a way to leave for the United States or South America like the Sarfattis. I knew Margherita through your mother when we lived in Milan, and she was considered as close to Mussolini's wife or *maîtress-en-titre* as possible. If *Il Duce* is telling her and her son to go to the Americas, I can assure you the handwriting is already on the wall."

"I promise, Father." Irene stifled her tears. "I will find a way."

Chapter Twenty-One

Bartie Maddox
Los Angeles
1938

LA's waving palm trees and constant daily sunshine could not mask the grim news; the following week brought forth the terrifying and jolting Orson Welles's radio broadcast, "War of The Worlds," about an alien landing—causing an actual public panic. And then reports of *Kristallnacht*, the "Night of the Broken Glass," the anti-Semitic persecutions in Germany sent shudders around the globe.

Despite the news reports, all Bartie could think about was a series of studio fixes that needed quick approval and execution: hiding a famous young actress's drug addiction and nymphomania, and squelching press rumors about a popular and happily married acting couple, the Sterling Dumonts, widely known in town as the "Destructive Dumonts" since broken glass and plates were always involved. They were on the verge of divorce due to his incessant cheating and abhorrent physical abuse. A budget for a studio makeup artist had been approved by Myers and Menowitz and dispensed weekly to their Hancock Park mansion to cover up the former silent film star Mable Dumont's recurring black eyes and bruises.

Within the year, Bartie had seen it all and would never again be shocked by the range of human emotions, actions, *and* depravity.

Then the impossible happened, and he saw how mercurial the Hollywood system was in action. Izzy Menowitz was not only fired, but also publicly kicked out due to an ill-fated studio fix that embarrassed and infuriated Myers in his most sensitive area, which insiders deemed "fag management."

It was inconceivable to all that the ultimate insider, Menowitz, was gone from the studio within twenty-four hours, but it was fact, though not before enduring an hour of screaming and invective from Myers that could be heard in all corners of the lot. And then, in the blink of an eye, Bartie was now elevated due to his former boss's botched PR plan. He knew his elevation was not due to his great talent or track record but the mere fact that there was no one else in the wings to fill the role or knew how to do any of it—akin to a Broadway understudy taking center stage and becoming an instant star.

Those in the know thought Izzy should have known better and deserved his decapitation as he had lost his touch, but tongues still wagged, and the news spread like wildfire through the lot. The gist was that SGM's newest young star, Duke Drake, was shacking up with Gorge Lamont in his Santa Monica beach house, dubbed by those in the know as "Pansy Hall." Myers had insisted Menowitz fix the issue. Without consulting Myers, he chose to address the problem head-on and set up a photo shoot exclusive of the two handsome bachelor roommates in *Motion Picture Magazine.* His strategy was to promote them as "lady-killer roommates on the prowl." When the story broke, there were myriad photos of the two male roommates side by side washing dishes in ruffled, gingham aprons with the headline "Searching for a Lady of the House." It was met with such derision and fury from Myers that he had Izzy's entire office put out onto the street, as well as the letters scraped off the glass door all in one afternoon—without so much as a goodbye or a stitch of severance, despite his extensive tenure. Izzy knew better than to cause a fuss lest he end up in a ditch somewhere, so he just hired a truck for his belongings and disappeared to the gaming tables in Vegas with his well-tailored tail between his legs.

It was later reported that none other than Freyda Myers, the president of president, had the final say. She had thought the story scurrilous and men in gingham aprons offensive. Not to mention Moira Menowitz had not sent a proper thank you or a handwritten note to her after she had hosted a hen luncheon at Hillcrest, hence, *the real issue*, pundits explained.

Having worked as Menowitz's trusty assistant for over a year, Bartie was now promptly elevated the old-fashioned way, without so much as a raise or further instruction. Myers had just called him, barked some orders over the phone, and expected him to do it. He knew he was out of his league, but he also knew more than most and less than he should have. However, Bartson Maddox realized, like parking the Nash and helping F. Scott, he had to just start driving. He also knew he hit the jackpot akin to having worked in the underground lab in New Mexico but not exactly having the atomic secrets. However, he was intuitive enough to absorb the lesson: to involve Myers in all major decisions (and defer to Mrs. Myers on all occasions), but best of all, if it was a good idea to let him, Solly Myers, think any great PR idea was *his.*

Within weeks, it was not unknown in the halls of SGM that the young, wunderkind, Bartie Maddox, was on the rise, a veritable *goyishe* Irving Thalberg of PR, they all said. Some thought it was due to his tall, lean, good all-American looks, professorial glasses, and polite manners, but Bartie possessed much more than the shiny exterior; he had an unflappable demeanor and none of the *Sturm und Drang* or neuroses of most New York-born film industry executives. He was a tireless worker who was always up for the task at hand and able to get along and deal with any problem without drama or issues, working side by side with emotional and difficult actors and actresses. He also notably found common ground with macho and hard-drinking, steak-eating, hetero directors like John Huston or Victor Fleming, who were gruff and demanding—in that order. They immediately took the preppy-looking Bartie under their wing, introducing him around to their crowd, mostly the non-Jewish technical side of the business such as the sound editors, grips, and lighting men. Occasionally, an Irishman or Italian would slip through the ranks to producer, like another young man on the SGM lot, Michael McDonough, an up-and-coming producer who would eventually become one of his best friends.

Most importantly, he was able to work with the most demanding and volatile man in Hollywood, Solomon I. Myers, and that stamp of approval from his boss was akin to money in the bank. If Myers liked you, that was one thing, but one also had to have a thick skin and a quick mind to get along with him on a daily basis; putting up with the incessant phone calls, screaming, and impossible demands was another. Within the year, Myers was so impressed by the young man that he started to consult him on some of the more pressing public relation issues facing the studio and let his cronies know how talented he was.

"He has a *yiddisher cup* that one," Myers would say to the Hillcrest crowd about Bartie, which meant he had given him his highest insider accolade that the very gentile Bartie had an innate Jewish head for business and was quick on his feet. This, of course, was the ultimate compliment from street fighters like Solly, who had fought their way out of the Lower East Side *shtetls*. Myer's sheer acceptance of his new protégé also connoted that Bartie was vetted by his macho boss, meaning there was no question he was an all-American, full red-blooded "male," which was code word for heterosexual swordsman. In the very beginning, Myers even went so far as to send a handsome young gay actor to Bartie's office and proposition him to test his proclivities and resolve. Bartie kindly said, "No thanks," when the actor put his hand on his thigh and asked if he wanted a blowie, quickly changing the subject to his next project. When the report got back to Myers, he shook his head in delight and laughed out loud with a grateful fist in the air. Young Barston Maddox had passed his ultimate test and now had a real future at SGM. He was *no fag like Lamont!* And while Bartie indulged, like most of his peers, occasionally in the joys of the casting couch, he was always known as being quite polite to the girls, even more so to the working girls. This endeared him to Solly Myers who, because he revered his mother and hated "fags," respected gentlemen and had it out for those men who mistreated women.

"Treat a tart like a lady, and you're apples in my book," was an oft-quoted Myerism.

Bartie's quick mind and aptitude for his engaging and seamless "fixes" became talking points among the staff. Yet, he wasn't a pushover and was able to go head-to-head with some of the toughest actors on the lot; notorious bruisers like Sterling Dumont, Greg Lancaster, and Spencer Tracy were often drunk and created a ruckus. These were hard men to please, and they all genuinely liked the hardworking and unflappable Bartie, thanking him over whiskey or Scotch. His helpful ideas and concepts whitewashed their press and clever movie campaigns that he was known to generate. The best thing about Bartie was that, deep down, he knew he was grateful for the job, and it never eluded him that he had been one step away from homelessness when he had first arrived in Los Angeles. It certainly colored everything he would ever do.

Over the next few months, his tireless work ethic, positive approach, manners, and discretion made him the perfect PR fixer. He evaluated each scandal with a steady hand and common-sense ideas. Best of all, he was a quick study and could come up with ideas in the moment. Whether it was covering up a stray abortion, killing an item on a gay star's vice squad bust, or misleading the press on married affairs, alcohol and drug addictions, he managed to do so with ease, aplomb, and discretion. As he grew in his position, he would also later learn how to trade items with the leading gossip columnists, who would erase a negative item for one star while they gained lewd information on another—what was termed the "*studio trade*". Those sacrificed were fallen stars or lowly contract players either on a downward box office spiral or ones that needed to be thrown under the bus for disobeying Myers's orders or ruffling the feathers of Madame Freyda Myers, who always kept score.

Weeks earlier, Bartie and the late Menowitz had gotten the brief on their newest acquisition and would-be-star, Duke Drake, from Myers himself who had promised Duke the moon and more. Myers knew that once Drake had been signed, he would fill an important slot in studio casting: that of the handsome, urbane cad or sophisticated, continental heir. Not many in SGM's ranks or town could pull off such sophisticated roles that were often foils for older female stars needing to work against type. Could a farm boy from Des Moines do it? No! But according to Myers, the friggin' *fagalah* English could and, therefore, he would be tolerated if he played Myer's game of "straight ball."

After Bartie briefly met with Duke in the commissary, they had an easy rapport, and Bartie found his new assignment quite charming, knowing he needed to craft a unique positioning and press story for SGM's newest male lead. As he worked on his press ideas, the studio also set out to remake and polish Duke through the ranks. After joining SGM Studios and seeing the rushes from his film test, the beauty technicians set out reshaping and thinning his eyebrows, tinting his luxurious lashes an even darker shade of black to make his baby blues pop even more, using darker tan tint in his cleft chin to play up the divide, and waxing the hair on his chest to make him seem even younger, leaner, and more aristocratic. Luckily, his teeth were perfect and white and needed none of the dentistry and capping so many midwestern farm boys and girls did.

He knew with Menowitz gone, Myers would want immediate results for any of his stable and needed to score big with his first big fix. Bartie stayed up entire weekends working feverishly around the clock on his campaign for the English star-in-the-making. When he thought he'd hit the jackpot, he arrived at Myers's office early that Monday morning waiting bright-eyed and bushy-tailed for his notorious boss. Myers was happy, and when he saw him, he ushered him in, so he could offer up his first major PR pitch and plan. Edna gave him a good luck wink as he walked the long runway to Myers's desk. Bartie took a deep breath and stood while he presented to a blank-faced Myers, who was settling into his oversized desk.

"Okay, Kid, you're on!" Myers scrutinized him, spraying seltzer from the blue glass siphon bottle into a tumbler which emphasized his point.

"Thanks, Mister Myers. So SGM," A flushed Bartie explained, "is going to present your newest find, Duke Drake, to the public as a 'real' English Duke from a famous, aristocratic acting clan 'the Drakes'"—he paused dramatically, "…the Barrymores of England."

"I like it." Myers exhaled and drank his seltzer and then his black coffee, while eating the hard-boiled egg Edna had silently placed on his desk, slicing it in half and popping the yolk into his mouth. "Good, Bartie, the Barrymore *schtick* feels like he has acting *loin-iage*"—soon to be another famous Myerism—"and acting *chops*, and that we paid more to get him! The public wants to know *we paid more*, Bartie. Don't forget it." He picked his teeth with a wooden toothpick.

"Yes, Mister Myers," Bartie exhaled and happily agreed that he was onto something.

Despite his mercurial nature, Bartie intrinsically knew that Solomon Myers truly believed in the star system, creating and caring for the stars, his "children" as he called them, all whilst providing the public with an entertaining and aspirational dream. Bartie also knew that Myers aped English manners and style like the rest of his new-moneyed set, and above all—the appearance of the handsome, aptly named English Duke presented the studio with a rare opportunity to, as Myers liked to say, "class up the joint."

Myers immediately approved the press release that stated "SGM Studios, Culver City, signs an important, handsome English Duke." Bartie would then arrange for a clever photo shoot of Duke in an English-style library, which would set the stage and build his image. Myers liked it all so much he immediately offered up the library of his friend's Brentwood mansion belonging to a director who had the "whole British shebang" down to the paintings of the hunt and "horns and all that crap." Myers shook his head gleefully. They would get the famous Hollywood photographer and image maker, Hurrell, to pose Duke against the carved marble fireplace mantel over which hung an oil painting of the hunt, with Duke smoking a cigarette in his Savile Row styled suit. The image would be that of a real, albeit impoverished English Duke, the son of a great Shakespearean actor. While no one in America had heard of Augustus Drake, Bartie cleverly added a line in the release that he descended from an acting dynasty whose patriarch was "a favorite of Queen Victoria and whose grand performances were the toast of European drawing rooms and greatest stages of Europe."

Stoke-on-Trent and Aunt Trudy were never to be mentioned again, and in the following weeks, the studio would invest heavily to vanquish Duke's lingering cockney accent, the new one polished by an on-staff studio linguist who encouraged an unusual combination of English aristocratic phrasing and mid-Atlantic WASP delivery. Once the makeover was complete, he would be sent to be fitted by Alice Henly-Jones, SGM's head designer of the costume department. Since Henly-Jones was a Brit herself, she was well-versed in English men's fashion, and Duke would be ordered to only be seen around town in English Savile-Row-style suits, starched white monogrammed shirts, and silk ties replete with cufflinks and a perfectly pressed white pocket square, which she instructed Duke how to fold to great effect. All was done in an effort to portray the chic nonchalance of the English upper classes.

Months later, when Duke had his first hit movie, as a bonus, Bartie thought, instead of cash, he should be given a uniformed driver and an English Rolls-Royce to further the image. Myers bristled at the expense but loved the idea, and Bartie had the studio art department create the Drake family crest. It was hand stenciled in gold on the side doors of the used, secondhand Rolls-Royce Phantom II, embossed on his business cards, and engraved on an antique silver cigarette holder. In a stroke of genius, Bartie and Henly-Jones then had Myers's jeweler make a gold signet pinkie ring with the bogus crest. They antiqued the gold to make it look like it had been a family heirloom for centuries.

In the follow-up meetings, Myers ate it all up and started calling him the "Duke *of* Drake"—what would become another well-known Myerism. He also demanded that when they had a visiting English VIP, Duke was always on hand for a tour of the studio, drink, night on the town, or a photo opportunity.

"Let the Duke of Drake handle all those visiting *swells*," Myers quipped, knowing he had nothing in common with café society. When the English politician Anthony Vaughn-Stewart and his wife, the daughter of Lord Lawrence, visited Beverly Hills and were offered a studio tour, they would be thrilled but slightly bemused by Duke's well-crafted and phony personae but were willing to overlook it since Duke was so handsome and projected an aristocratic image. When the Vaughn-Stewarts asked where Duke was from, he was instructed to say, "I was a vagabond dragged from one corner of England to the other by my father playing *Hamlet*, but that's life on the stage for you."

In the end, Bartie's two pages of ideas for Duke were all approved and eventually executed.

In the coming weeks as Duke's press started to build, Myers chuckled at The Duke of Drake moniker like a child who received a large box of chocolates and had a few each day. He gave Bartie a hard, approving slap on the back and then sent a bottle of French Champagne to his office. In fact, Myers was so thrilled with Duke's transformation and studio fix, he gave Bartie a $150-a -week raise, which provided a real boost in his lifestyle. With his raise and good standing with Myers, Bartie moved into a small apartment at the Garden of Allah on Sunset Boulevard in West Hollywood, originally an estate built for Alla Nazimova in the 1920s before turning into a hotel residence. It was perfect for a young bachelor and also boasted a swimming pool in the shape of the Black Sea that provided a built-in social life. Bartie also enjoyed being in the center of things and rubbed shoulders with his former employer, F. Scott, who lived there off and on with his paramour, Sheilah Graham, and writers like Robert Benchley and Dorothy Parker all stayed in the hotel side of the complex, enjoying the sense of creative community while on the West Coast.

Bartie's main focus was work, which had become all-encompassing, but it did not stop him from occasionally sampling the wares of the young actresses and starlets he met by the pool and were more than happy to accommodate him for an evening or afternoon of pleasure. More than one good-looking girl had suggested moving in together, but Bartie fled at the thought. He had no desire to ever be trapped like his poor mother had been.

On the job, after being immersed in the Hollywood scene and SGM politics, Bartie knew more and talked less. He knew that his ability to deal with the stars and permutations of their sexual peccadilloes without judgment would also secure his success. In fact, he never knew so many actors and actresses had wildly different tastes and desires. One young and beautiful Swedish actress was married but had open relationships with both men and women, and the ladies she gravitated toward were not attractive and looked like men, often with the hint of a mustache. Another female star who had a wholesome all-American image loved to have sex with multiple men at the same time. Bartie was once called in to kill an item and rumor that she had serviced an entire college football team at a victory party, her body being the prize. Her way of thanking Bartie was to let him know she would have a party with him and his friends, but Bartie chose to keep it professional.

As time went on, the items Bartie had to kill became more bizarre, with one or two older male macho stars dressing privately in women's clothes, and one former silent film star who believed that only a nightly dose of fresh semen would help him retain his youthful complexion. The list went on and on and was so extensive that he started to make notes and file them away in a locked box. Yet, Bartie was also smart enough to not ever use anyone's name and had code words for each star. Gorge Lamont was "the Peacock" and Duke Drake was "Lord Fauntleroy" should anyone ever discover his notes. He only marked one-liners next to the code name. The "peacock was lavender" was code for gay, and Lina May, the nymphomaniac, was called "Platty" for platinum blonde. Next to her name was written "the gang's all here." No trace was to be left and when, the following year, Lina May overdosed in a drug-addled orgy, Bartie took her index card and lit it up in flames with his lighter, throwing the ashes in the fireplace, never again mentioning what he knew about the tragic star.

Six months had turned him into a professional fixer, much like a weightlifter who can bench heavier weights over time. It was early Monday morning in late August, and Edna called, the phone ring jarring at 7:30 a.m.

"*He* wants to see you, Bartie. *Now*!" He heard the click of the phone and jumped to attention. He made sure his short beige hair was combed, slicked back, and tidy with Brylcreem and cleaned his glasses before running over the main building to see Myers. As he arrived at the studio, the bright California sun reflected off his lenses, and he waved to a few studio technicians who he would occasionally have beers with in the local tavern.

"Hey, Frank. Hey, Gene," he waved. They knew since he was rushing, he was on his way to see Myers.

"Poor kid. I can't imagine what he has to put up with." They all nodded, commiserating and knowing how mercurial Myers could be. Would he be walking into a happy Myers or a lion's den? He never knew.

"Go inside." Edna rolled her eyes upward, indicating it wasn't going to be good. Bartie pleaded with his eyes, but all Edna did was shrug with her steel-gray eyebrows in the shape of an arc.

The moment he got into Myers office, he detected his nervous energy exploding as he walked toward his desk.

"Good morning, Mister Myers," Bartie offered softly.

"None of this 'Mister Myers crap.' *You* created a two-headed monster, Maddox!" He threw his arms in the air.

"Who? What? Me?" Bartie shook his head in actual confusion and had an immediate pit in his stomach.

"Lamont is at it again," he lamented.

"At what? "

"*Grand Voyage* is a huge hit. I didn't think it would be that successful, but the public wanted to see Gorge Lamont after all these years." He paced like a wound-up toy soldier. "His absence worked to his advantage, and to tell ya the truth, in audience exit polls, they went in wanting to see how bad he would look and how bad he would act, and they came out saying he looks great, and his acting is even better. It's number one at the box office. I can't fucking believe it." He moaned loudly, slamming the paper on his white lacquer desk, pacing, his thin body swimming in his shoulder pads.

"But isn't that great?" Bartie could not comprehend what the issue was.

"It's great for the bottom line at the studio, but now Gorge Lamont has the upper hand. He insisted that if he got Duke to join SGM, this would be his last film under contract, so I agreed at the time, thinking he was a total washed-up, *fagalah* has-been."

"I see," he said, trying to comprehend the onslaught of Yiddish expressions.

"And that *Farshtunkene* campaign you did was *too fucking good*!" He groaned.

"How so?"

Myers flipped open a copy of *Photoplay* magazine to the ads and then threw it at Bartie.

"Your billboards and movie posters all said, 'See for yourself. The handsomest man in Hollywood is back in town!'" He read aloud and grimaced. "And that's what everyone did. They wanted to 'see for themselves' if he was still as handsome and if he could pull off a comeback role. You made this film a smash. It's terrible." Myers wrung his bony hands. "Don't do that again, Bartie," he lamented and cautioned.

"Do what? I am sorry, Mister Myers. I thought you liked the campaign."

"Yes, but you are a *mashugana* boy genius. I am telling you if we ever do another Lamont movie, I want your *worst* idea," he begged.

"Yes, Mister Myers."

"And this Duke of Drake fag…he's also now the toast of the town. Looks more royal than King George. Can't ya do anything right?!" he screamed so loud the windows vibrated. Edna came running and opened the door and bowed out as Myers waved her away.

"I am so sorry, Mister Myers. I thought you wanted him to be famous." Bartie looked pale and wan at the news.

"I do, but not *that* famous. Now I have to deal with two famous fags who live together. Don't ya see what happened to Menowitz?"

"Yes, Mister Myers."

"He tried to tell the public that Lamont and Duke were ladies' men. Looking for a lady of the house in checkered aprons. Can you believe it? Now we have to strategize. We have to find a way to get Duke Drake with some girl, or all hell will break loose. They're both getting too big," he pleaded.

"Yes, Mister Myers." Bartie looked down as if he had committed a crime.

"I want you getting Duke Drake with some actress or married—or go back to Spokane or wherever you're from."

"I'm actually from Sioux Falls," he mumbled under his breath for no apparent reason.

"Well, get Drake dating or married, or I'll *sue* ya, Mister Sioux Falls, and you'll be finished!" he screamed.

"How am I going to do that?" Bartie shook his head in disbelief.

"You'll find a way, Thalberg," he said, referencing the boy wonder producer.

"I'll try my best, sir."

"Try harder." He banged the desk and screamed so hard his face turned the color of a radish.

"Yes, sir."

"Now get out and get it done," he groused. "Oh, by the way, before ya go…"

"Yes, sir?" Bartie looked up as pale as a white sheet of paper.

"I had Mick McDonough sign this new contract girl. Her name is Carroll Madison. I'd like you to think of a handle for her. It's a favor to me. Her boyfriend, Marty Lester, is a legend in this town and gave me my first job. He must be close to a hundred and can still get it up. So, the girl must have *something*," he groused.

"Of course, Mister Myers. Mister Myers?" Bartie asked softly. "Um…for Carroll, do you want my campaign idea to be okay, very good, or great?" Bartie asked innocently.

"Great! Ya big louse. Now get out and get it done, pronto!"

Bartie fled the office.

"How did it go?" Edna looked up over her bifocals.

"I've had better days."

Edna had a soft spot for Bartie and walked up and put her arm on his shoulder. "Bartie…"

"Yes, Edna?" He looked up in surprise. Edna was known as the ice queen—never displaying a moment or hint of emotion. The last person to charm her, it was said, was Valentino.

"He only does that with people he respects," she said softly.

"Sometimes I feel like I can't win."

"You've already won."

"How's that?"

"He knows your name. Do you know how many people on this lot have worked here for years and have never even met Myers? He has no idea who they are. Don't get down, Bartic. You're doing an excellent job."

"Thank you, Edna. That means a lot to me."

"Now don't go telling anyone I told you that, okay?" She looked at him sternly.

"Yes, Edna. I won't." She suddenly reminded him of old Elsie, who ran the rooming house in Sioux Falls. He reached over and kissed her on the cheek, surprising her. "Thanks, Edna."

"You know what, Bartie? You could have been in movies yourself, but you're too smart for that." She nodded. Bartie smiled and made a mental note that next time, he would bring Edna some flowers, just like he did for old Elsie.

Chapter Twenty-Two

Madame Fritz Langenheim
Zurich
1938

The only good thing about her father's death was that the baron didn't live long enough to witness the much talked about and threatened Anschluss. He would have been more than dismayed at Hitler and the Nazi forces' triumphant arrival and the unanticipated, enthusiastically cheering throngs welcoming the German army through the streets of Vienna and all through Austria. The blood red and sinister black of the Nazi flags and chants were bold, feverish, and chilling, especially for those who were considered not Aryan: artists, Jews, Gypsies, homosexuals—all considered degenerates and enemies to the Reich.

The baron's regal funeral a few months earlier was extremely well-attended, and one senior imperial member was overheard, his quote oft repeated, "Von Mendelssohn's timing in the markets and life were always impeccable." Hundreds attended the Stadttempel Synagogue, which would be the only one left standing in coming months since it was in a residential zone; every other was set on fire and destroyed days after the jackboots landed on Austrian soil. It would be one of the last formal Jewish funerals with an imperial honor guard and a speech by Chancellor Schuschnigg and the ritual *shiva* period at the palais.

With the death of the baron, Princess Bonaparte encouraged Irene to open her Paris apartment and spend time there to take her mind off her grief and invited her to stay in her own Paris mansion as they were still painting and furnishing with Jean-Michel Frank's modern designs and only a few *objets* that were sent from the palais. They were only allowed just a few things to help avoid suspicion from both the authorities who were clamping down on Jewish immigration and Fritz, who somewhat suspected and disagreed with her true motives. It was a source of great tension and angst between the newly married couple that, more often than not, degenerated into heated fighting.

Weeks earlier, the princess had also heard from good sources and contacts in Berlin that the actual planned Nazi military incursion was likely to be in March or April and to leave before. As a disciple of the famous founder of psychotherapy and a fervent client, Princess Bonaparte was desperately trying to secure the Freud's family move to London, and eventually would be celebrated for paying for the Freud's family exit visa and negotiating the Nazi instituted burdensome flight tax. Jewish refugees now had to pay an onerous tax in order to emigrate, already having had to leave their real estate and all their worldly possessions behind—if they were lucky enough to get out at all. This would, after the war, be tantamount to the world's largest bank robbery. Despite not being able to convince Fritz to leave Vienna, as he was in the final stages of his opera, Irene left for Paris the last weekend of February, using Grace's birthday celebration as a ruse just in the nick of time as the Nazi machine rolled into Vienna on March 12.

Even as her long-term houseman, Gunter, was loading the car with her luggage, Irene ran back into the palais and up the five flights to the gilded music rooms and begged Fritz to leave the palais and join her in Paris, but he refused. He kissed her and promised to call and visit later in the month, once again stating his close friendship with the current chancellor, who was a fan of his work, would protect him. However, that was not to be.

Within days of the Anschluss, anti-Jewish legislation was enacted and enforced, and many of Fritz's friends in the theater were forced to scrub the streets of pro-independence slogans. Jewish actresses from the Theater in der Josefstadt were forced to clean toilets, and rabbis and Jews were beaten in the streets and shorn of their sacred locks to jeering crowds. Irene frantically called Fritz but, after April 1, no one answered at the palais, and he seemed to have vanished into thin air.

Without her father or Fritz to advise her, Irene had no choice but to quietly settle in her chic Avenue Foch apartment after a brief stay at Princess Bonaparte's *hôtel particulier.* Her dear friends Grace and Louis tried to comfort her, and Louis urged her to make the trip to Geneva to access her funds. He theorized it would protect her in the months and years to come, and Irene nodded her agreement through tears.

With her apartment in order and no news of Fritz, Irene decided that a visit to the Swiss bank was in order.

It was one of those clean, clear, and crisp days that only the Alps could boast, and Irene and Princess Marie tried to be equally even-keeled, although there was underlying anxiety in the dining car on the train due to Fritz's disappearance. Princess Bonaparte had agreed to accompany Irene and, on March 15, they made the trip together taking the overnight first-class train from the French territories to Geneva.

Upon the arrival of Princess Bonaparte at the Moritz Bank of Switzerland on the Rue de Lausanne with the young and beautiful Baroness Irene, they received top attention from the conservative bankers. They made a striking impression with their formidable titles, furs, and jewels as they swept into the stately paneled conference rooms. The senior staff were at their most charming attention. Café and strudel were summoned on gleaming silver platters, and they were ushered into an even more formal and spotless boardroom hanging with Swiss German portraits of bank founders. The bank's president, Dr. Rudolf Scheid, entered and gave a courtly bow to the ladies and kissed their hands in a most formal European and courtly style. After pleasantries were made, Irene explained that her father, the baron had passed away, and she brought forth his diary with the accounts and her bound bank books. She also had the keys to the multiple safety deposit boxes containing her mother's storied jewels.

"Yes, I see that everything is in order with *you,* Madame Langenheim." Dr. Scheid looked over the paperwork, his gray pallor ghostly in contrast to the robust and rosy cheeks of Vice President Kristian Bohrman.

"My condolences, of course, on the news of your father's passing. He was a true gentleman," Mr. Scheid said. "One question…do you have a copy of his death certificate? We need that in order to allow you access to the accounts and boxes since it's a *joint* account," he added, grimacing.

"Oh, dear," Irene gulped. "I was in such a state when Father passed, making all the arrangements for the funeral, I never thought to get a death certificate nor that I would even need one since my name is clearly on the account." She pointed to her name embossed on the small maroon bound book.

"We will need one in order to allow you access to the funds and the safety deposit boxes."

"Yes, but I am sure you know I cannot return to Vienna now given the Anschluss. It is not safe for me, given the recent news," Irene stated.

"Baroness, Princess...give us a few moments to confer." Dr. Scheid rose from his chair and left the room with Mr. Bohrman. A good twenty minutes passed, and when he returned, he had a somber look on his face.

"I am afraid, Madame Langenheim, it is bank rules. We must have the death certificate in order to allow you access to the bank accounts and contents of the safety deposit boxes since it is a *joint account*."

"Herr Scheid, you know quite well this young woman cannot go back to Vienna safely." Princess Bonaparte spoke strongly and clearly.

"I am sorry. Those are the bank rules, clearly written in our bylaws."

"Why, this is preposterous, a charade of the highest order! You all heard the news that the baron passed, and this is his rightful heir on the account stated in black and white in this bank book. She is in grave need of her funds, cannot find her husband, the composer Fritz Langenheim, who remained in Vienna, and fears for his life and safety."

They both shook their heads with a blank stare and folded their hands in protest.

"We have to abide by our *rules*!"

"Why, this is outrageous!" The princess shook her head at the news.

"I am sorry, Princess. Even if you, yourself, came to us in the exact same circumstances, we would not be able to do it. How do we know for certain he is dead? I did not see the body, nor did we read about it in the papers."

"Perhaps I can get a newspaper clipping," Irene offered.

"That would help, but we do need the formal death certificate. There is no other way possible. Rules are rules."

"Shame on you." The princess rose from her chair, throwing her silver foxes over her shoulder. "I will make sure this travesty sees the light of day, and one day you will pay for this. I can assure you if it was Princess Bonaparte and not Baroness Von *Mendelssohn*, you would allow me access to my funds. Swiss banking hypocrisy at its best."

"Aunt Marie, please…don't trouble yourself." Irene rose in ladylike fashion from her chair. "I can promise you, Doctor Scheid and Mister Bohrman, you have not seen the end of me, and one day when it is possible, I will return and claim what is rightfully mine. Don't you dare touch my account or those safety deposit boxes. They contain my inheritance, and I promise you I will be back to claim them. You are clearly not doing what you can to help me in any way as a client of your bank."

"I am sorry, Madame. That is our final decision, and I would be happy to see you again when you possess the death certificate. I will personally take you to your account and boxes."

"Yes, you will, *indeed*." Irene stifled a cry with her gloved hand, and the princess led her out of the office to the waiting, hired car to take them back to the train station. As the steam exhaled from the train, they hugged and kissed.

"I will call you from Vienna, my dear. I am sure I will hear news of Fritz, and I will do my best to try and get you that certificate, although I have heard it is utter chaos in Vienna with many of the public offices shut because of the Anschluss."

"Oh, life is indeed unfair." Irene shrugged.

"It is. I will pay the palais a visit after I see the Freuds and see what I can find out about Fritz."

"Thank you, Aunt Marie, you are one of the kindest, bravest, and most generous souls I have ever known."

"Nonsense! I just do what is right when things go wrong. That is all." She kissed her on both cheeks and held her beautiful, young face in her hands. "I know this is hard for you to hear, darling, but your father was right. I think, despite the new apartment, you may need to go to England or America. I hear from my sources in Berlin that Paris will be next."

"Paris? Oh no!" Irene gasped.

"It's unthinkable, but there's no stopping this madman. Worry about the money after the war. I will lend you anything you need, my darling—safety first." She thrust a stack of large banknotes into her hands.

"I'm not sure how I can thank you, Aunt Marie." She looked down and then kissed and hugged her.

"No need to thank. You are family." They emotionally embraced before her departure.

Irene took the overnight train back to Paris. When the young Swiss border guard saw just how incredibly beautiful she was and stamped her passport, he noticed the large red "J" engraved in the religion section of her passport. "J" for *Juden*. Jew.

"Juden? You're too beautiful to be a Juden!" he exclaimed, surprised.

"I am proud to be a Juden," she countered.

"I'm sorry, mademoiselle. I hope you do not consider me impertinent, but have you considered staying in Switzerland? Thousands of your people are trying to cross the border from Germany and even Austria, desperately trying to get in, and you're going to Paris." He looked at her forlorn expression. "Well, I guess it's safe for now."

"Thank you for your concern." She saw him look at her up and down, salivating. "Yes," Irene said, "safe for now, but thank you." She put the passport back in her crocodile handbag, clicked it shut, and sat, looking at the beautiful scenery chug by as she made her way to Paris. Her father had only managed to put one hundred thousand francs in her Paris bank account before he passed. And then five thousand from Aunt Marie. She knew besides her jewelry and the two paintings he was able to spirit to Paris, she'd have enough money without needing to sell anything for a year. And she now had a hard choice to make: England or America? And how to get there?

Chapter Twenty–Three

Duke Drake
Los Angeles
1938

The original meeting had been scheduled for an early morning Monday breakfast in the commissary. Given the nature of the discussion and Myer's discontent with Duke's personal status, Bartie changed it at the last minute, rescheduling it for a Sunday in his office using Myers's name as a surefire lure. He wanted to avoid generating gossip among SGM employees and the lascivious glances of Mavis, who was now a waitress in the commissary, continually pestering him for a date. He had continued to see her for a night of quick, hot sex when he was in the mood, and she was always accommodating, yet Bartie knew she was falling for him. He didn't want to encourage anything more than a casual relationship, although he had actually grown quite fond of her. In anticipation of Duke's early arrival, Bartie had fetched coffee and pastries at the local deli across from the studio as he sat waiting for Duke, looking occasionally at his trusty stainless Hamilton. He looked around the bungalow once occupied by Menowitz and felt a bit like a child playing dress-up, but was grateful it was not the case. Of course, the nonchalant Duke proved to be a half hour late, and the coffee was cold upon his arrival. Bartie had left a message for him the day before with their Japanese houseman, Akito, at "Pansy Hall" and hoped Duke had gotten the message that there would now be a change of time and venue. Finally, after thinking he might not have gotten the message or was not coming, Duke strode in looking a bit flustered and somewhat put out by the change of time and date. He sported a white cable-knit tennis sweater and cream-colored slacks, looking fit and tan and ready for a pleasure-filled yacht trip to Catalina Island or a tennis match, rather than a studio visit. They cordially shook hands, and Bartie motioned for Duke to sit in one of the opposing armchairs that his previous boss's wife, Mrs. Menowitz, had recently recovered in caramel mohair, before her husband's expulsion.

"Coffee?" Bartie asked.

"Yes, please, with cream," Duke ordered, as if he expected staff available to serve him.

"It's in the bag." Bartie pointed.

"I see." Duke sniffed as he opened the crinkled brown paper, inferring that he was now a real Duke and didn't do mundane things for himself anymore and sighed at being suddenly forced to.

"So, I got the urgent message yesterday that you wanted to see me in your office at Mister Myers's request." Duke looked at him suspiciously.

"Yes, I'm sorry to ruin your beach weekend, but when I have private conversations, I want to make sure they're kept private."

"Why couldn't you come to Santa Monica?" Duke asked in an accusatory tone.

"I wanted to have the conversation with you, *alone*."

"I figured. Gorge thought as much, as well," Duke offered.

"Of course…and how is Gorge?" Bartie inquired.

"I think he is quite enjoying his comeback moment. Thank you for asking…and for your great press campaign, although Gorge was less than pleased with my disappearance today. I don't assume it's for *fun and games*." He winked.

"Look, Duke, I'm going to level with you because that's how I do things. I think you know I am a straight shooter."

"Well, I know you're straight…I don't know how well you shoot." He raised an eyebrow, delivering the line as if it were in one of his screwball comedies.

"Okay, enough with the jokes. I hope you think I've done a pretty good job for you and Gorge both." He looked directly at Duke.

"I would say so. I like you, Bartie. You're one of the good guys here. Everyone says so—even Gorge—and he dislikes pretty much everyone here except for his gals like Joan and Lana. You know how he is." Duke got a hint that this was going to be a serious meeting and changed his tone slightly as he sat back and sipped his coffee.

"Yes, and that's the point of this discussion. I had a long conversation about you with Myers. I hope you realize he and the studio are investing a great deal in you and your image, and they want to make you a big star. They only have the best intentions—but it's a bit hard with you living openly with Gorge in Santa Monica. I'm getting direct calls from Louella and Hedda, and they're on the verge of printing a blind item about it."

"Well, just tell them we're roommates, that's all," Duke said flatly.

"Yeah, and I'm Rin Tin Tin." Bartie shook his head.

Duke sat back in his chair and laughed, revealing his perfectly-arranged white teeth.

"Look, you're smart, Duke. You know how to play ball, and that's why the studio has made such a large investment in you. And Gorge didn't, and look what happened to him."

"What happened?"

"Come on, Duke, let's not play games. We all know the score." Bartie shook his head and sighed.

"Okay, as you say in America, shoot." Duke leaned back, looking cool as a cucumber.

"I have a good idea for you, that's all. And it will be quick and fairly painless."

"What's that?"

Bartie came out with it.

"I want you to go out on a few dates with Lorena Smalls."

"Lorena Smalls? The hoofer? The minister's teenage daughter?" Duke shook his head in disbelief. "She's pretty and all, but I hear she is a Bible-toting prohibitionist."

"That's my point." Bartie eagerly leaned forward to stress his idea.

"What point, Bartie?"

"She's been a child star for a long time, and she's been brought up with an overbearing, religious mother. She's the only young girl on the lot who hasn't been corrupted. That's why she's known as 'the professional virgin.'"

"And why would that be good for me?" Duke asked the question with his hands.

"Well..." Bartie leaned back and lit up a cigarette after offering Duke one, which he declined. "You tell *me*, Duke?"

"Because...I won't have to sleep with her, and Gorge won't get upset?" Duke asked in a singsong manner.

"Correct—there won't be too much pressure."

"You know, Bartie," he smiled, "I think you're onto something."

"Look, here's my plan. The studio is going to throw her a sweet sixteenth birthday party, and you're going to show up and be her date. You'll present her with a corsage and a big present with a bow, and afterward, you'll take her out dancing at Cocoanut Grove. Of course, the date will be followed by the studio photographers, which I will set up. Her big musical, *San Francisco Stagecoach*, is being released next week, so the timing is perfect. Just take her out, let's say, once a week for a month or so—long enough for Louella to write about it, and we'll get Myers off your back...and mine." He took his glasses off and used his shirt to wipe away a smudge.

"Lorena Smalls is going to hate me, Bartie." Duke shook his glorious head. "And that mother of hers...." They both grimaced at the thought of the hulking, snarling woman constantly seen trailing her daughter on the lot like an interfering bodyguard.

"How so?"

"I drink. I smoke." He looked at Bartie and, sensing a real friend, added more or less to shock, "I suck cock. Does that bother you, Bartie? To hear that?"

"Duke, whatever floats your boat, but it's my job to have the women in America think you like *them*, not men. You're tall, dark, and debonair, and by the way...now a real," he coughed, "Duke." They both laughed at the pretense. "And for the record, Lorena won't say no," Bartie said with confidence.

"How do you know?"

"Look, I'll let you in on a little professional secret that you have to promise not to betray."

"Promise." They shook hands. "This isn't exactly a conversation I'm happy about either."

"The reason Lorena Smalls is still the professional virgin is she's just like you. She likes...*girls.* Myers had his people spy on her and found out she was going down on the high school tutor they had assigned her, this older girl, Janine. And if you must know, they've been together forever. She's also addicted to those amphetamines they gave her as a kid to get her on the set by 5:30 a.m. So, Myers had the same conversation with her and that mother, and they're willing to play ball. Just show up, and it's all sunshine and lollipops, and no one gets hurt. Let's just say you're both helping each other out."

"What's Gorge going to say?"

"He'll be thrilled. He knows damn well her hymen is like the hoover dam—it's not going anywhere." Bartie paused. "And one last thing."

"Yes, Bartie...what else do you want me to do? Sleep with Margaret Hamilton?" He raised an eyebrow at the thought of the mature and unattractive yet popular character actress.

"Can you, at least for the month, spend more time at Gorge's mansion in Los Feliz and less time at Pansy Hall? It's a great deal more private, and you guys really flaunt it at the beach with the weightlifting, the little bathing suits you strut around in. It's like you're begging for trouble with your romantic beach walks."

"Look, I'll talk to Gorge about it."

"So, you're in?

"I guess it makes sense." He flashed a dazzling white smile and held out his hand for a shake. "I'm in."

"Great." Bartie let out a sigh of relief. He knew Myers would be thrilled.

"You know, you're a handsome guy, Bartie. You sure you don't want to come over and have dinner with Gorge and I one night? We have fun parties."

"So I've heard. No, thank you, but thank you. I'm flattered."

"Well, it didn't hurt to ask. Lorena Smalls, right?" He leaned back and sighed.

"Right. Lorena Smalls, the professional virgin." He nodded and saw Duke starting to laugh.

"What's so funny?" Bartie looked askance.

"I just think if my stepfather, Augustus Drake, heard about this one, he'd have a field day."

"Well, you told me he was a man of theater."

"That he was."

"Then I'm sure he did anything to put on a great show. Just remember, great acting runs in the family. The English Barrymores!" Bartie slapped Duke on the back and walked him out of his office to Duke's navy chauffeured Rolls. He opened the door for him, the gold Duke family crest glittering in the sun. They chatted about his next movie, and Bartie said he would present the new PR campaign in a week. Bartie looked as the Rolls drove off and felt slight satisfaction at knowing Myers would be pleased by the news.

As he walked back in the office, he was startled to see a gorgeous, young, and very voluptuous blonde in the waiting area, a vanilla apparition, all cherries and whipped cream. He checked his watch and realized his ten o'clock was a bit early.

"Are you Mister Maddox?" she asked in a breathy tone, lifting her dark sunglasses.

"And you are?" Bartie raised an eyebrow and smiled.

"How do you do? I'm Carroll, Carroll Madison. We have an appointment through Mister Myers's office," she said, looking somewhat confused.

"Yes, nice to meet you. Call me Bartie." He surveyed her with a beaming smile.

"I didn't realize you would be so young and handsome. I was expecting some old-timer." She smiled and adjusted her slim pencil skirt and tight-fitting sweater set as she stood. Within minutes of looking her up and down, Bartie knew exactly what he was going to do with her.

Chapter Twenty–Four

La Marquise de La Faucigny
Le Vésinet, Paris
1939

Grace checked her makeup in the carved oval mirror over the 18th century giltwood console. She decided she needed more rouge and applied some along with a fresh coat of ruby lipstick from her 14K-gold case. She moved a diamond clip up to her shoulder and placed another one in her hair, displaying the dazzling deco jewels in a rather *soigné* way only old money heiresses knew how to do without overly thinking about it.

"I'd rather you not go to the movies tonight, cherie." Louis looked at her a bit sternly, his cerulean eyes more foreboding than usual. He played with his gold watch fob dangling from his black silk vest pocket in the grand salon of the Paris mansion, which had recently been refurbished under his supervision and Grace's healthy bankbook.

"I'm feeling just fine, Louis," she smiled and said in her usual jolly tone. "It's been three months, and it's been the perfect pregnancy so far. Aunt Rose wrote to me that I was born to carry babies," Grace said brightly, snapping her large crocodile handbag shut.

"Still, the doctor wants you taking it easy," Louis cautioned. "Remember you're carrying the next Marquis de La Faucigny."

"Or Marquise." Grace smiled and then saw his dour expression at the idea of a girl baby, and she quickly changed the subject, knowing she had put her foot in her mouth. Patrimony wasn't a subject to discuss with Louis or his father, she had come to realize.

"I promised Irene we would see the new American comedy, *The Weary Widow*, that is playing in town. She desperately needs some cheering up, and I thought a Mae West comedy would do the trick. There's this new dreamy actor in it everyone's talking about now... Duke Drake. Don't worry, darling, it's only the movies, and no movie star is as good-looking as my handsome husband." Grace walked over to Louis and straightened his tie in a loving way. "Now, don't be such a sourpuss! I'm just going to the movies, not riding."

"I'm just doing my duty, Grace," he said without humor.

"Why don't you come with us? It will do you a world of good to go to the cinema and forget politics for a while." She smiled.

"I have a dinner meeting at the club. The coalition government and Blum just resigned, so there is a great deal of anxiety in town." Louis put down a copy of *Le Figaro.*

"I know, darling. I read the papers, too." She shrugged.

"I am just more concerned these days with the baby coming and the world in such disarray," he replied, frowning.

"I've been telling you we should spend some time in New York. I hear it's great fun these days, and you would enjoy it. It's only ten days by liner, and my uncle owns the ships, which we never, ever use, by the way." She shrugged at the thought.

"Grace." He peered at her and shook his head. "Life isn't all about parties, travel, and the cinema." He looked at the Picasso portrait and its abstract face newly installed above the fireplace mantel.

"What's wrong if it is?"

"New painting?" he grimaced.

"Yes, it's supposedly a masterpiece of Picasso's mistress, Dora Maar," she mentioned in an excited fashion. "Though Picasso is an odd man—quite intense. When I went to the studio, he looked me over with the face of a bull like I was a piece of pastry."

"He probably wanted to bed you and then paint you."

"Yes, but I'm taken, and he is scary." She looked in the mirror and adjusted a wave set in her hair. "Kahnweiler, his dealer, told me I was very lucky to get it."

"Of course he would say that. He's his dealer, Grace, and you know how pushy *they* are." He paused, taking it in. "Why is her nose all the way over *there*?" He squinted.

"He's actually a very elegant man, and I had to beg for it, truthfully. And don't be so provincial, darling. We have enough canvases of bowls of fruit and wine in this place to start a grocery. We need a little energy among all these antiques and *relics* that I'm forced to live with. I can't even get rid of anything to really decorate because every canvas is a *relative.*" She looked up at another seventeenth-century portrait of a disapproving marquise in her powdered wig, peering down at her with disdain.

"I leave the art and decor to you." He turned away from the canvas with a raised eyebrow.

She laughed. "Well, you go to your meeting and spend time on all the world's problems, and I'll see a comedy. It's rather fitting, no?"

"Just be back and put your feet up as Doctor Peillon prescribed."

"Yes, of course."

"If I had my way, you'd spend your entire pregnancy in bed. And make sure Luigi has an umbrella and drives slowly."

"You know, you are being such a dear. I do rather think you love me." Grace reached up and gave him a peck on the cheek.

"I do, and our baby."

"I told you and your father I would give you an heir and a *spare*... no need to worry." Grace walked slowly down the grand circular staircase, her red lacquer fingernails grazing the marble banister to collect her warm sable coat.

"Why don't you meet us at Brasserie Lipp after the movie?" Grace offered. "I have been craving rémoulade!"

He held her tightly by the elbow as she walked down the grand staircase. "Grace, the world is changing, and I think you need to be more aware of the changes and be on the right side of things." He looked squarely at her.

"You think I'm the one who is on the wrong side, dear?" She smoothed her fuchsia silk maternity dress that Worth had created especially for her.

"Well, your politics have always been very *liberal*, I should say."

"You know I *hate* politics. I just love my friends."

"Speaking of your friends, if France falls to the Germans, I think you might consider *helping* your friends," he said slyly.

"I always help my friends. What do you have in mind, darling?" She lit up a Gitane when she reached the black-and-white marble entry foyer.

"Well, I was speaking to one of my German contacts in Berlin, and I think you might have your friend, Irene, deed us the rights to her father's vineyard in Bordeaux. Some of the smarter Jews are putting their properties in proper Christian hands, their friends' hands, so they have a better chance of keeping it if things turn out differently for them," he said in a low voice. "The Wertheimers are putting their interest in Chanel with a Christian representative," he informed her.

"Why are you so interested in Irene's vineyard?" Grace looked a bit startled at his suggestion. "You've mentioned it once or twice before."

"I wouldn't want to see her lose it, that's all," he said, playing it off. "And they do make the best Bordeaux," he laughed.

"I don't think that's a laughing matter." Grace shook her head.

"There you go again, Grace, taking everything so *seriously.*"

"Well," she paused, agreeing with him to avoid more unpleasant discussion. "maybe you're right, and that would be a smart idea for Irene. I'll talk to her about it."

"When?' he said in a loving fashion, trying to appear nonchalant.

"Tonight." Grace was uneasy about his clear interest in Irene's assets. "She has been quite upset, you know, after her father's death and with no news of Fritz, of course. Although Princess Marie is quite convinced Fritz was taken away to one of those horrid concentration centers."

"Yes, camps are popping up all over. Quite distressing and all the more reason to talk with Irene about the vineyard. Has she had any plans on leaving the country?" he asked, looking away and still trying to appear nonchalant.

"Aunt Rose told me that immigration to the US has slammed shut. It's quite upsetting."

"Then it's more important you talk with her about it. Do it soon, Grace. Don't wait." He tapped the gold carved lion on the banister nervously with his forefinger.

"Why? Do you know something I don't?" She turned toward the coatroom for her fur, her lady's maid returning with a sable muff as well.

"I only know that Hitler is gobbling up Europe in pieces and requisitioning all the good Jewish art and properties, so if you want to be a good friend, have Irene sign over the vineyard. We can protect it for her, and no one will mess around with the Marquis de La Faucigny—not even the Germans."

"You mean the *Marquise* de La Faucigny," she said with verve to prove a point.

"Yes, la *Marquise*."

"That's one of the things I've always admired about you." Grace smiled. "You always seem to know all the *right people*."

"It's not a time for music and movies, Grace. That's all I'm saying." He looked back as he climbed up the staircase. "Just be careful. *Je t'aime*."

"*Je t'aime*," she answered, as the butler opened the heavy gilded doors, and Luigi helped her into the polished Daimler's commodious back seat, placing the sable throw over her legs.

As they drove into town, Grace sat back and looked out the window with a certain unease. She had found the conversation about Irene's vineyard disturbing and was becoming uneasy with Louis's recent myriad anti-Semitic comments, his pro-Nazi sympathies, and contacts in Berlin—who he seemed to be getting closer to by the day. She felt odd about lying to Louis that her Uncle Reggie was secretly helping Irene with her US visa. He had secured one for her after she begged him to, and her uncle had specifically said to not tell a soul, especially Louis, or it would imperil Irene's chances and his own reputation with the state department. Grace hadn't told Irene and certainly not Louis, but she had sold her two iconic emerald and diamond bracelets to a jeweler on the Place Vendôme to pay the contact for arranging Irene's exit visa. She knew that Louis would object, even stop what she was doing as he had oversight to her bank records and didn't want to raise suspicion with a large cash withdrawal. She knew deep down that she was doing the right thing and that Irene needed to get out of France as soon as possible—although she would miss her chic bracelets! Now that the papers had come through, they were secured in her handbag, and she was excited to surprise her best friend tonight with them at the movies. She and Uncle Reggie had arranged for her to travel to the South of France and depart on a McClean Star Liner that weekend, and Irene would be safe sooner rather than later. Grace smiled at the thought and then sighed at her own predicament. She loved Louis and her future child; however, she was coming to terms with the fact that she was married to a Nazi sympathizer. Or worse, God forbid, a bona fide Nazi. The possibility made her shudder. She also knew deep down that Louis hadn't made love to her in months. She wasn't sure where he spent his evenings, but couldn't dismiss the gossip she had been hearing. Gossip that he was having a long-term affair with a young French actress, Ghislaine Garriaux, the star of a new movie, *Lumière des Étoiles.* That was the second movie they were seeing tonight. It would be a double feature as Grace needed to see the actress and was finally ready to size up her rival. For now, she would give Irene the ultimate gift and bask in the look of relief on her best friend's beautiful face while inspecting another beauty's face…for different reasons.

Chapter Twenty-Five

Baroness Irene Von Mendelssohn
Paris
1940

Perhaps it was the sight of a simple, golden, flaky croissant and a large frothy ceramic bowl of cappuccino that did it to her. She stifled an inner cry; all the delicious and mundane things, small and large, that she would miss. First, the apple strudel in Vienna and now something as simple as a Parisian croissant. It seemed silly, but it was the little things that did it to her.

Irene sobbed at the sight of the gift of her papers, more than grateful as she hugged and kissed Grace, knowing she would be leaving and separated from her dearest friend and not knowing when she would see her or her baby next. After a bout of frenetic packing and taking in her lovely apartment one last time that Saturday, she left in the dead of the night in Princess Bonaparte's chauffeur-driven Rolls, which would drive her south to the port at Marseille. She knew she was lucky to have such good friends, but Aunt Marie and Grace were more than that: they were truly sisters. She also knew how lucky she was, despite her father's recent death and the last terrifying report of Fritz being sent to a makeshift concentration camp in the Viennese railway station.

Her journey was to be done in utmost secrecy, and she tried to keep a low profile as she didn't want to attract too much attention before leaving France. The Raphael was sold for less than she wanted through Grace's art dealer, given there was so much Jewish-owned art on the market. She entrusted Grace with her father's Tiepolo, which Grace promised to ship once Irene arrived in New York. Irene was overcome by Grace's generosity and pressed Grace on how she raised the money without alerting Louis. Grace revealed the selling of her two bracelets to pay off the bureaucrats. Then, there was the fully-paid first-class ticket on Uncle Reggie's steamship to New York. It was all so incredibly generous. She also had fifteen thousand American dollars, which she had withdrawn and converted over time from her Paris bank without attracting suspicion, and she hid it in a small Louis Vuitton makeup case. She had her jewels, furs, and gowns, and she also knew she had her youth and beauty, but despite knowing she was luckier than most, a deep sadness and anxiety traveled with her. She had endured the last few years living in rarefied air that was quickly dissipating, and she knew with news of the Jewish atrocities surfacing in Europe, her beauty and title would do nothing to protect her. She needed to leave—and yesterday, at that. The thought of the ocean voyage and new land, where she could reimagine her own life on her own terms, was thrilling, yet terrifying.

"Grace, you are the sister I never had, and I love you as much as anyone can love," Irene cried and hugged her as they parted.

"Darling, my sister and best friend, I shall see you very, very soon in New York after the baby arrives." Grace wept as well.

"Grace, please thank your Uncle Reggie for me and tell him that once I find a way to retrieve my inheritance, I will pay back your kindness and generosity. I am devastated you had to sell your bracelets."

"Nonsense! People are much more important than *things.* Things can always be replaced."

"I promise you one day I will repay you and replace them," she teared.

"Please don't worry, Irene. Your safety is all that matters now. And I have more than enough jewelry, I assure you."

"Grace, one thing."

"Yes, anything."

"I'm a bit worried for you too," Irene treaded slowly. "Princess Marie confirmed your husband has already created an alliance with a few leading Nazis, and when they invade, and they will, you will be considered an enemy alien. I am also begging you to listen to your Uncle Reggie and go to London before it's too late. Louis's mistress is bad enough, but you need to get away from this man, and I'm worried he will hold you hostage for your money. Look at what happened to Fritz and the palais, not to mention nationalizing our family bank." Irene suppressed the flow of tears from her eyes. Grace nodded and looked downcast as well.

Princess Bonaparte had indeed called Irene with somber information after having visited the palais to learn that it had been immediately stripped of all the important *objets d'art*, including her father's priceless library and paintings, all shipped back to Germany. Fritz had been arrested and sent to a jail cell, where they forced him, under duress, to sign away the rights to her estate, the bank, and the palais, which was then requisitioned by the Wehrmacht. Then, Fritz was released and forced to scrub the streets on his hands and knees with the other theater and opera members, while kicked and beaten. He was last seen being sent to a makeshift concentration camp in the railway station. No one knew if he was dead or alive, and his friend, Chancellor Schuschnigg, who had opposed the Anschluss, would also be sent to a camp, tortured, and kept in solitary confinement until the war's end. At first, she had fought leaving Europe without Fritz, but everyone assured her that he was most likely dead and that she had made a deathbed promise to her father to leave for England or the United States.

Irene arrived in Marseille in the early morning hours and checked into a small luxury hotel on the Corniche overlooking the bay, Le Petit Nice. Marseille was as beguiling as ever, as if she were heading for a luxury *vacances*; the small hilltop villages beckoned, the winding streets, array of colorful flowers and pink bougainvillea blooming, and the lemon sun dappled roofs displaying a fake optimism. The residents went about their daily routines, not comprehending that their guests would have to escape the country or having any sense that Paris would fall to Germany a month later. Like her father, Irene's timing would later be noted as being seer-like.

It had all gone according to plan, and after a fitful night's sleep, she arrived to board early. She braved the photographers stationed at the ship entrance, who noted the departure of the stunning and glamorous baroness. They were routinely given the ship's passenger manifest, and Reggie had made the reservation under her maiden name instead of Langenheim. She quickly posed with a few other first-class passengers as she walked up the gangplank to the McClean Star Liner, personally welcomed by the ship's captain as a VIP guest and personal family friend of Reggie McClean. Her sixteen pieces of Louis Vuitton luggage were brought up to her stateroom within minutes.

Inside, she opened the bottle of Dom Pérignon and then artfully arranged the long-stemmed yellow roses in the large crystal vase sent by Reggie McClean, himself. As she heard the loud foghorns blow and the ship launch, she thanked God and said a prayer for Grace and her baby, looking out her circular porthole windows toward the sea. She artfully applied her makeup after freshening up and walked out to the upper promenade deck. She took in the stinging sea air, but refused to look back at the tugboats helping the liner out to sea. She would only look forward now, and promised herself she would come back to France and Switzerland to find out what had become of Fritz and claim what was rightfully hers when the time was right. She would do it on her own terms, and nothing and no one would stand in her way. As she took deep breaths of the sea air, she felt freedom for the first time and knew she would have to fight and find a way to succeed.

Chapter Twenty-Six

La Marquise de La Faucigny
St. Jean Cap-Ferrat, France
1940

It *should* have been glorious; the long sunny days strung one into the other as the unfurling tail of a kite, each one more relaxing and picture-perfect than the next. The scent of jasmine, burnt pine needles, and the sea converged into a natural eau de parfum. It would have all been wonderful if Grace hadn't miscarried the week before, but instead, she was still crying and convulsing from both the physical and mental pain.

Louis was bereft as it had been a boy all along, and she sighed as she sat on the worn terra cotta terrace of the Provençal butter-yellow stucco villa and admired the contrast of the vibrant olive-green shutters. *Only in Europe*, she thought. It all seemed so *alive* and dazzling as she overlooked the azure sea, the diamond waves, the elegant ilexes casting long shadows on the sloping, manicured lawn and listened to the hypnotic opera of cicadas. She had everything, but now had nothing. It had all been taken away from her...*them*...in a flash.

She sat and observed Louis taking his morning constitutional in the sea, his strong, lean strokes slicing through the rippling, glittering water off the Cap. He had been stoic, yet visibly upset.

"Why did you have to go out so much?" This was all he said before leaving the house, not coming back until the next day, his subtle blame lingering in the air like stale cigar smoke seeping into the damask of the sofa fabric.

"I'll have a bit more coffee, Lourdes, and some orange juice *s'il vous plaît.*" Grace tied the navy-and-white Chanel scarf around her hair and adjusted her sunglasses. It was only 11:00 a.m., but the sun was blazing, and she didn't want to burn.

"How are you feeling this morning, Madame?" Lourdes asked.

"After my croissant *et beurre*, I think I should feel better," she sighed. "But I don't."

"Of course, Madame." Lourdes did a slight bow, her crisp black-and-white maid's uniform contrasting with the weather.

Grace watched as Louis walked up the paved avenue to the main house in his trim navy swim trunks. Finally, he arrived, walked over, and kissed her hand, as was his fashion.

"Good morning, darling. You're looking chic and rested," he observed.

"Thank you. How was your swim?" she asked. "Coffee?"

"No, thank you, I have already had two espressos." He smiled.

"I have an idea," she said in a forced, cheerful way. "Let's take a drive and go to Èze today for lunch. The view is always so stunning once you get there," she offered brightly.

"Grace, you need to rest," he sternly advised.

"I have been, more than you know," she replied. "It would be fun. I think we need that," she said sweetly.

"I wish I could, but I have to go up to Paris today." He toweled his hair, the white-blonde ends spiking up.

"Again? But Louis, but you just got here." She looked down.

"Yes, I know, but I was called into a cabinet meeting.... Europe is in a bit of disarray, my dear, despite how idyllic it is on the Cap." He looked away, his blue eyes cloudy.

"Can't you stay one more day? I feel like I never see you anymore." She tried to be casual in an offhand way, despite her gnawing fears.

"I wish I could, but darling, it is an important meeting."

"When did you find out? I didn't hear anyone ring this morning?" she sulked, trying not to be the prying wife, but could not control her wifely instincts.

"Oh, I received a telegram late yesterday and forgot to mention it. I'm sorry, dear."

"I see, well, that is a shame. When do you think you will be back?"

"Next Friday." He looked off at the sailboats in the distance.

"I see," she said in clipped sadness, her large eyes downcast in pools of fear.

"I know. I wish I could stay, but my political career is taking off, and the country needs true French leaders to chart the course during this time." He stood squarely, putting on his navy terry cloth polo shirt.

"Of course, my darling." She rose to kiss him. "Until next week. We have a costume party at Jay and Florence Gould's. It should be great fun."

"Perfect, I adore them. I will see you this weekend, then." He kissed her on her forehead. "I'll call you. Rest!" he ordered and walked up toward the villa, disappearing from her view.

Upon his departure, Grace decided to take a nap by the patio overlooking the sea. She fell into a trancelike sleep and then had a fitful dream. It had her tossing and turning as she had a foreboding, terrifying dream sequence of flying telegrams and horrible news shocking her awake. She realized how hot she was as she had fallen asleep under the umbrella on the wicker chaise and saw from her wristwatch that it was 12:08 p.m. She was burning, perspiring, and jittery as she ran toward the house and up the back staircase into Louis's room, unable to control her premonition. She double checked to see that he had indeed left for Paris, and when she saw his Louis Vuitton suitcases were gone from his armoire, she walked briskly into the library. The sunlight highlighted the grain of the highly-polished mahogany wood desk, and she felt a chill at what she would discover. *Where would he keep his telegrams?* she asked herself as she rummaged through the top three drawers. In a top file of papers, she saw he had copies of her bank statements front and center. Suddenly she remembered, as it was a partner's desk, there were two locked drawers on the side facing the bookshelves, and they were indeed closed and locked. *Where would Louis keep the key?* She riffled through the drawers but could not find it. *Take a breath. Where would he keep it?* she asked herself, as she looked at the desk and the fireplace and then saw the distinctive mechanical clock. *Of course—that was it!* She often saw him winding the treasured, ornate mechanical clock that had been given to him by his grandfather, and he had showed her when they were courting that it needed to be wound by a small silver key kept in the clock's manual silver drawer under the base of the clock. She took a deep breath and calmly walked over to the mantel and withdrew the drawer, and, sure enough, there were two small keys. Louis was predictable and orderly, which made certain things easier. She walked over to the desk with the larger key, and the small desk door sprung open. Then, her spine went numb as she found a folder on one shelf. She silently and slowly opened it and saw a number of telegrams with the distinctive bold red official Nazi swastika emblem brusquely stamped onto the paper—so sad to see her dark thoughts confirmed. She quickly flipped through a few that mentioned meetings in Berlin. One telegram stood out, and she steadied herself against the desk. "When time comes, you will have an official position already approved by the Fuhrer." Why hadn't she bothered looking before? She hung her head in distress as she was always so trusting and felt immediately ill, her body reeling from the confirmation and the shock.

She looked at the third telegram twice and couldn't believe her eyes.

"Stop. Goring…pleased at offer of Chateau Von Mendelssohn. One of his favorite Bordeaux…stop."

She looked around some more and noted that there was, indeed, a typewritten official telegram with an invitation to a meeting in Paris for today. Out of the corner of her eye, she saw that it was signed at the bottom with the faint letters GG. She felt dizzy. It was all so strange but starting to make sense to her.

Grace felt panic-stricken and leaned on the partner's desk for support as she knew what she and Irene had discussed was now real. She remembered more of the nightmare, which was coming back to her in flashes; she had walked into the Paris mansion and discovered Louis in bed with the beautiful, young actress, Ghislaine Garrieux. At first, she thought GG had stood for her own initials…then it made sense. She looked down at the GG again and knew that the rumor Irene had told her, which she initially tried to brush off was true and probably had been true since before the wedding. Her Riviera idyll was now officially over. She, Grace Greystone de La Faucigny was married to an adulterous

Nazi collaborator, and if she listened to her Uncle Reggie, she needed to make her way to London and back to the US as soon as possible.

All before it was too late, or France fell to the Germans, and she became a real prisoner.

Chapter Twenty-Seven

Carroll Madison
Beverly Hills
1940

Hundreds of the most important industry players crowded under the grand byzantine dome of the Wilshire Boulevard Temple as it was standing room only for the legendary and beloved Marty Lester's funeral. As the throngs were taking their seats in the grand synagogue, a stunning blonde in all black floated down the aisle alone, to many arm nudges and a few gasps, before sliding into a pew, only a few rows back from the family. Carroll Madison knew the art of the entrance and wiggled her black silk-encased tush as she slid in slow motion and nodded to Bartie Maddox, who had saved a seat for her.

"Boy, Marty was right. She's some dish! And it's the main course, not the appetizer." Groucho Marx elbowed Myers as they sat in a pew a bit behind Carroll, right off the aisle. They had a prime view of Carroll's sumptuous, impressive rear as she had turned up in a hip-hugging black suit and large black picture hat with oversized dark sunglasses. She was visibly upset, weeping and also totally ignored by the family but smart enough to have made a late entrance where everyone in town would see her.

"He sure knew how to pick 'em," Myers whispered back. "Man was a genius."

"Who's the young guy with her?" Groucho Marx asked.

"The new Menowitz—name's Maddox, Bartie Maddox. Kid's sharp and has a huge future ahead of him," Myers said. "Marty asked me to help her out, and since his kids won't have anything to do with her, I told Bartie to take her here today. Not a bad job."

"I'll say," George Mackay said, leaning in from the row behind them. "The kid should be paying you!"

"Well, they keep getting younger and younger, and we keep getting older and older."

"The only thing I have to look forward to now is becoming a widower and, in my grief, finding a blonde dish like that when I'm Marty's age," George Mackay added. "I'm sure he went out with a bang."

"Yeah, get this. After we signed her, the kid came up with a great PR handle for her."

"What—*tits on a stick*?" Mackay said in a louder voice than he should have, a bit drunk from lunch. Two older matrons in the next pew turned and flashed him a derisive look.

"She has a bit part in the new Van Johnson movie, and the kid's billing her as *the tight-sweater girl.* Emphasis on the word tight. He put her in a sweater three sizes too small, and when Van Johnson pins her, you get this shot of the huge boobs in the tightest sweater, like *cashmere over* a *cantaloupe*—will cause a sensation," Myers said, his eyes twinkling at the thought. "We're negotiating with Breen at the Hays Office as we speak."

"The kid's obviously got it. You think he's bangin' her?"

"He'd be crazy not to. But she sure seems all cut up over old Marty."

"Yeah, and that the gravy train has come to an end. I am too, though. He was a true *mensch.*" Myers nodded wistfully. "They don't make 'em like Marty anymore, that's for sure."

As the crowd took their seats, and the rabbi intoned the prayers, there was a great deal of weeping over Marty Lester, and Carroll was leading the pack with theatrical moans and sighs. Bartie dutifully handed her a wad of tissue paper he was wise enough to bring in his pocket. Even Maude, herself, had made an appearance in all black, sitting in the back row, weeping for the loss of her best customer.

"The family will be observing shiva this week from 5:00 p.m. to 10:00 p.m.," the rabbi declared from the pulpit, "at the Lester home on North Linden Drive and tomorrow at the home of Lance Lester, 101 North Hudson Avenue, Hancock Park. We ask all donations be made to his beloved wife Sadie's Hadassah. The internment will be family only at the cemetery," the rabbi said before reading the final prayers in both Hebrew and English.

As the temple emptied, and people walked into the center aisle, Carroll slowly approached Marty's daughter, Francis, for directions to the burial.

"I'm so sorry for your loss, Francis." Carroll paused and introduced herself. "Would it be okay if I came to the cemetery?" she asked sweetly.

"Look," Francis turned in dismay, "I really don't think it's appropriate you come. It's family *only*." She shook her head.

"I loved your father. He was a great man, and I would really like to be there," Carroll pleaded.

"Look, Carroll or whatever your name is…everyone knows the score. What girl your age, who looks like *you*, goes with a ninety-two-year-old man?" She shook her head again. "And my mother would turn over in her grave." She teared with a hankie at the ready.

Marty's son, Lance, who was in his sixties, walked over to try and calm the situation. He ushered his sister on with his eyes.

"You must be Carroll." He seemed a bit friendlier, extending his hand.

"Yes, nice to finally meet you." She dabbed her eye. "I am so sorry for your loss. Your father was well…another father to me."

"My condolences." Bartie extended a hand. "I'm Barston Maddox. I work with Carroll and for Mister Myers at the studio."

"Thank you for coming. Look, Carroll, you seem like a very nice girl and all, but this is a difficult time for us, and we'd rather you not come to the cemetery. I'm sorry, I truly am. He is being buried next to our mother. I am sure you understand."

"I loved your father, and he loved me," she sobbed.

"Maybe so, but it will make my sisters very uncomfortable. I hope you understand. My sisters are very conservative." Lance's pale blue eyes were mournful.

Bartie held Carroll's elbow as she wept.

"The housekeeper packed your things, and your suitcases are in the hall closet. We would appreciate it while we are at the cemetery if you could pick them up before the shiva." He looked down.

"Mister Lester, I am so sorry for your loss," Bartie stepped in. "I know how close Mister Myers and your father were. He asked me to accompany Carroll today and help out. I will drive over now with Carroll to the house and get her things." Bartie nudged Carroll to not create a scene.

"Yes, of course," she cried, tears streaming.

"Thank you, Bartie."

"Mister Lester, you seem like a real gentleman like your dad. Thank you for understanding. I just wanted to pay my respects," Carroll said softly.

Lance Lester seemed truly touched by Carroll's grief. "I'm sorry, Carroll. You seem like a very nice girl, and my father did tell me you made him very happy. Honestly, it was hard for my sisters and I to accept the idea of you after Mom died." He withdrew a white envelope from his breast pocket. "I wanted to give you this too. I spoke to my father at the hospital, and there's a note in there for you and a little something he wanted you to have."

"Please, I don't want anything. That was never…my intention," she cried.

"He said you would say that." He handed the envelope to Bartie. "Please make sure she takes this. It was my father's dying request. Please," he said. "I don't agree with my sisters, but that is their wish."

"Yes, Mister Lester, of course." He took the envelope and shook his head.

"Mister Lester," Carroll looked up, her eyes rimmed with red.

"Yes, Carroll?"

"I just want you to know that Marty…well, he was the father I never had." She reached over and kissed him on the cheek, which totally disarmed him. "He was just wonderful, and I want you to know that Marty…well, Marty *saved me*," she cried.

"I see." Lance Lester looked down and processed the information, feeling a bit like a heel.

"My father was…well…" his tears welled, "the world's nicest man. I was so lucky to have him as a father."

Carroll tried to wipe away the torrent of tears, but they kept coming.

"Thank you, Carroll, I understand." Lance paused for a moment. "Bartie, look, will you…" he paused, "*and* Carroll stop by my house tomorrow evening for a drink and a bite? I'm observing shiva there. I will just tell my sisters that you are visiting *me*," he said kindly, realizing that Carroll had true feelings for his father.

"Mister Lester, that is too kind." Bartie looked at Carroll and smiled.

"Thank you, Mister Lester," Carroll smiled broadly. "That means more to me than you know. I will—we will—thank you."

They shook hands as Lance Lester walked forward, stopping to accept condolences from friends and relatives.

"You see, Bartie. Marty Lester was a real *mensch*," Carroll said, using the Yiddish term. "And apples don't fall far from the tree," she said as he held her by the arm and they walked out into the blinding sunlight arm in arm with all eyes on her real tears and her swaying *tush.*

Chapter Twenty-Eight

Michael McDonough
International Waters
1940

As the ship dipped into a swell, Michael McDonough stepped backward to regain his balance and adjusted his too-tight bow tie, running his fingers through his cropped ginger-blond hair as he strode into the first-class dining room of the SS *Rhode Island.* He was fairly immune to the opulence of the sparkling crystal chandeliers and the elegantly turned-out passenger list. It all seemed too fancy for his liking, like too much airy cotton candy and wanting solid food.

Suddenly, everything went into slow motion when he saw *her*, and she came into focus. Normally, he would have just scanned the posh surroundings, but he would later relate to his close friend Bartie Maddox at the studio that he couldn't get over his eyes, and the world literally stopped. It was as if someone were playing a joke on him as he had been in Europe for three weeks searching for locations and casting for another great Garbo replacement for his next hit movie, and he had come up empty-handed on fresh talent.

"Close, but no cigar" was his unfortunate motto. He would shrug at the screen tests of a sea of French and English starlets, all who came within a narrow range, but didn't have the on-screen magic, that facial luminosity, the... *unexplainable makings of a screen goddess.* It was the holy grail; you only knew it when you saw it—the camera weaving in and out among the cheekbones and lashes, rendering someone either pretty, beautiful, or the ever-elusive one-in-a-million—and no one in the capital cities of Europe was up for the task…until now.

And yet, after all the traveling and multiple cities, *there* she was sitting at the captain's table right before him. In fact, he had never seen anyone more beautiful, and he had been around a handful of the most beautiful screen goddesses throughout his whole career. His heart actually stopped momentarily at the sight of her, and he stood still, trying to regain his composure at the gorgeous apparition. Was she real? Flesh and blood or a figment of too much whiskey? Her perfect heart-shaped face and wide emerald eyes were set against the creamiest skin. A faint mole strategically placed above her lip and lustrous raven hair with the slightest widow's peak glowed in a glamorous ether with diamond star clips all making his pulse quicken. She turned now with a perfect profile, the upturned and regal nose, glittering white teeth, and she threw her head back slightly, vivaciously, as if she had no idea of the power of the spell she cast and just…laughed. She was, by far, the most beautiful young woman he had ever seen, and it took his breath away. She sat at the table making small talk, her long cigarette holder held in such an elegant way as to make her look like she was a modern Joan of Arc brandishing a sword with her long, lovely arms, her clinging white, satin evening gown and vanilla ermine shrug, her armor.

Michael McDonough wasn't a man easily given to sentiment or emotion. In fact, he was tough, a hard nut to crack as one of the few Irish Catholic film executives in a town started and run by mostly Eastern European Jews. Tall, fair, and handsome with golden, reddish hair, his almost transparent white skin was freckled and showed off his mossy hazel, twinkling eyes. He was rangy and broad-shouldered and had an athletic build that gave him a sportsman's agility. His leanness highlighted his tuxedo to perfection since it fit him like a glove, his broad shoulders overpowering his slim waist. The fact that he had little patience for formality and could have been wearing a pair of overalls allowed him to sport the tux with an ease and informality few could pull off. At thirty-two, after years of working at different studios, he had finally been lured over to SGM by Solomon Myers, himself, because he had earned a reputation for being smart and tough and no-nonsense with his pictures all coming in on time and on budget. While he hadn't received the public accolades of his rival Irving Thalberg, he quietly racked up hit after hit, and his low-key, respectful manner was a perfect fit to Myers, who could direct and control him but wholly respected his work ethic and choices. And more importantly, in Myers's mind, here was a man's man who loved pussy and had no "fag qualities", enough said, and everyone in town knew it. On a scale of one to gay, he was at zero, and it wasn't ever in question, especially after Myers hired him.

Michael had been brought up in a middle-class family in working class Leominster, Massachusetts, learned simple Socratic skills and manners from his Italian mother—a lovely grammar schoolteacher—and hard work and discipline from his father—the ruddy-faced and gregarious Irish policeman. He was instilled with a respect for authority and hardly ever had to raise his voice to get things done since he was so beloved by virtually everyone on the lot. His last film, *Grand Voyage*, was a loan out starring the former silent film star Gorge Lamont and had hit number one at the box office after twenty-two consecutive weeks. It had been the perfect comeback vehicle for Lamont. It also made a star out of relative newcomer, his own discovery, Paulette Lafarr, who would be nominated for an Academy Award for "Best Supporting Actress." Michael had spotted the gamine on the beach in Santa Monica and was impressed by her deep, soulful chesnut eyes and tawny mane of golden hair and, contrary to popular belief, she was one of the few actresses he had not taken to bed, as he preferred her older sister, Margaret.

"Monsieur McDonough, I presume?" The captain extended a strong, confident handshake to welcome him.

"A pleasure to meet you, Captain," Michael said in an amiable tone.

"And may I introduce your dinner partners, Missus Louise Flick from Des Moines and Baroness Irene Von Mendelssohn from Paris and Vienna," the captain announced, grandly.

"A pleasure, Madame." He gallantly kissed Mrs. Flick's thick, doughy, and age-spotted hand in the European fashion, a habit he had picked up at fancy parties on the continent, although he felt somewhat uncomfortable with the affectation. And then he did the same again, taking Irene's lovely hand clad in white satin with a dazzling array of deco diamond bracelets, and kissed it. *Of course* she *had to be a baroness, no less*, he chuckled to himself.

Dinner proved both torture and a dream: torture at having to make polite conversation with the stolid, heavyset Midwestern Mrs. Flick, whose late husband owned one of the largest feed companies in the US, and a dream at conversing with Irene, the ethereal baroness. Finally, when he could not bear any more information on the care and feeding of swine, he turned to Irene, who also turned after speaking French to her dinner partner.

"And how many languages do you speak, Baroness?" Michael inquired, hanging on her every word.

"Please call me Irene," she said softly. "Six. My mother was Italian and my father Austrian, so I was brought up speaking many languages, yet we only spoke French in the house. I also speak Hungarian as I had a Hungarian governess growing up, but enough about me." She diverted to conversation in a lilting tone. "And what brought you to Paris, Mister McDonough?"

"Please call me Michael as well. I am head of production for SGM Film Studios in Los Angeles, and I was in Paris and London last year shooting a film you may have heard of called *Grand Voyage*. I am prepping for our next film called *Au Revoir, Paris*, which needs a very clear shot of the Arc De Triomphe, but given the tenuous situation in Europe, I will have to be clever and make do another way it seems." He shrugged offhandedly.

"And what would you do?" Irene turned and leaned in, fascinated.

"Given the issues in Europe, I now had this idea to shoot in the evening at the arch in Washington Square Park in New York City, which, from a great distance, somewhat resembles the arch in Paris, and *voilà*... if you shoot at night *and* use a filter, we will have Paris in New York... at a discount." His eyes brightened at the thought.

"That's a wonderful idea! Quite enterprising," Irene said, smiling brightly at his easy charm and self-effacing sense of humor.

"I was also in Paris and London meeting with casting agencies and taking in the shows, meeting actresses for parts in the film."

"Well, I am sure you found quite a few." Irene nodded at his busy schedule.

"Not really. Very few speak English in Paris, and the ones who did in London weren't very attractive. Bad teeth." He appraised her with his wry smile. Irene revealed a pearl-like smile at the idea.

The meal flew by, and the bulky Mrs. Flick thankfully said her goodbyes after a double portion of Baked Alaska. Michael helped her to her feet as if she needed a crane. As the guests departed for the bar and smoking lounge, Michael and Irene lingered ever so casually. After the dining room emptied, he helped pull out Irene's chair. As she stood, he was taken aback by her flawless, lithe figure.

"Can I convince you to have a nightcap?" he hoped, thinking she would say no.

"Yes, that would be lovely." Irene smiled at the invitation without hesitation.

"Really, you would?" His voice raised in surprise, expecting a baroness to say no.

"Of course. I know not a soul on board, and you seem like just the right purveyor of nightcaps, Monsieur," she laughed.

He guided her by her satin-encased elbow toward the outdoor promenade deck, the salty sea air and fog slightly whipping like frothy egg whites. He was fascinated by her background and asked her about her childhood in Vienna, and she spoke about the recent death of her father. He was moved, and then, as they made their way to the men's bar, he stopped, gripped the railing, and looked directly at her, appraising a rare jewel.

"I hope I am not being impertinent since we have just met," he started.

"I have recently come to enjoy the idea of such questions and view impertinence as a new positive quality. One does not get anywhere being meek, it seems," Irene said slyly.

"Okay, then…have you ever thought about becoming an actress? You are so…well, very beautiful," he gushed. "And forgive me for being so forward, but your face is…so *cinematic*."

"Well, Michael," Irene laughed. "That's quite a compliment coming from you, though I expect you are quite the charmer with the ladies, Monsieur McDonough."

"No, I am being one-hundred percent honest," he said, with a healthy dose of American enthusiasm.

"Actually, it *was* a dream, but alas…not to be." She shrugged.

"What happened?" Michael surveyed her intently, not understanding.

"Well, I did grow up singing, and…" She shrugged again.

"You sing too," he marveled. *Of course she did, most likely like a songbird*, he thought.

"Yes, I am classically trained in opera, and I once performed at a state dinner my father hosted. Kurt Weill was a guest and offered me a part in his next production, but my late father made me refuse the offer." He steadied her as they made their way to the first-class paneled bar. "As he did with a summer position with Madame Curie and a ban on my former boyfriend—although he was right about that one."

"Why would he do all that?" Michael shook his head in disbelief.

"He was very formal and didn't believe a girl with my…upbringing should be on the stage, which he was brought up to believe. In his day, if a woman was an actress or singer, they were a *demimondaine*, like his own mistress."

"And what do you believe?" He stopped by the railing and looked intently at her.

"After my mother and father died, the Nazis seized our properties and nationalized the family bank as we are…Jews," she paused, tears in her eyes, "and I have had to flee Paris. I now believe I am free to do anything at this point that I would like to do." She looked a bit willful and downcast at the same time, which made her even more alluring. Michael was stunned; she was Jewish and a baroness—it all seemed so terribly exotic. He felt so vanilla with his Irish Catholic roots. "Well, that's a wonderful attitude." He caught his footing and added, "And I'm also very sorry for your difficulties, but I assure you, you will be *very* at home in New York and LA." Michael felt for her.

"And what about you, Michael?" Irene looked up at him with her doe-like eyes. "What do you believe, Monsieur McDonough?" she asked politely, but in the most direct and intrusive fashion.

He paused and was taken aback at the direct and insightful question. He decided to answer honestly.

"I believe in something I never believed in before." It was as if he was being transported; this was nothing he had ever felt with his estranged wife.

"And what would that be?" She looked into his eyes and felt as if she were falling into a hazel pool. Irene, as well, failed to mention her own husband, Fritz.

"I finally believe…" he was overcome by emotion.

"Yes?" Her eyelids fluttered.

"…in the idea of love at first sight." He grasped the railing of the ship to steady himself, and it was not the current that had him falling.

Chapter Twenty-Nine

La Marquise de La Faucigny
Paris
1940

"Why in the world are you taking fifteen trunks?" Louis fumed as he saw the lady's maids packing the array of Louis Vuitton steamer trunks for Grace's trip to London in her boudoir.

"Well, let's see...because I am *fleeing* the country!" Grace laughed out loud at the question. "Really, Louis! I have eleven trunks, not fifteen, and I usually travel abroad with twenty, and I am going to a royal wedding. The last time I traveled to Bootsie's engagement party I took twenty-four, isn't that right, Lourdes?"

"Twenty-seven, counting your hat boxes," Lourdes said, not looking up as she layered tissue paper between the garments.

Louis was pacing, ramrod straight in his riding gear and mud-splattered boots as he strode over to inspect her large shagreen jewel case.

"I see you're taking all of your jewelry as well?" he said angrily.

Grace walked over to the wall safe cleverly disguised behind a Modigliani nude and opened it for his perusal.

"You know, you really are a baby, but then again, most men are. Most of my important pieces are in the safe, take a look for yourself, many more millions than what I am taking for the wedding. I can assure you I only packed four or five of the parures and only one of my tiaras. The rest are in the safe—safe and sound. You really are acting paranoid, Louis." Grace lit a cigarette to stop her hands from trembling.

He walked over to the safe and rummaged around, taking in the remaining booty, which seemed to slightly mollify him.

"Do you think I wouldn't take my Aunt Rose's diamond choker that belonged to the Czarina if I was fleeing? It was her most prized possession, and it's equally as important to me as you are," she joked, kissing him. She saw him finger the original Fabergé case and inspect that it was still there. "So, I am leaving it, and you know I will be back," she laughed.

"You know I am just jittery about you going to London without me," he said softly, approaching her and giving her a soft, romantic kiss.

"That feels nice. You haven't done that in a while," she sighed.

"Yes, I have been busy with government meetings, but when you return, I booked us a long weekend at The Palace in St. Moritz. I know how much you love it off-season."

"Oh, darling, how sweet you are! I adore it there. What are the dates?" she asked like a schoolgirl.

"June fourteenth. I already spoke to the hotel and reserved your favorite suite. And hopefully we can start again."

She kissed him warmly with a hug.

"Nothing would make me happier," she gushed. "I am so excited you'll take the time. Really, Louis, why don't you come with me to London? It's going to be the wedding of the season, and I am so happy for Cousin Bootsie." She closed her jewel case.

"Maybe I will." He looked directly at her, calling her bluff.

Grace stiffened at his words, then tried to relax. "Fabulous, I will call Bootsie and tell her to add you to the seating plan. She will be thrilled you will be coming." She embraced him warmly, yet he shrank from her.

"No, I don't have the time with my meetings," he countered, testing her.

"It will only be a week, my darling, and I'm staying at Claridge's if you choose to pop over," she said gaily.

"One doesn't just 'pop over,' Grace. It takes a great deal of time and planning, time I don't have. You never seem to understand these things."

"Yes, of course, darling. I will try my best."

"I still don't understand why you have to go," he groused like a petulant child.

"Go? Why, I couldn't *not* go. Bootsie is my first cousin, and after all Uncle Reggie has done for me, it would be unthinkable for me not to attend. Remember that Bootsie and the entire family came for my wedding to *you*. And King has said he is attending with Queen Mary, given Bootsie's marrying Viscount Ashcombe. How could I miss that?"

He just shook his head and grumbled.

"Oh, don't pout, Louis. I'm sure you'll be fine given how busy you are."

"I just don't like the idea of you not being in France." He paced nervously.

"I love you, and I adore France and can't wait to get back. However, high tea and clotted cream and scones at Claridge's is definitely something I'm craving." She saw him go over and flip through one of the trunks suspiciously.

"You didn't tell me if you have spoken to Irene about the vineyard yet?" he asked in an offhand manner.

"Oh, yes, I did bring it up to her, and she thanked me for such a clever thought."

"And?"

"And she said she would think about it and would call me after her weekend at Princess Bonaparte's. I haven't heard from her."

"Well, when you do…urge her to do it. I'm having paperwork drawn up for her," he tried to be nonchalant, "to help her, of course."

"How *thoughtful* of you." She paused a lit another cigarette, nervously. "Louis, I know you are skittish about me going to London, but please don't be cross with me." Grace walked up to him and then, in a childlike fashion, presented him with a small, red-pebbled leather box.

"Here, I bought you a going away present." Her eyes sparkled.

"What's this?" His blue eyes brightened at the thought of an expensive gift.

"Just a present for my handsome husband."

Louis opened the box from Cartier. He looked down and saw stunning diamond cufflinks each in the shape of a diamond "G."

"So you will think of your favorite girl when you wear them!" Grace said so sweetly and innocently, kissing him full on the lips, which he was forced to return. She said it with the charm and innocence and a cunning guile he would later always associate with her. Neither made mention of the fact that the two "G"s were the initials of his wife and also his mistress, and the links would be her ultimate going away present.

Chapter Thirty

Bartie Maddox
Culver City
1940

"Start thinking of names! Pronto!" Myers threw the screaming ship-to-shore telegram at Bartie, who opened his chestnut-shaped eyes wider as he looked down and saw the contents. The slip of pale-yellow paper proclaimed, "Mr. Myers. Stop. I found next international star. Stop. On board SS *Rhode Island.* You won't believe. Stop. Baroness Irene Von Mendelssohn. Fleeing Paris. Prettiest woman I have ever seen. Stop. Six languages. Mick M."

"Must be *some* looker." Bartie whistled as he read the message. "Mick never ever thinks anyone's beautiful," Bartie added thoughtfully.

"Yeah, but that didn't stop him from sleeping with every whore in Hollywood. And that *meiskeit* wife of his ain't no looker," Myers smirked. "How he married that cow is beyond me."

"They married when they were very young, childhood sweethearts." Bartie shrugged nonchalantly to defend his best friend on the lot.

"Yeah, well, she ain't no child now. Looks like a grandma." Myers dished the dirt, which he pretended to hate, but clearly loved to do. "Look, he thought Lina May was ugly as sin, and Garbo is just an okay looker. This one must be quite something—or he's getting laid—but that never convinced him to sign anyone." Myers paced and shrugged. "He wants to give her a contract. I've never done it sight unseen, but if Mick says so. . . ." He waved his arms up in the air signifying how generous he was. "I just threw the standard one-fifty a week. He had the gall to write back and say two-fifty! What does she have, a platinum-plated pussy? So, since he's such a *macher,* let's start thinking of names."

"Names? The girl's a baroness. That's a hook?" Bartie offered.

"Yeah, but the public won't buy it. Too many German and Austrian refugees in this town already. If she's as beautiful as he says, we have to make her into a real international movie star. I'm sure if she's a countess..."

"Baroness..."

"Whatever she is, she has *class up her ass.* So, get to it the way you did the *Duke of Drake*. I dunno, but you figure it out—that's why you get paid...ya big louse." Myers scratched his bald pate.

"Yes, Mister Myers." Bartie smiled. "I have an idea right off the top of my head." Bartie knew that with Myers, his one great asset was his off-the-cuff thinking.

"Well, out with it already! What's takin' ya so long?" Myers screamed for Edna. "Edna, bring me some coffee and a bagel."

"Yes, Mister Myers." Edna came running.

"Ya want something? Bagel and *shmear*?" Myers said in kindly way, his bark louder than his bite.

"No, Mister Myers."

"Edna, bring in a bagel and *shmear* for Bartie. The boy's gotta eat—look at him, he's too skinny. He'll fall over on those big clown feet of his," he laughed to himself. He rubbed his red, chapped hands together like a child waiting for a Christmas candy cane.

"Michael is a good friend."

"Yeah, you *goys* sure stick together!"

Bartie ignored the comment, like most.

"And if he says she's the prettiest girl he's ever seen, I know he means it," Bartie opined. "I think if she's fleeing Paris..."

"Out with it already. Whaddya waitin' fer, New Years?"

"So here it is...something *French*," Bartie opined. "Everyone thinks French women are beautiful. I looked down the roster of actors and actresses the other day, and we don't have any current female French stars—even Deitrich is German." Bartie dispensed the tidbit as if it was caviar on toast points. He was always nervous to offer his creative thoughts but excited to be in Myer's presence.

"Good point. French is good." Myers stood up and paced. "I like F-R-E-N-C-H! No one thinks Germans are sexy these days except for Dietrich, and she looks like *a man* anyway. Yeah, I agree." He let the thought marinate. "French!" He leaned back and lit up a cigarette, then sat and put his feet on the desk, his custom English shoes gleaming. "French is the way to go. Good, Bartie. Yeah, I like it. Hey, are you sure the broad speaks French and everything isn't *Achtung*? *Von what*?"

"She speaks six languages; I am sure one is French."

"I don't understand how all these foreigners speak so many *foreign accents*," he blurted out in what would be one of his most classic and oft-repeated Myerisms in years to come.

"Once I have the name…" Bartie blocked out his hands. "We can bill her as 'So and so: the most beautiful woman in the world,' or 'France's greatest gift to the US since the Statue of Liberty.'"

"I like both. I like the 'the most beautiful woman in the world.'"

They both sat there enjoying their brainstorm. Twenty minutes went by, and Edna brought in bagels and cream cheese and coffee from the commissary.

"Eat, ya skinny *malink*," Myers commanded.

"Yes, Mister Myers."

"You think she's a beautiful as he says?" His eyes misted over at the thought.

"Yes. Mick has an impeccable eye. Look at Paulette Laffar. He found her on a beach, and she's become an overnight star."

"I can see it now." Myers eyes twinkled. "A new international star sparkles at SGM!" He threw his hands up dramatically.

"I like that, Mister Myers."

"Now, finish your damn bagel and get me a *name*!"

"Yes, Mister Myers. On it."

Bartie was summarily dismissed as Myers was called into a production meeting, grumbling that the movie being discussed was over budget and that the director was a lush. Bartie walked back to his office in a haze. He always wanted to please Myers, and he knew he only had hours or a day or two to come up with a name for the new star, or he would be itchy and call him every five minutes, which he did when he wanted something. So, Bartie sat at his desk and took out his dictionary then decided he needed more source material.

He left the lot at 4:00 p.m. and drove his old secondhand Ford to his favorite bookstore in West Hollywood to buy a few books on France for his research. It was a dilapidated old store on a seedy part of Santa Monica Boulevard, but it had a deep library and overflowing stacks of books on travel all organized in a haphazard way, as if the owner had his own system but wouldn't tell anyone what it was. The door had that familiar chime, and Bartie tipped his hat to the owner, an elderly man who had come over from Berlin and opened the store a few years earlier. He asked the owner where he could find the section on French books and great French writers.

"Here, Bartie, this one is from the back." Mr. Stern, the kindly proprietor, trudged slowly, handing him a book on famous French authors. Bartie thanked him and bought three books, got a receipt, and left looking forward to diving in when he got home.

He brought his book bag and writing pad to the far end of the pool on the faded lounge chair as the orange sun receded at the Garden of Allah under a malachite palm and scanned the books for an hour or two. Then, his eyes immediately fell on the sixteenth-century French writer, Michel de Montaigne. He thought it was also interesting that he was thought to have some Jewish-Marrano blood, something he would keep to himself and not tell Myers. He looked at photos of the great buildings, religious and otherwise, and streets in Paris, and the Avenue Montaigne came up again as the Grande Dame of Parisian streets. He scribbled the word "Montaigne" on a piece of paper and shook his head in a yes fashion as he thought it had a great sound to it. Then, he started thinking of first names. *Madeline Montaigne. Marie Montaigne*, he brainstormed; he liked the alliteration. He became more excited by the thought of two "M"s. He looked at a list of French women's names. And there before him was the perfect name staring back at him. *Mirielle. Hebrew derivation.* Totally French. Perfect name and nod for the beautiful Jewish baroness whom Mick had discovered. *Mirielle Montaigne.* It was perfect. Mirielle Montaigne! It had the mellifluous sound of the next great international star.

He always knew when things came quickly to him that it was a good sign, and this name had been the fastest he would ever create. He had a feeling it would be one of his best, which put him in a good mood, and he felt he could now enjoy his dinner date that evening with Carroll Madison. Since the funeral, they connected and had a fun, easy friendship, always dinner at a place where Carroll could be seen and then a round of casual sex in the car or at his apartment at the Garden of Allah. It was a perfect setup for both, whose careers came first and who wanted a bit of fun with no strings attached. He ran the name Mirielle Montaigne by Carroll at dinner at Chasen's, and she whistled, saying, "Now, she's someone a girl could get into a real *catfight* with in the powder room!" She sparkled, admitting she even liked it a bit more than her own name. Bartie thanked her before kissing her, but reassured her that her name was perfectly suited for *her* and no one else. He dropped her off at her rooming house on the early side, knowing he had an 8:00 a.m. presentation with Myers and needed his energy.

The very next morning at 7:30, Bartie was sitting across from Edna's desk with coffee, donuts, and a spray of simple flowers for her. She was touched and smiled, which was a rarity.

"Bright and early, I see." Edna smiled and arranged her steel-gray coif.

"These are for you." Bartie handed her the simple bunch of lilacs.

"You shouldn't have, but I'm glad you did. I'll put them in a vase. Thank you, Bartie. This is a first!" Edna gave a small, wry smile.

"My pleasure."

"So, you have it…and in only twenty-four hours!" She beamed for him. "He loves the timing. Most people take days or weeks, which he *hates.* I knew you would."

"Do you want a sneak peek?" Bartie asked coyly.

"No, don't tell me—tell him first," Edna said in a warm, conspiratorial tone.

They both chatted about studio gossip until Solly Myers rushed in the door. His face brightened at the sight of Bartie.

"Eight-*thoity*! Good." He looked at his watch "Okay, if you're here early, you must have something. Out with it here. Edna will tell you if she likes it or not. She liked Paulette Goddard, whose real name was

Marion Levy, and I hated it, and then she married Chaplin, so what do I know about names? But I do know a star when I see one," he bragged.

Bartie handed Edna a sheet of paper with the name *Mirielle Montaigne. The world's most beautiful woman. And France's greatest gift to America since the Statue of Liberty.* It was written in black ink in his neat cursive writing.

"Oh!" Edna shook her head in clear delight. "That's *good. Very, very good!*" She smiled and handed the sheet to Myers, whose eyes sparkled.

"Mirielle Montaigne…huh…well, let's just hope when we see this broad, she's as pretty as your name." Myers laughed and walked into his office, slamming the door behind him.

Chapter Thirty-One

Duke Drake
Los Feliz
1940

The 1920s Mediterranean mansion reclined on a leafy knoll above LA's twinkling lights and was one of the more lavish in a neighborhood of already massive and stately hilltop homes. It had a distinctive and grand double staircase leading to the front door and an octagonal Spanish, tiled foyer with a monumental wrought-iron chandelier designed to overpower and impress. It was a masculine, imposing castle built originally for a great, now forgotten silent film director who died in a car accident. Gorge Lamont had snapped it up two decades earlier with the proceeds from his first hit film, and it suited him with its elegance, grandeur, and over-the-top masculine decor. Duke's driver entered the imposing gates and dropped him off at the side entrance, and he walked into the darkened house through the pantry, dropped his keys on the marble-topped console in the foyer, and then walked slowly upstairs to the paneled library. Gorge was sitting like a philosophizing buddha in the dark in his royal blue satin robe, smoking a Cuban cigar, the swirling smoke ascending to the beamed ceiling.

"How's your *girlfriend*?" Gorge declined to look at him, his handsome face already contorted in anger, which had been building for hours the later Duke was.

"Gorge, please don't start. You know I'm just doing my job." Duke rolled his eyes.

"Well, maybe you're doing it *too well*," he said in a snarky tone.

"Lorena Smalls is a child, and that mother of hers is always lurking in the background. It's not exactly a day at the races," Duke replied, frowning.

"It's the fifth time you've gone out with her in three weeks," he snarled.

"It's the deal I made with Bartie and Myers. You know I'd rather be home with you or at the beach." His eyes pleaded a bit to soften the anger.

"Well, we can't even go out to the beach anymore," Gorge lamented petulantly. "In fact, we can hardly go *out* anywhere," he griped. Duke walked over and massaged his massive shoulders from behind, trying to change the subject.

"What are you reading?" Duke scanned the open script on the leather-tufted footstool he had tossed there.

"Oh, my agent sent me a new script from Warners. Now that I am a free agent, the offers are starting to come in again." Gorge's features softened.

Duke walked over and took off his tuxedo jacket and placed it on the circular ottoman and then turned, leaned down, and kissed Gorge on the lips. "Don't be a baby, that's great news." He picked up the script. "What's it about?"

"It's called *SS Corinthian*. It's basically a rip off of *Grand Voyage*. I'm now king of the ocean liner movies, it seems." He nodded.

"So, are you going to pass on it?"

"Hell no. This one will be sure to drive Myers crazy." He laughed. "So, when is this charade with Lorena going to end already? Hedda wrote about your budding romance in her column. Isn't that enough?" Gorge frowned, not letting the subject go.

"Gorge, I think you are sounding a bit unreasonable. When I go out with her for dinner, she makes me say grace with her. She's sweet, but a total religious wacko."

"Yeah, does she say grace when she's going down on her tutor? Or a novena?" he said in a bitchy tone.

"Don't be mean. She's a little crazy, but actually a very nice girl. She's just living the same lie we all are, trying to do her best."

"So now you feel sympathy for her too?" Gorge finally turned to inspect his reaction.

"No, for *us.*" Duke moved to the leather stool at Gorge's feet. "We have something great. Your career is back on track, and mine is taking off, so I have to go out on a few dates and be seen around town with little Lorena. It's only good for my career too. Tonight, I even met Thalberg, and he complimented me on *The Weary Widow.* It's been good, okay?" Duke laid out his case in a business-like fashion.

Gorge looked at him and saw his gorgeous face and melted. "Okay." Duke leaned over and hugged him, and they started to play wrestle. Gorge got him in a headlock.

"Look, I know it's your first day of shooting early tomorrow morning, so I got you a big present to celebrate, from me to you…to let you know how much I love you."

"Gorge, that's totally unnecessary. You know I have a hard time accepting gifts…the watch for my birthday was enough." He motioned to his solid-gold Cartier tank.

"Just follow me." He stood and motioned Duke to follow him upstairs into the bedroom. When he walked through the door, Duke froze, and then smiled.

"Meet Private Gregg Smyth." Gorge motioned to a naked, muscular, tattooed young man lying in bed, his arms behind his head revealing his sculpted biceps and a smooth compact physique.

"Hey, nice to meet ya," the young man said, winking at the pair.

"What the…?"

"Our friend Jerry Stein filled his cavity—among other things," Gorge laughed.

Gorge walked over and pulled the sheets from his waist revealing a cock the size and girth of a pepper mill.

"When I said a *big* present, I really meant it." The private just laid back and had a smirk on his face. "I thought you needed something *big* after all the time you are spending with Lorena *Smalls,*" he joked, but was serious at the same time, knowing he wasn't going to risk Duke's affections for the pretty, young actress.

Gorge also dropped his satin robe and, totally naked, and got onto the regal bed.

"Who loves you, baby?" Gorge said as he lay with his arm around the young private and motioned Duke to join in. Duke smiled brightly as he started to disrobe, ready for the sexy menage.

"I figured, if Myers is making us keep our lives private, I might as well *hire* one." He laughed as Duke dove in for the fun.

Chapter Thirty-Two

Baroness Irene Von Mendelssohn
International waters
1940

The sea was oily gray: dismal, churning, frothing, and rough, as if one was staring down the mucilage of a carnivorous plant. The ship chopped and rolled, throwing many of the first-class passengers into a roiling and nauseous discomfort, heaving overboard.

Irene woke up, quite alert, despite the vibrating steely light pouring in through the large portholes of her stateroom and the roller coaster crashing waves, which seemed to diminish the ship's size, making her feel even more insignificant. Ironically, Irene wasn't affected by seasickness, having larger issues on her mind. She looked over at this strange man in her bed and smiled, not quite fully understanding how he got there. Michael slept soundly, totally naked next to her, his dedication to sleep as even-keeled and forceful as his nature. Theirs had been an instant, intense attraction, and both felt the heat of lust and were touched by the rays of love. It was so unlike her to give herself to someone she had hardly known, but it felt so entirely natural. There was an unspoken force between them that actually pulled them together as if they had known each other for a thousand years, and there was no way to possibly avoid the destiny and outcome of their meeting. Perhaps they had, indeed, had previous lives as it seemed they were picking up, overlapping, where they had once left off.

As he gently snored, she looked over at the broad map of his back and marveled; it visually communicated he wasn't a boy, but a man, with its networks of connecting sinew and muscle under a sheer freckled wrapping. She didn't want to make the comparison with Fritz, but it was inevitable and struggled with the idea of telling Michael about her marital status and Fritz's disappearance. Yet at the same time, she had remorse at feeling *no* remorse for her actions. Deep down, despite the horrific political environment and his horrendous predicament, she now felt Fritz had a larger share of blame by putting his head in the sand, given his intransigent attitude and the options available, which were not afforded to everyone.

Irene clearly knew the man lying in her bed was a different species altogether, that he had had other women, or was, perhaps, married, but until now, she had no desire to know and sensed he had no desire to tell her as well. She also realized that despite her fear for her husband, she was deeply angry with him—boiling mad in fact. She had gone against her loving father and had been willful, clearly having made the mistake he said she would. Had Fritz been another type of man entirely, he would have listened to mature reasoning and foresight, been able to read the tea leaves, to negotiate and navigate the perilous times and not put her in a position to have to fend for herself. She now saw Fritz for who he was: a temperamental genius, a prodigy, but just that…a child, nevertheless. In the last week with Michael, she felt the outside waves crashing down, and she realized she did love Fritz, but she was not necessarily *in love* with him, and sorrowfully, possibly didn't even *like h*im. Now, in comparison to Michael McDonough, she saw Fritz in the light he was intended, and it was as if their weeklong affair was there to shatter her illusion and bring her to a newer, brighter, shinier place in her life. All this made her even more frightened and more apt to cling to this new foreign man in a way she had never imagined. Suddenly, as if she were appraising him, he turned over and caught her in the act, slowly opening one gold-flecked hazel eye, as he peered at her.

"Morning, Baro-*ness*," he chuckled and yawned, seemingly able to read her mind, which was both off-putting and sensual at the same time.

"Good morning, Michael." She pulled the covers up under her chin, not used to a man seeing her naked breasts. "You can sleep through anything, I see. Half the ship is heaving overboard." She grazed his gold rust hair with her lacquered fingernails.

"Really, I didn't notice. The only thing I am thinking about is you, how beautiful, intelligent, and sexy you are." He raised himself on one elbow.

He then sat up, and she was even more surprised by how natural it was to see this man in bed with her. *Who was he, and how did he get here?* she marveled.

"Irene, this has been…" he started.

She touched his lips and smiled. "I know."

"We only have two days left on the crossing, and I wish it could last forever." He closed his eyes shut as if to freeze the moment in his memory.

"It's been the happiest time of my life," Irene said.

"Mine too." He reached for her silky hand and intertwined his fingers in such a loving fashion.

"We've never discussed…" They both knew the subject they were talking about and avoiding.

"I know…"

"Should we?" Michael grimaced.

He lay back in bed, and she nestled into his chest, hearing his steady heartbeat. Finally, she decided it was time and, for the next hour, she opened up to him about Fritz, their meeting, courtship, marriage, and his reputation as a prodigy—along with his stubbornness and attraction to the palais. Now, he was missing, and she feared he might even be dead. She spoke about how she begged her best friend Grace's Uncle Reggie McClean and Princess Bonaparte to see if they could use their contacts to find out any information on his whereabouts, but when they did, they had come up with very little. She didn't want to be overly critical of Fritz but now shared her father's point of view and her own disappointments. Michael listened and nodded and felt deeply for her predicament yet was visibly angry that Fritz had not had the good sense to leave Vienna and had put her life and fortunes in danger. Then, it was his turn. He also slowly opened up and revealed he was married to a childhood sweetheart, Mary Katherine, the marriage souring over her brittle nature, her jealousy over his long hours and his career, the pretty actresses he had to work with, and that, at the same time, they had been unable to conceive. He then quietly broached the subject of his many affairs and his inability to get a divorce given his wife's religious objections, her being a staunch Catholic. They were separated but still tethered to each other, and he had never looked for another meaningful relationship—just a physical outlet for his stress.

"Well, it seems we are both locked in marital purgatory." He uttered the words based on his wife's long-standing Catholic faith.

"All I know is that these last few days, I have been happy," Irene said, "and I haven't been happy in a very long time." The ship rolled and took them down, and they both laughed nervously.

"Well, we're in the same boat—literally," he joked, and she laughed out loud as well. It was no secret at the captain's table and on board the ship that they had become lovers, and most of the other passengers looked at them with a dose of jealousy, wry smiles, and humor as they were trying to conceal something so obvious and powerful.

"Irene." He got up and walked toward the window to see the silvery, churning waves. He picked up a robe to cover himself.

"I know you were meant to go to New York." He turned to her. "I have another idea for you—for us." He paused slightly, not sure of how to present his case. "Come with me back to California. You will love it!" Michael said with passion.

"California?" she said, slowly pronouncing the foreign word for the first time. "In New York, I can get a job as a translator or an editor like I did in Paris. I never even entertained the thought of California." It sounded so foreign to her, like Timbuktu.

"I told you I am head of production at SGM Studios" He looked at her gorgeous face intently. "I hope you won't be mad, but I've already cabled my boss, Mister Myers, and asked him to give you a contract at SGM. *I'm* giving you a contract. From the moment I saw you, I knew you were meant to be an actress, a star. And I want you to know up until now, I have never, ever mixed business with pleasure. I have pretty much free rein to sign actors and actresses and…well," he continued in a slightly boyish way, "I think you have the face to be on the big screen and what it takes to be famous. "

Irene sat dumbfounded at the news.

"And two-fifty a week to start!" he added with a bright smile.

Irene looked at him as if were insane and then was hit with another wave of emotions, both joy and excitement. Was this a dream or real?

"You're not being serious? I've always *dreamed* of being an actress, but never thought..." She sighed and caught her breath. "Two-fifty a week! Why that's a thousand dollars a month. That's quite a lot of money, Michael." She sat up fully naked, her soft pink, luminous, pearlized breasts so young, perky, and alluring springing free. She felt entirely at home in this natural state as opposed to the sharp contrast with Fritz, where she had snuck into bed covered in a demure nightgown and had little desire to see him naked, feeling embarrassed at his scrawny, milky body.

She threw her arms up against Michael and kissed him passionately.

"So? Is it a yes to sunshine, palm trees...and me?" Michael looked at her with his big puppy-dog eyes.

"Yes, of course yes...how could I turn that down? Are *you*...sure?"

"More than I've ever been."

"I just can't believe it! An actress!"

"Look, it's going to be hard work and difficult for you. The studio is tough place, and it's political—not to mention the sharks."

"Sharks?" She looked at him with a dose of fear.

"Not the ones out there," he said, motioning to the sea. "The ones that will soon be circling *you.* And they will when they see fresh meat."

Irene smacked him. "So, that's how you see me? Sirloin by the pound?"

"No, but you don't know Hollywood and how...hard it can be."

"If I can handle the Nazis, I can handle Hollywood, I can assure you," she stated with all seriousness.

"Clearly, but do know they'll most likely give you a new image with a new name. It all goes along with it. I have a good friend whose head of PR on the lot—Bartie Maddox. He's a bit of a boy genius and in charge of all that. You have to know they will turn you into another person...

but I'll be there every step of the way. At least until you become famous, and then…throw me over." He looked down at the thought.

"Never, you have made me the happiest girl." She kissed him passionately.

"Are you sure, Irene?"

"Yes. And clearly, I've never been more ready to be…*someone else.* And to be with someone else…with you." They kissed, and Michael lifted her up in his strong arms, and despite the rocking, or perhaps enhanced by it, they came together with a frisson neither had experienced before. Or ever after.

Chapter Thirty-Three

La Marquise de La Faucigny
London
1940

Her chic, whimsical, violet-and-yellow fascinator perched on a rakish tilt seemed to almost squawk with its colorful plumage and its half-net veil appearing as a veritable bird cage. Grace sat in the foyer and reading room of Claridge's and tried to hold back the tears as the wait staff silently brought the crustless tea sandwiches, scones, and clotted cream on the silver tray stands. The only thing visible to the other patrons was the stack of glittering diamond bracelets that shimmered as she dabbed her eyes with a discreet lace hankie and her old mine diamond ring that had belonged to Louis's grandmother.

"Well, it's clear there is no going back." Uncle Reggie looked pale and drawn at the news, the steel shot at his temples now giving him the look of an elder statesman. He had aged so much in the recent years; she felt sad at the thought.

"You cannot consider going back—are you, Gracie?" He looked at her askance as her emotions seemed to buckle. He sipped his tea, his hand slightly shaking with his advancing age.

"I'm not sure," she wept quietly. The prior week of wedding festivities was well-attended by the royals and widely covered in the international press, and his daughter Bootsie and the next Viscount Ashcombe seemed to be the perfect match. It was an esteemed turnout at St. Paul's Cathedral and a social triumph for the McCleans with the king and queen in attendance. As her first cousin and the grandly-titled Marquise de La Faucigny, Grace was not only the maid of honor, but also given prime seating next to the attending royal family.

It was an emotional week for Grace as she saw her younger cousin married off. "I'm so very happy for Bootsie; at least someone got it right." Grace smiled in a downward way, showing her despair even while happy for her cousin. With Bootsie's simple and delightful enjoyment of the country life with a solid and fairly boring squire with a large country estate to manage under the nose of her father, it was the perfect setup. Why did it seem everyone else had it so much easier and got it right on the first go-round?

"Louis expects you home in two days, I assume?" Uncle Reggie scowled.

"Yes, however, he already suspects something as he called in a fury that he had seen a news clipping of Irene departing on one of your ships from Marseilles, screaming that I had arranged the whole thing and that we lost the chance of her vineyard. Can you imagine? Of course, I stuck to our story that Princess Bonaparte arranged it all, and I knew nothing, but he doesn't believe me."

"That's the definition of a scoundrel." He paused. "Grace, I hadn't wanted to tell you this, but right after you announced your engagement, he had his lawyer send me these papers insisting that he be in control of your trust or, at the very least, be one of the trustees. Now, I do understand his having the right to control a trust if you had a child together—that is not unreasonable—but I found his initial maneuver quite distasteful. And, of course, all the bills we have paid on the chateau."

"Bills?"

"Why, yes, you do know quite well you have spent half a million dollars so far on upgrading all his family properties. You did approve it."

"Oh yes, Uncle Reggie. I just forget the details sometimes," she managed to say, although she had no idea about it and didn't want to appear irresponsible. Now, she was feeling taken advantage of by her conniving husband.

"Now, dear, I have friends in Washington who helped arrange for Irene's visa, and they have told me it would be quite dangerous for you to go back to Paris at the moment. If Germany invades—which is highly likely—you would be considered an enemy alien and would end up being a chess piece, I am afraid, for Louis's ambitions," he cautioned.

"What do you suggest, Uncle? I feel so badly." She wrung her hands at the thought of leaving permanently.

"I think the best thing is for me to call Louis and confront him on his having a mistress. You did keep the notes she wrote him?"

"Yes, I have all three telegrams like you instructed." She opened her purse and gave her uncle an envelope filled with the telegrams and correspondence. "The other ones are in there as well."

"Good, that will be the excuse for why you are staying. He cannot argue that point with the proof, and I will say that you are very upset and unhappy about it, and that it is an open secret he is in love with this actress Ghislaine so and so, and that you are going to need time to think about it. Of course, during that time, we will know a bit better where the world is. I would not mention his Nazi affiliations yet and the other set of telegrams that clearly show he is collaborating. I will hold those in case I need it for future ammunition."

"Uncle Reggie, how did you get to be so smart?" she marveled.

"Good old American ingenuity. These old aristocrats can't compete." His sipped his tea. "Oh, and by the way, I think it's time you moved out of Claridge's and came to stay in the country with us. It wouldn't surprise me if Louis decides to show up and try and...*collect* you."

"Do you really think so?

"Of course. I do think you will feel safer in the country, as will I. Grace," he touched her hand gently, "I understand how badly you must feel." He chose his words carefully. "Do know that great fortunes are also a burden and a responsibility and can be met with great peril. You will have to always be on guard for fortune hunters and those who will want to try and control you, but one always needs to be on the right side of things."

"Thank you, Uncle." She reached over and lifted her veil and reached over and kissed his cheek. "I am quite lucky, though, to have you, Aunt Rose, and Irene."

"Yes, I was happy to see she made it on the ship safely. Such a terrible situation for her and her people—and the news about Fritz."

"News?"

"I was only able to find out they had him arrested. He was kept in a Viennese prison until he signed over the rights to the family bank and assets since Irene was no longer in Vienna, and the baron had died, and he was next of kin. Then, they shipped the poor chap to some camp, a concentration camp called Auschwitz-Birkenau. . . ."

"Oh, that is horrible news! Does Irene know?"

"I think she might have some idea from Princess Bonaparte. And that is the last we have heard of Fritz, I am afraid."

"Oh dear, how awful for him. . .and for Irene."

"You know, the situation at hand has made me think of this ancient Chinese curse: 'May you live in *interesting times*.'"

"How true, Uncle!"

"Like Fritz, we all have choices to make. Grace, make sure you make *less* interesting ones. Come to the bucolic English countryside, at least for now."

Chapter Thirty-Four

Bartie Maddox
Los Angeles
1940

"Hop to it! We're goin' to Maude's!" Sterling Dumont barked, slapped the back of Bartie's head, and slammed down a dark, caramel colored whiskey on the rough-hewn counter of The Big Lucky dive bar and ordered his drinking partners to accompany him to the elite industry bordello off Sunset Boulevard. The popular character actor had a remarkably elastic and malleable face, which seemed to come in handy for all of his varied, nefarious roles. In fact, he was so often cast as the villain, murderer, or henchman at the studio, that he kept a handgun, a whip, and a knife in his dressing room just to scare his co-stars and get into character before shooting a scene.

While Sterling Dumont wasn't considered a traditionally-handsome leading man, he had been one of the most successful and hardest-working actors in Hollywood when he wasn't drinking, whoring, or beating his wife and girlfriends. The last few years, his hard-living reputation had caught up with him, and he was getting fewer roles as the studio brass felt he was less reliable, which made him even more polarizing and angrier—a vicious circle. Bartie had been assigned to come up with a slogan for his last thriller and then developed something of a friendship with the older actor, who was more drunk than sober. Dumont took a shine to Bartie, loved having an entourage, and started inviting him out for drinks and dinner with some of the tougher studio actors and directors. There weren't a lot of younger, red-blooded gentiles in the business to carouse with, and Bartie easily fit in as the mascot.

Initially wary of the invitation, he knew—despite the constant issues he had to clean up—the star enjoyed immense popularity with the public since he still delivered solid numbers at the box office. Bartie enjoyed his time with hard-nosed actors and seasoned directors like Billy Mackay, and they had invited him out for a boys' night as he was working on the promotion for Dumont's new *film noir* movie, *Isle of Innuendo.* They all loved his tagline for the poster: "There's no escaping the Isle of Innuendo."

Dumont and Mackay were considered "talented trouble" but were held in high esteem by Myers since, in his book, they were "red-blooded men's men." Bartie knew if he could keep up with the tough duo, Myers would approve since they were both entertaining and considered the "hardest nuts to crack" in the film colony—and the hardest to manage. He was smart enough to know it was all "work" but was flattered they wanted to accept him. He had always tried to keep it somewhat professional, but when they were out to dinner and had that endless supply of drinks, it became harder to keep things under control when the evening degenerated into a drunken mess. He also knew that going to Maude's was considered a rite of passage where "the Kid," as they called him, would hopefully be able to keep up with their late-night carousing and whoring.

As he was the only sober one in the group, Bartie drove Sterling's Pierce-Arrow and needed to be the responsible one or he knew he would be working overtime the next day to have an item cleaned up with the press. Maude's was located in a musty English Tudor mansion in a remote, yet prime spot off Sunset, with a garish red velvet interior and high iron gates to keep out any snooping press or civilians. Not many people in the industry knew that Maude's was also partially backed and secretly co-owned by none other than Mr. Solomon Myers, who found this a substantive way to indulge his passions and also keep track of his star's sexual peccadillos.

"Had this whore last week. Was made to look like Joan Blondell," Billy Mackay groaned. "She wouldn't kiss me, but swallows. Seems like a weird rule, don'tcha think?" He drank whiskey from a silver flask extracted from his navy overcoat.

"Nah, it's a whore thing. And there's this new piece who loves to fuck. She's a machine," Dumont offered. "Yeah, I gave it to her good last time. I hope she's there tonight," he growled.

They drove up to the gate, and an ominous guard emerged from the darkened guard house and looked in with a flashlight. They gave Dumont's name since he was a regular and—although married—had absolutely no sense of indiscretion or shame.

"Hey, Frankie." Sterling shook his hand through the window.

"Hi. Mister Dumont, just wanted to make sure it's you."

"Say hello to a new member of my crew…the Kid. Works at the studio." He motioned to Bartie, who seemed somewhat out of place as the fresh-faced, conscientious driver.

"What's your name, Kid?" Frankie asked with a clipboard.

"Bartie. Maddox." He gulped.

"That's Maddox, with an X?" He peered into the car, noting his arrival, most likely a report to Myers.

"Yes, sir," he said in his polite tone.

"*Yes, sir*!" Dumont laughed and slapped his thigh. "He's in a whorehouse and *sir-ing* everyone. Kid, it ain't Buckin'ham Palace." He slapped him on the back. "But hey, that's what we love about you. Kid here's got manners. You'll probably sweet talk the whores too. I just slap 'em around." Dumont's eyes lit up at the thought.

Bartie had a painful searing memory of his mother in bed with the traveling salesman and tried to excise it from his mind.

He drove the car into the car park, and a young college kid darted out, taking the car and the keys. Bartie noted that not too long ago, he knew that would have been him.

They walked up the slate steps into the gothic mansion and were greeted by Maude, herself, positioned as a sentry at the top of the stairs and who looked more like a conservative businesswoman than a madame. Her gray pageboy fit her like a crown, and her simply-cut navy chiffon dress to the knee and low heels conferred a no-nonsense demeanor that meant all business. While she greeted everyone with a kiss, her tough inner core kept most people in line. She surveyed her regulars like a sergeant appraising his troops.

"And if it isn't the bad boys club." She offered her hand as any lady would at a ball. "And who is this?" She appraised Bartie from the top step with her hand on her hip.

"The Kid—the *new* Menowitz, Myer's fixer. They keep gettin' younger, Maude!" he sneered. "And we keep getting' older. Although this one is a good egg. Smart too."

"A little young in the tooth to be the new Menowitz, don'tcha think?" She walked up to his chin to see if he was shaving yet as Maude raised an eyebrow.

"Yeah, but he's a friggin' wunderkind like Thalberg. Myers's flavor of the week."

"Oh, I see. Well, if that is the case, welcome to Maude's, Kid." Maude extended a firm grip.

"Very nice to meet you, Missus—"

She laughed. "What manners on him! It's Maude. Plain Maude. And you are?"

"Bartie Maddox."

"Well, you'll always be the Kid to me with that baby face. Do ya shave yet? Any whiskers?" She laughed out loud. "Anyways, go inside. I got a few new gals tonight. Got Rita Hayworth tonight and a Harlow that will knock your socks off. You'll see! Remember Maude's motto: 'Treat them like a lady, and they'll treat you like a man.'" Go easy on 'em, Dumont." Maude winked.

"Yeah, yeah! They love it!" he grumbled.

"The whiskey's all set up for you gents on the grand piano in the bar. We have a new girl singing tonight. She's gonna be something. Bette Desiree's the name."

Sterling Dumont walked in like he owned the joint and was greeted warmly by Enrique, the suave but older Latin bartender.

"Enrique here is a real gentleman. Kid, meet Enrique. He'll set you up."

"Nice to meet you, sir."

"Enrique, fill 'er up."

"Yes, sir, Mister Dumont."

Once they walked into the bar, the beautiful café au lait singer in a blue satin gown and rhinestones sang a haunting version of "My Man" as the girls started to walk in for their preview, two at a time. They were all heavily made-up to look like a particular movie star, and all sported a selection of skimpy multi-colored lingerie with corsets and garters. The men looked up, salivating at the parting sea of dyed blondes, brunettes, and redheads and which facsimile of a particular Hollywood star they would want to sample. The men ogled their ripe young breasts, lean bodies, and curvaceous asses, and many whistled under their breath as they whiffed the cheap perfume.

Sterling and George sat in leather arm chairs as the array of girls all came toward them and sat making small talk until they would be "chosen." Suddenly, a heavily made-up, familiar-looking platinum blonde girl entered the lounge in a black-and-red cheap lace brassiere, panties, and high heels. Bartie did a double take; he spotted her across the room as she was made to look like Harlow. They both knew better than to greet each other hello, and Bartie walked over to the men's lounge, out of view, as the blonde followed him.

"Mavis," he whispered, shocked. "What the hell are you doing here?"

"I dunno. You think I look like her?" She shrugged and applied more lipstick.

"Kind of. But Mavis? Working at Maude's?"

"It was either slinging hash in the commissary or doing this, and honestly this is the only thing I'm good at, Bartie," she said with little emotion.

"Come on, Mavis, you can do better!" He shook his head.

"Look, I tried to make it as an actress, and all I got were bit parts. Anyway, it's all the same. I ended up on my back for that too. I know the girl Carroll, who was the Harlow here for a year, but she met a producer at Maude's, and she is getting real acting gigs. So, the Harlow spot opened up, and she even gave me her wig for free." She said it as if she won the lottery. Bartie wasn't shocked at the news about Carroll, but would keep it to himself and file it away.

"At least here, I get to sleep days, and I only have to work three or four nights, and my nut is covered." She shrugged. "And you weren't interested." She shrugged, knowing she was making him feel bad but defending her choice. He noticed that she was wearing a lot of heavy pancake makeup, and she looked a bit dejected and worn.

"Okay, I guess," Bartie said sweetly, not knowing what to say.

"Listen Bartie," she whispered quickly. "You gotta help me. Sterling Dumont has a thing for me, and he's a mean drunk. Either he falls asleep and you get paid, or he starts hitting and punching. Last time, I had a bruised eye and almost blacked out. Maude just shrugs it off, but I'm scared he's gonna really hurt me one day or even kill me." She had real fear in her eyes.

"I have an idea. Just pretend we never met, okay?"

"You've always been quick on your feet." She kissed him lightly on the cheek.

She nodded as Bartie walked into the men's room and washed his face with cold water as the bathroom attendant handed him a linen napkin in black tie. When he walked quickly back to the bar, he sat on one of the armchairs, and Mavis walked in with a forced smile. Sterling Dumont's eyes seemed possessed at the sight of her. "Hey, Harlow, come on over and meet the Kid!" he commanded. She slowly walked over.

"Hi, nice to meet ya." Her eyes pleaded.

"This here is my new piece." He smiled like the evil characters he played on the silver screen. He grabbed her ass, and she winced at the pain. "She can suck a watermelon through a hose with that mouth." He broke up. "Now, in this town, that's what I call talent."

"Hi, Jean, I'm Bartie." He shook her hand, playing along with the gimmick. "She sure is pretty, exactly like Harlow." Bartie looked her over.

"Whaddya think?" Sterling reached up and twisted her nipple as she howled in pain. "Want some of this?'

"She sure is something," Bartie eyed her lasciviously.

"You know what, Kid," he said, slapping him on his back in a grand gesture. "I'll take Rita over here tonight." He walked up to the girl made to look like Hayworth and slapped her ass so hard she jumped, the sound reverberating through the room. "And you take Harlow, my piece. On me, Kid. Best blow job in town, and she *loves* to fuck, don't ya, *piece*!" Dumont reached up grabbed her by the jaw and squeezed so hard it left marks on her face.

"Yessir," she whimpered in pain.

"Whaddya say, *piece*?" He boasted an evil grin. "I wanna hear it. You give the best blow job in town…say it!" he bellowed.

She hesitated for a moment and then as he twisted on her jaw, she gave in to the pain. "I give the best blow job in town," she said, trying to get the words out.

"Louder!" He released her. "Yell it from the rafters!"

"I give the best blow job in town!" she said in a loud voice, stifling a sob.

"And I love to fuck like a jackrabbit." He ordered her to repeat.

"And I love to fuck like a jackrabbit." She looked down, her voice breaking.

"Good girl." He slapped her face for good measure. "Now you take the Kid upstairs, and you work him over the way a young man needs to be. And Kid, if you don't tell me it's the best piece ya ever had in this damn town, then you're…*Gorge Lamont*." He laughed out loud as they all cracked up. "Best piece of meat in all of LA." He slapped her hard again, and she buckled at the pain.

"Thanks, Mister Dumont," Bartie nodded.

"Should we watch the Kid?" Bill Mackay asked salaciously. "That could be a fun warm-up?"

"Nah, I think Rita over here needs a good one, don't ya, Rita? I'll fuck her first, and then you can have her." He emitted an evil laugh "Sloppy seconds, just like your film career," he laughed, "getting everyone's leftover scripts."

"Well, off with you two." Dumont waved them up to a bedroom.

"Thank you, Mister Dumont. You're the best." Bartie smiled widely.

"You're welcome, Kid." He thrust Rita's arm backward again, and she moaned in pain.

Mavis took Bartie's hand in her own under Maude's steely eye, and she walked him up the creaky, carved oak staircase to one of the ornate bedrooms. While Bartie would later regale Dumont and Mackay about the whore's sensual skills and how she looked exactly like Harlow, Bartie spent the evening holding Mavis as she wept silently in his arms.

Chapter Thirty-Five

Duke Drake
Los Angeles
1940

Like a flash lightning storm, the screaming was so loud and thunderous it could be heard all across the lot—so much so that one take of a nearby film needed to be reshot due to the audio interruption. Bartie had been summoned to Myers's office and sat tall and at attention, hands folded in his lap, taking the position of a scolded schoolboy. He knew he had to suffer through the interminable ranting and raving even though they both knew he had nothing to do with it, but Myers needed a punching bag, and he was it.

The legendary feud between gossip columnists Louella Parsons and Hedda Hopper had erupted into a volcanic free-for-all, flowing lava of gossip, innuendo, and one-up-manship, and there was hell to pay! Bartie knew he was being forced onto the hot coals and into a no-win situation.

Solomon Myers had, over the years, developed a warm and open relationship with Louella, the earthier and kinder of the two syndicated columnists, and a more complicated one with Hopper, who had been a contract actress in the '20s and who was known for her hardline views, revenge, and carrying out and executing grudges, so much so that she, herself, christened the Beverly Hills manse she lived in "the house that fear built." Yet, both industry columnists had millions of readers and could make or break stars, studios, and film releases and—despite the viselike grip they both had on celebrity gossip—it was virtually impossible to please one without upsetting the other.

Hopper was a card-carrying hard-nosed, self-described Republican patriot who thought men like Solomon Myers were all left-leaning communist liberal Jews at odds with her reactionary views. They all knew that Hedda might have been softer had she achieved her earlier goals of becoming a movie star in her youth, and she, in turn, might have turned out *nicer*. Yet, she had finally arrived after a hard-earned career and was now powerful *and* vindictive, and industry insiders trembled. Myers and his fixers were always smart enough to try and keep on the right side of both women and cleverly doled out exclusives, first to one and then one to the other, so they both knew they were up at bat at least once a month. That said, if one's feathers were ruffled, or it got too heated, the volcano cone could easily blow. Scores were kept on a mental scorecard and tallied, and it could take a week, a month, or a year before a damaging news story would emerge out of nowhere. And blow it did.

Hedda had been steaming over a certain incident over the last few months. It had all taken place before the filming of *Grand Voyage.* It was the day before the SGM announcement, and all heads in the Brown Derby were agape as Gorge Lamont entered and met not one of his boy toys, but was lunching with none other than his archnemesis, Mr. Solomon Myers. Heads swiveled and tongues wagged, and all mouths dropped to the floor as the inconceivable pair and such noted long-term enemies were breaking bread, especially at a public place like the Brown Derby. However, dine they did and with such conviviality that they looked like great old friends catching up for a college reunion. The decision had been made to give neither of the women the exclusive as it was such big insider news, one of the columnists would have been greatly offended. The idea was to show up when they knew both would be having lunch that day, as they always did. It was the right and smart strategy, but as luck would have it, Hedda happened to be late from a hair appointment that afternoon.

And then the inevitable: without being invited, Louella casually bellied up to Myers's and George Lamont's banquette, planted herself, and broke her notepad out of her purse and scribbled notes for her readers. Hedda Hopper just happened to be walking into the restaurant at the exact same time when she spotted the threesome, her own mouth agape, and turned beet red in anger thinking that Louella Parsons had been given the exclusive and went into a total rage. She stormed out of the restaurant and went on an anti-SGM rampage. That wasn't enough, though, as she saw the moment and the optics as the ultimate betrayal, and no one would ever one-up Hedda!

Her campaign went on for months, giving Myers the silent treatment and horrible stories about his films despite his explanation, sending flowers, candy, and even a diamond bracelet. He offered juicy exclusives, but Hedda returned everything and wouldn't play ball. And Myers knew that he would have to take the beating just the way he had originally punished Gorge Lamont. Hedda was smart enough to bide her time, and just when Solly Myers thought she had exacted enough revenge, and everything was peachy keen, she shoved her poison pen like a dagger directly into his *kishkes.* It had to be one of her great strategies. The previous night they had all dined together at Humphrey Bogart's, and Hedda was as charming and as sweet as sugar with Sol and Freyda Myers, so much so that Sol told his wife that he thought the feud was over. And that's exactly when she struck like a snake in the foliage waiting to pounce. Today's paper, thrown at Bartie's head, was her final revenge and pound of flesh.

When Bartie picked the *Los Angeles Times* up off the floor and saw the headline in Hedda Hopper's Hollywood syndicated column, he turned ghostly white. The headline screamed, "Duke Drake's Secret Life Unveiled," and a provocative subhead boasted, "What Lorena Smalls doesn't know will hurt her, and why she'll never walk down the aisle with Duke Drake. The untold story…" and on and on. Although the article vaguely hinted at Duke's homosexuality, it was a thinly-veiled piece that was skillfully written to suggest but not actually say it outright. A first shot across the bow to make it clear Hedda Hopper was more powerful than the people she documented. Phrases like "Duke's secret love won't allow him to commit" were close enough to do damage without going over the line. Worse, the scandal rag, *Confidential,* picked up the story and showed a photo of Duke and Gorge weightlifting in bathing suits, along with shots of the two in aprons at the beach house from the infamous Menowitz spread.

Bartie, of course, always knew he needed to ideate in the moment with the mercurial Myers and had something up his sleeve for a while, an idea for a studio fix, which he had been dreaming up for Duke, and when he floated it, it seemed to calm Myers, who told him to "get it done and quick, ya louse!" That was, if only Duke Drake would go for it.

Later that afternoon, after Edna tracked down Duke at the beach house, she summoned him to Bartie's office with the curt phrase, "Be there!"

Duke appeared outside his small cottage on the lot looking pale as clotted cream and somewhat chastened having read Hedda's column. He knew that his next film, *The British Cad*, was being released in a month's time, and the studio had invested a great deal in him and the upcoming film. It starred the popular actress, Joan Bennett, as an heiress who falls in love with a real British aristocrat who pretends to be a fake one until he falls in love too, played and written specifically for Duke. It was his first film as a leading man, and the studio had high hopes for the tongue-in-cheek comedy of manners that, after seeing the rushes, was rumored to be a surefire hit. That is, if the scandal didn't sink it before it was released. Upon meeting outside Bartie's office on the lot, the two men shook hands cordially and said little.

There was an embarrassing silence that now pervaded their interaction as if Duke were a child who had been caught stealing a piece of penny candy.

"I'm in deep shit, aren't I?"

"You said it. I didn't." Bartie rolled his eyes. "Come with me. I have a surprise for you," Bartie said as he walked toward Duke's gleaming navy Rolls-Royce.

"Where are we going?"

"You'll see." Bartie instructed the driver to an address in Bel Air.

"I can't imagine it's a good one after today's article. Does Myers have a torture chamber hidden somewhere in the hills?" Duke asked, looking like a handsome, frightened puppy being taken to the pound.

"Not exactly." Bartie waggled an eyebrow.

"Why are we going up to Bel Air, Bartie? Are we going to see Myers?" Duke asked anxiously.

Bartie remained silent knowing his terse stance might help soften Duke's point of view as he nervously lit up a cigarette.

"You'll see."

"So secretive. It's all quite alluring, Bartie." His hands shook ever so slightly at the suspense as he lit a cigarette with a gold monogrammed lighter Gorge had given him.

"How's Gorge?" Bartie asked, looking toward his left out the window.

"He's now under fire as well. Jack Warner saw the paper and read him the riot act this morning and basically ordered him to start acting like a real man, or they would drop him after this next film. It's been impossible."

"Ah, the price of fame." Bartie shrugged.

The car wound its way up to one of the highest vistas in Bel Air. Bartie asked Duke's driver to pull into the address he had given him, past two huge iron gates, and into a capacious cobblestone car park. Before him was a veritable seventeenth-century English Tudor castle, much of it shipped over from the English countryside in the early '20s by a now impoverished tin tycoon.

"Who lives here?" Duke looked wide-eyed at the castle.

"You do." Bartie looked him straight in the eye.

"I do?" Duke looked quite perplexed.

"Well, you will…" He paused dramatically. "If you're smart enough."

"Okay, Bartie, enough of the charades, please…what's going on?"

"How old are you, Duke? Real age, please," Bartie asked.

"Just turned twenty-four."

And how old is Gorge?" Bartie looked at him with a sly, knowing look.

"Thirty-two…" He smiled. "Okay, thirty-seven."

"Two famous, grown men who have real money and who aren't teenagers or in college just don't *room* together," Bartie noted, summing up the situation. "Gorge has his own house, and you need yours. No one and I mean no one, including Myers, is saying you can't…" he searched for a euphemism, "…enjoy each other's company. It just can't be full time."

"Bartie, can I be honest?" Duke implored.

"Yes, of course, Duke." He softened his stance as Duke poured out his heart to him.

"I know you're, well," he paused, "…an *all-American* kind of guy, and this may be very hard for you to hear and understand, but Gorge and I love each other deeply." He paused, trying to explain. "The way a…husband and wife love each other, and we hate being apart." He stopped talking as Bartie looked down.

"I'm sorry, is that hard for you to hear? It must be, that two men can actually *love* each other?" Duke looked out the window.

"Actually, yeah. What can I say? It's not what I *know*…but I also can't understand why Sterling Dumont hits his wife and beats up hookers. I just have to deal with it and clean up the mess."

"It's not the same thing."

"Okay, but it is to the publicity department at SGM. Duke, your career is at stake, and if you love each other so much, do it in different houses so Hedda *frigging* Hopper can't say you're shacking up in Pansy Hall. Look, let me tell you something about me. In the height of the Depression, my mother died, and I only had money left over from a pocket watch to get me to LA. I was one step from the streets. When I landed here, I worked as a busboy and then as a valet and as typist for F. Scott and all the way up to being a press agent. Myers believed in me, and now I'm no longer in poverty, and I will do anything to protect the studio. So, while I understand you two lovebirds want to live under the same roof, you can't be 'two famous male movie stars in 1940 who live together!' And no, I can't understand why living in two separate mansions is so frigging tough. No one is crying for you given what's going on in Europe, so Duke, buck up!" he said, forcefully.

They sat in a long silence. Finally, Duke opened the door, and the chauffeur helped him out.

"Okay. Show me the house, Bartie." He looked over, teary-eyed as he tried to smile. Bartie smiled back sweetly, knowing he had touched a nerve. "Where did you come up with this one?"

"One night I went to Maude's, and it was in an old Tudor mansion, and it gave me the idea...for *you.*" Bartie patted him on the back.

"So, you're thinking about me at a whorehouse. I'm flattered."

"You should be. So, I asked around about any English mansions available, and this one has been on the market for over a year. Used to belong to King Vidor, and since it's so big, it's a white elephant, a bargain. You can afford it, Duke. Get it? 'The Duke and His Castle.' I see the article now." He blocked it out with his hands.

The uniformed chauffeur lit up a cigarette and whistled at the view as Duke took in the opulent surroundings, replete with spires and acres of slate roofing.

"Here's how I see it..." Bartie went into his pitch. "With the launch of *The British Cad*, we get *Photoplay* magazine to do a spread on 'the Duke in his castle.' And it's called...?"

"Duke's?" he offered sweetly.

"No, that sounds like a restaurant on La Cienega! We'll take your family crest and put it on the gates, and then," Bartie beamed, 'Welcome to Drake Manor.' The public will know that the English Duke lives alone in his castle, and your fans will think...where's the Duchess? Maybe it can be *me*! A fantasy for all your young female fans that the position of Duchess needs to be filled—in a bona fide castle. We don't have to say anything. No more roommate gossip or Pansy Hall when you can have *all this*...unless, of course, you don't want it?"

Duke paused at the splendor. "I didn't say that."

"Are you worried what Gorge will say? Because if that's the issue, you and Gorge can continue to live together, and you both can look at opening up a very successful interior design business in a year or two and say goodbye to your movie careers. The choice is yours."

"How much?" Duke gulped.

"Was originally listed at ninety-five-thousand and has been reduced to sixty-five-thousand. And Mister Myers said he would give you the down payment of ten-thousand as a bonus just to get you out of Gorge's house. Then, the studio will loan you the money, and you'd pay it out of your salary." Duke just sat and marveled at the castle without saying a word.

"It's Gorge, isn't it?"

"Warner is tougher than Solly Myers. I think, given his comeback, Gorge is getting a bit more realistic too." He shrugged.

"That's good to hear." Bartie breathed a sigh of relief.

Bartie and Duke were met by the dapper real estate broker and the butler who opened the house for them. They walked into the massive stone castle, replete with a suit of armor and stone and oak staircase, worn and faded aristocratic oriental carpets, and ancestral portraits hanging in carved, gilt frames. It was as if the English countryside was ten minutes from Santa Monica Boulevard, all which took Duke's breath away. The poor boy from Stoke-on-Trent now was going to be king of his castle, even if he was called a queen and not actually looking for one.

"You know, Bartie, I have to hand it to you. You really are quick on your feet. This morning, I thought my career was over before it started."

"Thanks, Duke. Look, I told you the studio is heavily invested in you, and I already gave Myers my word you're smart and will want to play ball, and this will just give you a fresh start…for now."

"For now?" He looked surprised but didn't press it. "Well, I won't say no." Duke shook Bartie's hand.

"And Bartie?"

"Yes?" He ground the cigarette into the stone drive.

"Thank you," Duke said, with a genuine tear in his eye.

"Of course—but one last thing." Bartie put his arm around Duke's shoulder.

"Yes, what's next?" he sighed.

"The Duke and his castle is eventually going to need…a *duchess.*" Bartie looked him straight in the eye.

"Of course." He looked down and paused. "I understand."

"Good. Welcome home to Drake Manor, Duke."

Chapter Thirty-Six

Mirielle Montaigne
Los Angeles
1940

The sparkling, dancing cut-crystal chandeliers of the Hillcrest Country Club's main dining room reflected the light of the diamond brooches and art deco bracelets, the freshly-polished silver cutlery, celebrities flashing enhanced smiles, and movie deals being done over bagels and borscht. The grand room had all the accouterments of a gentile club, but also had lox, blintzes, and the Marx Brothers on the menu. In fact, so valuable was a membership to the prestigious club that Groucho Marx would eventually will his own to his son when he passed. While it didn't have the exclusive WASP patina of the Bel Air Country Club, as they didn't allow "entertainment people," it was the epicenter of Jewish power in LA, and that was everything to the industry. While Hedda Hopper privately bristled at "those New Yorkers," publicly she was triumphant at being seen and seated with Solomon Myers at the prime table and enjoying her smoked salmon sans bagel. In fact, they made quite a humorous pair, the diminutive and overdressed Myers and Hopper in one of her legendary and extravagant hats nodding across the room to the star members Al Jolson, George Burns, and Milton Berle—who would all come over and pay their respects after rugelach and coffee.

Hedda, being Hedda, was only lightly chastised by Myers for the Duke Drake incident but was taken to a very public lunch at Hillcrest and then, after the entrée, as she knew would happen, given a grand exclusive as a peace offering. And today's offering on the menu would be Mirielle Montaigne. After all, Myers and everyone else in the dining room knew that Hopper had a staggering thirty-five million readers in her syndicated column and, besides Parsons, wielded a virtual lock on Hollywood gossip impacting the success of films and their stars.

"I'm telling ya, Hedda," Myers leaned in. "She's the world's most beautiful woman. An actress, singer, and…get this, also some countess or something *royal.* We pulled out all the stops to get her—get this—two-fifty a week to start. Can ya imagine?" he whistled, acting the part of the beneficent big shot. Myers also failed to mention he hadn't ever laid eyes on her. He was sweating at the thought, but hopeful that "the Mick" knew what he was talking about, or he would have his head on a platter. Hedda looked slightly askance under the wide-net veil of her hat at the description, and she was weary of studio overhype and lingo but nodded and said she was eager to meet Mirielle and "review." Then, she added for good measure, "You know, Solly, you studio types can't pull a fast one over on me. If she's not the real thing, *I will know.* I know royalty, and I'm not some Midwestern pushover like *Parsons* who can't differentiate between…sterling and stainless." She sniffed and adjusted the veil on her chapeau.

"I'm telling ya, Hedda, she is the *gen-u-ine* article, some French princess *thingy,*" he said with pride as she rolled her eyes under her veil. He tried to recall Michael's list of her attributes despite being somewhat foggy on the subject.

Michael had indeed phoned Myers and Bartie from New York, where he and Irene were staying in separate suites for appearance's sake at the Plaza, all on SGM's dime. They had arranged for first-class tickets to Los Angeles on the Super Chief, known as "the train of the stars," which was the way most of the rich and famous traveled to either coast, replete with pullman sleeping berths and gourmet dining cars; the place where café society and Hollywood met and socialized, mingling on the luxurious journey. The days and nights with Irene on the ship, sightseeing in New York and on the train were dizzying with joy and pleasure—a honeymoon he never had experienced with his own wife, given her brittle and stingy personality. At night on the train, in the privacy of her compartment, Mick had given Irene a virtual dossier created by Bartie for her to study. He coached Irene on her new name and bio, which she needed to stick to for studio press purposes when they arrived in Los Angeles, knowing it would be her biggest acting role ever. From here on out, she would no longer be known as Irene Von Mendelssohn, but Mirielle Montaigne, born to an Austrian mother and a French count. When her parents divorced, her mother, Brigitte, a great beauty and actress, married Maurice de la Montaigne, another Baron and boulevardier who adopted her. Later her mother would marry many more times, creating a dizzying record no one could possibly keep up with—neither the press nor the public. This was a common part of a particular kind of studio *fix*, creating a story so elaborate and complex, so chock full of facts, that by the time the story was told and retold, no one could remember much of anything—especially reporters who were more used to Jack Daniels than doing their research.

Irene was instructed only to speak Franglish, a mix of French and English with an overt French-tinged accent. Her signature song would be co-opting and white-washing Josephine Baker's "J'ai Deux Amours," the lyrics highlighting her two loves being Paris and New York, which she would eventually sing at rallies after Germany invaded France. The story was that her beauty and talent were so extraordinary that the head of production at SGM studios had rushed to Paris to see and sign her for the upcoming, surefire hit, *Au Revoir Paris*, starring opposite legendary film star Charles Boyer. An array of studio photographers would be on hand and stationed outside the train station in Los Angeles as SGM's newest star stepped onto the platform. As the train pulled into the station, the new creation, Mirielle Montaigne, emerged and would be given a grand welcome. Not to mention the exclusive gift from Solly Myers to Hedda Hopper.

Exactly ten days later, the clear and sunny California morning had the train pulling into the station with boundless energy, yet as the train came to a melodious stop with its screeching wheels, Mirielle suddenly felt a pit in her stomach and her knees wobbled. Michael steadied her by the elbow and kissed her, grazing her lips with his stubble.

"Mirielle, my darling, you can do it!" he whispered and kissed her again, one last time before she exited the train and became public property. She tentatively adjusted her silver fox cape as the porters unloaded her multitude of Louis Vuitton steamer trunks before she descended the steps to the platform and the press. It didn't go unnoticed by Irene that she had left Europe as a refugee in a panic and was now arriving on the red carpet with a new name, new identity, and film contract all thanks to her new lover, Michael McDonough.

Solomon Myers was personally on hand to meet his newest star, with Bartie trailing to inspect the goods and to welcome her to California and the SGM studio family. Michael emerged first and then there was a gasp at her beauty as he extended a hand to help her off the train. The press went wild and applauded her, and myriad photos were snapped as a beaming Myers walked up to meet her with a large bouquet of red roses. His broad smile gave away his thoughts, as he could never conceal his emotions. He was dazzled at her luminous beauty and by her glamorous style and international chic. Most young women came to LA and had to be invented by the studio, but here was the real thing already bathed in luxury.

"Mademoiselle Montaigne, welcome to Hollywood and SGM studios." He smiled, and they turned to the camera. The flashbulbs crackled, and Irene, now Mirielle, was instructed to smile and say, "*Merci beaucoup,* Monsieur Myers. *J'adore LA et* SGM Studios." She tilted her hat, revealing her movie star face and then, for effect, added in Franglish, "Thank you very much!" to applause and laughter. She bared a hint of a naked knee as she raised her skirt with a sexy flourish—as she was instructed to do.

"Ya hear that? That's real French for *yous,*" Myers offered the press, lighting a cigar for good measure. Myers, Mirielle, and Michael then all posed and smiled for the camera.

"Mister Myers, are you happy to have Miss Montaigne in LA?" a reporter shouted.

"Reports of her beauty reached my office, and I can honestly say that she is more *bee-ootiful* in person. Don'tcha think?" They snapped the photos. "Just look at her." He marveled. "She's the most beautiful gift from France since the Statue of Liberty," which he pronounced "*libeddy*." This would be her official line as he had merged Bartie's two thoughts.

"Hey, Mick." Myers took a very long pause and then let out a deep breath and a sparkling laugh and patted him on the back.

"I'll never doubt ya again. That's *platinum-plated pussy*," he whispered to him and Bartie as he motioned them off to the side to have a quick chat. Myers struggled to put his arm around Michael's shoulders since he was a head shorter and whispered, "She *is* the most beautiful girl in the world. Whadda face! You really know how to spot em', ya Irish genius."

"Thanks, Mister Myers," Michael beamed.

"Hey, Mick, welcome home." Bartie pumped Michael's hands enthusiastically and smiled.

"And how about that name, huh?" Myers whispered off to the side. "Mirielle Montaigne—boy genius over here came up with it! Nice, huh? By the way—can she act?" Myers probed.

"Yes, she read a few pages for me. A natural," Michael beamed.

"She can really sing too?" Myers marveled.

"Like a songbird."

"You fuckin' her?" Myers directed a laser focus at McDonough.

Michael's silence denoted a triumph for Myers.

"Well, well, the Saint Michael McDon-*ovitz* finally done it," he joked and laughed gleefully. "Mixin' business with pleasure! Glad I know, or I would have had her bent over the desk with her royal ass in the air. But look, it proves you're a *hoooo-man* being like the rest of us. Imagine that, Mick and the baroness. Ah ha!" He laughed out loud, rubbing his chapped hands together in glee. Bartie quickly changed the subject, sensing Michael's discomfort.

"Mister Myers, don't you think Miss Montaigne and you should have a photo next to all her Louis Vuitton steamer trunks? It'll look like she is the real deal." He motioned over to the trunks stacked on the platform.

"Good, Maddox. Ya see…he's as smart as a *yeshiva bochur*."

"Right this way, Mister Myers." He led Myers away from a bruised McDonough, who was at a loss over the personal revelation.

"Listen, Mick, over here," Solly called, sensing he had possibly overstepped his bounds, which was rare for Myers.

"Days like this call for a celebration. Why, I haven't been this excited since I brought in ZaSu Pitts! Wait 'til Hedda meets Miss French Fancy Pants over here. You're both gettin' raises and a night at Maude's on me!" He smiled, revealing his oversized caps brightly. "And where did she get those clothes and jewelry?" Myers surveyed and whistled at her Paris couture as Mirielle chatted with one of the studio photographers, who was posing her in a certain way to get a glimpse of leg.

"Mister Myers, she's a real baroness," Michael said proudly. "It's all hers."

"Well, she's better dressed than my wife! Don't introduce her to Freyda if you know what's good for yas. What can I say?" He threw his small hands up in the air at her chic couture and enchanting manners. "I didn't know Jewish gals like that on Pitkin Avenue!" he whispered and slapped Michael on the back with a guffaw.

"Maddox…"

"Yes, Mister Myers?"

"You get those photos of Montaigne and high tail it over to Hedda Hopper's house. She's gonna love her." He paused, sizing up Bartie's lean and intellectual college-boy look. "And I have a feeling she's gonna like *you* too." He smiled, realizing the very fresh-faced and gentile Bartie Maddox might also just do the trick.

After all, Solomon Myers was in the movie business, and nobody better understood the need for good casting more than him.

Chapter Thirty-Seven

La Marquise de La Faucigny
London
1940

The telegrams, calls, and flowers from Louis were endless and all-encompassing, flooding Grace's palatial suite at Claridge's, a virtual tsunami of guilt and panic. Each elaborate floral arrangement from Mayfair's top florists was received by her lady's maid, placed on the polished deco console, card opened, noted, and then sent directly to the concierge to then be delivered to an old age home or public maternity ward. The handwritten notes with the family crest and declarations of love were promptly tossed in the garbage. "The love of your bank account," Uncle Reggie shook his head, "is what *he* cares about." Grace's slow, simmering anger, however, was a pebble on the beach to the wave of Louis's guilt, rage, and ambition. While privately furious with her, he knew the goose that laid the golden egg had decamped for London and had outsmarted him, taking her unlimited checkbook with her. Even her grandmother's diamond choker in the safe was eventually discovered to be a paste copy made by Uncle Reggie and placed in the original case as the ultimate chess move. He tossed and turned and took his rage out on Ghislaine by not seeing her for a few days until her hysterics and his sex drive brought him back to his senses. He also knew that Grace was being sheltered and supported by the wealthy and powerful McCleans, and their possession of proof of the affair would do little to help lure his heiress wife back to Paris—not to mention his knowledge of the impending invasion. He plotted and planned and, as Uncle

Reggie had suggested, made the expected "surprise" trip to London, arriving surreptitiously at Claridge's unannounced, where he found Madame la Marquise had conveniently checked out. Then, shaking his silky blonde hair and adjusting his gray cravat, he wearily hired a car and made his way to Compton House, Reggie and Victoria McClean's huge fifteenth-century country pile, to no avail.

The head concierge at Claridge's had called and given Reggie the heads up that the marquis was indeed poking around and had ordered a private car soon to arrive. When the enraged Louis showed up at Compton House in the early evening as expected, Reggie was waiting for him, exited the castle, taking his hunting rifle as a greeting, and pointed at Louis.

"I will not hesitate to use it on a philanderer, Nazi collaborator, and fortune hunter, and I have proof," he challenged Louis as a uniformed butler emerged from the castle with a large silver platter encased with a polished silver dome. When the servant raised the dome, Louis's telegrams were in full view, including the red Swastika stamp (Reggie would dine out on this part of the story for years to come). Louis immediately and reluctantly fled without saying a word or being able to see Grace in person. She hid in the upstairs bedroom and had watched the altercation from above, peeking through a curtain. Louis knew he had lost and hightailed it back to London and then to Paris empty-handed, and the timing was exactly as Reggie predicted: right before the Germans attacked and invaded France.

On May 10, despite Reggie's advance information, the rest of the world was stunned when the German armored units advanced through the Ardennes and the low countries, attacking France and taking Belgium, Luxembourg, and the Netherlands. The French populace wept openly in the streets.

Grace knew that she had narrowly avoided personal disaster and that if she had had her baby, she would have been living under Nazi rule. Over the next few days, as she processed her imminent divorce, she took in the rolling hills and verdant lochs of the English countryside. It was a miraculous tableau, and she wished she'd had a camera or paint and easel to capture the vast beauty and majesty of the landscape, yet she found the weather depressing. She would go on long walks returning for a lazy afternoon nap, reading a musty copy of Disraeli's *Vivian Grey,* which she found in the well-stocked library of another period under the lead-paned Elizabethan window.

In the end, it would take a $1.75-million-dollar payment for Reggie McClean to secure Grace's divorce from Louis. When the funds hit the account in a neutral bank in Monaco, Louis became engaged to Ghislaine within days. With the newspapers reporting the divorce and Louis's engagement to the young French star in the London papers, Grace was on the verge of not being received in polite society once again as a scandal magnate and divorcée. She took stock of the social situation and wrote to her dearest friend, Irene, who urged her to come to Los Angeles. Grace and Uncle Reggie decided that perhaps the sunshine and stars of Beverly Hills seemed the best possible solution, given her new unfortunate social status. After much consideration, she finally used her family assets and booked passage on her uncle's ship to the new world… and hopefully a new life. Crossing over.

Chapter Thirty-Eight

Bartie Maddox
Los Angeles
1940

Michael joked in a bawdy fashion that walking into Maude's was like entering an oversized, red velvet vagina. Maude herself seemed to have taken the cliché of bordello interior design rather seriously, and it was a tableau of overstuffed, gilded Victorian furniture covered in scarlet, red, and gold-flecked velvet. There were over-draped windows in matching crimson velveteen spilling onto the floor in puddles with golden pulls, fringed red satin lampshades, and a replica of a Western saloon-style bar. It actually all worked rather well with the dark, vast Tudor architecture. It had been created by SGM's head of set design, a noted lesbian, Sacha DeVine, in exchange for a year of barter. One almost expected Dietrich to come out in saloon regalia and reprise her throaty ditty from *Destry Rides Again.*

"I feel like I'm cheating on Mirielle." Michael looked downcast as he walked through the immense stone foyer and handed his raincoat to the voluptuous hat check girl, who sported a robust figure in a black lace corset. Her homely face damned her to a life in the coat closet and small tips. "Poor girl has a great body but a face like Margaret Hamilton. That's who *she* could pass for," Mick observed as all the girls were to be cast as a current star.

"Wait, you're married, but you feel like you're cheating on your girlfriend?" Bartie laughed as he handed his overcoat to the unfortunate, buck-toothed damsel. "Interesting concept!"

"Something like that." Michael raised a bushy ginger eyebrow. "You know we're married in name only. Mary Katherine has been living in Boston most of the year. She detests me but still won't give me a divorce for religious reasons."

"That's difficult," Bartie nodded. "But maybe it's good you don't live together." He paused. "You're really in love with Mirielle, aren't you?"

"She's everything I've ever dreamed of and never expected to get—not to mention completely out of my league."

Bartie and Michael walked into the oak-paneled bar and each shook hands with the legendary Enrique, the suave bartender, who immediately started fixing their favorite drinks. He knew his clients by name and mentally filed away their drink preferences. Everything at Maude's had been carefully designed to fulfill the ultimate male fantasy, from the inflamed red velvet divans, the perfectly stirred and preferred whiskey cocktail, to the ersatz female stars, the sexual positions and combinations which were all noted by Maude, herself, and then sent in a discreet report to Myers weekly.

All the industry players knew each other at Maude's, and it was considered a private and elite club on Thursday nights as everyone would say they were working late at the office. Fridays and Saturdays were designated for their wives. Michael and Bartie waved across the room and shook hands with colleagues from Warner Bros. and Fox, the sense of normalcy a large reason for Maude's success. In fact, more often than not, a real louche female star would often be spotted at the bar for a drink and to hear the jazz music, usually in a group setting, offering up a sophisticated aura and sometimes even seen on the staircase with a girl of her choice.

"I can see why you feel that way. Mirielle is quite possibly the most beautiful woman I've ever seen, and one of the smartest too."

"I'm screwed," Michael sighed, scanning the room for talent.

"Do you think Mary Katherine knows about her?" Bartie asked.

"She went back to Boston right before Irene…I mean, Mirielle arrived, but she always suspects something. Honestly, she would have been better off taking the habit. She dislikes me intensely. We never have had a real sexual relationship, and she hates LA. The only thing we have in common is we're both Catholic. I think she hates the Italian in me on my mother's side—says it's sinful passion."

"Well, she's not wrong." They laughed and both looked around the room at the heavily made-up women.

"Yes, so that's why I'm here. If I don't choose a girl tonight, Myers will think I'm as in love as I am, and then he'll find a way to lord it over me and use it against Mirielle as leverage."

"So, who do you have in mind?" Bartie asked as they both scanned the room. Suddenly, they both stopped in their tracks.

"I can't believe it." He pointed to a girl who looked exactly like Rita Hayworth, the sexy movie star. "Wow, she really looks like her." Her flame-colored hair was cascading; she was wearing a tight, black lace bustier to highlight her lovely breasts and wore garters to display her long, silken, showgirl legs, giving her a sense of both sensuality and elegance. Michael walked over to her. He had worked with the real Rita on two movies, and he walked closely to check to see if it was really her, only to find a close facsimile.

"Hi, doll." She perked up and noticed his interest as Michael looked at her sideways as she strode over to the bar.

"Hi, again." She turned to Bartie.

"You two know each other? I didn't realize you were such a regular at Maude's. I'm impressed." Michael laughed and slapped his young friend on the back.

"I came with Dumont and Mackay last week. It was a command performance."

"Oh, I see." He nodded.

"What happened to you?" Michael looked down as he caressed her arm and noticed the multiple bruises she had tried to cover up with makeup. The Rita lookalike just shrugged and nodded to Bartie with a knowing look.

"Sterling Dumont is rough with the girls." Bartie shook his head.

"So I've heard," Michael said. "He once beat up an extra in his trailer. She went to the police and Menowitz had to do a fix, a payoff."

"Rita, let me ask you…" Bartie asked in a low voice. "Where's Mavis? I mean Harlow?"

Rita shook her head and looked down in fear. "I don't know nothin'."

"Meaning you know something?" he asked, wide-eyed.

"She's in a bad way." She looked around and whispered. "Dumont roughed her up a few nights ago."

"I see." Bartie gave Michael a knowing look.

"When you see her, tell her to call me, okay? I want to check in on her." Bartie looked concerned. "There's a girl I know who works here who used to work for Menowitz," he explained.

"Got it. Dumont is a bad seed."

"Wanna buy me a drink?" the faux Rita asked as she saw Maude approaching and changed the subject. She flirted with Mick as she saw Maude eyeing the room and making sure everyone was engaged.

"Hey, Kid," Maude walked over. "Good to see you."

"Nice to see you too, Maude. Looking lovely as ever."

"Love his manners. Hey, Mick." She looked over. "Nice you see you too. Haven't seen you here in a while—must be serious." She smirked.

"Just traveling."

"Yeah, and I'm twenty-five. I keep tabs on my boys." She had a hand on her hip.

"Maude, where is that girl Harlow?" Bartie asked in an innocent fashion, and Maude tried to hide her concern.

"Oh, you liked her? She's quite popular. She's at home with a bellyache, that time of month." Maude was stone-faced.

"I see," Bartie nodded.

"Here…if you like Harlow, let me introduce you to Lana Turner." She snapped her fingers. "She's one of my new girls." She motioned over a sexy, cheap blonde imitation.

"Lana, this here is the Kid and Mick. Two of my important friends at the studio. Take good care of him. You're lucky. The Kid is a real gent."

"Hey, Kid." The ersatz Lana cracked her gum, thrusting her voluptuous figure at him, her taut breasts straining the black lace negligee.

"Hi, Lana," he said, then turned. "She's very pretty, like the real Lana, Maude," he said as Lana walked over and sat on Bartie's lap and stroked his hair.

"She is the real Lana, Kid." Maude tried to keep the illusion intact by never breaking the fantasy.

"Think I seen you around," she whispered. "I thought you were cute then and cuter now. Wanna go upstairs?" She leaned over and licked and nuzzled against his neck.

"Sure," Bartie gulped, taking in her innate sexuality on display. "Just let me finish this." He toasted her with his whiskey.

"Here, I'll help you." She sipped it, laughed, and stroked his cheek.

"Have a good time, all. I want my boys to always have a great time at Maude's no matter what!"

"No matter what." Bartie also thought of Sterling Dumont and what the girls had to endure at his hands and fists.

Chapter Thirty-Nine

Mirielle Montaigne
Los Angeles
1940

Across town in the buzzing hive of the Culver City studio, Mirielle's glamorous transformation was underway, and while it was all very thrilling, it was also somewhat exhausting as well as confusing. First, the studio team conducted and then put through Mirielle's screentest to the beauty department to analyze her teeth, smile, hairline, nose, skin, and anything else deemed appropriate to change or enhance. The famed head of the department, Madame Lou, was stunned at her perfectly symmetrical face, exotic and stunning green eyes, and flawless skin. Her teeth were also perfect, as were her profile and hairline.

"Not much to do with you, Frenchy. You're going to put us all out of a job." She puffed on a cigarette as she looked at her through her black cat-eye glasses and a magnifying glass. "Only thing we need to do is dye that hair of yours red, and you'll take this town by storm."

"Red? They never told me that...." Irene seemed shocked at the idea and looked in the mirror touching her glossy blue-black waves." I'm not sure I want to dye my hair," she said with trepidation.

"It's not up to you, doll. The script calls for a French redhead dancer at the Moulin Rouge who is a noblewoman in disguise and that, my dear, is...you. You'll get used to it. You got to become one with the character if you want to succeed, and the character is a...*redhead*, and with your green eyes, no one will compare." And that was that. She sat back in the chair before the mirror and remembered what Michael had told her: she was no longer Irene—she was now Mirielle, SGM Studios property, and if they wanted a redhead, so be it.

She sat for hours while the chemical process smelled and burned her scalp, but when they spun her around to look in the mirror, she could not believe the transformation. Someone else less mortal, more bombshell was staring back at her.

That week, with her new look as the redheaded French starlet about town, she created a sensation. Bartie Maddox, her publicist, filled her in and gave her the lay of the land over lunch in the commissary with Michael. One was expected to be "seen" dressed to the nines, dancing and mingling at the high society clubs like the Trocadero or Cocoanut Grove, attending industry dinner parties in Beverly Hills and Bel Air, and then be perky and fresh by 6:30 or 7:00 a.m. for hair and makeup on the set. With the news of the German attack, the shooting of *Au Revoir Paris* was rushed into production, and Mirielle's timing, like her father the baron, was impeccable.

It was a rare, lazy Sunday, which saw her taking a much-needed swim under a substantial picture hat that bloomed like a water lily from above at the pool at the Garden of Allah. Bartie had arranged for a hotel room for her to live in temporarily until she found permanent housing, and she loved the general atmosphere and eclectic collection of artists, writers, and directors, who all rubbed shoulders in the rarefied enclave when they ventured east to west. There were many German and Polish émigrés, but despite their questioning her, she stuck to her script. No one bothered to press it as everyone, it seemed, had a new name, a new nose, or a new career, and the Garden had the air of an exclusive and urbane private club. Michael and the leading "woman's" director, George Cukor, had ordered her not to gain weight or get tan. Taking her orders seriously, she swam slowly under the broad-shaded brim, which cast an umbrella-like shadow over her, and the large saucer-esque dark sunglasses also gave her a movie-star look. Mick admired the cinematic, aquatic sight with pride as he saw other sunbathers lift their sunglasses to get a better glimpse of the enchanting vision of the striking nymph swimming by. McDonough sat at the opposite end of the pool in his navy swim trunks looking pale but fit with his Irish complexion, talking to Bartie, who had been devising a public relations plan for Mirielle's launch. She had come to truly like and respect Bartie, and she and Michael double dated with him and Carroll a few times, whom she thought was fun and amusing. Bartie continued to date Carroll on a casual basis as he really liked her, but he rationalized that, to an extent, it was part of his job, and anything close to real intimacy made him totally uncomfortable, as it did for her. He ran from it always, as did she.

"*C'est divin*!" Irene swam up to the shallow end and emerged like a beautiful mermaid, her stunning and elegant figure highlighted by a lavender one-piece bathing suit, which set off her slightly slanted, sultry, and hypnotic jadeite eyes and soon to be exquisite world-famous profile.

"Oh, Michael. I forgot to tell you. I am so very happy." She smiled brightly as she toweled off, the entire row of lounge chairs peering at her over lifted sunglasses.

"With me?" he laughed. "You're welcome." He and Bartie laughed out loud.

"That too. It's just I had wonderful news today. My best girlfriend is coming to Los Angeles to stay, and she booked a bungalow at the Beverly Hills Hotel, so I shall be rooming with her when she arrives."

"The Beverly Hills Hotel? Why, she must be very fancy. Who, pray tell, is it?"

"You may have heard of her, Grace Greystone, La Marquise de La Faucigny." She laughed merrily.

"Really—I thought you told me she was in London?" Michael looked slightly confused.

"Grace Greystone, *the heiress*, is your best friend?" Bartie looked somewhat shocked at the news, but not totally surprised. He thought back to the newspaper story about her custody trial in the press when he was just a kid.

"Why yes, we met in Switzerland and were roommates in Paris. She is the most wonderful person, and I owe her everything for arranging to help me leave France."

"That's great news, Mirielle." Michael was conflicted at the news of having to possibly share her.

"Well, it's actually tragic. She was pregnant and lost the baby, so now she has decided to come back stateside, and I convinced her to come to Los Angeles. She needs to recuperate after her divorce from the marquis who turned out to be…how do you say in American, *le stinker*?" Mirielle touched up her face in her compact, pursed her luscious lips, and struck a pose with her perfect upturned nose, the siren song of female beauty. "I think we need to find her someone."

"That's like winning the lottery." Michael laughed as Mirielle playfully smacked him.

"Do you think she would like yours truly?" Bartie joked, drinking a beer, pointing to himself as he sat at the edge of the pool and flexed.

"Bartie, you're dating Carroll, and she's adorable."

"It's not serious, and we're not dating each other exclusively."

"Regardless, we've double dated, and I could never do that to another girl. We'll have to find her someone else. Grace is very lovely and also fragile, and I am sure she will say she is not ready."

"That's what you said when I met you," Michael laughed. "So now we will have to rendezvous at the Beverly Hills Hotel. Very posh."

"I think I see 'a story' in it, if you don't mind," Bartie stated with a bit of a hand gesture.

"I will have to ask Grace as she's terribly sensitive about the press. I am not sure how she would feel."

"What does she think of your new career?" Bartie asked.

"She is absolutely thrilled for me. She loves my new name and knows I always wanted to be an actress, although I am not so sure what she will say about my red hair when she sees me."

"You're magnificent," Michael said firmly.

"You don't think she wants to be an actress as well?"

"Oh, no, Grace has never had any desire to be in the public eye. It's actually quite the opposite. She tries to avoid scandal, although it seems to follow her."

"I see." He let it all sink in.

"Bartie, I see the wheels turning." Michael smiled. "You're onto something, aren't you?"

"Well, let's just say if it's not me…I *think* I have the perfect guy for her." He looked over after Mirielle toweled off, and he smiled brightly. He innately knew Grace Greystone was above his own paygrade and offered, "And if la marquise likes him, it could be a fabulous match."

"Who is it?"

"I can't say yet, but when does she arrive, Mirielle?"

"In two weeks. I'm so excited as I haven't met many women here I like, except for the writers like Dotty Parker, who have any substance at all."

Bartie smiled to himself. It was perfect. It was as if the news about Grace Greystone was Heaven-sent, and it could be the solution to all his and Myers's problems. While he wasn't going to share his idea yet, he thought perhaps, with the release of the smash movie, *The British Cad*, there was possibly a match at hand.

After all, there was a handsome, single Duke in town who had just moved into a castle and needed a duchess. And perhaps the well-known heiress would be as interested in a Duke as she was in a marquise—a match made in Hollywood royalty. Of course, it would only be possible if Grace Greystone was not looking for true romance, if she needed to restore herself emotionally—as well as her reputation and image—which Bartie knew had been tarnished by the European press. So, in fact, Duke could be a *temporary* solution to *her* problems as well.

He smiled and sipped his martini by the pool. Which had a higher ranking? A duke or a marquis? He would have to find out.

Chapter Forty

Bartie Maddox
West Hollywood
1940

The sun was his alarm clock, and it went off at exactly the same time each morning as the radiant beams broke through the flimsy curtains and shone directly in his eye, startling him awake. Then, after groaning and pulling up the covers for one last bit of sleep, he arose to a hard-working cup of black coffee and a cool shower as the hot water system was often on the blink. On the way to his car, there was a message resting in his cubby hole at the front desk that Myers wanted to see him and pronto, that it was important, which always created a pit in his stomach when he saw the pink slip in his inbox.

Bartie never knew what to expect when summoned by Edna to Myers's inner sanctum. Would he be seeing the happy, generous, and sparkling Myers? The irate and irrational Myers? Or the vindictive and aggressive Myers? Today would be a Myers he had never encountered or seen before.

Bartie arrived with such haste he was tucking the tail of his shirt into his slacks as he made his way through what seemingly was the "mile-long walk of intimidation" to the famous white oval deco desk.

"Take a seat," Solomon Myers indicated in a low, dismal voice, his hand-painted silk necktie of palm trees pried slightly sideways, like a noose. Would the subject be his friend Amelia Earhart's famed disappearance in the Pacific, or the Nazi invasion of Paris, which was on everyone's minds? Or Duke Drake's number-three film at the box office? None of these, however, would be on the menu that morning.

"Bartie." He had rare bloodshot eyes. "Can I trust you?" He looked like he hadn't slept in days. "I'm a bit *fatootsed.*"

"I'm sorry?"

"Don'tcha know English? Fatootsed…disoriented!"

"I see."

"Can I trust ya?"

"Of course, Mister Myers."

"No, *really* trust you, with…top *secrets.*" He stood and paced.

"I am fully committed to you and SGM Studios." Bartie sat up at attention. "I am a vault. I hope you know that, Mister Myers. You took a chance on me when no one else would, and I am eternally grateful. Again, I hope you know that," he repeated.

"Good. Bartie, you have done a good job, and I think I have been generous, no?" He opened his hands as if rain was falling and he was catching imaginary drops.

"Yes, Mister Myers, you have been incredibly generous to me, which I greatly appreciate." He slicked back the pomade in his light brown hair, trying to tame his Midwestern cowlick.

"Good. It goes both ways, Bartie. What I am about to tell you is…" He struggled to find the words. "Whadda they call it, privileged information, ya understand?"

"Yes, of course. I promise." Bartie looked nervous.

"Good."

"What is it, Mister Myers? Is it something I did?" He looked concerned.

"No, not you, *dummkopf*…one of our stars." He nervously lit up a Chesterfield and tried to light the gold lighter, which wouldn't take. "Look, here's the situation." The flame finally emerged as if to confirm that nothing and no one disobeyed Myers—not even the flame. "I am not sure how to say this…there is this girl and…well, she turned up…" he paused in a grave tone, "…*dead.*"

"Dead?" Bartie's eyes opened wide. "Is this a script for a new movie?"

"I wish," Myers exhaled. "I got a call, and it seems there was this whore, and well, Sterling Dumont had rough sex with her at Maude's and...well, she ended up in the hospital. You know these damn cunts. They want it, and they ask for rough sex, and Dumont gave it to her, and well, she was in the hospital and died. We need a fix on this one, Bartie. I need you to help me and the studio. Sterling's new movie is out next month, and it would cost the studio a fortune if there was a scandal."

"I see." Bartie looked down and felt a wave of nausea rise over him.

"Any ideas? Your best ideas are off-the-cuff." Myers lit up another Chesterfield as the room started spinning for Bartie.

"I went to Maude's with Dumont one night..." Bartie said softly.

"Yeah, I know. With Dumont and the boys."

"Well, um...was it...um, the girl, well...who used to work here and used to play Harlow there?"

"Work *here?* We don't have whores working here." He paused. "Well, I mean actresses run around and all, but," he became increasingly flustered, "you know what the fuck I mean." Myers puffed furiously.

"The girl worked for Menowitz. Her real name was Mavis, so I got to know her, and she was a good egg and showed me the ropes here."

"I bet she did."

"Not only that way, Mister Myers, but she was a nice person. When she started working at Maude's, I know Mister Dumont had a thing for her, and she was scared of him—she told me so, herself." He shook his head at the news.

"Look, Mavis or Harlow or Cleopatra for that matter, was a low-down whore...who *asked for it.* Dumont told me so himself. She liked it rough! It was her kink, and he just didn't know his own strength. Look, let's just figure this out. We need a plan, and I know you are quick on your feet," he bellowed.

"Yes, Mister Myers, of course." Bartie looked at him, and the room seemed to spin. "I just need some time to think on this one."

"What, your ideas dried up when I need 'em most?"

"This one is serious. I need some time."

"Okay, Einstein, meet me here tomorrow at 8:30. I'm running into a production meeting the whole day for the next ten slate of films, but we'll figure out a plan. I know you can do it, and remember: loose lips sink ships."

"Yes, of course, Mister Myers." He walked out of the office with his head down, trying to avoid Edna's questioning gaze.

Bartie went home and spent the day and night as if in a trance. He lifted and looked at the solitary bottle of whiskey on top of the icebox and evaluated it. The last time he had a shot alone was on the anniversary of his mother's death, and he missed her so much and toasted her again and again until he fell into bed stone-cold drunk. Now, he poured shot after shot and finished half the bottle without thinking. He tried calling Mick for advice to no avail as he must have been working late at the studio. Soon, he felt queasy on an empty stomach and, like the last time, fell into bed with his clothes on, sleeping fitfully. The dreams about Mavis were vivid and so real as to be entirely disconcerting. Dreams, nightmares of his mother and the fat man he discovered on top of her, strangling her, and her with Mavis's face, and he woke up, bolting upright in bed in a cold sweat.

At six in the morning, Bartie rolled out of bed, and without showering or shaving, threw on the clothes he had been wearing the night before and went directly to see Myers. He knew exactly what he needed to do and felt as if he had compressed twenty-four hours into one hour—a claustrophobic one at that. He arrived at 7:00, but Myers was in even before Edna. His door was open, and Bartie peeked his head in.

"Well, *look* at what the cat dragged in." Myers took a puff on his omnipresent cigarette, dangling from his mouth as if it were somehow attached to his lip with glue as he saw Bartie sheepishly walk the "walk of intimidation." He looked him over and saw the rumpled state, which he had never encountered before.

"Whaddya do, go to Maude's again and bang a few more whores as homework?" he snarled. "You seem to like it there."

"No, Mister Myers. I went home and I slept on it."

"Any good ideas?"

"Yes, Mister Myers. I have a very good idea of what I am going to recommend."

"What is this, a guessing game? Out with it already, ya louse." He banged the desk, his sapphire-and-platinum cabochon pinkie ring with diamond baguettes slamming into the vanilla wood veneer.

"Mister Myers, I gave it a great deal of thought and…I'm…I'm going to need to hand in my…" he paused, "resignation." He looked down.

"What? You call that an *idea*? I call that suicide," he yelled. "What's the matter with you? This is a *goy* joke, correct? Like April Fools' or Easter?"

Bartie took a deep breath. "No, it's not. First, I want to say, I actually like Sterling Dumont when he's *sober,* which is a rarity."

"Yeah, well he's a guy's guy. And let me remind you…number two at the box office 1930 through '33."

"And he's a mean drunk…which is about every night. He's also a wife beater and strangles hookers."

"Ah…so, you wanna get…technical?"

Bartie placed a manila file on Myers's desk.

"I don't keep detailed files on all the studio fixes, but Menowitz obviously thought it was a fine idea." Bartie gathered strength he didn't know he had.

"Leave it to that friggin' moron!" Myers fumed, fingering the file.

"Mister Myers, are you aware that according to these files, SGM has had over seven lawsuits because of Dumont that had to be covered up and paid off, including one girl's family who claimed she also died at his hands?" He looked down and breathed deeply. "I…I cannot cover up my *friend* Mavis Robert's death. I won't. He's sick, and he will continue to do this when he is drunk, and you and I will have blood on our hands." He looked over and pleaded. "Mister Myers, you have a wife and daughters."

"Don't you dare compare my wife and daughters to a…*whoooooore*." He drew the word out like an unraveling kite string.

"I'm not, but Mavis Roberts was somebody's daughter too." He paused. "Do you know we send a studio makeup artist over to Hancock Park every week to touch up Missus Dumont because of the bruises?"

"Yeah, well, I'll have you know Mable Dumont is a *has-been alchy*… who's just about banged everyone on the lot when she was a star, and she's livin' in luxury. Why, I had her bent over my desk a month before she married Dumont, beggin' for it, like the whore she is." He shook his head.

"Sterling Dumont is a monster when he's drunk, and if we cover it up, he's going to do it again and again. I want no part of it, and I want justice for my friend." Bartie stood his ground.

"You're soft, Maddox—weak." Myers paced and belted out the words. "You don't have what it takes. I thought you did." He stroked his bald head with exasperation.

"Maybe I am." Bartie shrugged. "Mister Myers, can I say something?"

"You already did, ya *pisher*." He shook his head again in disdain.

"I look up to you—we all do—but you're *better* than this. The studio is. Look at Fatty Arbuckle. Paramount survived his rape scandal and trials, and I am telling you, it will enhance the SGM's image. You must go to the police."

"And say what?"

"Tell them the news and let them run with this. I promise you, it will be good for the studio in the end and a testament to what kind of man you are. This isn't you, Mister Myers! Dumont is a serial murderer who needs to be arrested and brought to justice."

Solomon Myers was taken aback and sat back in his throne-like chair, letting it all seep in while the phone and intercom buzzed. He sat and said nothing for a full minute, which, for Solly Myers, was eternity. Then he spoke.

"You know what, Maddox. I'm confused. When did you become a priest or a rabbi? It's aggravatin'." He gave a long pause. "But you know…you speak like a true *mensch*. You know what that is? A good person, a person of integrity and honor. Look, I will give it some thought, and I will give you my decision tomorrow, but for sure I do not want you leaving SGM."

"I won't stay if we cover up murder. I even went down to enlist, but they won't take me because of my eyesight."

"Enough playin' the hero!" Myers groused. "What about if I get someone else to do it? We can have someone else handle it?"

Bartie shook his head at the audacity of the request.

"Even more so." He looked down.

"I see." Myers sighed deeply and sat down like he had been crushed. "Let me sleep on it." He looked nervous and added, "But I'll tell ya one thing, Maddox. You—you're not going *anywhere. Ya hear me?*" He yelled at the top of his lungs. "Edna!"

Chapter Forty-One

La Marquise de La Faucigny
Los Angeles
1941

January 20 saw President Franklin Roosevelt being sworn in for a third term; Myers reluctantly agreeing to Bartie's demands about Dumont; and Grace Greystone arriving and upgrading her suite to Bungalow Number Four, Howard Hughes's accommodation of choice at the Beverly Hills Hotel. Since her much heralded arrival on the West Coast, it was clear Grace Greystone, La Marquise de La Faucigny needed more room for the vast array of Louis Vuitton steamer trunks, myriad hat boxes, and infinite collection of hand luggage and jewel cases. This fact, of course, was noted by Hedda Hopper in her popular column and radio show after a lovely and timely lunch at swish Perino's with Bartie and Mirielle, her new young acquaintances. Grace was not on the main menu just yet.

At the behest of Myers, who had thought of this particular introduction once he saw Mirielle walk off the liner, Edna had set up a lunch with the press doyenne for SGM's youthful publicity head, Barston Maddox, and their newest star, Mirielle Montaigne. Bartie nervously confessed to Edna he didn't think he was ready for Hedda on his own. She smiled and soothed his fears.

"You'll do just fine. You're smart and also all-American, not to mention very handsome," she stated and then added, "She will appreciate you, Bartie. You're a different sort in this town." She nodded to him without being overtly explicit. "And don't forget Mirielle will be with you."

Bartie was a bit shy about his new expense account but took his cues from Edna, who also assured him that being able to handle Hedda would enhance his position and elevate his status at the studio.

"Mister Myers hates to have to wine and dine the press dragons." Edna looked at him with her steely eyes. "Having a direct line to the press is a big part of your job, but I don't have to tell you that," Edna explained in a motherly fashion.

As Edna and Myers suspected, Hedda was indeed happy to have a young, handsome, and attentive Midwestern studio executive to interface with after all the "Lower East Side peddlers" she always griped about having to deal with. It was also apparent she was immediately taken with the gorgeous and chic Mirielle Montaigne when she arrived at Perino's in a Paris hat and Lucien Lelong couture creation. When Hedda took in the refinement and education—not to mention the glittering array of Cartier and Van Cleef jewels—it was not hard to detect the young star was indeed the genuine article. Mirielle was smart enough to have emptied much of her jewel box onto her person, which she had festooned in a chic yet opulent way. When she casually puffed on her onyx-and-pave diamond cigarette holder and turned to exhale, accenting her newly dyed luxurious red waves, green eyes, and exquisite upturned nose, the otherwise bejeweled Hedda was wide-eyed and truly in awe at the sixteen-carat emerald-and-diamond ring and diamond earrings. She had never seen a symbol of such excess, luxury, and French chic. When Mirielle plucked her engraved Cartier lighter from her woven 14K-gold Van Cleef minaudiere, Hedda swooned. She was wearing a fortune and hadn't even done one movie yet. And when Hedda found she was staying at the Beverly Hills Hotel with her best friend, none other than Grace Greystone, the heiress and Marquise de La Faucigny who had recently arrived in LA, Hedda Hopper went into a virtual social frenzy. *Myers had been right*, she marveled. Mirielle Montaigne was indeed the genuine article; filet mignon after having been served so much chopped meat for so long by shady studio executives. She had also been kept abreast about Grace's arrival in the *Times* and was eager to hear all on the subject.

"But we must all do a girl's lunch, Mirielle. We have so many friends in common." Hedda salivated at the thought of dining with her new, chic French friend and getting her claws into the titled heiress and rubbing everyone's noses in it, especially her nemesis, Louella Parsons, whom she felt couldn't pass muster with chic creatures like Mirielle or Grace.

"*Mais, bien sur,* I am sure Grace would love to meet when she is settled," Mirielle said in her French-tinged accent, which she laid on a bit thicker than usual. "I do want to mention in advance that Grace is actually press adverse. It stems from the early days and her youthful custody trial," She confided, exhaling petite and well-groomed, ghostly blue-white smoke rings.

"Well, of course. It was the custody trial of the century. Well, that's a novelty in this town. *Finally*, a woman who wants to stay *out* of the press and not get in it!" Hedda laughed, trying to navigate Chasen's famous chili in an elegant fashion with her fork and pinky raised. "When did she arrive?" she asked.

"She traveled to Galway from London and, of course, had passage on one of the last McClean ships out. She's had a very tough time, you know, having unfortunately divorced recently. I think Los Angeles will do her a world of good."

"That's quite awful." Hedda shook her head with reverence at the news. "Poor dear, I can't imagine what she has been through, with The Blitz and all."

***

Grace had indeed arrived in Los Angeles with a star's fanfare. She was met at the Super Chief by Mirielle, Michael, and Bartie with press in tow, in an emotional embrace. As a titled American ex-pat heiress returning stateside, Grace received more than her fair share of publicity and interest from the American public who knew and were fascinated by her ongoing trials, tribulations, and marriages. When she stepped out of the train into the dazzling California sunlight, the newly-christened Mirielle ran toward her, and in a press bonanza, Grace fell into Irene's arms, overcome at being reunited with her best friend given her recent losses.

After being introduced to Michael and Bartie, the young press man wisely turned and asked the cadre of photographers to hold their photos until the two women had a chance to reconnect, and Grace and Mirielle had an opportunity to reapply their makeup. It was a keen move from an intuitive professional. It was also immediately clear to Grace, and unspoken, that the handsome studio producer named Michael attending both women was her friend's lover. Grace immediately thought he was charming and handsome.

"Now, he is, as my aunt's friend Maybelle Carson used to say 'a tall, handsome drink of water,'" Grace whispered in a smile after the initial tears had dried, before hooking arms with Mirielle.

After her tumultuous departure and checking into the Grand Dame of LA hotels, Grace's first days in Beverly Hills were marked by lazy days at the already iconic pool, recuperating from her divorce and the choppy crossing from Europe. Unlike Mirielle, she loved the sun and wasn't under contract or studio orders to shield herself from the rays. She had two chaises set up, one in the sun and one for Mirielle, protected under the deep shade of the striped, green-and-white umbrellas.

"Irene, I adore your hair," Grace said; she would continually call her Irene in private, the way Lauren Bacall was called Betty by her close friends.

"Do you really like it? I prefer my original color."

"No, darling. Irene, the *sirene*." She laughed and turned an attentive eye toward her. "It *is* going to take me some time to recognize you across a room, though," she laughed.

"Well, if you say so. How do you like Los Angeles so far?"

"It's quite the tonic. I just adore the sunshine and the palm trees, especially after the dampness of London." Grace sighed as she puffed on a platinum cigarette holder. "I am so very happy for you, *Mirielle*," she teased. "It's your dream come true as well. I think after Fritz, your father would have approved." She shook her lovely soft waves and attended to her skin with a pearlized white suntan crème.

"I hope." Mirielle smiled. "This Friday, I want you to come with me to the premiere of *Mr. and Mr. Smith* and to meet some of my new Hollywood friends. Carole Lombard is such a dear—so lovely and funny, and she has been so kind to me," she confided.

"You know Carole Lombard?" Grace's eyes lit up as if she were reading a movie magazine.

"Yes, of course. She has gotten great reviews as one of the best actresses and comedians. They call her films out here 'screwball comedies,'" she offered. "She's also very down to earth. I want to thank you, Grace. If it wasn't for you, none of this would have happened."

"I'm not so sure. Just look at you and that face of yours. It was inevitable."

"You are too sweet, but Grace, enough about me. How are *you* feeling?" Mirielle asked softly, not wanting to avoid the subject entirely, but not wanting to bring up the divorce and Louis's affair.

She sipped an opalescent martini and chose her words carefully as she stirred it, tapping the olives.

"It was awful, just terrible, Irene." Grace turned her lovely eyes wounded in pain toward her friend. "I feel very betrayed...." Tears suddenly fell in large, copious drops.

"I am so sorry, Grace," Mirielle reached over and caressed her hand. "There's nothing anyone can say." She took hold of her hand and teared up as well. "I am just glad you're here with me."

"Oh, I just *adore* the sunshine." Grace tried to put on a good face. "It's so...I don't know. It has a healing quality and reminds me of our time at Breiner's. Remember those white starched smocks they made us wear out by the lake?" She chuckled at the thought.

"And the raw food—quite something," Mirielle reminisced.

"By the way, I want you to know I like your Michael. He strangely reminds me of your father."

"You think so? I never thought of that, but come to think of it, they do have similar ways of approaching life. Do you really like him, Grace? It means so much to me."

"Yes, he's perfect for you."

"I just feel so guilty about Fritz. I don't know if he's dead or alive. I have nightmares of him being taken away from the palais. It's terrible. Princess Bonaparte is trying to help get any information for me on his whereabouts in that horrible camp. I have heard the most terrible things. She said not to be hopeful given what she heard. It's a dark cloud over my head."

"That's exactly how I feel."

"I know, darling." Mirielle squeezed her hand.

"And Michael?"

"He is married as well. They're Catholic, and the wife won't consider a divorce."

"You see, you're a perfectly matched set." Grace blew smoke rings. "Look, given the war in Europe and what is going on, you know my philosophy has changed. I used to believe in fairytales, and now I know it's all a sham. If you find love, Irene, I think you should grab it like the brass ring and enjoy the ride."

"You think so?"

"I know so."

"Then the same goes for you, *cherie*. Once you're feeling up to it, we'll go to a few premieres, parties—nothing serious, just fun for now." She reached inside her pocketbook. "I have a present for you too!" Mirielle took an elegantly-wrapped present out of a small, tailored shopping bag. The gift box was slim, long, and made of rich velvet.

"Present? Why, that's not necessary." Grace seemed surprised.

"If it wasn't for you, I wouldn't be here."

"And neither would I." Grace smiled.

"Just open it please, *cherie*." Mirielle's gorgeous eyes pleaded.

Grace looked down and smiled like a little girl as she opened the navy, velvet jewelry box. It was from the famed Beverly Hills jeweler to the stars, Paul Flato. She opened it and gasped. It was a stunning platinum-and-diamond ribbon bracelet set with large cabochon emeralds and diamonds in a repeating, geometric pattern.

"Oh, Irene, it's just *divine*. Just look at it!" She held it up to the sunlight as its rays cast a prism-like effect. "You really should not have!" Grace scolded her softly.

"This is just an advanced gift until I have enough to get you the other emerald bracelet you sold for my visa. I promise when I earn enough money or get back my inheritance, it will be the very first thing I do. For now, this is from my first few paychecks at SGM," she said proudly. "I'm earning a real living."

"Darling, you're just getting settled. I cannot believe this. That said, it's gorgeous, beautiful, and I adore it!" She fastened the bracelet on her wrist. "Oh, Irene, it's just stunning." She reached up, kissed, and thanked her.

"I hope and wish you will enjoy LA and meet someone fabulous here. I am so sorry for everything. It seems Louis wasn't what we all thought he was," Irene said quietly. "And worse!"

"I am just glad to be rid of him." She shook her head. "And Irene, I never told you, but he actually tried to have me get you to sign over the vineyard as 'protection,' the way Chanel tried to outmaneuver the Wertheimers." She scowled at the thought of someone trying to take advantage of their Jewish partners due to the horrifying racial laws.

"Really? Well, that's not surprising. I could tell he was overly interested in my Swiss bank accounts."

"And Ghislaine Garrieux—they're now engaged."

"I am so glad you listened to Uncle Reggie." Mirielle paused. "You will find love, I promise."

Perhaps it was the discussion about Louis and adjusting to a strange city, but a wave of emotion swept over Grace. The torrents of tears finally came as her best friend reached over and comforted her. The pool boy adjusted the umbrella and brought fresh towels.

"I promise you will be happy here, Grace. Maybe not now, but one day, you will."

"Well, it is quite clear what they say is true."

"What, *ma cherie*?"

"Money can't buy you happiness, but sunshine and martinis are quite the tonic."

Chapter Forty-Two

Duke Drake
Culver City, Los Angeles
1941

Bartie picked up the morning papers on his way to work and shook his head proudly at the blaring headlines that were front-page news and not only in Hedda and Louella's columns: "Sterling Dumont Held for Manslaughter," and "Dumont's Distress. Actor charged with Manslaughter of actress and Party Girl," and "Mabel Dumont's Daily Torture and Torment," splashed across all major outlets. The town was rife with rumors, and even his wife, Mabel, had publicly turned against her abusive husband with a divorce as they led him away in handcuffs. Bartie had also organized her public relations by leaking a photo of the former silent star with a blackened eye and the headline, "Mabel's Murderous Madman."

Sterling Dumont's arrest was one of the town's biggest scandals to date, but a nail-biting Myers was a nervous wreck and impossible to deal with until he started to receive sympathetic calls from other studio heads congratulating him on doing the right thing—and only then started to embrace and then flaunt the arrest, strutting like a peacock. Once the arrest was made and Sterling was taken away in handcuffs, Dumont became persona non grata, and his films were shelved and pulled from distribution into film vaults. Myers and the studio were in the hole for a few million but now also saw a financial benefit in backing Mabel as a way to retrieve some of her soon-to-be-ex-husband's lost revenue, and an exploitation film called *Save Me* about a silent film star who marries a murderer and keeps her prisoner, locked up in a Sunset Boulevard mansion, would eventually earn her a best actress nomination. Bartie was called in to deal with her and, at first, he had felt sympathy for Mabel, but it quickly turned to a problem when Bartie went to see her in her Hancock Park hacienda. In her day, Mabel had been a vivacious young star who was known for her golden brown curls and pouting cupid lips and dubbed "the curl girl." Years of alcohol abuse and living with Sterling Dumont had ravaged her curls, looks, and body, and the studio was soon to pay for a facelift for her next role.

"You see this?" She opened her silk robe and showed Bartie the bruises on her back and legs. "He tried to kill me. You and Myers *saved* me! She threw her arms around Bartie in a drunken cloud. "You're young and handsome." She dropped her robe and tried to pull him on the couch, her breasts sagging, and her hot breath at his neck. "Come on, give it to Mabel. I wanna thank you, and she needs it," she said in a raw, guttural tone.

"I'm sorry, Missus Dumont." Bartie blushed and stammered. "I can't. I could get fired for this," he said, pulling away from her with distaste.

"Nobody ever turned Mabel Dumont down." She looked up in surprise. "*Nobody...because you're a nobody*!" she screamed at the top of her lungs. She took a heavy glass ashtray and threw it at his head. "Get out, you motherfucker. You won't fuck me, then *fuck you! Get out! I never want to see your fag face again.*" Bartie fled the house, and in the next few days, would communicate with her through Edna. When Myers berated him on the subject, Bartie demurred.

"I didn't think it was professional," he stated, eyes downward.

"Professional, fer Chrissakes. A hole's a hole, you dumbass. Why couldn't ya have bent ole Mabel over and given her one for *Ole Glory.* What, are you now turning into some kind of...fag?"

"No, sir, I was trying to protect the studio."

"Your problem is you're spending too much time at Maude's with tight pussy. Yer just *sperld*," Myers ranted.

"*Sperld*?"

"*Sperld*. Like a *child*."

"Oh, spoiled."

"That's what I said, ya dumb fuck. Don'tcha know English!" he quipped as he walked out of his office and slammed the door.

***

With Sterling Dumont now banished forever and then hanging himself in his jail cell two days later, it had been a tough week at SGM—and it was about to get even more so. It was a Monday morning, and Myers's creamy mood turned sour like two-week-old milk when Duke casually walked in to their scheduled catch-up meeting in a new tailored suit with a new agent in tow, the natty Charles Feldman. Duke had wisely not said a word that he would be bringing a guest and certainly not a new agent—the most powerful in the business. After moving into his castle, the resulting press Bartie had set up, and with the release of the smash hit *The British Cad*, Duke's fan mail had immediately jumped from 500 to 1,000 to 4,000, and then to almost 9,000 a week, not beating Valentino's 10,000-a-week haul, but close. With his handsome face appearing on the covers of *Motion Picture* and *Photoplay*, Duke Drake and his aqua-blue eyes and distinctive cleft were everywhere, and his on-screen magic, effortless sense of humor, and continental elan made him a bona fide superstar, not to mention he had an empty castle, and women across America dreamed of moving into the ultimate fantasy. Myers, of course, wisely knew that with success would also come the never-ending demands from agents and managers, not to mention the stars themselves as it wasn't his first trip to the rodeo. Duke Drake fan clubs were popping up all over the US with scheduled appearances, and Duke sent his male fans advice on how to dress with English panache.

In fact, Bartie now commandeered a small office and two secretaries on the lot to handle the avalanche of Duke's recent explosion of fan mail. Feldman, however, was on a different level; an industry insider who knew the ropes was now advising him.

"I'm going to kill that cock-sucking fucker Gorge Lamont," Myers griped the moment he saw him, knowing he had advised his boyfriend.

"Feldman!" Myers bellowed. "Wasn't expecting *you* first thing. I didn't think your damn ass was up before ten!" He glowered and shot a stern look at Bartie, who had immediately been summoned to his office to attend the meeting. Charles Feldman was known as one of the toughest and smartest agent handlers in town, and Myers was loath to admit he was impressed that Duke had fired the sketchy Virgil Lindstrom and hired Feldman, and it was going to cost him now for sure. They stood up and shook hands with both Duke and the suave, legendary agent.

"How're Freyda and the girls?" Feldman switched on his famous charm.

"Fine, and Jean?" Myers asked after his wife, the former actress and silent film star, Jean Howard.

"Wonderful."

"Send her my best. She's still one of the great beauties, and class!" Myers raised an eyebrow. "So, when did you start representing the Duke of Drake?" Myers scowled, surveying Feldman's hundred-dollar Savile Row suit, silk tie, and handmade shoes.

"I have been talking to Duke since you took interest in him, and now that his career has taken off, he's signed with me. And with the release of his new hit film, we want to talk turkey." Charles Feldman pumped Myers's hand, and his eyes sparkled.

"*His* release...puh...lease! We made him a star. *I* did. SGM and Myers...and don't you both forget it," Myers protested. "You know, Feldman, you agents are all the same. The studio creates the stars, and then when they become famous, you guys get hired, and *we* get shafted." Myers lit up a cigar and sat back in his chair as the two men took to the armchairs.

"I see it somewhat differently, Solly." Feldman lit a cigarette by cupping his hand and handed the other to Duke in a conspiratorial fashion.

"The man upstairs created that face." He pointed to Duke. "Not you—you're just showing it off to the public. Duke Drake would be a star at any studio, and you know it. You just were smart enough to sign him first. That's *your* talent, Myers. You're a star *maker*...because you're a star *picker*! And best of all, you get there first!"

"Okay, okay." He broke into a grin. "At least you understand what I do. You see, Bartie," Myers said, smiling brightly, "that's why Feldman here is one of the best agents—'cause he *gets it.* He gets what we do, what I do, to get there *foist*. Not like some of these *schmoes*, and it ain't just his pretty face. Why, when Feldman first moved to LA, Bartie..." He looked over and reminisced. "I'll have you know I offered him a movie contract. I wanted to change his name to something like Van Stephens, but he didn't take the bait. He's not as handsome as Gable, but close."

Charles Feldman smiled at the compliment. He knew he was noted as one of the most handsome and debonair men in Hollywood with his distinguished looks and snappy pencil mustache, but Charles Feldman liked two things more than fame, money and beautiful women. Why not be on the other side of the camera without a morals clause? And as the agent who was noted for creating the "package deal," Feldman was also known for raking it in—for his clients *and* himself.

"Sorry to hear the news about Sterling. I dropped him as a client a few years back when he beat up a starlet I was handling. Virginia Hoff. I give you credit, Solly, brave move on your part." He took a sip of water, belching slightly.

"Thank you." Myers stood up a bit taller at the compliment. "SGM is a family company. If he did it, he deserved the electric chair. That's what I say," he said, proudly puffing his chest out. "We already lost a helluva lot of money on his last picture. I shelved it, but that's life. The poor *goil* was somebody's daughter too. Ain't that right, Bartie?" He winked.

"Yes, Mister Myers." He nodded.

"Well, just be glad *The British Cad* is number two and going to be number one any day now, so you can recoup some of those losses," Feldman pointed out.

"Yeah, yeah, but we also overspent on that picture, so this one over here could be a star and parade around town with his Rolls and all. So, whadda you lookin' fer, a raise?" Myers coughed. "I'll have you know he already got one. Duke went from five-hundred a week to fifteen-hundred. Plus, I got him a Rolls-Royce and a chauffeur and the down payment on his castle in Bel Air. In fact, I would say he's already rolling in it! Don't be a *schnorrer*."

"I think we should be smart about this, Solly. You know he deserves four-thousand a week...but we are willing to build his career with you and settle at twenty-five hundred."

"Why that's highway robbery!" He turned beet red. "Nobody gets that."

"He will after he completes his next few pictures."

Solly Myers sat back, thought about it, and surveyed the room. Then, he took control.

"Ya know. I say twenty-two-fifty, and it's a deal." He paused. "But contingent." He smiled, the points of his incisors showing.

"Contingent? On what?" Charles Feldman knew it wasn't going to be this easy.

"No problems with the vice squad, and no more visits to Pansy Hall on the weekends." He folded his hands on his desk as he dropped the bombshell.

"What are you talking about?" Feldman played dumb.

"What I am talking about is we can't pay him that much money if he's corn-holing it with super queer *fagalah* Gorge Lamont in Santa Monica every weekend in full view of the Hollywood brass."

"He lives alone like you requested," Feldman countered.

"Yeah, in a castle we paid fer." He wiped away imaginary perspiration on his forehead.

"And he just goes to the beach on the weekends with his...roommate," Feldman lied through his teeth.

"Roommates, my ass!" he roared. "They are a bunch of *fagalahs*, and you know it. Sorry, Duke, and I love ya, but you're a handsome poof, plain and simple." Duke sat in his chair and blushed.

"We take offense. Duke Drake is all man...why, here," Feldman reached into his briefcase and thrust a sheaf of papers at him. "I have a doctor's report of his latest girlfriend's abortion."

"Ya gotta be kidding me."

"We're not." He shook his head vigorously.

"Okay, okay, I get it. You want Drake here to be treated like a real man with a real raise."

"Something like that." Charles nodded.

"Great, I am happy to hear that our newest star in the SGM firm-a-*ment* loves *pussy.*" He smiled, his caps glistening. "So, I'll sweeten the deal and throw in a year's free trip to Maude's. Bartie will go with him and see what the girls have to say." He smiled like a kid at the thought.

"Sure," Duke nodded nonchalantly.

"Okay, Duke, who's your latest?" Myers looked squarely at him.

"Latest?"

"Yeah…Bartie here wants to PR your latest affair in the press, so who are you bangin'?" He looked him straight in the eye.

"Um…well…" he stuttered and paused. "I'm in between dates."

"Yeah, sure. A handsome stud like you can't find a date? Yeah, and Santa Claus is real. What does your 'roommate' think of this…recent development?"

"Gorge Lamont, haven't you heard? He's engaged to Letitia St. Clair, the sugar heiress," Charles Feldman stated.

"Engaged?" Sol Myers was truly floored. "The damn faggot couldn't keep his mouth off a cock while he worked for me, and *now* he's engaged! Boy, Warner must have really worked him over or offered him a small fortune."

"Word is Gorge Lamont is going to be nominated for an Oscar for *SS Corinthian.*" He paused, letting the news sink in. "We're happy for Gorge and the Oscar buzz, but he was only Duke's roommate."

"Yeah, and I'm Snow White. And if they are just roommates, why is Gorge over every evening for a nightcap and vice versa?"

"They play cards."

"*Cards!*" Myers screamed so loud that Edna came running. "I never heard anything so fuckin' funny." He sat back, now relishing the conversation. "Well, Duke, since now you're a lady-killer, we'll be happy to find you a great girl, won't we Bartie?"

"Yes, Mister Myers."

"So, Bartie here is going to get you someone nice to date, and that's that. Enough of this crap. Bartie, who do we got fer Duke here? I want him fixed up…pronto. And not with some dyke virgin like Smalls." He glowered.

"In fact, I think I may have the perfect person for Duke," Bartie offered off the cuff.

"Great, since now Duke is a lady-killer—aren't you, Duke?"

"For twenty-two-fifty a week, he'll go out with Marie Dressler," Feldman coughed.

"Marie is a saint. She's box office. Remember that, Duke: she is beloved by the fans. It's a good lesson," he said of the matronly and homely character actress. "Anyway, Bartie, we're all ears. Aren't we, Duke?"

"Yessir. Is it Mirielle Montaigne? Now *she's* a real beauty," Charles added, salivating at the thought.

"Actually," Bartie raised himself in the low chair. "One better, since Mirielle is well, as we say, spoken for, but it actually happens to be her best friend. I would have to speak to them both first, of course, and see if they would agree, but it's...." He paused, keeping everyone on the edge of their chairs. "Grace Greystone, La Marquise de la Faucigny. She just moved to LA from Europe, and she's lovely, pretty, funny, and..." He let the facts speak for themselves.

"And rich." Myers actually let out a cool whistle and then added, "Ya see, that's why the Kid here is number one in my book. He's the Thalberg of PR." He walked over and gave a Feldman playful pat on his well-tailored arm.

"Can ya imagine that? Grace fuckin' Greystone! That's who he dreams up for Duke. Well, I want thanks for this one. Over two thousand a week, a Rolls, a castle, and now one of the richest girls in the world. Feldman, I should be getting a piece of that deal."

"Hell, give her to me, and I'll divorce Jean," Feldman laughed, referencing his wife, the gorgeous former star, Jean Howard. "But you're right, Solly. We are very appreciative, aren't we, Duke?"

"Yes, Mister Myers. It all sounds wonderful." He sat fairly mute on the subject. "I would be happy to take out Grace Greystone," he said in a morose tone.

"So, then here's how I see it," Charles Feldman started his classic wrap-up overview. "Since *The British Cad*'s success, I propose that as a new star, Duke Drake deserves twenty-two-fifty a week for the first year, three thousand a week for the second year, and onward. Then five-thousand a week in his seventh year and it will be paid for the fifty-two weeks, not his current forty-one weeks. SGM has the right to exercise an option for the eighth and ninth year at seventy-five hundred a week. I suggest an expense account of two-fifty a week to squire around dates such as Grace Greystone, since he will be hopefully taking out the heiress. Additionally, we request the studio pays for a fencing instructor, his riding lessons at the stables, a Swedish masseuse once a week, and will pick up the cost of all his alterations and suiting. Then we agree to curtail our visits to Gorge Lamont's beach house in Santa Monica. I do want to add, however, that since Gorge Lamont is getting married, and Duke is going to hopefully be dating or engaged at some point, we cannot dictate his social life, and if he wants to play *cards* with his married friends at night in the privacy of their homes in Los Feliz or Bel Air, that is not subject to the deal. And Solly, none of your private investigator henchmen snapping photos at who's playing in their card games."

"Henchmen? Me?" Solly raised an eyebrow and batted his eyes innocently.

"Now, we wouldn't want to break up anyone's card games," Feldman said. "Imagine if I said you couldn't play pinochle with Berle and Jolson at Hillcrest or croquet with Harpo at Hawk's place in Palm Springs. How would you feel?"

"Yeah, yeah. Okay..." he relented.

"So, do we have a deal? Duke?" Feldman's eyes danced.

Duke smiled thoughtfully and shook his head yes.

"Deal." Myers shook Duke and Feldman's hands.

"Thank you, Mister Myers," Duke said. "I'm very excited. I just want to make sure I don't break up..." he paused and shot a discreet but pleading look to Feldman, "my card game."

"You got it." Myers agreed. "But I am holding you to evenings at Maude's. It's important to be seen in *all the right* places."

"Don't worry, Mister Myers," Bartie offered cheerfully. "Duke can come with me."

"If Bartie takes me, I'll go," Duke said like a little boy agreeing to have his friend walk him to school the first day.

"Perfect, Bartie is multi-*poi-pose*. And if you can get Miss Fancy Pants Greystone to go out and be seen with the Duke of Drake, you get a raise too, Maddox." He beamed.

"Thank you, Mister Myers." Bartie smiled.

"Don't thank me—just get my favorite new movie star here fixed up, dating, and married like his friggln' *fatry* pal, Gorge Lamont, whose arse was being plugged in the air in the gas station…so he can get nominated for an Oscar too," he barked.

"I'll have the papers memorialized this week." Feldman twirled the end of his dapper mustache.

"And by the way, make sure Duke goes on the Hollywood Victory Caravan to entertain the troops in between pictures."

"Of course, Solly. He'll be part of the lineup."

"And remember, no entertaining the troops that way! Fa Chrissakess!"

Chapter Forty-Three

Gorge Lamont
Los Angeles
1941

After the Academy nominations were announced, with Gorge in the "Best Actor" category, the negotiations and bartering in town began as they always did like a high-stakes chess game. Hedda immediately arranged a very social private lunch at Perino's with Bartie in her private banquette to begin the dealing. Hedda knew that Bartie had often advised Gorge Lamont for press advice through Duke, and she was as direct as General Patton; she wanted and demanded an exclusive, and she promised Gorge Lamont a huge industry favor in exchange for the Oscar interview if he were to take home the prize for "Best Actor."

"What's the favor, Hedda?" Bartie gave her his broad Midwestern smile.

"I get the interview. In exchange, I'll be 'kind' to his new fiancée in my column." She smiled back and took in his still-glowing cheeks misted with freckles.

"The timing of their nuptials is most interesting, don't you agree, Bartie?" She tippled her martini, taking an extra swig from the chilled glass. "A committed bachelor for most of his adult life and only *now* Gorge Lamont gets engaged with weeks to go before the Academy Awards?" She smiled her frosty, knowing smile. "Jack Warner has a way of putting old Solly Myers to shame," she clucked. "Now *he* gets things done—if you ever want to meet Jack, Bartie?"

"Hedda, you know I am very loyal to Mister Myers."

"You're too good for him," she declared, not as a thought but as a statement of fact.

The lunch was sealed with lush chocolate cake and a kiss from the steely Hedda. That's the way Hollywood press negotiations worked; the deal was that only *she*, not Louella, would have the exclusive Academy interview for her column and radio show, and in return, she would omit mentioning or hinting, in her usual snarky way, that Gorge's wife-to-be, Letitia St. Clair, was known to keep the company of women, or as it was called in LA, the Sewing Circle. In addition, she would not mention that she would be wearing her controversial uniform to their elopement in Vegas: a man's black tuxedo jacket, black trousers, and high heels, and would also be knocking back Jack Daniels and puffing on a Cuban cigar. All which would have alluded to what everyone in the film colony already knew—that Gorge's forty-year-old bride-to-be was rich as Croesus but also a notoriously eccentric "butch dyke." Letitia also resembled the actress Katherine Hepburn so much they were often mistaken for each other, having both attended Bryn Mawr and affected the same accent and mannerisms of the upper-class Connecticut breed.

The match, though, was widely welcomed by studio brass and film publicists alike; in fact, word around town was it was a perfect coupling as, despite her dressing like a man, Letitia had three things Gorge Lamont didn't have. One: a vagina. Two: an acerbic wit. And three: a trust fund. And in return, Gorge had the one thing Letitia craved as a bored, rich, single woman living in LA: *fame*. Having a real connection to the film industry would be the sprinkles on the ice cream cone for the attractive, bored heiress since she didn't possess any apparent talent in writing, directing, producing, or acting.

Despite her sexual proclivities, Gorge's new fiancée knew that whether it was a lavender marriage or not—like Cole Porter's or Charles Laughton's—*her* engraved stationary would soon proclaim the newly-minted *Mrs. Gorge Lamont*, putting her on a different level, socially. And if he won the Oscar? Well, she would now be part of the reigning star system, welcomed at the elite, closed-door dinner parties in Bel Air and Beverly Hills, on the red carpet and ushered to prime seating at the best restaurants and clubs. Having a famous husband would also give her the social stability her conservative Southern family craved for her—and the cover she needed, so she could still sleep with any woman she desired. It was a perfect fix.

"Hedda, I will call Gorge and recommend the exclusive."

"Thank you, Bartie. Oh, I did want to mention something…before we finish," she paused. "Something I…*heard* from a reliable source…." She made friends with the lone olive resting at the bottom of her martini glass.

"And what did you hear, Hedda?" Bartie knew she was going to offer some information that could be traded.

"Well, I know that you have been seen around town with that *peroxide blonde Sweater Girl.*" Her eyes widened as she spoke.

"Carroll Madison. She's just a friend," Bartie blanched and shrugged innocently.

"Friend? I'm not so sure. She's quite attractive, but I want you to know that on good information, I heard that Carroll started her career at Maude's, and there are photos and a stag movie circulating. I thought you should know." She looked in her compact while delivering the news.

"Really, photos? A stag movie?" Bartie couldn't believe his ears.

"Yes, men's calendars, that sort of *sordid* thing." Hedda shrugged.

"Well, thank you, Hedda. I'm glad you told me."

"On a personal note, I wouldn't want you falling for a girl like that, Bartie. You're too special."

"That's kind of you, Hedda. I promise you we're just…casual friends."

"I hear she has *a lot* of friends." Hedda raised a well-plucked eyebrow.

"I'm under no illusions."

"Good, so I will kill the item on Carroll, but…"

"Yes?"

"I want the Oscar exclusive with Gorge. And by the way, can you make that introduction to Grace Greystone I have been asking for? Of course, we have so much in common."

"Yes, Hedda, anything for you." He nodded as he paid for lunch on his SGM expense account and noted he would have to do something about Carroll's photos and film.

"I am setting up a dinner date with Grace, Duke, and some friends next Saturday night at The Grove. Please come, and I'll make the introduction," Bartie offered.

"Grace and Duke? Why, Bartie, that's a genius idea if she'll play ball. Really, you are smarter than your age, dear." She thought of the possibilities. "Fine, I'll be there for dessert." She smiled widely. "*And*... I'll bring my photographer."

Way down south, Gorge and his fiancée were driving in his new bright yellow Cadillac roadster on the dusty highway toward Las Vegas.

"Dahling, I do hope you know I am eloping with you only for the *restaurant reservation*!" Letitia threw back her head, her lustrous auburn hair in waves and puffed on her short, stubby Cuban. She laughed in a gravelly tone as Gorge motored to Vegas in his new 6-series convertible, a wedding gift from the St. Clair sugar trust.

"And I do hope you know I am eloping with you for your *trusty trust fund*." Gorge laughed and paused, switching to a serious tone. "Do you think I should be disappointed that Duke isn't attending as best man?" Gorge looked in the rearview mirror.

"Not at all. He was upset at the news," she cautioned.

"He was, but he understands Jack Warner is a tough son of a bitch and that with the Oscar nomination, well..." Gorge shrugged in a defeated tone.

"I rather thought Duke liked me." She blew a puff skyward.

"He adores you. He just didn't think I'd make it official so quickly."

"He's done quite a few things to advance his career from what I've heard." She puffed.

"I still wish he'd be there to wish us well," Gorge said sadly.

"Dahling, it would be a farce to have him there, and he is shooting. The only man you should be thinking about right now is gold and named Oscar." She ran her fingers through her waves, a twenty-five-carat star sapphire-and-diamond ring glittering in the afternoon sun.

"We've both become more realistic, which is quite boring." Gorge shrugged. "Although, when I asked him what he was doing this weekend, he said he's squiring around Grace Greystone. Threw it in my face."

"You see, he's doing the same, all in the name of the Hollywood press. I think money, fame, and power are more interesting than great sex, so I salute you both." She looked out the window at the desert landscape flying by, the puffs on the cigar blown to the highway side.

"Clearly, they're having him woo Grace Greystone," he grimaced.

"Dahling, I'd like to woo *woo* Grace Greystone." She turned, her aristocratic profile and Connecticut private girl's school accent laden with appealing upper-class privilege.

"Did you hear that Myers said she had a 'platinum-plated pussy?'" He laughed out loud. "Another great *Myerism*, but he isn't wrong."

"Well, I'd like to get a gander at that. And you, my dear, look very handsome today." Letitia surveyed her husband to be.

"And you are handsome as well, my dear. I think I am going to enjoy being Mister Letitia St. Clair." They both roared with laughter as he floored the roadster's pedal.

"Poor Hedda. I'm not sure she knew what to say, but she was actually very congenial on the subject, not that she believed a damn thing."

"That's because they want us all to fall in line like little soldiers."

"One can't blame the Hollywood machine." Gorge blew a perfect smoke ring. "You know, I hate to admit it after all these years, but I have come to believe Myers may have been right all along."

"Interesting. I won't broadcast that." She nodded.

"Please don't. I have resurrected my career, been nominated for an Academy Award, and now will have a wife and respectability. And all we have to do is live in my mansion with separate entrances. And you and I get to fuck all the guys and gals we want."

"Why do you think I agreed to this? Besides, you're also damn handsome and so is Duke. I like being around the beautiful…and the *damned.*" She exhaled dramatically.

"That's what I love about you, Letitia. You're funny but…mean."

"Would you rather me be sweet and boring?"

"I'd rather kill myself and be a decorator."

"But that's where your real talent lies…besides sucking cock." She guffawed. "Maybe they should give you a statuette for swallowing and Custom *Valances.*"

"And maybe you should enter the best supporting actor category, 'Best Dykness.'" They both laughed merrily.

"You know, I think we are going to enjoy being married."

"Will you mind having Duke around?"

"He is entertaining, and he's famous, so it will lure all the girls I want to sleep with."

"You really have thought this all out?"

"I'd rather be a star's wife than another single lesbian in the Sewing Circle."

"I believe the two-bedroom suite at El Rancho will work out quite well." Lamont nodded.

"Yes, but Gorge, you can't go inviting the first handsome bellboy you see in for a *cock...tail* on this trip. It will be our *honeymoon* after all, and the press will be alerted," she advised. "I will be your wife and need to protect you from scandal."

"Fine, Florence Nightingale. I'll make a mental note of that when you go to a party with your strap-on." He paused and looked at her. "You know you will have to wear a dress to the award's ceremony and at Grauman's when they give me cement shoes."

"Why? Dietrich wears a tux." She looked at him squarely, her strong jaw and high cheekbones highlighted by the sun. She was unusually attractive in a mannish sort of way.

"She can get away with it because she's Dietrich."

"And she once licked my pussy in the powder room. How can I show up in a dress? No one will recognize me. It's like asking me to go in *drag!*"

"That's the point."

"Oh, you are a cruel, cruel fag." She shrugged.

"Here's how I see it. You wear a gown in two weeks to the Oscar ceremony, which I think you will look quite pretty in, and if I win, you can use it as bait with any starlet you like."

"That's a fair trade."

"Yes, my dear. I get to wear your lace panties, and you get to buy me anything I want. It's simply marvelous."

"And what do I get?"

"Hopefully an Oscar dildo…and my name, darling. My name *engraved* for extra stimulation."

And with that, Gorge Lamont kissed his soon-to-be new wife on the cheek and sped up to sixty-five miles per hour to Vegas without taking his eyes off the road.

Chapter Forty-Four

La Marquise de La Faucigny
Beverly Hills, California
1941

It was another typical, balmy Angelino afternoon; regal palms were swaying in the glittering, turquoise sky, which is why it seemed so odd when the rain started in waves like synchronized lawn sprinklers. Bartie had parked his modest car on the perimeter of the cemetery and walked the distance, getting lost once or twice, before he finally found the simple grave, suddenly feeling older than his years. When he came upon the headstone, which he had anonymously paid for, he laid the simple bouquet of flowers before it and said a silent prayer for his friend. He inspected the carved letters on the stone, which simply read *Mavis Roberts 1915–1941.* It somehow reminded him of his mother, and a tear streamed down his cheek, which he neglected to wipe away as it merged with the raindrops—which seemed only fitting. As he drove back to town, he felt a release that he had made a small difference, and he was hopeful about trying to do more.

He changed the subject in his head to more pressing matters at hand and bit his lip knowing he had artfully arranged the blind date between Grace and Duke as just a casual evening out on the town among mutual friends. At first, he had confided in Michael and Mirielle about his and Myers's plan and had asked Michael to do him the favor, confidentially. "Would you talk to Mirielle for me and ask her if she can arrange a fun night on the town with Duke and Grace? Nothing serious, just a fun night out for press purposes."

"Of course, Bartie, anything for you! Mirielle said Grace needs to meet people anyway since she's been a bit down due to her divorce, so I am sure she'll agree. Duke is certainly handsome and fun company."

"Duke is actually a really nice guy and will be a total gentleman."

"Well, that's a given." Michael laughed knowingly. "He's English and famous, which should brighten her mood." He shrugged.

Later that evening, when he broached the subject over dinner, Mirielle thought it was a fine idea and that Grace could use a night out, and it would do her a world of good, despite the rumors about Duke's sexuality.

"Who cares anyway? It's just a fun studio publicity date, which happens all the time," he countered.

After a number of successful fixes, Bartie was awarded his first real raise and his own secretary, an older woman named Doreen, and he had her call for reservations from SGM studios for six at the ever-popular Cocoanut Grove nightclub at the Ambassador at 3400 Wilshire Boulevard. Once the reservation was secured, Bartie went into planning mode and thought a larger group would create more press interest; Michael, Mirielle his casual squeeze, Carroll, and of course, Duke Drake and Grace would certainly guarantee a prime table, attract attention, and garner an item—especially from Hedda. Despite the extravagance and beckoning menu of shrimp cocktails, sumptuous steaks, and sparkling pink Champagne, Bartie knew Myers wouldn't gripe at the expense on this particular outing, once the evening arrived.

That afternoon, the sun burned off the clouds, across town and in the privacy of the very opulent Beverly Hills bungalow, Grace fussed like a schoolgirl going to her first prom as she and Mirielle tore through her steamer trunks looking for the perfect thing to wear. Glorious couture was tossed in the air and thrown into silk and satin and crinoline heaps until they came across a Charles James satin evening gown, and Mirielle's green eyes lit up the room.

"Oh, Grace, you must wear this! This is perfect for coloring, and the cut is just exquisite!" she exclaimed as she held up the extravagant gown, admiring the sheen of the purple satin ruched bodice with an aqua tulle train under the lights of the chandelier. As she lifted the couture garment, the delicate layers of tissue paper used as packing material fell away like a delicious *mille-feuille* confection created in a Parisian pâtisserie. James's creations weren't as well-known yet with the West Coast set, but he was gaining a reputation among certain European society women for the most flattering, artful, and exquisitely constructed evening gowns.

"I had it made for one of the Paris balls, and I hope I can still fit into it." Grace looked down and gave her hips a quick pat.

"You will. You still have the tummy of a teenager," Mirielle advised.

"This is like a dream come true," Grace exhaled. "Remember when you and I saw *The Weary Widow* in Paris?" Her violet eyes seemed to sparkle a bit more at the idea of a night out with a dashing movie star, and Mirielle was thrilled for her friend's excitement, notwithstanding the rumors about Duke. She was not inclined to bring up the subject lest it spoil Grace's mood since it was most likely a one-time lark after all. She had also heard from Michael that despite Duke's long-standing relationship with Gorge Lamont, he had also been known for sleeping with a few of his co-stars and oversexed women like Tallulah and Joan, who were skilled at fellatio and were known for their ribald off-screen antics. Maybe he liked women too every now and again, she shrugged with European sophistication—not to mention, who was she to judge?

"I remember at the movie theater, the French actor who had dubbed him was terrible, but I have never seen a more beautiful man than Duke Drake in real life or on the big screen. Louis was quite handsome, of course, but Duke Drake is…well, Duke Drake." She laughed as she stepped into the gown and crinoline. Mirielle helped her with the hook and eyes and zippered her into it, which highlighted her lovely waist and visually slimmed her hips.

"There—you see, *parfait*! Not even a pull." Mirielle smoothed the satin material of her gown. Mirielle had chosen for herself a simple green Grecian-style Madame Grès in silk jersey for the evening, which she would pair with her mother's prized emerald ring. "Green for money!" she laughed.

"Irene," Grace said softly. "I'm excited, but I feel...I don't know... a bit insecure." She sat on the edge of the bed as Irene selected diamond-and-emerald Van Cleef earrings at the vanity from her own jewel case, which she knew would bring out the mossy green in her own eyes.

"Insecure? About what, *ma cherie*?" She turned and appraised her friend.

"My looks. I mean, Duke Drake is perhaps the handsomest man in the world, and I'm just...ordinary. Why in the world would he like me?" She shrugged.

"Oh, my darling, you have this all wrong." Mirielle walked over and hugged her. "Duke should be lucky to go out with you or be seen about town with you. He's just an actor with a mixed reputation, and you're Grace Greystone!"

"Still, he's gorgeous."

"Darling, let's just go and have fun. It happens all the time here. The studio likes its stars to be out and about, so there should be no pressure," she said. "And Grace, you're beautiful, funny, smart, and at the top of the social heap...Madame la Marquise!" She clucked like a mother hen.

"Well, that hasn't done me much good 'til now in the male department." Grace shrugged.

"You are being much too hard on yourself," Mirielle cautioned.

"You can say that because you're movie-star beautiful." She sat somewhat glumly on the bed. "I know what I am, Irene. I'm attractive, even considered somewhat pretty, I know that...and super rich, and that makes me appealing to a certain kind of man, but I just want true love like everyone else—like you and Michael."

"Grace, stop this nonsense right now! You are indeed beautiful—you just need to think you are. After all, everyone says so."

"They do?" she asked like a little girl questioning if the tooth fairy was real.

"Yes, you are magnificent." She lied a bit to Grace. Mirielle observed her friend anew. While she had many lovely attributes, her violet eyes, beautiful skin, and silky hair, she overlooked her long, strong jaw and heavyset hips, legs, and ankles. The floor-length gown hid her thick calves, and the cinched waist gave her a slimmer appearance. Mirielle did her friend's makeup, and she played up her lovely lips and eyes, trying to bring attention to her best features as she had learned from the studio makeup artists. With the makeup, gown, fabulous jewels, furs, and the looming hint of endless riches, there was no doubt that Grace Greystone, the finely turned-out product, could hold her own with any starlet at SGM.

"Just relax and enjoy it. You, my dear, deserve that!"

The evening arrived suddenly and would later be remembered as truly Hollywood fabulous, with shimmering stars, sensual dancing, and confetti-like laughter. After five bottles of pink Champagne, it was clear to the other members of their dinner party that Duke Drake only had eyes for Grace Greystone, la Marquise de la Faucigny. Perhaps her title, her thirteen platinum-and-diamond bracelets, or her thirty-carat diamond-and-sapphire earrings offered an inviting clue. Or maybe it was the way she blew smoke rings from a solid-gold cigarette holder, or how the sheared mink wrap ever so casually fell from a satin, vanilla shoulder, or the combination of all, but when Duke and Michael arrived at the hotel to pick them up, Duke seemed immediately smitten and hung on her every word. She felt his eyes on her and, for the first time in a long time, she felt like a sensual, beautiful woman with a handsome movie star paying her solitary attention.

The Cocoanut Grove was jumping as the group entered the club to lingering glances and whispers. Duke Drake was having his star turn, and every woman—and more than a few men—wanted to catch a glimpse of the town's newest reigning screen idol in person. When he entered with heiress Grace Greystone, the room had a momentary lapse of conversation. Then, when Mirielle Montaigne and Grace Greystone went together and finally emerged from the powder room and joined their dates in their Paris couture and jewels, even the likes of Mrs. Ann Warner and Edie Goetz, two reigning social queens of Hollywood, turned and eyed them with admiration and envy. They each knew these weren't typical contract girls trying to hook a producer, and all of Hollywood society was aflame. In a rare instance, the Hollywood queens decided to have mutual friends make their Introductions, and soon Mirielle and Grace would be coveted dinner guests at the more important LA dinner parties.

"We are the luckiest men in Hollywood this evening." Michael stood and made a toast on behalf of himself and the other men at the table. Bartie and Carroll joined the merry group after a series of introductions as Carroll looked like a true, glamorous Hollywood pinup in a red satin gown, showing all her curves. Grace was astonished at how low cut her dress was, and Michael hoisted a glass of Champagne and toasted the group.

"Grace, you are ravishing. Welcome to Hollywood! Mirielle, you are gorgeous and divine." Michael paused. "And Carroll, we are all not exactly sure what you are doing here with our friend Bartie, but he will do until that producer over there finally comes and gets your number." They all laughed good-naturedly. Carroll was indeed making eye contact with a well-known producer at the next table. "Here, here!" The men all laughed and clinked glasses.

"Grace, would you care to dance?" Duke asked in a soft, clear voice, leaning in.

"That would be lovely, although I am not the most graceful dancer. I am afraid I tend to lead," she confided, thinking herself rather clumsy as she saw the real and amazing Rita Hayworth dancing the rhumba with Fred Astaire.

"That suits me perfectly," Duke said. "I rather like when a woman takes control."

"That shouldn't be too hard." She let him rise and, as good manners dictated, he pulled out her chair and led her to the dance floor. It was a festive evening with none other than Xavier Cugat's Latin-themed orchestra in full swing.

"Well, Bartie, it seems that you have very good instincts for PR and matches," Mirielle said as they surveyed the elegant couple.

"I think you can bank on your next raise." Michael toasted Bartie, who basked in the glow of a hopeful studio fix.

"They do look quite marvelous together." The table appraised a well-turned mambo. "He needs a woman with height." Michael smiled and commented to Bartie. "She's exactly as tall as Gorge."

"Now, Michael, don't start," Mirielle whispered. "There are men who enjoy *both*, you know. In fact, I have had quite a lot of women at the studio invite me into their dressing rooms. At first, I was shocked, and now it seems more the norm—in LA, that is."

"Is there something I should know?" Michael seemed shocked.

"Don't worry, I'm not built that way, Cherie."

The laughter and intimacy continued over gin and tonics at the famed hotel bar. The evening was glamorous, entertaining, and fueled by endless bottles of bubbly and gin. After Hedda's grand introduction, steely kisses and posing for her photographer, the group all bid each other a good night; the couples exited the club to great fanfare while she scribbled in her writing pad. Duke offered to have his chauffeur take Grace back to the hotel for a nightcap at the Polo Lounge.

"Isn't he just gorgeous?" Grace whispered to Mirielle in a stolen moment.

"He is just darling." Mirielle smiled, putting her stole around her shoulders. "Grace, I'm glad you are having fun. You deserve it, but take it *slowly.* I just don't want to see you get hurt, that's all," Mirielle said softly, before kissing her goodnight.

"Hurt?" Grace looked at her friend.

"I'm just saying, you don't know each other yet. *He's...*" She tried to advise Grace, but Duke appeared and quickly escorted Grace to the coatroom to fetch her sable.

"You know, I have been looking for a girl like you my entire life." Duke batted his long, lovely eyelashes at her as he helped her on with her fur.

"You have? Well, I can't say I haven't been looking for a duke as well, since I've already had a marquise." They both laughed.

What they could not have known was that despite each other's personal deficits, each was outwardly appraising the other, basking in the idea of a world-famous match that would stir the imagination of the studio PR department and, most importantly, the public. The fact that, on the surface, they were both beyond reproach but desperately needed each other was the secret sauce that would propel their relationship in the press to the American public. And later, to the altar.

Chapter Forty-Five

Mirielle Montaigne
Beverly Hills
1942

The lilting March breezes did little to calm the nerves of most Angelinos who were on edge due to the war in Europe and still reeling from the news of the January plane crash of one of the film industry's brightest stars, the thirty-six-year-old actress, Carole Lombard. She, her mother, and agent were snuffed out on her return from a successful war bonds tour in the mountains of Las Vegas. Carole had wanted to get back to LA quickly, and they did a coin toss for airplane versus train. Carole won, and her plane crashed into Double Up Peak southwest of the Las Vegas airport. Her husband, the mega-popular film star, Clark Gable, would never fully recover, and the grief felt within the film colony for the gorgeous and popular madcap star was palpable. Mirielle was devastated at the news of her new friend who had been so warm and welcoming when she first arrived in town.

The tragic event fell on the heels of the next month's scandal, the so-called "Battle of Los Angeles," when the Air Force fired heavy artillery—exactly 1,400 shells—at an unidentified flying object. It turned out to be a weather balloon mistaken for an enemy aircraft, and this action resulted in five civilian-related deaths and other frayed nerves at the possibility of an enemy attack on American soil after Pearl Harbor. When Bartie received the panicked call from Michael to meet him and Mirielle at the low-key Frolic Room bar on Hollywood Boulevard, it suggested something critical—or another newsflash—was also at hand, hence the dive bar, on the wrong side of town.

Bartie hung up the phone, smoothed his hair as best he could, and grabbed his room and car keys, but knew something was amiss. Michael hardly ever called at night, and by the tone of his pleading voice, he knew whatever the news was…it wasn't good, especially since he wanted to meet in an out-of-the-way location. Bartie reluctantly left his cozy apartment at the Garden of Allah, and as he walked outside and smelled the lovely distinct smell of gardenias, he heard the strains of his new neighbor, the famed Rachmaninoff, practicing his "Piano Concerto No. 4 in G minor, Op. 40" and realized how lucky he was to be surrounded by so many talented émigrés fleeing, and their artistic genius, which was currently fueling the ranks of Hollywood talent. He walked to his parked car, turned on the ignition to the new Buick sedan he'd bought with his last bonus from Myers, and made good time since it was long after work hours.

When he arrived at the dimly-lit bar, his eyes adjusted to the low-key lighting, finally spying Michael and Mirielle sitting side by side in a back booth, engaged in deep conversation. Mirielle wore a simple black dress and a dark hat with her strawberry tresses pulled back. Despite trying to dress down without makeup or jewelry, it was impossible for her to not to look like a movie star; her face was that cinematic.

"I know you can't tell me you've both gotten engaged, so what's so important?" He slid into the booth before shaking Michael's hand and quickly leaning over and kissing Mirielle.

"I ordered you a whiskey in advance, straight up." Michael pointed to his waiting drink.

"I love the service." Bartie picked up his glass, swirled the amber liquid with the melting ice, and toasted the couple. "But perhaps not the reason why. Pray tell?"

"Thanks so much for meeting us spur-of-the-moment and late at night." Mirielle touched his hand lightly in a grateful gesture.

"Look, I know you have an early day tomorrow, Bartie, and I'm not sure how to say this, so I will just come out with it." Michael looked bleary-eyed. "Mirielle's pregnant."

"I see." Bartie looked wide-eyed. "I would say congratulations, but I do understand the implications."

"The studio will insist on an abortion according to the contract like they did with Lana and Judy," Michael stated plainly, his turbulent eyes downcast.

"I won't give up the baby." Mirielle put her head in her hands. "I won't! No one can force me." Mirielle's red-tinged eyes filled with tears. She had recently gotten rave reviews in *Au Revoir Paris*, and was currently filming the large-scale color musical *L'amour L'amour*, playing a soubrette dancer at the Moulin Rouge who captures the heart of a French nobleman. The scuttlebutt around town was that the movie would make her a bona fide *international* movie star.

"Does anyone else know?" Bartie asked softly.

"Only her doctor." Michael swirled his rock's glass.

"And Grace," Mirielle added.

"Can she keep a secret?" Bartie looked concerned.

"Yes, of course. I trust her completely," she offered.

"I just don't trust Duke. You know *they* gossip a lot."

"She promised me she wouldn't tell him. I just want to know what to do." Mirielle looked down into her glass of gin.

"You have to give me a bit of time to get my head wrapped around this one. You're still married, and you don't know if Fritz, your husband in Europe, is dead or alive? Correct?" he said, gathering the facts out loud as he usually did.

"Correct," she said.

"I'm sorry. I know I talk out loud. It's just how I work things out," he said. "And nothing's changed between you and Mary Katherine?" he asked Michael.

"I wish," he grumbled. "The joke of it all is when we were first married and did try to have children, she couldn't conceive."

"Bartie, we called you because we are...*desperate*," Mirielle cried.

"I understand." Bartie nodded thoughtfully at the irony and gave a long pause, downed his drink, and motioned to the old waiter for a refill.

"Well, I might—and I said *might*—have an idea." He took a final swig. "It was something I saw in old Menowitz's files about this exact issue. He was hardly discreet about his notes," Bartie confided.

"You do?" Mirielle perked up. "I knew he could figure a way out, Michael."

"When are you scheduled to shoot *Marie Antoinette*?" Bartie asked of the lavish costume drama he knew she was slated to play the lead against the wildly enigmatic Olivier, as it was high on the studio lineup.

"Next month on April 22," Michael answered for her.

"And how far along are you, Mirielle?" Bartie jotted down mental notes.

"She's one month and fifteen days," Michael immediately answered.

"I can answer for myself, darling. Just because I'm in the family way doesn't mean I've turned into a babbling baby, myself."

"The timing is good because the eighteenth-century costumes will hide her stomach," Michael added. "You really have an idea, Bartie, on how to handle this?" he asked. "I would have suggested she marry Duke, but Mirielle's already married."

"Yes, but this one is going to need a fairly complicated fix. No one at the studio is allowed to have a baby out of wedlock, especially if they are already married. If the public found out, it would end her career before it even started."

"That's why we called you." They all looked grim.

"We really need your help on this, Bartie," Mirielle pleaded. Bartie sat back in silence and then spoke.

"Of course, but in order to get this done, you're going to have to let Myers know."

"He's going to kill me. I could get fired over this." Michael downed his whiskey.

"No, he won't. You're too important to Myers. Look, I have an idea. I'm not going to lie to you and tell you it's an original idea."

"Go on."

"About a year ago, I found Menowitz's file notes with names and dates on all his fixes. I kept them as I could not believe my eyes," Bartie confided.

"Wow, no wonder he got canned."

"So, I was reading up on all the things he and the studio concocted over the years, and there is one amazing fix about a Catholic actress, who we all know, who got pregnant with one of the world's most famous actors on our lot and wouldn't have an abortion for religious reasons."

"And?" Mirielle's eyes suddenly brightened.

"So, here's the story, and here's how I think we are going to work it out. It's quite complicated, but you're going to have to completely trust me." He started to fill them in, and when Mirielle heard there could be a solution, she started weeping.

"I'll try anything. After all I've been through, I have to keep this baby."

"If you agree to everything, I can help. And Myers too. He's a tough bird, but deep down—and I mean when you dig *deep*—he's a good man." He raised a concerned eyebrow. "But don't worry, Mirielle, I will handle it. Leave it to me." They sat for the next hour going over the initial plan as Michael and Mirielle started to realize there might be slight hope for what seemed like a hopeless situation.

"It really worked in the past?" Mirielle asked.

"It really worked," Bartie declared, "but you have to trust me."

"You're my best friend. How could I not trust you?" Michael said with a deep exhale. "Anything you say, right, Mirielle?"

"Anything! *Merci beaucoup*, Bartie," she said, slightly relieved as she wiped away a tear.

"*Bien sur*," he replied with his South Dakota accent, which made them both smile.

"Oh, by the way," he said as he rose from the table, "I need a little favor in return."

"Anything, Bartie." They nodded in agreement.

"I heard now that Gorge Lamont got married, Duke is squiring Grace around town."

"Yes, they are actually dating. They really get along quite well," Michael said.

"I'm a bit surprised, but Grace is having a wonderful time with him. She says he's great fun and so charming." Mirielle shrugged.

"Would you ask Grace if she would have lunch with Hedda Hopper? She's dying for a lunch date and keeps asking for it. And we have to keep her happy, especially now knowing you might need her down the line."

"Of course, I'll make sure she does," Mirielle replied, nodding.

"Now that Grace's ex-husband, Louis, is married to that French actress, I think she actually likes being in the press with Duke." Mirielle shrugged. "A bit of female revenge, you know? It's only natural."

"Perfect," Bartie sighed in relief. "Can you imagine Duke and Grace?"

"Stranger things have happened in this town," sighed Michael, raising an eyebrow at the thought. "Stranger things."

"Yes, stranger things." Bartie thought about his latest fix and his newest one, soon to be in the works and not sure if both were on the up and up and up for the task.

Chapter Forty-Six

Grace Greystone-de La Faucigny-Drake
Las Vegas
1942

Over the next few weeks, Duke and Grace's whirlwind romance took flight to shocked Hollywood insiders and press, and the glamorous couple was seen at all the Hollywood hotspots: Chasen's, Romanoff's, and the Cocoanut Grove. Mouths were agape at their laughter, body language, the rhumbas, and the stolen French kisses on the dance floor; it certainly appeared they were having a grand old romantic time of it and seemed to bask in each other's company, and that real romance was in the air.

"Duke's not *that* good of an actor—yet!" Hedda keenly observed and quipped.

Perhaps it was that Duke had felt the sting of Gorge's quickie marriage and Oscar nomination and suddenly had more time on his hands, and that Gorge's new boss, Jack Warner, had insisted they keep their distance until after the Oscar ceremony. Not to mention that Duke was the perfect diversion for Grace, who kept reading about the sexy French starlet who had captured her former husband's heart and was now the toast of Nazi-occupied Paris, often seen out on the town with Coco Chanel and her Nazi-officer boyfriend, Hans Günther von Dincklage.

When he and Gorge secretly caught up at the cozy bar in the Bel Air Hotel, Gorge had raved to Duke about Vegas, and Duke, feeling the sting of jealousy over his new marital status, decided on a whim to take a similar road trip as well with Grace. When he asked Grace for the weekend, she seemed delighted, had heard it was great fun, and had her lady's maid start packing for the trip. Duke was pleased to get out of town as he was tired of Gorge's hypocrisy and ongoing Oscar press junket, not to mention Mrs. Gorge Lamont was now the toast of old Hollywood. *What's good for the goose is good for the gander!* Duke's anger simmered.

"Las Vegas, here we come, darling!" Duke exclaimed in the back of his navy Rolls, knowing it would drive Gorge crazy once he heard the new couple was headed for the desert strip.

In the back of his mind, he also thought he might just have the courage to pull off what Bartie and the studio wanted him to do. He truly enjoyed Grace's company and was entranced by her wealth, image, and personality, and the last couple of weeks, after drinks at her bungalow, things had become more intimate. One thing had led to another and, after a flirtatious exchange, Grace invited the handsome young star back to her bedroom—an invitation he quickly accepted. Grace was smart enough to turn down the lights as the accouterments were removed from her body, and they fell into bed in a most natural way. Duke liked Grace's chic femininity, her small yet supple breasts, and boyish body and lay back on the bed in a receptive position as she fellated him. He was surprised and pleased that she was not unwilling to engage in oral and anal sex. Afterward, they fell in an exhausted tangled web as she feasted on his wondrous physique. Duke had been bisexual for his career when he needed to be, but now it was something he wanted, enjoyed, and best of all, he felt confident in feeling like a man with a woman he was starting to really care for. In the back of his mind, he was deeply anxious of what Gorge would think, but he also knew he had put his career first, as he would now do. The drive to Vegas was hot and dusty, and the couple was photographed as they went out on the town after checking into the El Rancho Hotel in two separate-yet-connecting suites. They started drinking at 3:00 by the pool and didn't stop, ending up with two crushing hangovers.

"Why, Duke Drake, fancy meeting you here! Can I have your autograph?" Grace emerged from under the rumpled sheets in the early dawn, jutting forward, naked and the color of rose petals, and took in the handsome, chiseled specimen beside her. She sighed, feeling dizzy as the room spun like a child's kaleidoscope. "Darling, why is the room spinning? I think I need some black coffee and quick." She lay back in bed.

"It's on its way. I called room service, Missus Drake." He gave her his best toothy and dimpled close-up smile at her. "Fancy meeting you in Las Vegas!" Duke said.

"Missus What?"

"Missus Drake! When shall we call and let people know?" Despite his own hangover, he beamed like a little boy.

"Let them know what?" Grace sat up in a panic, the room not quite coming into focus, only primary colors.

"That we got married last night, my darling," he said in an animated tone.

"Oh, that! I was so tipsy, Duke. That wasn't real, was it? It was all a lark, right?" She snuggled up to him, struggling to remember the series of jumbled events due to her hangover.

"Only that we went into a Vegas chapel, and now you're all mine, Grace Greystone de la Faucigny...*Drake.*"

"Wait. Duke, last night was crazy, and I had *so* much to drink. Don't tell me that we *really* eloped?" The color drained from her already pale face. "That it was *legal*?"

"We really eloped," he laughed.

"I thought it was a Vegas lark, or I was dreaming."

"You're not dreaming, and I hope you are not having cold feet, are you?" He put a muscled arm around her.

"Darling, my extremities are generally cold, but it has nothing to do with *this.*" She rubbed his muscular calve with her cool arch as he jumped, reached over, and kissed her.

"Don't tell me you want to have this *annulled*?" He looked at her with slight fear. "It's not giving up the title, is it?"

"Title? That was more like a prison sentence. I just don't usually do things spur-of-the-moment, but maybe I should now that I'm in America," she laughed. The phone in the capacious suite rang, and they both looked at it for two rings before answering it and then turned an ashen shade of gray.

"Yes, of course, I'll hold the line." Duke raised an eyebrow. "It's Hedda," he mouthed in a whisper. Grace feigned a terrified look and giggled.

"Why, hello, Hedda, how are you this morning?" Grace heard him say in his clipped accent. "Yes, Grace and I are in Las Vegas. How did you know?" He paused.

"Yes, well you do *know* everything, Hedda. Of course...and have people everywhere...yes, it is *your business* to know." He paused and listened. "Well, yes. I couldn't be happier. *We* couldn't be happier. Here, I'll let her tell you, herself." He handed Grace the receiver. She tried to brush the phone away, but he threw it at her like a hot potato as they both tried not to laugh.

"Hello, Hedda dahling." She caught her breath and paused, pulling the sheet over her naked breast. "How are you?" She listened quietly. "Yes, Duke and I are in Las Vegas having the most marvelous time. He's great fun, you know."

She turned to Duke and saw him looking at her with pleading eyes, his smile and white teeth lighting up the room.

"Why, yes. You can let your readers know that we did indeed... elope. I think!" She looked at him. "That was a joke, Hedda. Yes, my divorce was final months ago, and I am very, very proud to be Missus Duke Drake. Yes, you are the *first* to know, after *me*. Yes, I am sure he will call Mister Myers after this." She paused. "Why, thank you, Hedda, I will. Well, you know it was love at first sight, and I have been married to a marquis and now Duke, and take it from me, dukes are better, Hedda. They really know how to treat a lady." She listened quietly.

"Yes, Hedda." She paused and then looked flustered. "Why would you ask such a thing? Of course. Given I have been married before, so I do have something of a comparison," she said in a flustered tone. "Yes, you can print that. I can assure you, dukes are bigger and better in *all* areas than marquises. And you can print it, or as you say, on the record." She giggled. "And Hedda, it's all true. Yes, thank you for your good wishes, and we will have you to the wedding party once I get my bearings straight in LA."

"Well, there's no going back now." Duke leaned back and raised an eyebrow once the phone was in the receiver. "The price of fame."

"Darling, I do think you should call Mister Myers. I am sure he will want to know before it hits the Hollywood press."

"Good idea. You are already acting like a good wife." He reached over and kissed her.

"What else did Hedda say? Something…inappropriate?" Duke bit his lip nervously at what she could have revealed.

"Well, she mentioned your friend Gorge's marriage and wanted to know if our honeymoon…was, well real and *intimate*." She looked down.

"I see." Duke looked down as well. "I'm sure it has to do with the rumors we talked about."

"Don't worry, darling. I know what a real man you are. I understand you had a few *youthful indiscretions* as you told me, but that's all behind you now!" She thought back to an earlier conversation she'd had with Irene when she had finally brought up the subject of Duke's sexuality and then asked him about it.

"Darling, I'm just worried your head is being turned by his looks and fame," Irene had said bluntly. "He's gay. It's a known fact in town, Gracie."

"Well, he's not gay with me. He's a wonderful lover." She sipped her martini, looking wounded.

"Then maybe he likes both." Mirielle tried to be conciliatory.

"I can change him, Irene. I can. He told me he did have experiences, but that he would change for me." She said it in such a way that Irene knew it was a lost cause and dropped the subject since Duke Drake was clearly making her best friend happy. She did not want to rain on Grace's parade, and it was not mentioned again.

"I promise to be a wonderful husband, and you're the only woman for me." Duke removed a small velvet ring box from the bedside table. "I bought this from Flato in LA."

She opened it up and saw a fifteen-carat glittering, round diamond in a platinum setting as he got down on one knee.

"Grace, my darling, will you be my duchess?" His eyes sparkled as much as the ring.

"Oh, my darling, of course. A thousand times yes! Oh, Duke, it's just…magnificent," she said, surveying her newest bauble, before slipping on the glittering blue-white orb almost ready to lift off into space.

"Let's get breakfast and get back to LA," he said as he kissed her forehead. "But not before we call Edna and get Myers and tell them we eloped."

"Do you think he'll be happy at the news?" Grace asked naively.

"Oh, more than you know." Duke smiled proudly. "More than you know. And I also have to make another important call."

"To whom?"

"Bartie Maddox." He smiled.

Chapter Forty-Seven

Michael McDonough
Culver City
1942

With the way Michael felt, it could have been pitch-dark, charcoal clouds descending like a hovering thunderstorm rather than the flaming West Coast sunshine peering in from the lot outside. Michael, who was naturally milky white, paled further at the strenuous and fabled walk to Myers, which would have been punishment enough once Edna uttered the words, "Mister Myers will see you now," and pointed with a raised eyebrow to the forbidding white lacquered deco doors. Michael thanked her profusely and hung his head low as he walked into his inner sanctum. Edna was privy to all, and her tone was that of derision and disdain, which only let Michael know it was going to be bad—very bad.

He was forced to endure the distance as Myers stood looking grim, hands folded, awaiting his victim with Bartie seated beside him looking anxious and drawn. As Michael looked up, he saw Myers's draconian expression and pallid face, which gave him pause. He knew it was going to be very bad, but now it seemed...*terrible.*

Mick, who had always been so confident in his daily swagger, viewed the prolonged walk to Myers as the walk of shame. Solomon Myers sensed it as well and hovered like a sleek panther waiting to pounce, his reflexes primed for the kill. Despite being short in stature, on that particular day, Solly Myers appeared larger, his moral superiority making Michael McDonough shrink even further.

"Mister Myers, Bartie." Michael's voice croaked. "Thank you for taking the time to see me on such short notice," he said in a barely-audible whisper, sheepishly extending his hand, which Myers immediately brushed away.

"Ya damn right! Had to cancel my whole morning because of the likes of…*you, you momzer*!" Myers sneered, picking imaginary lint from his cream linen blazer, which seemed slightly incongruous to his pallid visage.

"I hope the family is well," Michael gulped.

"Dispense with the family shit," Myers barked, as he knew he would. "Sit yer dumb Irish ass down. Haven't ya heard of a fuckin' condom? Or are you that *stoo-pid,* ya louse? Or did you intentionally set out to fuck the studio too?" He leapt at him, his darting tongue leaping like a snake hanging overhead from a dangling tree branch.

"I'm sorry, Mister Myers. I should have used my head."

"Yeah, the other one, you fucking stupid piece of shit. You could have had the usual twenty-four children with that *meiskeit* wife of yours, but do you think you can randomly knock up my stars? One of my biggest assets? *Do you*?" He screamed so loud, Edna peeked her head in and then set out to efficiently bring him in a Bromo-Seltzer on a silver tray as he turned all shades of blotchy, beet red.

"I know it was a terrible mistake, and I am very sorry, Mister Myers."

"You should be!" He raised a clenched fist. "I brought that dame over from Europe at your suggestion, and we invested hundreds of thousands of dollars in making her a star, and you decide you can knock her up like a common barmaid?"

"I'm so sorry." He hung his head lower.

"Yeah, yeah, so was Brutus. Do you know if this ever got out, it would ruin me and the studio. Every *goil* in America dreams of being a movie star, and they all come here—and their mothers let them because they think people like Solomon Myers will protect them, that we are their father figures. Let me ask you. If you had a sixteen- or seventeen-year-old daughter, would you go to one of their movies or allow her to come to Hollywood after reading that a married woman is pregnant with someone else's baby who's also married? *Would you*? I lost millions on Dumont's last movie, and do you know what? Every mother in America thinks their daughters will now be protected from being *strangled* if they come here. And I had to pay up, so that now they can believe that SGM is the studio with *morals.* Tell him, Bartie, boy wonder. And now this? If I didn't fucking *love you,* I would *KILL YOU!*" he exploded, in one of his most famous Myerisms to date. After excoriating him and turning him into a virtual puddle, Bartie was left to clean up the mess.

"Michael." Bartie's voice croaked, as he encroached slowly. "I spoke to Mister Myers. Because of your good, hard work to date, and the studio's investment in Mirielle, he has generously agreed to help execute our plan. I stressed that you and Mirielle have promised that you are both going to work with us, do whatever it takes, and we mean *whatever* for the sake of Mirielle, her career, and the best interests of SGM."

"That's right, and one wrong move with the *fix,* one disagreement or leak, and you and Frenchie are canned! Thrown to the curb. Do ya hear me?" Myer's voice went up another octave.

"Yes, Mister Myers. Thank you."

"Just look at what ya did!" he wailed. "She was beauty and a class act…" he lamented, his bony hands skyward. "Now, she's a fallen woman. It's a Shonda!" he moaned.

"I love Mirielle more than anything in this world. Please, you can fire me or whatever, but I don't want Mirielle to suffer. It wasn't her fault. I forced myself on her," he cried.

"Oh, cut the crap. She wanted the bone, and you know it. They're all *whores* beggin' fer it." Myers paced. "Even if she was a countess or whatever she was. But you know what you did. You did what no one has ever done before. That's right, you turned a countess into a *cuntess.*"

"We're in love."

"Save the sob story for the Salvation Army. You're married and so is she. Her damn husband is hangin' by his thumbs in a concentration camp somewhere in Europe, and you're bonin' her? The censors would have a field day. I already have one scandal with Dumont 'cause Bartie over here is a *saint*! Give me a break and some credit."

"I couldn't help myself. I am deeply sorry," Michael lamented and hung his head in shame.

"I don't know which is worse—if you were a cock-crazy fag like Lamont or not being able to keep yer dick outta *fresh* pussy! Fer Chrissakes, I have to deal with this crap. If Hedda found out, she'd rake her, you, and SGM over the coals."

"I promise you we will do whatever you would like."

"First, no more sex with Miss Fancy Pants. If you have to drop a load, do it at Maude's. You can use my house account, ya damn louse, and second, once we get this fix in place, get back to working on yer next picture. Make me some money to pay me back for all the money I'm losing 'cause of...*you.*" He pointed a well-knuckled finger at him and wagged it.

"Mister Myers also appreciated your help in getting Duke married to Grace Greystone." Bartie tried to be positive.

"What are you saying? He deserves a raise?" Myers barked. "He would have already been fired if he wasn't *good*...like you. You both have it in fer me 'cause I didn't come over during the potato blout." He screwed up his face like a prune.

"Blight."

"Whatever, you dumb fuck. Everyone hates the Jews," he said, pointing. "And you do too, which is why you tried to fuck me," he lamented.

"Mister Myers, we have great respect—"

"Tell it to *Grand*-ma...." he quipped.

"Mister Myers, please, we are distraught for Mirielle. She won't, however, get the usual abortion," Bartie said.

"Of course she won't, 'cause she has dough stashed away unlike these floozies who would sell their mother and their cooch for a ten spot. Ya know, I've had enough of you today. Bartie, tell him the plan, and then I don't want to hear a peep outta yas. Do you hear me?"

"Yes, Mister Myers." Michael nodded and looked at his shoes.

"So, Mick, here is what Mister Myers and I have decided we will do."

"Whatever is best for Mirielle."

"You're damn right!" Myers opined.

"Okay, okay...we all agree Michael was irresponsible, but let's try and move forward."

"Don't you lecture me—just spill the beans." Myers shook his head at Bartie.

"Firstly, Mirielle has to complete *Marie Antoinette*," Bartie stated.

"And I don't want to hear one complaint or late notice, or I will be happy to replace her with some other floozy. At this rate, I'll just go to Maude's and put one of the whores in a powdered wig, and we can use *her*." Myers shook his head.

"And we will get the costume department to cover up the stomach." Bartie paused. "The studio did it once before with Jeanette Murray when she had Dumont's baby a few years back."

"Really," Michael whistled. "I had no idea."

"That's the point, ya moron...no one has any idea. It was the studio fix *fer Chrissakes*." Myers paced.

"Mirielle will finish her next film, and then she and Grace or someone will hopefully go on a much-needed vacation...a four-month cruise to South America, where she will stay in her stateroom most of the time."

"I see."

"Grace just got married. She can visit part of the time and keep Mirielle company when Duke starts shooting *Deb-on-air*. I am sure he will be happy to have some free time on his hands."

"Yeah, with his real wife, Lamont! The fag!" Myers groused. "And *you* will be nowhere in sight," Myers commanded Michael.

"You don't mean..."

"You are to stay away from her until the baby is born."

"I can't see her?" He hung his head and moaned under his breath.

"Yes, that's unfortunate," Bartie explained. "So, here's the fix. We will let Mirielle have the baby, and then once it is born, we will deliver it to the Catholic orphanage, who will receive a ten-thousand-dollar donation, which you will pay for out of your salary. Mirielle will then, two or three months afterward, adopt twins, one being her own baby, and I'll get another one...to make it look impartial," Bartie explained.

"Bartie here will do the press with Hedda to make her look like a saint like we did with Murray, the other slut." Myers grinned at the thought.

"Then, the real mother will come and collect the other one, saying she changed her mind, and Mirielle will keep her own son or daughter."

"By the way, I forgot to ask ya, Maddox, where ya gonna get the other brat? It's not like you can walk into Macy's and buy one." Myers was skeptical.

"There's this girl I know at Maude's."

"Which one?"

"Veronica Lake. She got knocked up. I already spoke to her. She agreed to give us her baby and then take it back."

"And what does she get, boy genius?"

"A studio contract and a new name."

"*Poy-fect!* See, I told ya to go to Maude's. Think of all the contacts you're makin' there, ya louse. Can't keep it in his pants either, like a kid in the candy store." He rubbed his hands and smiled. "The Kid here is a real stallion!"

"Wow, that's some idea. Do you think it will work?" Michael looked on, wide-eyed.

"We just told ya, *thick*-head. We did it with Jeanette. She adopted her own baby. Why, it's almost... *bib*-lical!" Myers smiled.

"How so?"

"Like Miriam who was called in to nurse Moses after Pharaoh's daughter adopted him from the basket in the river. Don't you know the Bible, ya moron?" Myers shot him a look.

"I guess I'll have to brush up."

"Yer damn right, and that's how we do things here at SGM, with style and with class, all for our public. They don't want to see two *fags* living together or knocked-up women having babies out of wedlock. Why...? It's *un-American.* What are ya, two commies?"

"This way, Mirielle gets to keep her baby," Bartie offered.

"Bartie, it's really a very ingenious solution. I can't thank you enough." Michael's eyes teared at the thought.

"And then…" Myers paced. "We'll pay off that dog wife of yers, get you a divorce, and then once we can prove Mirielle's husband is dead, you can both get married, and everyone lives happily ever after. Simple, right?"

"I'm not sure what to say."

"How 'bout thank you to your friend over here who is as brilliant as you are stupid."

"Yes, it is brilliant." Mick put his head in his hands. "Thank you, Bartie"

"And if I ever catch your dick in another star's pussy at SGM without it being wrapped up again, I will personally see to it that you never work in this town again. Do you understand me? And I will pay good money to fly over a *leprechaun* from Dublin to fuck you up the ass, the way you fucked me." He, again, screamed so loud Edna came running and brought him another Bromo-Seltzer.

"Anything else, Mister Myers?"

"Ahh, I'm just disgusted. Now just *go*."

As they both took the long walk out the office, Bartie turned to a trembling Michael.

"I know that was tough, but it went as well as it could have with Myers. Now that we removed the splinter, he'll calm down."

"Thank you, Bartie. Thank you."

"No need to thank."

Michael walked out of Myers's office feeling demoted in mind, body, and spirit but also somewhat relieved at the fact that he had been suitably chastised and that there was indeed a plan in the works. More importantly, if all went according to plan, he and Mirielle would be able to keep their baby.

As they exited Myers's office, Michael and Bartie noticed the stylish and effervescent Fanny Brice, the noted singer and comedienne who was waiting to speak to Myers about a new project, sitting in the waiting room. Glamorous Fanny looked chic and dressed to the nines in a well-cut navy suit, luxurious silver foxes, and long, opera-length pearls. She nodded at the two men.

"Miss Brice, I am a great fan." Bartie extended a cool hand to the well-known, former Ziegfeld girl and radio star. "It's such an honor. I'm Bartson Maddox, head of SGM publicity."

"So young and handsome," she whistled. "Why, there are more good-looking single men here than in the Army," she cracked. "I should come more often. By the way, which one of you was getting yelled at?"

Bartie pointed to Michael.

"Well, I want to know *you.*" She walked over and caressed his lapel in a comedic fashion.

"Really, and why is that?"

"Any guy who can get Myers ranting and raving like that is somebody worth knowing. You can't be a *nobody* and get Myers worked up like that. Whatever you did, it must have been a doozy."

"It was. Thank you, Miss Brice."

"Call me Fanny. And you are?"

"Michael McDonough, head of production."

"I should have known it was the *fighting Irish.* But don't worry, I've known Myers for years. He'll forget about it by tomorrow."

"That would be nice."

"Miss Brice." Edna looked up. "Mister Myers will see you now."

"I hope your meeting is better than my meeting," Michael laughed ruefully.

"Oh, don't worry, it will be." She stood and then in the blink of an eye, as if turning on a light switch, raised herself to her full height with regal posture. With a hint of décolletage and the turn of a lovely calf, the fifty-one-year-old aging star transformed herself once again into the former *Ziegfeld* girl descending a staircase to applause. Edna opened the double doors with extra pride as she took the long and graceful walk to Myers.

"Now, *that's*...a star!" Both men looked on in amazement, shook their heads, and nodded in agreement.

Chapter Forty-Eight

Gorge Lamont
Loz Feliz, Los Angeles
1942

The headlines screamed "*SILENT STAR LAMONT BECOMES TALKING OSCAR WINNER!"* declaring the incredible comeback at the famed LA Biltmore Hotel. Interestingly, *Citizen Kane* failed to win best picture, but Gorge Lamont exacted a win for "Best Actor" to a standing ovation. In his victory lap, newspapers were stacked in myriad piles around his living room to great effect and overrun with wilting congratulatory bouquets from stars, executives, and studio heads, alike.

Yet, despite what should have been a scene of happiness and revelry, smoke puffs seemingly emanated from Gorge's glistening, well-formed ears like a bull in the ring charging the red *muletta.*

"I'm asking you if Grace *knows*," he bellowed at Duke, "the way Letitia *knows*!" Gorge assumed the charging position, knocking back a caramel-colored whiskey from his glimmering bar set, his rage getting the best of him. The high flush of his cheeks and the tensing of his rippling musculature only made him maddeningly more attractive.

"It's not the same!" Duke nervously lit a cigarette, blowing smoke out of the corner of his mouth. "Grace doesn't go for women."

"So, you just up and eloped without letting me know, so I could read about it like everyone else in Hedda's column?" Gorge fumed and paced his oak-paneled library, the chalk-white cigarette smoke curling to the vaulted, pecky cypress ceiling against the rich patina of wood and stucco.

"It wasn't a planned thing, but who are *you* to talk? You've barely returned my phone calls, just got married yourself, and told me we had to cool things until after the Oscars. So I have. What are you saying, Gorge?" Duke sat like a chastened child trying to defend himself in a bedroom corner.

"Yes, but I married the biggest dyke in Hollywood—it's different." Gorge shook his head, his silky blond locks suddenly becoming untamed and unruly.

"Something tells me there's more between you two." Duke shook his head.

"She just uses me to get straight girls she wants to sleep with into bed. It's a perfect arrangement."

"Don't tell me you don't get a few blow jobs out of it."

"As a matter of fact, I don't." He slammed the crystal tumbler on a marble side table.

"Your loss."

"My, how we've changed—since when did you like girls so much?" Gorge peered at him through angry, slanted eyes.

"When *you* did," Duke challenged. "The person who has actually changed is *you*. The moment you were nominated for the Academy Award, you became a different person." Duke crushed a half cigarette in a silver deco ashtray and lit up another Chesterfield out of the pack, tapping it nervously on the coffee table.

"I just became a bit smarter after all these years," Gorge explained.

"And then when you won, you hardly even acknowledged me," Duke lamented. "I called, sent telegrams, and now have to answer to your *wife*, who is basking in the glory and entertaining half the town, not to mention the ultimate insult of having an Oscar party and not even inviting me. How do you think that made me feel?" Duke walked over to the window, toying with the silken, braided pulls of the brocade curtains, looking out toward the flickering lights of the city.

"I told you that Hedda was exclusively covering the party. We discussed that if you attended, she would have considered the marriage a total sham in her column. Bartie traded an exclusive for good press before the Oscar ceremony."

"Okay, Mister Best Actor. And I went off to Vegas and eloped too, and it's helped *my career* and *my relationship* with Myers, so I don't see why you are being such a hypocrite."

"Because," his voice got louder, "I have a deal with Letitia, and you don't with *Grace*."

"You don't know what I have or don't have because you haven't been around to ask me!" he shouted back. "Once Oscar came into the picture, I went out with yesterday's trash."

"So, you're telling me Grace Greystone knows about us?"

"What's left to know? We hardly see each other anymore. And for your information, I did tell Grace that I'd had…*experiences.* And so did Mirielle. It's not a secret in this town, Gorge." He looked at him with his doe eyes, like the lost boy he once was.

"*Experiences*? That's a laugh. You've probably fucked more guys than she has."

"Gorge, you're the biggest whore in this town, and everyone knows it, and now you fancy yourself American royalty. Since when do you have upstairs and downstairs maids, a butler, and personal secretary? *Mister Lamont will see you in the library*," he mimicked—delivered in his clipped accent—and rolled his eyes.

"Letitia likes to do things the St. Clair way," he shrugged.

"Well, my wife likes to do things the Greystone way, and she has more money than *your* wife."

"So now it's about who has more money?" he raged.

"You started this."

"I don't know what to say." He walked up to him and changed his tone, trying to modulate his posture for full effect. "Duke, I love you, don't you see that?" Gorge's voice cracked.

"When it's convenient."

"I won the Academy Award. Aren't you happy for me?" He paced. "I supported your career when I was out of work. I gave you your first agent, my agent. Don't you remember any of it?" Gorge paced.

"Yes, and that's when we were happy."

"I'm telling you I love you, and you're not even acknowledging it?" He walked up, and Duke brushed him away.

"You love Oscar…more."

"Hey," he walked over and touched his handsome face. "I do love my Oscar, and you should love it too, for *me.* Do you have any idea how it felt to be banished to Siberia in this town for ten years? Do you? You cannot imagine, and when I met you, and you were getting roles and I wasn't, I was supportive and happy for you, even though deep down my heart was breaking." Gorge started to tear up.

"I am sorry."

"And now my career is on fire, and I'm not going to lie to you and tell you it's not a big deal for me. And one day *you* will be nominated…and do you know what? When you are, mark my words, you will do anything to win it not because of vanity, but because it'll prove we were *here* and we *mattered,* despite who we love and sleep with. So yes, it helped me to marry Letitia, and I understand why you married Grace. The difference is *you* haven't told her the truth…and I have," he said angrily.

"You shoved me off to the side, Gorge—all for a gold statuette."

"I still love you."

He shrugged. "It just hurts that I couldn't be a part of it."

"I'll try to make it up to you." Gorge walked up again and reached out and caressed his face.

"I am happy for you and proud. It was just very hurtful, Gorge. And mean."

"I am so sorry. I got caught up." His eyes started to tear again. "Can I make it up to you?" He put his hands on his shoulders as Duke pulled away.

"I have my own life and career, and being married to Grace is the best thing for me—the way Letitia and the Oscar was for you. It's my one chance…" His voice broke in a pleading tone.

"Chance for what?"

"To be…" He paced and paused. "*Normal.*" He emitted a lone sob.

"Oh, so that's it." Gorge shook his head and mocked him. "*Normal* Norman?" he sneered bitterly. "You and I…we're not *meant* to be normal." He approached him again and gored him like a bull with his hardness straining his pant leg.

"It's the one thing Grace Greystone will never have." He angrily unzipped his pants and pulled out his massive cock.

"Don't." Duke turned away.

"You never said no before." He thrust himself at him.

"Do you know how many men in this town want me that I've said no to?" Duke coolly threatened, stepping back. "Younger men, richer men, more powerful men than you. Men who like women. And they have all made it very clear..." he taunted him. "You wouldn't believe it if I told you...."

Enraged, Gorge walked over to Duke and backhanded him across the face, not afraid of leaving a bruise. Duke fell backward in shock toward the bookshelves.

"Don't you *ever* tell me that!" he screamed. "You're mine, my property. I'll never let you go. I'll kill you first and then kill myself!" Gorge raged out of control while Duke struggled and tried to throw him off. Gorge raised himself to his full six feet, four inches, overpowering him with his strength. In his fury, he angrily ripped at Duke's clothes, tearing his pressed white shirt off his body into two strips.

Gorge, who had been a high school wrestler, put Duke into a painful headlock as he tore at his boxers. Duke resisted, and in his fury, bit his hand, breaking the skin. Gorge howled and, in anger, slapped him across the ass with such force, it created a huge raised red mark, which erupted as Duke groaned.

"Stop, Gorge, you're *hurting* me!" Duke pleaded, his feminine lashes wet with tears.

"No one else owns you. I do. I made you!" He spit on his hand.

"No. Don't!" Duke whimpered. "Stop, Gorge, please!"

Gorge pulled Duke's legs apart in an obscene manner, pulled down his boxers, and forced himself on him as he screamed in pain.

"You're my bitch, and don't you ever forget it." He overpowered him, losing control in the rhythm and the fury of his grunts. Duke lay crumpled, sobbing.

"That was..." he gasped for air, "...rape." He cried, Gorge still beet-red, who snorted with a subtle grin.

"Say whatever you want." Gorge flexed his massive biceps, and struck him, with one last painful, crisp slap across his ass.

"You're mine and you love it." Gorge taunted him as he took his massive hand and ground Duke's beautiful face into the pattern of the oriental carpet and listened to him sob with deep and immense satisfaction.

Chapter Forty-Nine

Mirielle Montaigne
Panama
1945

The year 1945 was a year of contrasts: the Allies won the war, having entered the atomic age with bombs dropped on Hiroshima and Nagasaki, and Anne Frank died of typhus in Bergen-Belsen. Despite the horrors of war, conservative public taste in America saw crooner and actor, Bing Crosby, as the top money-making male celebrity in Hollywood; Les Brown and Doris Day's "Sentimental Journey" topped the charts. And it was also the year in which the French ingénue and import, Mirielle Montaigne, became an international film star. Her impossibly gorgeous face would be splashed on the covers of every major magazine and iconic movie poster on theater marquees in cities all across the country—and eventually, the globe. A sexy, illustrated color rendering of her in Jean Claude's's emerald-green, tight-fitting satin, strapless evening gown and matching long green gloves, emeralds at her throat, a cigarette holder pointed skyward, and dazzling jadeite eyes contrasting her cascading tawny red tresses would prove to be one of the most enduring and iconic movie poster images of all time. Its idealization of the female form—hip jutting, tiny waist, and uplifted, perky breasts—would be seared into public consciousness. And then at the height of her interest and adulation, it would also become the year she would entirely disappear from public view without a trace.

The lavish technicolor musical entitled *L'amour L'amour* launched like a heat-seeking missile onto the big screen, and war-weary audiences, hungry for lighthearted entertainment, were fully entranced by the racy storyline of the redheaded Follies dancer who captures the heart and pulse of a young French count against his aristocratic family's will and German occupation. Her elegant sex appeal, coupled with an angelic singing voice, would captivate an entire generation and had more than the onscreen aristocrat falling for her. Mireille Montaigne was so ravishing that the word *Montaigne* would become synonymous with enduring sex appeal. One iconic scene from the film, where she was featured *se déshabiller* in the dressing room, in a black lace bustier, would titillate the movie-going public and require negotiation with the conservative Hays office, which governed onscreen morality. Her penultimate line as she unhooked her foundation garment, freeing her breasts, purred, "American women know how to tease…" and as she eyed her prey, the darkly handsome Franchot Tone, she added, "French women know how to *please*." It instantly became part of popular culture.

Wide reporting had accompanied her highly-anticipated next film, *Antoinette*, where she held her own against Olivier, despite second billing. It would prove to be a solid and critically-acclaimed performance, also proving Montaigne had true acting chops. Oscar buzz was in the air as audiences identified with the naive and doomed queen, and Mirielle pulled emotionally from her real-life experiences fleeing the Nazi mob in Vienna. SGM was said to have lavished $250,000 on period costumes, and it was noted that she wore a diamond parure that had belonged to her own grandmother, Countess Franchetti. Bartie had planted that item in various magazines to play up her aristocratic yet vague upbringing. He also assumed that no one in the US would know that the Franchettis and the Montefiores were Italian-Jewish nobles. This was meant to give her an authentic international and sophisticated air without any religious issues for the seemingly unsophisticated public to digest. Gorgeous blonde stars like Lauren Bacall and Kirk Douglas, while also Jewish, were not profiled that way for the American public's consumption, as they were considered unable to process such "complex" issues at a time when the horrors of the Holocaust were also coming to light.

Myers took a hardened, critical stand considering her situation and tersely insisted on a staggering social schedule for Mirielle while she could still be seen in public. He was less concerned with her condition than her image since, according to him—she had brought "her downfall" upon herself. She quietly obeyed, kept up the grueling schedule, dressed to thrill, socialized in the evenings, and up for hair and makeup at the studio by 6:30. Each night, she was gowned and gloved and seen dancing at The Trocadero and the Cocoanut Grove at the town's elite dinner parties and feted by the society hostesses. She was courted by notable swordsmen Chaplin and Flynn, all who salivated at the thought but couldn't seem to crack or lure the elusive beauty home to their beds. She had captivated studio heads and their wives with her beauty, jewels, and Paris couture, and everyone in town worth knowing agreed that the magical Mirielle Montaigne had simply taken Hollywood by storm. And then once *Antoinette* wrapped, she simply…*disappeared.*

It was all going according to plan as Bartie had put the complex studio fix in motion by wisely hiring her an older, aristocratic social secretary, a bankrupt White Russian Princess Yusupov, who elegantly handled, telephoned, and sent all of Mademoiselle Montaigne's regrets. Original reports of her being exhausted and losing weight were highlighted in the press, planted by Bartie. The standing curt and regal response to any inquiry or invitation was, "Mademoiselle is currently indisposed," which gave reporters and social wags no information, and her secretary spent her days at the studio sipping mint tea and repeating the same obscure lines with little emotion. Hedda and Louella found her imperious gatekeeper impossible and wrote about the star's apparent disappearance in their columns. Was she ill? Had she eloped—or worse? Had she suddenly died? No one knew. That is until, after intense pressure, Hedda Hopper received a call and an exclusive from Bartie at a lunch at her regular booth at Perino's on Wilshire Boulevard, for which she was eternally grateful. It proved to be one of her best scoops and a satisfying lunch with her now-favorite pressman. She now "owed" Bartie, and they would continue to barter and cement their very own friendship and future press deals. Bartie was indeed getting the knack! The news was on the record and printed the very next day as Mirielle's fan mail had started mounting with hysterical and angry fans demanding answers regarding her whereabouts. Hedda was more than happy to oblige in her column and radio show.

> *HEDDA HOPPER'S HOLLYWOOD*
>
> *EXCLUSIVE: MYSTERIOUS DISAPPEARANCE OF MONTAIGNE—SOLVED.*
>
> *Mirielle Montaigne, the elusive and glamorous international star of the mega musical hit* L'amour L'amour *has surfaced of all places in Panama…hats, yachts, and all.*
>
> *Rumors of her illness and demise have been greatly exaggerated. Word from SGM is the elusive star is visiting her mother, a baroness who is thrice married to a Panamanian coffee mogul for a much-needed rest in between film projects—not that she needs beauty sleep! Montaigne's traveling companion is none other than the divine Mrs. Duke Drake. That's heiress Grace Greystone, La Marquise de La Faucigny for all those who haven't kept up with Hollywood's musical chairs. Over the last few months, word was Montaigne was everything from ill to ashes. Now we know she has been formally shipwrecked. After all, one can get "lost at sea" when one's best friend owns the world's largest yacht. All aboard the* Auntie Rose, *the 250-footer named after the late Queen of Newport Society, Greystone's own Aunt Rose McClean of the Floating McCleans, who raised her after her world-famous custody trial. A slew of handsome armed guards was said to be on board to protect the gorgeous gals and their oodles of jewels from pirates. It seems a girl's trip was in order after Montaigne finished* Antoinette, *setting sail in April. Montaigne and Greystone are due to arrive in Los Angeles next week, where Montaigne will start filming her next movie, the Hitchcock thriller,* Immortal, *with dashing Paul Henreid, while Greystone will reunite with dreamboat husband, Duke Drake. After weeks at sea and*

> *lavishing her new husband with his own polo team, the former marchioness and so-called "Duchess of Drake" will be just in time to attend the premiere of his latest movie,* Deb-on-air. *It seems rich girls are different and just want to have fun in the sun in their Panama hats!*

What the release did not reveal was that Mirielle's baby, Kyla Frieda, was born in an austere private clinic in Panama City. Bartie and Myers had picked Panama as the unlikely spot for Mirielle to give birth since, unlike Mexico, the little known Central American country was not a place that had shown Mirielle's films; therefore, she could enter and exit as a private individual without any attending press or fanfare. Michael had arrived for the birth with a private nurse in tow on a military transport set up by Myers, and they had chosen the seasoned nurse to secretly accompany him and the baby back to the orphanage in Los Angeles. The baby would be under the watchful eye of the nurse and Michael until she was formally adopted by Mirielle.

It had been a grueling few months of separation for the love-struck couple, and Michael wept when he first saw Mirielle and the baby. The chief rabbi of Panama City had been summoned to give blessings and named the baby after Mirielle's mother, Frieda, her father, Karl Frederich, and also Fritz. In Jewish tradition, a Hebrew name with the same first letters are given after the deceased, so the baby was blessed into the Jewish religion as Kyla Frieda.

"Kyla is Hebrew for *victorious*," Mirielle explained to Michael as they both wept at the sight of the baby's amazing coloring. She had bright emerald eyes from her mother and ginger hair from Michael. She knew that the birth was difficult for Grace, having just had a miscarriage, yet she took joy in seeing and holding the baby and acting as godmother. Although they had only been married a few months, Duke had been sworn to secrecy on Mirielle's pregnancy with Myers, even giving him an explicit warning that "loose lips sink ships." His complicit flexibility also earned points with Myers, and he was quite understanding about Grace's needing to accompany her best friend for a few weeks. He was shooting a small but important supporting role with a wonderful ensemble cast that Feldman had pushed him to do. They both agreed on a week's honeymoon on her return on the yacht to Catalina Island and his wrapping the movie. Duke also knew the break with Grace away would also free him up to see Gorge, once they had made up after a number of heartfelt apologies and time apart. They just couldn't seem to quit one another.

Grace joined Mirielle for the last six weeks of the leg of her trip and, despite the rest and relaxation, she was itching to get back to Los Angeles and to Duke, but knew she was an important part of the cover.

"I pray for you too, Grace. I know it will happen for you as well," Mirielle said as she held Kyla in her arms.

"She is my niece and I love her," Grace said cheerily. She then presented her with a small diamond line bracelet. "For when she's older."

Grace handed the baby back to the happy, reunited couple and went into the hallway to give them their privacy.

"I'll give you two time to be alone," Grace said after warmly embracing Michael and greeting the matronly nurse who waited in the hallway.

"I know you only have a few hours before the flight back home," Grace said gently, walking toward the garden area for a cigarette.

Michael sat at her bedside as Mirielle rocked the baby, swaddled tightly in the white-and-pink striped blanket.

"She's so beautiful, like her mother." Michael looked on with pride, a tear in his eye.

"I don't want to give her up yet. I can't bear the thought. Please," Mirielle cried.

"I'll be with her every step of the way." Michael tried to appear strong.

"It's so unfair and difficult," Mirielle cried. "Why can't I be like everyone else when they have a baby? A normal person?"

"Because you are special, Irene." He called her by her given name.

"I wish I was utterly normal." The tears fell like raindrops. "This is so painful. I won't see Kyla for two or three months."

"I will be with her every day and so will the nurse and the nuns." He took her hand. It gave them both comfort that the baby was being placed in Our Sisters of Mercy, a Catholic institution where

Michael had donated large sums and had a warm relationship with the Mother Superior.

"I've missed you so much." He looked at Mirielle's eyes and into his new daughter's beautiful face. "She will be in wonderful hands until she is back in ours. You have no need to worry."

"I know, and I'm truly grateful, Michael," she wept. "I've missed you more than you know." Mirielle looked away. It was very painful, both the reunion and their planned departure.

"It's been very hard," she cried. "Here." She reached over to the side table and handed him a slim white parchment envelope from Paris. The writing paper had the royal seal of the House of Bonaparte. As he read and digested the contents, his eyes misted over.

"I see." He lingered over the cursive script and looked up. "I'm so very sorry, Mirielle." Michael took her hand. News of the death camps had started to surface in the press with firsthand accounts of the horrors from the liberating allies and few survivors. Auschwitz, where Fritz was said to be sent, was considered one of the most horrific.

"Princess Marie confirmed from her best sources that Fritz is dead, on a death march before the camp was liberated."

"It's horrible, Mirielle. I am so very sorry." He looked down.

"It wasn't supposed to be this way." She rocked the baby with tears in her eyes. "Can you imagine? A man as brilliant as Fritz, reduced to having to lead the concentration camp orchestra. Those animals! They made them play Beethoven as they marched people to the crematoriums while they were forced to play the same music over and over. What a cruel, cruel end." She sobbed.

"I am so sorry. It's beyond imagination." They both sat in silence, not knowing what to say.

"I called Aunt Marie after I received the letter. She said she found a violinist from Vienna who last saw Fritz. When they received news of the allies winning the war, the Nazis stepped up the killing machine and marched many of the prisoners east. They're calling it a death march, and most people already sick and starving were shot or died or froze to death. He believes he saw Fritz walk onto the line where they made everyone dig a pit and...shot them."

"I see." They both sat in silence for a long while, and then he added softly, "That's nice that her middle name is Frieda." It was all Michael could think to say.

"It's the very least I can do." She wiped her tears with a lace hankie. "Poor Fritz, he always had stars in his eyes. He thought his friendship with the prime minister would save him, and in the end, he was sent to a camp as well."

"It's madness." Michael paused.

"I also know you must be pleased with the studio," she said slowly, "that they secured your divorce from Mary Katherine."

"In the end, Mary Katherine took the money. It's hard to say no to Myers and to one hundred thousand dollars. He told me they also gifted her Boston church twenty five thousand dollars for a new roof and rec room and a scholarship for the orphans."

"It's just not how I wanted to become engaged—in death, horror, and bribery," Mirielle wept.

"No worries, my darling." He leaned over and kissed her forehead. "We'll take our time. We have to think about Kyla. She's what matters most."

"I just need to process all the news about Fritz."

"It will all take a few months anyway. Let's get you back to the States and focus on the adoption, and we can discuss all this later."

"I love you, Michael. I do know that I am blessed. It just feels like I've gone from cursed to blessed to cursed. It's been so very hard."

"I know, life throws us all curveballs. When I was growing up, I never thought I would be divorced. I was an altar boy."

"Is *this* all okay for you, Michael?" She did not want to disregard his feelings.

"Yes. Love always finds a way." He kissed her. "I only thought it was in movie scripts...until I met you and now Kyla."

"Love finds a way! I like that." She dried her tears.

"Perhaps I'll have a script written around it. Good title." He tried to joke for some levity.

Later that afternoon, Grace stayed with Mirielle as she kissed Kyla and fell to pieces as Michael and the sturdy nurse took the baby from her arms. It felt like her soul was being ripped from her, and she gasped for air. The two best friends sat in the clinic in Panama and wept together, each in a sea of tears for the baby that was taken from them. Each finding solace in their love for each other and the sisterhood that kept them both going. Unlike the Hollywood press and Hedda's column, they both joked if only the public really knew the extent of the ruse and the lengths she had gone to enact the studio fix and be able to keep her baby.

"Hats and Yachts in Panama." Mirielle shook her head. "Makes us look like spoiled rich party girls, which I once was!"

"Don't apologize. My Aunt Rose McClean used to say, 'You can have a good cry for twenty minutes a day, and then you have to get on with it,'" Grace said, trying to give her best friend strength as she took her hand in hers.

"Is that the Protestant way?" Mirielle asked with a wry smile.

"Yes, dahling." Grace lit up a cigarette.

"No wonder you all rule the world."

Chapter Fifty

Bartie Maddox
Garden of Allah, Los Angeles
1946

All Bartie wanted was a cold one—hair o' the dog to solve his New Year's Day hangover. He was still in a piss poor mood; columnist Louella Parsons had taken revenge on her rival Hedda getting the Montaigne scoop and was punishing him and Myers by ignoring the item about Grace and Duke's reunion and, more importantly, ignoring a promised feature on his latest film release, *Deb-on air.* It was now all radio silence. He sighed as he opened the screen door and used his key to push open the locked wooden one and stopped in his tracks as he heard the sound of running water.

"What the…?" He turned his head around the corner of the small apartment and saw the familiar sight of a beautiful, buxom, twenty-something blonde in a white satin torpedo brassiere and panties and an apron with pointy-toed high heels cleaning a pan in the sink.

"Surprise!" Carroll Madison turned and gave him her best high-wattage smile.

"Carroll, what are you doing here?" Bartie was astonished at her presence. "Who let you in?"

"I thought you'd be glad to see me." She lifted her ample bust. "I just asked at the front desk, and they gave me the key." She winked. "I told them I was your sister visiting from Sioux Falls."

"I'm sure they believed you. My sister, really?" He laughed sarcastically.

"Why wouldn't they? They let me in alright," she shrugged. "I've been here before."

"No one's gonna turn *you* down." He shook his head at the thought of the platinum bombshell and old man Reilly at the front desk. He would have opened the safe for her if she asked.

"Hey," he said, "what are you doing here?"

"The dishes, can't you see?" She was tidying up in his little kitchenette.

"I can see fine, but you've never surprised me before. Knowing you, I think there's more to it than you wanted to just hang out and cook for me," he laughed.

"Well, that's your take."

"You know how much I enjoy our time together, but I was very upfront that I live alone, and I like my…privacy." He walked over and nuzzled into her neck and felt her luminous breasts from behind.

"I know what you said, but the one thing I learned about men is that they never mean what they say." She turned to him and nonchalantly unhooked her torpedo satin and lace brassiere. "Aren't you happy to see…*them*?" She giggled.

Bartie couldn't deny his immediate erection at the sight of her wondrous, high, full, firm breasts—nor her madcap personality. She was one of the few women who could actually make him laugh. Although Carroll had perfected the art of the dumb blonde, she clearly wasn't.

"Really, I mean you, they are…*beautiful,* Carroll." He reached out and felt the high soft pillows of her breasts. "Really beautiful." He started feeling her all over, unable to control himself.

"I just thought you might be hungry, so I came over and made you peanut butter and jelly sandwiches over there." She pointed to a small plate. "I got all fancy and cut the crust off for you," she said in a singsong voice.

"Wow, that's very domestic of you." He laughed, running one hand over her erect nipple and the other around her tight, lean waist. He leaned down and started sucking on her lovely pink nipples, as she reached between his legs and started stroking his cock through his chinos.

"Yeah, I put macaroni and cheese in the fridge for you too. I wanted you to have a really good home-cooked meal since you probably haven't had one in a while."

"Among other things."

"Well, all you need to do is just call me." Her naivete was so disarming; he delighted in her little girl quality and forgave her by kissing her neck, his five o'clock shadow tickling her.

"And why are you doing all this for…me?" He breathed heavily.

"Because you said you would help get me into Hedda Hopper's column for my latest walk-on, and you did…and I wanted to thank you properly," she said.

"I would say you already thanked me properly last Saturday night, but I'm happy to be thanked again and again."

"Well, you're handsome and funny and sweet, not like a lot of the awful guys I meet here, and I have a thing…for older men." She started unbuttoning his shirt and caressing the light hair on his chest. "You remind me of my high school gym coach, and he was older and handsome too." She snuggled into him.

"I'm not that old, Carroll. I'm twenty-four. They consider me one of the younger ones on the lot."

"That's *ancient* when you're nineteen."

"I thought you told me you were twenty-two."

"Who cares about details?"

"And did you also thank him?" He kissed her, his breath heavy against her cheek.

"Who?"

"Your gym teacher?"

"Oh, him, as much as I could behind the bleachers." She deftly unzipped his trousers, crouched down on her heels, and pulled down his boxer shorts. She kissed his penis and then started licking the tip.

"Yeah," he said as she put her luscious lips on him.

"He loved being thanked."

"Wait!" He suddenly froze in place.

"What?" She looked up at him, quite surprised.

"What's that?" Bartie pointed to a beat-up plastic aqua suitcase.

"What's what?" She shrugged.

"That?" He pointed at the suitcase again.

"Oh, that! Just a few things."

"A few things of what?" His eyes flickered, and his dark, bushy eyebrows furrowed together.

"Oh, Bartie, I just need to stay for two days. I couldn't pay my rent this month at the boarding house since I bought a secondhand mink stole for a movie premiere, and my landlady locked me out." She paused. "I have nowhere to go, and payday is on Friday. Only 'til then."

"What happened to all the money Marty Lester's son gave you?"

"I bought that mink coat and a pair of diamond earrings."

"And you can't pay your rent?"

"I need to *look* like a movie star if I want to *be* one," she said with the total seriousness of a student in medical school and their new prized stethoscope.

"So, you have a mink but nowhere to live? Makes sense. Seriously, Carroll, this is not what I agreed to. You can't move in with me," Bartie sputtered in pleasure.

"Please—pretty please—with sugar on top?" She dropped to her knees and started licking him again. "Just two lil' ol' days ol'…Bartie."

"Umm…yeah, just like that. Where did you get to be so good at that? Hmm hmm." Bartie rested back on his haunches against a table.

Carroll spit on her hand and artfully caressed the head of his penis as she answered, like she was on a job interview for a serious law firm.

"Gorge Lamont," she said nonchalantly.

"What?" He stopped in awe. "Gorge Lamont taught you that?"

"Well, everyone knows around town he has the *best* technique for head. So, my friend Connie is friendly with him, and we all got drunk one night, and he showed us how to give a great blow job by practicing on a banana. Like this." Carroll deep throated Bartie in such a way that his eyes rolled back in his head.

"Thank you, Gorge!" he exclaimed, before adding, "And does that bother you, two men together?"

"It's just fucking. You know what they say, a hole's a hole." She giggled as she reached up and played with her pink nipple as he watched her and stopped, just as he was getting even more excited. When she reached between her legs and started touching herself, Bartie started stroking himself at the amazing sight of the blonde pinup pleasuring herself and moaning. It was almost too much for him to bear.

"Please," she licked her lips. "I want you inside me," she moaned.

Bartie reached over and thrust his middle finger into her hot, wet pussy, and she responded by writhing all over him.

"Okay, okay, you win. Just a day or two," he acquiesced as he eased into her after he struggled to put on a condom he had extracted from his wallet.

"Just for two days. I promise you won't even know I'm here. I'll cook, I'll clean, I'll food shop, and when you want me to be here, we can do this any time you want, I promise." She gave him a dazzling smile.

"Sure, just keep doing what you are doing, and don't stop," he commanded as they both fell to the floor.

"Anything you say, Bartie. Aren't you glad I came over?" She moaned, and they rolled over.

"Yeah, Carroll, *whatever you want.*" Bartie let her do all the work as she pumped away and rode him. She quickly brought him to climax as he looked up at her monumental tits.

"Whenever I want?"

"Sure." He groaned. Carroll Madison, he thought, may not have been Bette Davis, but she was Academy Award material in the sack, that was for sure.

"Bartie?"

"Yes, Carroll?"

"Since you offered," she demurred. "I haven't had a *real* role in a while. I mean with…*lines*." She snuggled into his neck. "Pretty please?"

"Yeah, sure, Carroll."

"Promise? With *lines*?" She stroked him.

"With lines. Promise."

"How?" She stopped stroking.

"Don't! Stop! I'll call my friend, the director, Bill Mackay," he said in a moment of unbridled heat.

Chapter Fifty-One

Bartie Maddox
Culver City, Los Angeles
1946

"Look, Kid, you did a great job with Mirielle's fix, and I decided I'm giving you a raise to two-fifty a week. By the way, that was what Menowitz was making, the schmuck." Myers slapped him on the back with pride.

"Why, Mister Myers, well, that's just..." He beamed, wide-eyed. "All I can say is...wow," Bartie answered. "Thank you so much!"

"You really are that...*nice*, huh?" Myers surveyed him like he was seeing a bizarre circus act. "Unlike these snake oil salesmen I have to deal with from New *Yawk* who want more and more without a damn thank you." He smiled, revealing his oversized caps. "I just want you to know it was a great fix, and it also seems to be working out with the *fagalah*. The Duke of Drake and the rich *goil* too. You hit a triple, maybe even a homer."

"Thank you, Mister Myers."

"You know, I'm going to give you a little advice," he said hoisting the 14K-gold lighter on his desk. He kept sparking the fire and then letting it go and then sparking it again with his calloused thumb and forefinger. "'Cause I like you. I tol' Freyda I like that kid. So, use your *kop*, take the money, and put a down payment on a small house. Don't keep throwing away money renting at that Garden of um...*Alice*." Bartie smiled, as he couldn't help but keep his Myerisms in check. "I'll front you the down payment! You don't want to turn around and end up with *nuttin'*," Myers advised. "Get yourself a little house and start building your future."

"Really? Thanks so much, Mister Myers. That's incredibly generous of you. And of course, anything you say. I know how smart you are."

"That's because I had to be…growing up in an *orphanage!* Edna!" he yelled. "Bring Bartie here a bagel! This Kid needs to eat, the skinny *malink*." He looked him up and down. "And the press wasn't all that bad either. Louella's punishing us, but Hedda did a nice job, as usual. How is everything going with the adoption?"

"Great. Michael visits the baby with the nurse and the Mother Superior every day. The adoption on both babies will go through shortly."

"Great, send Hedda some flowers from me. She also did a good job for us on the lovebirds' reunion. She made it out that Duke likes women and does the *doity* deed…."

"*Doity* deed?" Bartie asked perplexed.

"In the front door!"

"Front door?"

"What's wrong with you…the ole *pussoir. The doity deed in the pussoir.*"

"Doity?" Bartie looked up in confusion.

"Yeah *Doity. Doity*!"

"Oh, dirty."

"That's what I said. Ya need a hearing aid, Kid? Anyway, Hedda's happy now."

"She loves Grace Greystone." Bartie shook his head knowing how impressed she was by the heiress.

"Of course she does, the old hag. Thinks Greystone's bank account will rub off on her."

"Well, Grace seems to be very happy with Duke." He smiled.

"Yeah, but you know these rich gals. It's all a lark. Not like Freyda and me. Thirty-one years later, and she still rips out my *kishkes*." He swallowed his Bromo-Seltzer. "Anything else before I run?" He looked at his slim, gold wristwatch. "I'm having lunch with Berle and Burns at Hillcrest. Don't wanna be late for the brisket sandwich."

"Actually, one last thing, Mister Myers."

"Shoot, boy wonder." Myers sat at his desk with a look of both pride and annoyance.

"It's more than an idea for a campaign. It's actually a way to promote a movie and maybe build a new star."

"Okay, shoot, who is she? Who are you bangin' now?" He leered at him. "That's why you look so pale and thin. She's suckin' the jizz and life out of you."

"It's not like that Mister Myers, but I think I may have a good idea."

"Yeah, yeah, okay, who's the dame? Out with it." He cracked some black walnuts with an ornate silver nutcracker and swept the shells and debris on the floor as he chomped on the meat of the nuts. "I would tell ya to stop bangin' the trim, but at least you're a normal, red-blooded, all-American, and not some…" he grimaced, *"fag* like Queen Lamont and his carpet-muchin' wife!"

"Well, I got this script for one of the B movies. I know we don't always push them on the PR front, but I read the script, and this one could be a real money-maker. It's called *Blondes from Outer Space.* I know it's low-budget, but it's about aliens who capture big, busty blondes to procreate after Los Angeles is hit by a nuclear bomb. I think it's timely," Bartie explained.

"Whose directing?"

"Bill Mackay."

"Figures. The friggin' *hack!*" A piece of nut spittle flew from Myers's mouth. "The King of the Bs."

"But with public interest in the atomic bomb in Hiroshima, I think this could actually be a real sleeper hit."

"Okay, so who's in it?" He genuinely seemed interested.

"They're talking about Claude Rains. Bill hasn't cast the female lead yet, but I have an idea on who it should be and a way to spin it."

"Okay, okay…she must be some piece if you're *pitchin'*!" His eyes sparkled at the thought of Bartie getting some.

"You know Marty Lester's old girlfriend, Carroll Madison? You asked me to come up with a handle…." Bartie asked softly, blushing.

"You mean your girlfriend?"

"She's not my girlfriend. She's my friend."

"Yeah, and Gorge Lamont loves pussy." He laughed and winked. "I'm impressed you got right in there, doggin' ole Marty's gal. Boy, she's some *numbah*! Gettin' some of that trim." He salivated, licking his lips.

"She's fun, and she'd be perfect for this," Bartie offered a bit too weakly.

"Her?" He racked his brain. "She's as dumb as a brick I hear. Must be great in bed if you're all revved up about her." He salivated at the thought.

"I'm telling you, Mister Myers, this girl is special. She has the makings of a real sex symbol, and she's funny...like Lombard was."

"Really? And the tits?" He cracked another nut.

"I have to say, they are two of the ten wonders of the world."

"Really?" Myers licked his lips salaciously. "So, what's your big idea, big shot?"

"We give her the lead in the movie, and I came up with the perfect idea for her...Carroll Madison." He blocked out his hands. "Harlow was called the 'platinum blonde.' My idea is to call her the 'Anatomic Atomic Blonde' or the 'Atomic Blonde.'"

Myers sat back and listened and then whistled out loud and actually nodded. "You know, Kid, you might be onto something. This town hasn't had a blonde bombshell since Harlow and Lombard died. Can she fuck?"

"She puts the whores at Maude's to shame."

"Not bad, Bartie—ya think she can act?"

"I'm not sure, but she created a sensation as the Tight Sweater Girl in the Van Johnson movie, *University Blues*."

"Okay...arrange it."

"You wanna screen test her?"

"No way—just arrange for her to come and see me. I want to see if this Carroll Madison is all you say she is, in *pois-on.*"

"Poison?"

"Poisss-on."

"Oh, person."

"Ya gotta get that hearing of yours checked, ya dumb fuck."

"Sure, Mister Myers. Regarding Carroll, I'll have her contact Edna for an appointment."

"Are you crazy? She'll go right to Freyda." He paused. "Can I trust ya?"

"You know you can, Mister Myers."

"I can't be out on the lot, like you, scouting fer *new* talent. Fa Chrissakes! This week, you and I will say we're working late," he whispered, "and you can bring her after Mussolini out there," he pointed at Edna, "goes home, and then you can drop her off, so I can inspect and sample the goods. Wait, you're not overly sweet on her, are you?" He looked at him shrewdly, squinting his left eye.

"No, I mean we do have the occasional tumble, but she's great fun, and I think she can be a real blonde star."

"I mean, I just wanna get a look at her in person…get my drift…to see for myself if she has star quality! Ya know, to sample the goods," he repeated, wanting to make himself clear.

"Of course. I'm sure she'll be thrilled to meet you."

"You know, Bartie…I'm liking this idea more and more. And if this Carroll Madison is all you say she is, I am going to double the down payment on that house of yours. *The Atomic Blonde Bombshell*! I like it!"

"Wait, Mister Myers, that's better than what I suggested."

"What is?"

"Atomic Blonde Bombshell."

"You said it."

"I mean the way you phrased it."

"Bombshell Schmamshell. I just wanna see those…*tits*."

Chapter Fifty-Two

Mrs. Duke Drake
Hillcrest Country Club
Los Angeles
1946

Twelve weeks into her marriage, Grace was finally getting the hang of it—or so she thought. The social firmament in LA was quite different than Grace had experienced in Europe, which had been more snobbish and rarified based on royalty, family lineage, and titles. On the West Coast of Los Angeles, beauty, money, and fame reigned supreme, especially the beauty and the fame. And Mrs. Duke Drake was just trying to adjust to her new role as a Hollywood wife.

After a lovely and relaxing week-long honeymoon reunion with Duke on the yacht to Catalina Island, she had moved her remaining things from her Beverly Hills bungalow into Drake Manor and was starting to accept social invitations from the town's leading hostesses for lunch and card parties while Duke was on set. And word in town was that all the savvy hostesses in town knew not to mix her with the other leading Hollywood wife of the moment, Leticia St. Clair-Lamont, for obvious reasons.

The handwritten invitation hand delivered by Mrs. Solomon Myers's Scottish butler for lunch at Hillcrest Country Club was akin to a royal audience in London and was immediately accepted knowing the couple had now been admitted to LA's version of rarified air. She and Duke debated her fashion choice, picking a demure Chanel suit that Coco, herself, had fitted for Grace, along with ropes and ropes of pearls to meet her husband's boss's wife. She agreed that an understated, more conservative fashion statement was more appropriate as Duke explained that while Freyda Myers was not a fashion plate herself, she had an equally frightening reputation as her husband for passing judgment. She was known for being as tough and direct as her husband was, often using her influence with her spouse to either promote friends or to settle petty scores with anyone who didn't sufficiently bow and scrape to the "President of the President" as she was called. Unlike Hedda or Louella, she was not known to ever be *forgiving*; in fact, the word was not featured in her vocabulary.

"It's Freyda Myers's way or the highway!" was her own frightening Myerism. Freyda, like her husband, appreciated the art of intimidation, and when, word had it, one well-known yet inebriated film actress failed to recognize her and sufficiently bow and scrape in the powder room of the Beverly Wilshire, her pending contract was not picked up, terminated without explanation, and her things tossed in the studio lot in a junk heap. When her friends and directors started to protest, Freyda took it one step further and terminated their contracts as well. From that moment on, Freyda Myers had ruled LA with an iron fist; some talent had to be sacrificed to let everyone know she meant business. She had learned from her husband, or vice versa. The gray streak in front of her bouffant gave her the look of a menacing ghoulish actress in a horror movie—and that's how she liked it.

"Did you hear the latest? The Mackays are getting a divorce!" Freyda Myers intoned, peering over the embossed leather menu with a pair of ebony reading glasses. "You know the old joke, once she turned forty, he decided to cash her in for two twenties. Men are the worst, especially… *directors*."

"Who to?" the entire table asked at the same time.

"Some tramp he met on his new picture. Get this title: *Blondes from Outer Space*. I told Solly he has to buy me a diamond necklace if he's going that low, but he claims it's going to be a big success, so I expect bigger carats." She chuckled, though with serious intent.

"And who's the girl?" The chorus of women all leaned in, their diamond bracelets jangling in unison.

"Some tramp called Carroll something or other. He hasn't officially proposed to her, but word is he is crazy for her and didn't come home for a week straight. Oh, I forgot! She was Marty Lester's old mistress."

"Smart girl," the hens clucked.

Freyda adjusted a precise curl in her hair, which had been freshly set that morning by a studio stylist sent over each morning to their Del Air mansion. She summoned the waiter with the turn of her eye and invited the women to order as the staff trembled. No one would ever say she was either young or pretty, but she enjoyed the role of the Grande Dame and exercised her position bloodlessly. No one can say she wasn't also an original. She kept herself rail thin and was a noted vegan before anyone embraced the concept. She drank no alcohol—only fresh juices—and did yoga with a swami. She was known for an entirely white house, embracing modernism long before it was in vogue and only wore navy as she detested black and colors of any sort. Navy and diamonds. Diamonds and navy. Freyda Myers knew she would never be a great beauty, but she was rich and powerful, and she willed herself to be chic and formidable...and she was. Referred to by Hedda as the *Queen of the Navy*, it offset her sharp features which proclaimed her queenly status. In Freyda's book, lunch at the club with Grace Greystone, La Marquise de La Faucigny-Drake was a social triumph, and she wanted to be the first to arrange a suitable star-studded lunch and rub it in everyone else's noses. Her guest list included Arlene Gladstone, known as "America's Sweetheart" and one of the town's richest stars, and Zsa Zsa Gabor, the glamorous Hungarian blonde import who was married to Conrad Hilton. Freyda was given her husband's centrally-located power table in the dining room as he took his lunch with his cronies that day in the men's card lounge. He would never have countered his wife's request for his table, and it was also widely known that Edna sent her white long-stem flowers every Friday night with an "I love you" note handwritten from her trembling husband, Solly.

It was a legend in LA that when the young and broke Solomon Myers had first arrived in LA trying to produce silent film reels to distribute on the East Coast, he met the studious Freyda through her sister, Bessie, whom he had asked out before her. Their father owned a string of burgeoning movie theaters, and when Freyda saw his own anxious ambition and East Coast energy, she threw over her own sister, who never talked to her again, persuaded her father he would be successful to his dismay, and married him within weeks. Freyda Myers knew a winner when she saw one, and she staked her claim and would never let him go. While Solomon Myers ruled SGM studios, the steely and shrewd Freyda ruled Myers and never let him live it down that he had "married up" and that her father had lent him the money to start the studio after working for his mentor, Marty Lester.

Freyda perused the menu, relaying the news about the director leaving his wife for a mere contract girl.

"Helen is beside herself. Thirty years of marriage down the drain, all for a peroxide tramp," she sighed. "You know how men are in this town, and if you're a *semi*-successful director like Bill, you have every young thing throwing themselves at you. It's a wonder anyone stays married for as long as they do." Her whimsical Cartier Tutti Frutti bracelets added a bit of expensive glamour to her chic navy suit.

"Dahling, she clearly has other forms of ammunition," Zsa Zsa laughed, breaking the table up.

"Not that I should talk," Grace offered the group her opinion, "but in Europe, it's quite different. The good families go back generations, and the couples often stay together for the sake of the family lineage. In Paris, it's not unusual for a man to see his younger mistress between five to seven and then be home for dinner. The French actually have a term for it called *a cinq à sept*. It took a bit of getting used to." She blew a ghostlike, circular smoke ring and laughed, as did the other women at the table, her monumental diamond ring capturing attention.

"Then why did you divorce, dahling?" Zsa Zsa batted her eyelashes.

"He was a Nazi *and* a philanderer." Grace stood her ground. "I could forgive the second but not the first."

"Well, I'm glad someone at the table has morals," Freyda toasted.

"Yes, a cheater is one thing, but a Nazi is another," Arlene Gladstone, the retired silent film star who was considered cinematic royalty, said. "When I turned fifty, I just told my husband I was closing up shop, and he could do whatever he pleased. We are coming up on our twentieth anniversary. I honestly didn't want to muss my hair since I go to the beauty parlor twice a week." She gave a knowing laugh.

"Dahling, you know *vhat* I *alvays* say," the gorgeous Gabor offered, every man in the room staring at her impressive and luminescent bust. "Getting divorced just because you don't love a man is almost as silly as getting married just because you do." She checked herself in her jeweled compact. Grace noticed that all of the women she met in Los Angeles were very "done" and took immaculate care of their hair, and their nails were incredibly turned out, whereas the women she knew in France, while incredibly stylish, were somewhat less intentional in their desire for perfection—and used less hairspray.

"Leave it to Zsa Zsa to have figured it out." The entire table erupted into laughter at the Hungarian beauty.

"Well, at least we have one newlywed at the table," Freyda proclaimed. "How was your honeymoon with Duke, dear?" she asked politely, avoiding his curious reputation.

"It was divine. We took the yacht to Catalina Island for the week, and it was heaven. We read and sunned. I felt like I was in Cap-Ferrat," she laughed.

"I heard you bought him a polo team as his wedding present?" Freyda repeated the news to the table.

"Yes, in Palm Beach. We both love to ride. I did offer him a B-1 bomber, but he turned that down." The table laughed despite Grace being entirely serious.

"Well, Sol told me that while Duke was filming *Deb-On-Air*, you were in Panama with Mirielle Montaigne. How was your girls' trip? I hear you two are the best of friends," she clucked.

"It was lovely. I'm very close with her and her mother, who has been married more times than all of us put together, and Mirielle needed a rest after the last two films." She stuck to Bartie's carefully orchestrated script at Michael's request.

"Is she really the daughter of a baron?" Freyda inquired, gathering information for her husband.

"Yes, I knew her father personally. He was one of the most elegant men in Europe."

"She has a divine face." Arlene blew a puff of smoke. "How did you two meet?"

"On vacation in Switzerland." Grace offered up her white lie and omitted the Swiss sanatorium. "We were both at a house party of a mutual friend's villa in Geneva and have been best friends ever since. Mirielle was always destined for stardom, but her father never wanted her to be on the stage or screen, but that is normal in those circles. He preferred that she marry well, and I, myself, made the same mistake."

"Everyone has, darling. Arlene's been married three times!" Freyda filled her in.

"Yes," she nodded. "The first was Basil Sherwood—actors are a big mistake. The second was the screenwriter Heywood Sykes-Browne, who was always drunk. And then I got smart and upgraded to a producer, Linus de Barre, my current ball and chain," Arlene said with a wry, knowing smile. "And then I retired, and *he's* producing, so it still works. That and separate bathrooms are the key to a good marriage." She smiled and waved to Louella Parsons across the room.

"You look so fabulous, I don't understand why you retired." Grace marveled at her still-exquisite features.

"That's what all my fans say," Arlene smiled, "but they don't know the truth about this town."

"Truth?" Grace seemed honestly perplexed.

"Should I fill Grace in on the sad reality?" Arlene shook her teased hair.

"Yes." A chorus resounded around the table.

"Retired? My ass!" she cackled. "After forty, you're lucky if they hand you a grandmother role in a black-and-white B horror movie. I started when I was fifteen years old, and I was a little, cute cornfed hoofer from the Midwest who became famous overnight. But there are realities to being a young ingénue." She lit a cigarette and inhaled.

"Such as?" Grace leaned in. She was intoxicated by Arlene's close proximity and revelation. After all, Arlene Gladstone was cinematic royalty, having acted in the '20s with Chaplin.

"At age fifteen, my call time was eight-thirty," Arlene reminisced. "When I arrived, they primped me in hair and makeup for a few minutes and sent me off to do my scene. After working with Charlie, I was the studio darling. Then a few years later, they wanted me a bit earlier—eight—to do hair and makeup when I was having my star turn with *American Doll*. Then years later, when I turned twenty-six, they moved it to seven-forty-five. At thirty-nine, and with talkies, my call time for hair and makeup was five-forty-five…can you imagine? Just so they could spackle me to make me look fresh. Finally, they couldn't go any earlier, and I wasn't going to play an axe-murdering aunt, so with no roles and a substantial jewelry collection from all my beau, I decided to *retire* from the silver screen. There's a moment when you realize it's better to go out on top," she revealed amidst the clouds of cigarette smoke.

"Grace, did you know that you and Arlene are now neighbors? Fair Acres sits above Duke and your mansion in Bel Air," Freyda offered.

"You own Fair Acres?" Grace looked at her wide-eyed. It was considered one of the grandest estates in Hollywood as it had been constructed on a former ranch in California during the '20s on fourteen prime acres in Bel Air. Grace was suddenly intrigued.

"Oh, yes, for many years."

"Oh, I had no idea." Grace had read in fan magazines that it was the largest mansion on the West Coast, a palace brought over stone by stone from France.

"You must come over," Arlene said, "but you will need to give me advance notice since it's quite large, and I have to find people. They tend to get *lost* when they arrive," she quipped.

"Arlene is the only woman in this town that Sol is jealous of. She was one of the first women to invest in a movie studio and lives in a palace."

"Now, I just finance movies instead of star in them."

"Well, that's equally impressive," Grace added. "And Fair Acres is just above the bend. I see the mansion from my bedroom terrace."

"Yes, though you do have to tell that handsome husband of yours his late-night parties and all the cars cause a traffic jam." She shrugged.

"Parties? Are you sure?" Grace cocked her head sideways at this tidbit, never having witnessed one.

"Why, yes, at least twice a month…always on a Thursday night, and it's always jam-packed. And one car almost drove me off the road. I have a feeling the young boy had been drinking a bit too much."

"Oh, I'll have to ask Duke. Perhaps Thursday is his boys' night card party." She shrugged innocently.

"Yes, that's most likely it." Freyda Myers raised a well plucked eyebrow and flashed Arlene a seemingly indiscreet and glaring look not to proceed on the subject.

"I apologize on Duke's behalf," Grace offered, the women at the table flashing knowing glances. "I am sure he will be horrified he caused you any inconvenience," Grace said, taking a puff of her cigarette, the women at the table entranced by her ropes of priceless south sea pearls and her chic Chanel couture. "We must make amends and have you all over for a proper dinner now that his bachelor days are over."

"Now, Grace, don't you mention a thing to Duke. Boys will be boys," Arlene offered, at which Freyda kicked her friend under the table for good measure. The lunch wrapped, and Grace kissed and thanked Mrs. Myers for her hospitality and her generous wedding gift of an entire service of English silver.

"We must have you and Solomon over once we are unpacked. You will be my *very first* dinner party."

"That would be lovely," Freyda said in a clipped tone that ensured if they weren't the first and guests of honor, there would be subtle hell to pay. "Sol doesn't usually go out much, but I am sure I can persuade him *this one time*." She then added, "You'll send me dates when you are settled."

"Lunch was divine. I have dinner tonight with Lily Pons and Andre Kostelanetz, and I have to have my hair done, so I am off to the beauty parlor. Would anyone care for a lift?" Grace offered.

"I *vould* luff one. I think I am coming down with a bit of a migraine," Zsa Zsa said, rising, while every man in the room was glued to her stunning figure in her aqua satin dress. She hadn't been Miss Hungary 1936 for nothing, like Irene, fleeing the Nazis, with her Jewish-born mother and sisters.

It was only 2:15 when Grace had her chauffeur-driven Rolls-Royce drop Zsa Zsa back at her mansion off Sunset.

"Zsa Zsa, I do hope you feel better. Use a hot rag on your forehead. I always do when I am getting a headache," Grace instructed, thinking she was ill and gave her a hug and double kisses.

"No, dahling, I *vant* one in time for *vhen* Conrad comes home, if you get my drift." She smiled, her exquisite diamond-and-ruby earrings sparkling in the sunlight.

"Duke and I would love to have you and Conrad over for dinner when I have set up house."

"Of course, dahling. I have one piece of advice, Grace. Just make sure you are a good housekeeper." She patted her hand.

"Oh, I have five in-staff," Grace said.

"No, dahling. *Vhat* I meant *vas*...I'm a marvelous housekeeper. Every time I leave a man, I *keep his house*." She laughed at her own *bon mot*, throwing her stylish and luxurious mink around her shoulders as she exited the car.

As the stylish and feminine Zsa Zsa disappeared from view, Grace suddenly changed her mind and asked her driver to take her back to Drake Manor to retrieve her own diamond-and-ruby chandelier earrings. Being around such incredibly glamorous and artfully turned-out women like Zsa Zsa and Arlene Gladstone made her think she needed to put more effort into her appearance. She would show her hairdresser the earrings in advance, and perhaps he would want to do an upswept style when he saw them. She wanted to look equally as fabulous for her famous and handsome husband, given the competition at hand.

The car entered the imposing gates and climbed the long drive to the car park area. Grace exited the car as the chauffeur opened the car door and once inside the English manor, she took off her heels, as her feet hurt her and it was a long climb and good exercise up the grand wooden and slate stone staircase.

The mansion was eerily silent and empty of staff as if they had all been given the afternoon off, which felt odd to her. As she approached the landing, she turned left and walked down the dimly-lit hallway, past an antique suit of armor toward her bedroom to access her jewel case which rested on an antique writing desk in her boudoir. She passed a suit of armor which, seemed comical given its lack of provenance. *That will have to go*, she thought to herself. She had been given permission by Duke to redecorate at her own expense. She understood his need to live in an English manor house given his image, but she wanted a more feminine, lighter, and more welcoming home as she found Tudors dark and oppressive.

While she passed the upstairs library, she suddenly heard a tangle of male voices and a series of strange noises, even one that sounded like a slap. She cocked her head and walked gingerly toward Duke's bedroom. She wasn't quite sure if he was home but remembered he had said he was doing a photoshoot at the studio with the photographer, Hurrell, that evening. She entered his suite as the door was slightly ajar, and as she walked inside, she froze in place, stupefied. Duke was on his back in a strange position with his legs in the air, wrapped around the torso of a muscular blonde man, who was slapping and grunting. The realization and shock set in as she saw Gorge Lamont on top of her husband, fucking him. While she had many homosexual friends, she had never seen two men together in bed having sex, and it was beyond her comprehension. Clearly, she now knew the rumors she had heard were true.

"Duke…?" She gasped as she looked on in horror as both heads swiveled, and Duke looked at her in a panic.

"Grace!" he shouted as he looked up in shock and surprise. "Please…" He tried to untangle himself from Gorge as Grace fled the room, running toward the grand staircase as he ran after her in the nude down the stairs.

"Grace, it doesn't change anything! Please!" he begged as he ran.

Grace turned and looked up.

"We're still…*newlyweds*!" She looked up at him, tears in her eyes.

"But you knew…" he cried. "I told you…."

"Not this—I didn't agree to *this*!" she shouted. "I'm your wife now, and you promised me you'd *changed*."

Gorge's blond, muscular figure emerged and appeared on the landing wrapped in a terry cloth towel as he looked down on her in disdain.

"You may be his wife for a few months, but he's been my *wife* for years." And he stood there laughing scornfully at her. "Now, Duke, get back up here. I'm not done fucking you yet." His laughter resounded and echoed through the house as Grace ran from the English castle and from another man who had, once again, broken her heart.

Chapter Fifty-Three

Carroll Madison
Hancock Park, Los Angeles
1946

A nude, beached Bill Mackay lay wheezing on his back in the new apartment he had rented for Carroll, his prodigious stomach rising and falling as he gasped for air. It was a sublet given to him in the Ravenswood Apartments in tony Hancock Park by an actor he knew who was moving back to New York to do theater for the year. He caught his breath and wiped his brow after a particularly active romp on her circular bed. It was so intense, he thought he was on the verge of a heart attack. *But if I'm going to go out, I might as well go out with "a bang,"* he thought to himself, laughing. He knew his old, crazy, and tragic crony, Dumont, would have appreciated that one!

Mackay had surprised Carroll with the rental when their affair first started, as they needed a place to tryst outside the prying eyes of the studio and his wife. When he gave her the keys and told her Mae West lived in the same building, Carroll did a little scream for effect and batted her false eyelashes with the realization she was now her neighbor. She was more than appreciative, and it didn't escape her that she had come a long way from her rooming house and ignominious start at Maude's. Bill, in his largesse, also let Carroll decorate the new place in what Gorge Lamont would later call the "Rococo meets Bordello period." Regardless, Carroll was in her glory at the new gold moldings and pink satin sheets. It was a sexy den of iniquity, but the overall effect rendered it somewhat comical to the trained eye.

To Carroll, it was heaven, and she set out to make it into a sensual, expensive, and alluring love den for her and her newest paramour. While primarily known as the ultimate B director, or a successful hack by industry insiders, Bill Mackay was the brass ring for a contract girl like Carroll. It meant she was now "going places" with his support. After they had gone through an hour of Kama-Sutra-style lovemaking, they lay in bed exhausted in a sheen of perspiration and mascara.

"I saw the rushes yesterday." He lay back against the large down-filled pillows, talking above his shallow breathing and lighting up a Camel. "After twenty-five takes, you actually have a few that are quite exceptional. Star quality, I would say."

"Well, I want to thank you again and again for believing in me." She intertwined her hands through his.

They both laughed at the ordeal and how they had initially come together.

***

It was the first day of shooting, and Carroll didn't sleep the night before due to overall nervousness. She had been a principal extra in a few B movies, but she only had one real scene as an actor with one line—only having to utter "Oh, my darling, yes!*" when Van Johnson presented and pinned her tumescent breasts encased in the all-too famous cashmere sweater set scene. Now she had, as Bartie had promised her, a real lead and real lines to memorize. The problem was she had no idea how to memorize anything and did not know how to pronounce the larger words. After showing up early for hair and makeup, Carroll was to play opposite Claude Rains, the seasoned actor, which was intimidating enough. The script was a surreal post-war nuclear black-and-white thriller. The plot was somewhat bizarre; the earth had been destroyed by an atomic bomb and space blondes appear to repopulate and save the world as Claude Rains is the only remaining man! Lucky him! Carroll's role as Princess Zara, a futuristic space alien, was "the atomic anatomic blonde showcasing her prodigious wares." Much had gone into creating a futuristic metallic brassiere so spectacular that when she finally emerged on set, the brassiere, with Carroll in it, got a standing ovation. At first glance, Bill thought she was sensational—until he found out she had real trouble with her lines.*

When he proclaimed, "Action!" and Claude Rains said, "Why are you here?" Carroll froze. Then they yelled, "Cut!" which made her more nervous. Then, she was fed the line and she still blew it. She was supposed to say, "I've been sent down to earth to procreate and help reestablish the kingdom."

"It's not po-cate!" Bill yelled from his director's chair after eight flubbed takes. "Or PO-CRATE—it's pro-CRE-ate, as in you ate my cock, you stupid cow," he shouted. Carroll was so embarrassed and devastated, she ran from the set and barricaded herself in her small dressing room.

Finally, after waiting half an hour, Bill Mackay realized that he may have overdone it and, in the moment, had forgotten that Myers himself had put in a word for her. So, he bit his tongue and decided to pay his lead actress a visit in her dressing room. He'd had enough experience with nervous actresses over the years that he would have to hold her hand like a baby. But if it was Myers who wanted it, so be it—although he knew he would also be taken to task by the man if the movie was over time and over budget. He was a gruff man by nature, but gently knocked on the door.

"Carroll, I want to apologize for losing my temper. You are a talented and stunning young actress. Everyone is nervous on their first day on the set," he offered, thinking only of an angry call from Myers. The door opened, and he saw her red-eyed as she looked up at him like a little girl. He felt terrible at the sight of her tear-streaked face.

"I want to apologize too," she said, wide-eyed. "I love a man who can say he's sorry, and so can I."

"Here's the trick. Don't take it all so seriously." He took her hand in his.

"Yes, and I can show you how sorry I am." She pulled him right into the dressing room and dropped to her knees. At that moment, Bill Mackay knew he had hit the sexual jackpot.

Later, when it came to her nervousness, Bill told her to think of the entire crew in their underwear. Then, he had a great idea. He said he would drop his pants, as would the entire crew, and then it wouldn't be so serious. The crew surprised her in their tighty-whities, which got her laughing, and then she delivered her lines on the first take, which were also phonetically spelled out on a large board behind the camera. But the best part was that it wasn't good; it was brilliant. Carroll may have been the sexiest girl anyone had ever seen, but she also possessed a real vulnerability that made her few lines sparkle. And each day, Bill and Carroll flirted and became more intimate. No one had also gotten Bill to laugh, and Carroll had the unique capability to break him up. But most importantly, not many had given Bill Mackay his due, and when Carroll Madison arrived and treated him like Cecil B. DeMille, he knew what he needed to do, and that was to get rid of the harridan of a wife who was always complaining about something.

Why not live with an atomic blonde even if it meant blowing up his family?

Chapter Fifty-Four

Mirielle Montaigne
Culver City
1946

It had started out as just another uneventful day in Beverly Hills, yet those basking by their swimming pools and en suite bedrooms heard sounds of war. However, since the Allies had already prevailed, the sense of looming disaster was even more shocking as they craned their well-groomed heads to see and hear none other than Howard Hughes's massive gleaming prototype, the Hughes XF-11 reconnaissance plane, lose altitude on its maiden flight and crash into one of the wealthiest enclaves in Beverly Hills on North Whittier Drive. Later, according to Hughes, himself—who had been critically injured and burned—he had tried to land the plane on the golf course of the Los Angeles Country Club. Yet, as the plane lost altitude due to an oil leak, he missed the course by 300 feet, careening downward, clipping and crashing into three homes before bursting into flames. It was a busy news week indeed. There was also front-page reporting of the Nazi monsters being tried at the Nuremberg trials, which captivated the American public. It was noted as well that given the busy news cycle, Mirielle Montaigne still received a featured item in Hedda's column.

HEDDA HOPPER'S HOLLYWOOD

Breaking Baby news! Mirielle Montaigne admitted today she is a mother...by adoption. The devoutly Catholic

French singing star confirmed she has adopted two beautiful baby girls from Our Sisters of Mercy orphanage in downtown Los Angeles. The gorgeous star has said her greatest desire is to be a mother, and this selfless act, after the horrors of the war, allows her to continue her skyrocketing career without any absences from the silver screen. Given Montaigne's reported newly negotiated $2,500-a-week salary—only to rival Duke Drake's—we know these two girls will be brought up with silver spoons in their mouths at their mother's new Camden Drive estate. Rumors are circulating that there's also a lucky man on the horizon, and he's a well-regarded producer. Not many are Catholic producers in this town, so you do the math!

Solly Myers put down the copy of his paper as he whistled. He asked Edna to send Bartie a case of French Champagne. It was a happy day on the lot.

Mirielle had a white wicker bassinet with a huge pink satin bow sent by Freyda and Sol Myers, which they set up for Kyla in her studio bungalow, and she and a nanny doted on her every second she could when she wasn't filming. The "other" baby girl that had been adopted was soon taken back by the birth mother within weeks and paid a hefty salary for "lending" her baby for the ruse by private SGM slush funds, as well as giving her a new name and the promised studio contract. She would end up marrying a well-known producer and, in later years, be known as a pillar of the community. The fix, which was PR'd in the press, was that the young mother had a change of heart, which took all the focus off young Kyla.

With the fix in motion, Mirielle was now back at work in the coveted role in Hitchcock's new movie, *Immortal.* Every gorgeous actress in town had vied for the role of a legendary ex-Nazi spy who falls in love with a United States senatorial candidate who must choose between her and the presidential nod. The actual script was so controversial, in fact, that the movie was almost shelved by the state department who had gotten wind of it and thought it might implicate the former Nazis now secretly working for the government on the nuclear program. Myers prevailed, and the script was fast-paced and intense, sure to be a huge hit. Before getting the role, Hitchcock had asked her agent, the iconic Charles Feldman, whether Mirielle could affect an authentic Austrian accent and was shocked when she spoke to him in perfect upper-class Viennese German—as did her leading man, Paul Henreid. She had gotten the role and was thrilled to be working with the fabled British director, who promptly fell in love with her. The master of suspense was so consumed with her and her image, he even picked out the lipstick and clothes she wore. They had started shooting within weeks after her public adoption, and that alone seemed to save her from his growing obsession with her. A few weeks into shooting, she announced her engagement to Michael McDonough, and she sported a five-carat round diamond to the dismay of the portly director.

Despite Hitchcock's unwarranted and misplaced attention and resulting cruel behavior on set, it was a happy time for Mirielle and Michael, and she finally had come to feel a sense of joy, happiness, and peace. Working with Hitchcock was intense, and he often changed his mind, expecting a great deal both physically and emotionally from all his actors and vast team. He had hired a noted German émigré film composer, Rudolf Holberg, who was often on set and looked at Mirielle quizzically as she spoke in her English-German tinged accent. Rudolf, whose complex compositions perfected the art of raising a scene to a nervous climax, often with angry violins, sat quietly in the back of the studio and took notes for each scene, often writing the score. She had noticed his gruff exterior, but paid him little attention.

After one scene where her character, Hedwig, had hidden herself on a fast-moving train, Hitchcock yelled, "Cut!" and she took the opportunity to run toward her small bungalow on the lot to see Kyla. As she was walking out of the cavernous film hangar, she saw Rudolf sitting in his canvas chair next to a pale, gaunt man who was also writing away. He saw them both look up at her intently, but as a star, she was used to unwanted attention.

She had a light lunch of soup and salad in her bungalow with Michael sent in from the commissary and held and played with Kyla.

Then, she made her way back to the sound stage. As she walked in and nodded to the script girl, she was handed four fresh pages with a few new changes from Hitchcock and veered toward the makeup artist, who she knew would want to touch her up.

As she slowly walked while reading her lines, she passed the spare camera equipment and, out of the corner of her eye, noticed the gaunt man following her. He was tall, painfully thin, bald, with sparse wisps of hair, large ears, and was swimming in an out-of-date woolen suit. She was used to people trying to approach her and assumed he was an assistant working with Holberg. She looked down, scanning the new pages of the upcoming scene. Hitchcock had rewritten the dialogue, and there were some illegible markings that he had crossed out along with difficult-to-read additions.

"Excuse me?" She turned toward the man who'd dared to tap her on the shoulder as she jumped backward. He looked at her like he had seen a ghost, pale and bloodless with red-rimmed eyes, which were totally frightening.

"Irene?" the gaunt man whispered, his tinny voice cracked with despair.

She heard the name and looked up in terror.

"Irene—*meine geliebte*, my beloved, it's.... It's me...Fritz," he uttered. It seemed as if an ice pick pricked her spine as she looked and saw the familiar yet now hollowed, dead eyes, the long half-moon scar on his cheek, and knocked-out teeth. It was the last thing she heard as Mirielle Montaigne, the star of *Immortal*, promptly fainted onto the cold cement floor as Hitchcock yelled for the actors to take their places.

Chapter Fifty-Five

Bartie Maddox
Garden of Allah, Los Angeles
1946

It was the male form of heaven; the favorite pastime of most men, lying prostrate on the faded green-and-brown nubby couch reading the papers, scratching his privates, and slurping a stale, warm beer. Nothing could compare. Bartie heard a subtle knock at the door and immediately thought it was Carroll, who had come by to surprise him once again for one of their intimate sessions and for more favors despite now being "Mackay's girl." He wouldn't put anything past Carroll. Bartie immediately smiled at the thought of her juicy, supple body and her fabulous high tits that Myers had salivated over and had greedily taken possession of for one hour each week after promising her the part in *Blondes from Outer Space*. In an interesting twist, Carroll had been told by Myers to "find someone and quick!" when spies told Freyda there was a new blonde bombshell circling his office. Freyda had her own paid spies at the studio, and Solly was able to demure when he said the lies were false, and she was not his, but Bill Mackay's gal.

Perfect timing, Bartie thought as he grabbed his beer and walked toward the door. He was half undressed anyway, and the thought of a hot fuck with the sexpot immediately had him straining his shorts.

"Hey, sexy!" he said lightheartedly through the screen door, expecting her. He opened the door and blanched, feeling awkward as he realized it wasn't Carroll, but none other than Grace Greystone, Mrs. Duke Drake. Surely, she had seen his hard-on, and he blushed.

"Grace? Is everything okay?" He froze.

"Bartie, I'm so sorry to bother you, but would you mind if I came in?" Grace asked softly, and he immediately knew something was wrong as he saw her red-tinged eyes.

"Of course, please." He nodded and ushered her in. "Just give me a second to put on a pair of trousers." He ran toward the tiny bedroom alcove and shook his head as he slipped on a pair of tan chinos. He felt the need to be more formal with her and also threw on a long-sleeved, crumpled white shirt.

"Oh, Bartie, no need for that. I am so very sorry to disturb you," she said as he ran to open the screen door.

"You're not disturbing me. Please make yourself at home. I wish I knew you were coming. I would have straightened up a bit." He paled, shrugging at the messy bachelor pad as she entered and looked around.

"I am so sorry, and I know it's late, but I've been driving around LA with nowhere to go. I've been in Mirielle's driveway for hours, but she must be late at the studio. And I don't know who else to talk to."

"Please come into my humble abode," he joked. "Yes, I heard Mirielle is still at the studio with Michael. I think something important came up. I can't reach either of them as well. I've been trying all day."

"Is everything okay with Kyla?" Grace looked concerned.

"I just think they are probably shooting overtime with Hitchcock."

"Oh, I see." She looked around. "I love your place. It's darling." She was unaccustomed to being in an average, strange man's apartment. *So, this is how most people live*, she thought.

"Please, have a seat." He ushered her into his small living area and took her plush mink but had nowhere to hang it, so he carefully laid it over the arm of the lone side chair. Clearly, he was not used to having women like Grace Greystone over, and she was not used to visiting strange men in tiny and messy hotel suites.

"I'm so sorry for barging in, Bartie, but I honestly had nowhere else to go and there are very few people I know and can trust in this town. I thought of you and remembered you said you lived here. I really need your advice." She sat, promptly put her head in her hands, and started crying, filling him in on what she had seen and discovered with Duke and Gorge. He sat there and listened as she was so upset, she could barely put the words together.

"Honestly, I thought that the two of you dating would be great press for both of you," Bartie explained. "And you two seemed to be having a ball. So, when it got serious, I just *assumed* you and Duke had discussed his relationship with Gorge and had come to some kind of compromise or understanding." Bartie was saddened and somewhat ashamed he had been the cause of her distress.

"I can't go back to that house. I can't." She was visibly shaken.

"I see, Grace. I'm so sorry, but we were all sure you *knew*!" Bartie scratched his head. "I mean, I feel terrible. I was the one who set you two up in the first place, but it's the worst-kept secret in Hollywood. He and Gorge have been together for years."

"Well, he did tell me he'd had *experiences*, but he didn't really elaborate, and he was *normal* with me. Mirielle tried to warn me too but, for some reason, I chose to ignore it and thought I could change him. And he said he would change for me, and I believed him. Then we eloped, and it all happened so fast. I think his being so good-looking and famous turned my head. Bartie, I am such a fool with men." She gulped. "But he charmed me. He really did!"

"Well, first let me get you a drink. I only have whiskey." Bartie saw the hurt in her eyes and felt like a heel.

"I've never tried that, but it sounds perfect." She tried smiling, looking around at his small, messy kitchenette.

Bartie got up and washed two glasses in the small sink and then took the whiskey from on top of the icebox and poured two tumblers full.

"This is only for *special* occasions." He handed it to her. "I am sorry that this is such a sad bachelor pad. I know it's not what you are used to, and I have to admit I'm honestly a little embarrassed." He handed her the whiskey as they both clinked glasses.

"Embarrassed? No, Bartie...please. I think it's really...*charming*. And what I'm used to doesn't seem to have worked out in my favor either, that's for sure." She sipped the firewater. "Wow. This is strong." She coughed after a swig.

"Now, Grace…" Bartie went slowly. "Do you think it's something you can live with? I mean, with Duke, in the long run?"

"I'm so confused. I do think Duke loves me—or part of him loves me, anyway. And we did have…um…*relations*," she said softly. "He was very attentive, and I really thought he had changed, like he told me."

"I understand it must be very confusing." Bartie nodded.

"And Gorge got married as we were dating, so I ignored the rumors."

"Yes, to the town's biggest lesbian," he retorted.

"I see." She paused and looked down. "I guess I am the only one in LA who is that naive *and* big of a fool. I only believe what I read in Hedda's column."

"Most people do," he consoled, "and I'm the one who crafts the lies…the studio fixes. I'm so sorry, Grace." He looked down. "I never thought I was doing something wrong until now."

"You're not. You're just *very good* at your job, Bartie." She shrugged.

"No, you're sweet and smart and…and well, so pretty and deserve better."

"That's so nice of you to say."

"So, what do you think you want to do?" He combed his hair from his forehead with his fingers.

"I don't want to stay married this way. I can't say he totally lied to me, or I didn't know. It was always in the back of my mind, but it's what they call the sin of omission." She took another sip and coughed at the strength, but motioned for him to pour more.

"Go easy!" he laughed.

"Thank you! It's just that my marriage to Duke is very public, and it will be seen as another scandalous failure, and so soon as well." She paused. "But I can't go back to that house again, ever." She shivered, and Bartie walked over and put his arm around her as she wept. He looked down and thought, *What kind of man would ever let a woman like this go?* Certainly not him if he ever had the chance with someone like Grace Greystone. He immediately remembered the photo of her when he was a mere kid in Sioux Falls.

"I'm such a fool. I have always been in love with the idea of being in love since I never grew up with it."

"I understand." He looked at her and saw her in a new light.

"Do you?"

"Yes, of course. I'm the same way, but I'm the opposite. I've been running from love, I guess, my whole life," Bartie confided.

"Well, what's worse?" She looked at him without makeup and the all the accouterments and looked simply fresh and beautiful in that moment.

"I'm not sure." He paused again. "Listen, here's what we are going to do. Trust me?" He smiled his broad, impish smile.

"I trust you. I really do." She looked up into his kind eyes.

"Look, I feel totally responsible here since I made the introduction. I think what you need is what we call at the studio a *fix*, and I'm going to fix this, I promise. "

"I think I understand." She nodded.

"I'm going to call and meet Duke on Monday, and I'll dream up some way to handle this with the press. Duke is also my client, and he trusts me, so don't you worry about a thing. Would you like me to drive you back to the Beverly Hills Hotel?"

"It's so late." She looked at her diamond wristwatch.

"Well, you can always stay here."

"Can I? I think I need the company." She said, feeling quite woozy.

"Of course. I'll take the couch, and you can have the bed."

"Oh, Bartie, no need, but that is so sweet of you."

"No, I insist, and I promise to be a total gentleman."

"That's been my problem. I thought every man I've been with was a total gentleman. Maybe I should look for the reverse." She looked down and shook her head.

"*Maybe.*" He laughed too.

The next few hours, they stayed up talking, laughing, and crying, and Bartie told Grace everything about his childhood, including the most private things about himself and his mother. It felt good to be able to unburden himself and talk to someone so naturally, and Grace did the same about her difficult childhood, her mother's suicide, her court case, and loveless marriage. Later that night, as she tossed and turned, she made a decision. She sat up in bed and looked at the fine young man lying on the sad, lumpy sofa. Even though she was embarrassed earlier when she had spied his erection in his shorts, she found it endearing and sexy. Wearing the oversized T-shirt he had given her, she crept slowly from the bed and slipped next to him on the sofa. He hadn't been sleeping either, awake with one eye open due to the sexual tension.

"Are you sure about this?" He looked at the lovely sight beside him and smiled.

"I'm not sure about anything anymore." She paused, caressing his adorable cowlick and sweet face.

"*But this.*"

And as they lay in each other's arms, they cuddled, caressed, and kissed each other—though both held back from going further.

"I have to tell you, Grace…"

"No need to say anything."

"I am going to fix things, but we need to wait here, so I can make things right. And I do have a big job ahead of me."

"And what's that?"

"I have to talk to my client… and your husband first."

Chapter Fifty-Six

Madame Fritz Langenheim
Culver City
1946

The set was immediately cleared as the grips and the sound technicians ran toward Mirielle when she fainted as they yelled for a doctor. Within minutes, the assistant producer called Michael, who rushed to the set and surveyed the situation at hand and, on his orders, the studio doctor and a uniformed nurse arrived and helped a shocked and dazed Mirielle to her bungalow, where the studio doctor administered a punitive-looking injection of a sedative. Fritz followed and glowered at the English nanny and the baby as they quickly retreated to the small office off the bungalow bedroom, sensing something was amiss. After the sedative, Mirielle slept quietly and soundly on the couch as people hovered about her.

The specter-like Fritz paced like a tiger, looking intently at his prey, as if to check if Mirielle was not a figment of his imagination. He then huffed and sat in an armchair, staring off in an agitated trance, as Mirielle slept.

The level of chaos was finally tempered by Myers's arrival once Michael had reached him privately in his office. Myers shook his head in disbelief.

"Who the fuck gets outta a death camp alive? Of course, it has to be her damn husband," he groused.

They both entered the bungalow in a respectful way, though, with trepidation as they knew the situation was potentially explosive.

Mirielle, whose engagement had only been recently announced as an exclusive in Hedda's column the week before, looked like a sleeping angel on the sofa. Myers had called Hitchcock in advance to let him know that Mirielle was off limits for a few hours and had confided to him it was "women's problems," which the rotund director seemed to accept, calming his fury at the expensive delay and break in his tight shooting schedule.

"Mister Langenheim, may I introduce the head of the studio, Mister Solomon Myers," Michael said, breaking the ice and making the introductions.

"Nice to meet ya!" Myers extended his hand.

"Yes." Fritz shrugged and offered a papery, transparent, and skeletal hand to both men.

"How is she?" Myers asked Michael as he saw Mirielle's prostrate form lying on the sofa.

"I don't understand why the doctor gave her an injection," Fritz said in a strongly-accented tone.

"She fainted, Mister Langenheim," Michael offered. "It was a shock to her system as I am sure you can imagine. She told me you are her long lost husband."

"And who are you?" Fritz looked at the handsome and fit Michael suspiciously. He was aware of his own facial scars and physical disintegration and talked with his mouth closed to avoid revealing the missing teeth. Fritz, however, was beyond pure vanity; he was in anxious survival mode.

"I'm Michael McDonough, the head of production at SGM."

"A shock? She should be doing the *hora* to see me!"

"The doctor gave her something to calm her, so she's sleeping."

"Mister Langenheim, it's very nice to meet you and make your acquaintance." Michael extended a hand, which was barely acknowledged. "She was searching for you for many years."

"Why didn't you call her to let her know when you arrived in LA?" Myers asked somewhat brusquely.

"I, myself, didn't even know it was her." Fritz shook his head. "Her hair is a different color. Irene had a small beauty mark on the right side above her lip. When I saw her picture on a movie poster in Paris after the liberation, I thought there was a remarkable resemblance, but I did not see the mark until I was hired to be the assistant composer by Rudolf on the set."

"Mister Langenheim, may I call you Fritz?" Sol Myers stepped into his role as head of the studio.

"Yes, of course, Herr Myers."

"*Mister* Myers. We are here in America. I have heard of your being in that horrible camp." He surveyed the gaunt and emaciated composer with a bit of horror.

"Yes, Auschwitz." He looked down. "Not many survivors."

"And I am sorry for that. I cannot even imagine what you went through." Even Sol Myers was shaken by the news reports of the gruesome death camps.

"You have no idea. Hell on earth." Fritz touched Mirielle's sleeping arm. "Only the idea of Irene kept me going."

"First, Mister Langenheim," Sol started slowly, "Michael here told me how talented you are and that Billy Wilder suggested you to that composer of Hitchcock's...what's his name?"

"Rudolf Holber...?" Myer's struggled.

"Holberg," Michael confirmed.

"Yeah, *HO*-berg. And we here at SGM try, and as a good Jew, to help all the victims. I do hope ya know that," Myers continued. "And we know you're gonna do a great job on this picture, but we all have to work together now." He dangled the work carrot.

"Work together? I don't understand what you mean." Fritz eyed Myers suspiciously.

"The situation here is...um...a tough one. Ya know what I mean?" Myers looked him over.

"Know what you mean? I don't understand." Fritz shook his pale head.

"Well, you must know that Mirielle thought you were...well, killed in the camp. We all did. Mirielle searched for you, and we even paid for an immigration lawyer to try and find you."

"Well, I'm alive as you can all see," he said in a vacant way. "And her name is Irene, not this Mirielle," he said swiftly.

"Well, that's just it. Don'tcha know that Irene is no longer Irene. She is now known as Mirielle Montaigne, a French movie star. The studio has invested close to a million dollars in her, and she is the property of SGM and now a mother with an adopted baby…and has a fiancé."

"She is my wife. She is no one's property."

"Mister Myers, let me," Michael interceded. "I am sure you can understand what a shock this is for Irene, Mirielle. Of course, she is thrilled you are alive and well. We all are."

"Not so alive and not so well," Fritz remarked under his breath.

"Like you, she fled Europe for her life. She searched for you for years. I know, because she personally asked me to look into it many times, and we at the studio called the state department and also her friends in Europe to try and find you."

"As she should have! I am her husband," he said blankly.

"Yes, but I also happen to know because she searched so long and hard, she was told that you, well…had not survived." He looked down. "So, this is a great shock to her."

"As it is to me. Irene is *Baroness* Irene Von Mendelssohn. Her family is one of the most important in Vienna. She is not this Mirielle whoever…a common tramp."

"Yes, I understand, but in Hollywood, actors and actresses change their names all the time. Whether you agree or not, Mirielle, Irene, is now an international movie star. That is how she is known around the world."

"Well, to me, she is my Irene."

"All we are saying is it is important to understand she is a public person now, and there are implications for the press and the studio."

"What implications? I want to be with my wife, that is all. And now that I found her, I want to take her back to Vienna."

"She adopted a baby. She just became engaged, and it has been announced in Hedda Hopper's column, which is read by millions."

"I don't care whose column she was in." He lent a steely gaze.

"Is he gonna play ball with us or not?" Myers turned his head and hissed a bit too loudly to Michael. "I don't understand what he is saying?"

Michael took him aside. "Mister Langenheim, may I call you Fritz? Mirielle is also working on the same picture as you. You must understand it's a job."

"Irene. I said her name is Irene."

"Look, Fritz." Myers was starting to lose his temper.

"Mister Langenheim."

"Mister Langenheim, the public thinks that Mirielle is engaged to another man. It would be terribly confusing and could kill her career if this got out. And it would hurt my studio."

"What? I deal with the Nazis and now this…this *propaganda*! Just as bad. Her career is as *my wife*!" he shouted, pacing nervously.

"Mister Langenheim, you are in the room with one of the most important and powerful men in the movie industry," Michael whispered. "Mister Myers is your *boss*. He is trying to help you. He also wants you to understand that your wife, Irene, is now Mirielle Montaigne, an international movie star, and the studio backed her career when she first arrived in LA."

"No one is my boss. She owes no one either, only me. Irene was known as the most beautiful woman in Vienna, and her father, the baron, would never have allowed this!" He continued to pace like a tiger in an agitated fashion.

Mirielle awoke slowly, and when the room came into focus and she saw everyone gathered around her, she smiled weakly, but was clearly confused. When Fritz walked over and took her hand, she immediately started crying.

"My Fritz-*ele*, I am so happy to see you are alive." She took his hand in a gentle fashion.

"Barely," he whispered. "And you…" he paused. "I might have thought you would have waited for me!" he said angrily. "I waited for you!" he said with an anguished cry. "Just look at you!" he said with obvious disgust.

"You wouldn't leave Vienna, Fritz. My father and I begged you to leave, don't you remember?" Her voice cracked.

"You saved your own skin, but regardless, Irene, you and I are still married—tell them!" he said forcefully in accented English. "They are trying to convince me you are someone else."

"Yes, Fritz is my husband," she said in a low voice. "But Fritz, I thought—they told me—you had died. Even Aunt Marie said so. I am so happy you are alive—it's a miracle." She reached for his hand, which he withdrew in an instant.

"So, you just ran off and had a baby and got engaged the minute they said I was dead?" He was getting angrier with each passing minute. "Did you even say *kaddish* for me?"

"Of course I did."

"A whore and a slut with an illegitimate baby!" His anger knew no bounds.

"Fritz, she's adopted," Mirielle begged.

"You think for one minute I believe that with those green eyes, she is not your child? I may be half dead, but I'm not a half-dead fool." He looked at her and shook his gray head with distaste.

"Fritz, this is a shock to everyone," she said weakly.

"And your name is Irene—why did you let them change it? And your hair is now orange? Who are you?" He raised his voice.

"We all did what we did to survive," she explained.

"In the camp, when I was forced to play Beethoven over and over, and they beat me as the thousands marched to the gas chambers… you…" he pointed a bony finger at her, "the image of you kept me alive, but you are no longer you. You are a fabrication. You are still beautiful…but you are grotesque—you and this studio of yours and your *image* and your perfect baby. Whose baby is it?" he shouted "*Whose*? I have a right to know since I know it isn't mine." The baby started crying in the next room due to the noise.

"Mister Langenheim, I think you need to calm down. You just woke Kyla," Michael said instinctively.

"So, it's *you*." Fritz noticed his ginger hair. He pushed Michael, his voice climbing. "You're the one who screwed my wife while I was being tortured, and you cheated on me? Shame on you, all of you!" he shouted loudly.

"I think we need to get him outta here. Someone will hear," Myers hissed to Michael.

"You." Fritz walked over to Myers. "You think you are better than me? You want me *outta here—outta here*!" he replied, mimicking him.

"I have a business to run, and you are creating a scene. I understand you are upset, but it's been years, and Mirielle was told you were dead."

"Irene!" he shouted. "Her name is *Irene*," he lamented.

"Fritz, you cannot do this." She put her hand to her mouth as she saw things spiraling out of control.

"Mister Myers, please, he's very upset. It is a great shock," she said. "Fritz, you have a job here," she pleaded.

"And this baby?" he screamed. "Do you think your father would have stood for your being a whore in the palais?" He spoke to her in German.

"Stop, Fritz, please," Mirielle begged and started crying again, "for the sake of everything."

"You're upsetting her." Myers became agitated. "Men shouldn't make women cry."

"Stay the hell out of this. She is *my* wife." He poked Myers in the chest with a bony finger. "Not yours."

"Don't you talk to me like that! This is my studio. No one curses here."

"Your studio? Your studio? You're just a low-class Jew. In Vienna, I wouldn't have let you polish my shoes or hers. A real *Galitzianer*, this one!"

"Nobody speaks to Solomon Myers that way, in *my* house!" He pointed a finger back into his skeletal chest. "I don't care what happened to you." He shouted for them to get the security guard.

"They would have taken you away first!" he screamed.

"You're fired, you ingrate! Get him outta here. I'm through talkin' to this nut."

"Please, no," Mirielle begged. "He's not in his right mind."

"You're not in your right mind," he screamed back at her as Mirielle cried hysterically.

"I think we should get the doctor and give Mirielle another injection to calm her." Michael thought he was doing the right thing as he shook his head in disbelief.

A beefy security guard who always trailed Myers appeared and strong-armed a shouting Fritz out of the bungalow and shuttled into a waiting car, which would later dump him in a remote location a few miles away. Mirielle screamed and cried hysterically amidst this living nightmare.

"Please, no. Fritz," she cried. "Please no...."

Later that week, when Mirielle had regained a bit of strength and some clarity, she desperately tried to locate Fritz—at the very least to give him money and talk things through, to no avail. Then, on a rainy Thursday, she received a call from Myers, himself, who quietly told her that the police had discovered that the former Viennese composer had hung himself at a boarding house in downtown LA. He offered his condolences, as did Freyda.

The following week, a small obituary would run in the paper prepared by Bartie and sent to the *LA Times* through Hedda. It mentioned that the well-known prodigy and classical Austrian composer, Fritz Langenheim, who had gained accolades and was renowned in Europe for his famed opera, *Die Liebesgeschichte und die Herzensbrecher*, had committed suicide in Los Angeles. He had been forced to lead the death camp orchestra at Auschwitz. The last line mentioned he was thirty-one years of age and that he had no family and no survivors.

It was one of the saddest fixes of all.

Part Three

Chapter Fifty-Seven

Bartie Maddox
Los Angeles
1946

Many years later, over a crisp, green McCarthy salad, sheltered under the striped awning at the Beverly Hills hotel pool restaurant, Bartie would reflect and wonder how he managed to pull it all off. Sipping his dry martini with olives, he thought back on the propitious year… *1946.*

By that point, he had created and pulled off many intricate fixes that were accepted by the public. Sometimes late at night, in the wee hours when he was all alone with his solitary thoughts, he wondered whether he was doing the right thing—whether it was PR or lying to the public. He had broached the subject with Michael a few times over late-night drinks, and he held the same view as Myers that they weren't lying to the public but protecting them; that their public was not ready to accept the human frailties and actions of their stars and that their royalty needed to be whitewashed, so the public could have sparkling dreams to believe in. Something pure to hope for.

The last few months had seen some of the oddest and most unusual fixes of his career, but nothing surprised him anymore. After Mirielle's tumultuous baby fix, Myers had called in a panic that another stunning young star in the making needed a quick fix for a brewing scandal. SGM had just signed and gave a starring role in a romantic musical to Maria Shane, the sensual brunette beauty and singer who had been discovered in a Broadway chorus line. Just as they were in the first days of shooting, she was blackmailed by her absent birth father who had contacted the studio revealing he was Black and threatening to go to the press.

"If anyone found out Dax Montgomery was kissing a "*schvartze*", the Hays Office will shut down the studio," Myers lamented over the inhumane segregation policies. Since her first movie was already in production, they acted quickly; Myers paid off the father for the birth certificate, and Bartie and Mick changed her name and race from Maria Shane to Maria Conchita Marquez, which would explain her *café au lait* skin. Changing her nationality and giving her the moniker of the *Brazilian Boom-Boom Girl*, costumed in a kitschy fruit laden turban, would complete the transformation as well as an accent coach to help her now speak a vague sort of "Spanglish"—even though if she was Brazilian she would be speaking Portuguese, but it was all the same to the public. To seal the deal, Bartie contracted the very Latin Enrique, the older bartender at Maude's, to have him now claim to be her birth father for a hefty fee. The movie, which was only in its first week of shooting, changed sets and locations overnight and the movie title went from *Revenge in Reno* to *Revenge in Rio*. Changing someone's race could have capped his crazy career resumé, but to Bartie, the next fix was the one in million. It was one he would be most unsure of, yet eventually most proud of for its sheer ingenuity and magnitude. Certainly, he knew the bold presumption that it could have failed or been laughed off. That said, he needed to swing for the fences as there were no other options; had the situation been left unattended, it would only have fared far worse. He later likened it to emergency surgery done either to stop the bleeding or, in some ways, to avoid a larger catastrophe in the future. That Myers had approved it with a hefty budget, *all of it*, slapped him on the back at the sheer daring nature of the plan, made him swing even higher and harder. It was his shining moment, his *ultimate Studio Fix.*

As he and Michael unfurled the copious silverware in the pink fabric napkin at the Polo Lounge, he knew that it was at that very moment of creative inception he had been born for the job. It was a gift that was either divine or genetic, like being an opera singer or a great artist at the easel.

"Bartie, I have to hand it to you. I thought Kyla's fix was brilliant, but this is truly epic," Michael and Mirielle marveled. It was so complex, it was almost surreal—since it was not only professionally ambitious, but also deeply personal.

He had worked all weekend long, going over every detail in his mind on a blackboard with chalk, only breaking for dinner with Michael at the Polo Lounge and Grace at Dan Tana's. He had been amused that they now had a Grace Greystone salad on the menu named after her as many of their high-profile guests' names preceded their favorite dish listed on the menu. After a careful planning session with Grace, he returned home and called Duke to set a time and place to meet. He didn't think he would have reached him on the first call, but the sullen actor was moping around the house and waiting for all hell to break loose. He answered the phone personally, to Bartie's surprise, his voice a blank sheet of paper.

"You need to see me, right?" Duke stated blankly.

"Yes, Monday first thing. I'll come to Bel Air. On Myers's orders."

"You'll come to me? That means it must be *really serious*," Duke said in a monotone voice as he already knew the answer.

"Yes, I would say it is. Monday morning at eight-thirty. See you then." Bartie hung up the phone and went to bed to refuel his energy. He would need it. He had explained that to Grace, and she understood why he had not spent the night. He felt slightly guilty seeing Grace and then Duke but pushed the thoughts out of his mind. It was all too fresh and too complicated.

"It's too important for you." Bartie kissed her passionately. "Like an athlete, I'm in training mode." They both laughed as he lunged at her, not wanting to leave but knowing he should.

The next morning, he drove his sensible navy Buick through the imposing gates and into the circular car park at Drake Manor. He walked up to the entrance of the grand estate, knowing some people got to live like kings but perhaps were also imprisoned in their castles. He rang the doorbell and waited longer than he should have had to, almost turning on his heels. And then, just like *that*, Duke answered the door, unshaven and disheveled with a hangover. Despite his unkempt state and questionable hygiene, Duke was still a handsome devil—there was no denying it—but he looked and smelled like he had rolled out of a pigsty.

"Hi, Bartie, thanks for coming by." He ushered him in.

"You want a Bloody Mary?" He slurred his words as he casually led him through his grand manse into the stately oak-paneled library. The regal room was strewn with cocktail glasses and ashtrays overflowing with half-smoked Chesterfields and an array of empty bottles of vodka and gin, one having found a way into the crevice in the sofa and another rolling onto the zebra carpets on the floor.

"Where is everyone, Duke?" Bartie looked around at the eerie stillness. "What happened to your staff?"

"I gave them the long weekend off. I couldn't face anyone, certainly not even the butler. Gorge has been ringing and ringing, and I won't take his calls." He shrugged as he approached his bar, tinkering with a new bottle of vodka, his only clear salvation.

"Duke, you have to lay off the sauce. It's not even nine a.m.," Bartie cautioned.

"I know, but even though I feel terrible, I feel worse when I'm *sober*. I can't believe how stupid I was." He threw his elegant hands up in the air, the gold-crested pinky ring punctuating his distress.

"In what way?" Bartie probed.

"To have had Gorge here. I keep replaying it over and over in my mind. I should have only met him at *his* house," he said with anguish. "I'm so embarrassed Grace had to see me like that."

"Like what?"

"Fuck you, Bartie." He peered at him angrily. "You know damn well being fucked in the ass in a *compromised position.* Or maybe you get off hearing I was on my back with my legs spread in the air as Gorge gave it to me. Is that what you want to hear?"

"No, spare me the details. I just wanted to know if we are both dealing with the same set of facts." Bartie looked less than amused.

"Are we?" Duke lamented.

"I would say so."

"And I fucked up by doing it in the *marital bed*," he groaned.

"Wait," Bartie said as he sat down on the English club chair. "Duke, don't you hear yourself? You have no remorse about *what* you did," he paused, "just *where* you did it? Or that you got caught? It makes no sense to me."

"But she never would have found out if I was more discreet," he moaned.

"You know, Duke, in all the time we've known each other, I've never held your lifestyle against you." Bartie led the conversation.

"Well, I would like to hold *yours against mine*," Duke sadly mimicked W.C. Fields through bloodshot eyes.

"Enough. Not funny. I fought for you and Gorge to be able to do what you wanted to do. That's *your* life. But with Grace, you took advantage of a wonderful gal. You lied to her, and you hurt her."

"I didn't lie to her. I told her…" he offered slowly, "…*things.*"

"Well, you didn't exactly tell her the truth about you and Gorge. Honestly, you used and hurt her—she feels like a fool. I set it up initially as mutual and amusing, but she truly fell for you—and I thought you were upfront with her about compromises, and yes, deals must have been made, but it's the sin of omission, and you know it."

"I guess you're right, Bartie." He poured more vodka into his glass of tomato juice. He screwed up his face and looked him in the eye.

"So, she's not coming back…is she?"

"No."

"And…" Bartie stood after delivering the hard news and paced like a lawyer in a courtroom scene. "You now need a fix—you both do. I now have to figure out a way to make it right in the press for your career and the studio." He paused and looked at him. "And, last but not least, for Grace."

"I'm all ears. You have this game down. I'm impressed. Any ideas, Bartie? Because I'm honestly baffled as to how I get out of this one. By the way, cheers!" He toasted and knocked back another Bloody Mary.

"Actually, I do have a few ideas, but first I have to tell you about a new movie I'm promoting."

"New movie? What has that got to do with me?" He looked at him askance, his stubble reflecting the overhead light.

"Just listen. It's called *Blondes from Outer Space*. And it's about these blonde, big-busted aliens who take over the world to repopulate after an atomic bomb."

"Now I'd go to see that! What a concept," Duke whistled. "Who's in it anyway?" he asked.

"Claude Rains," Bartie paused for dramatic effect, "and the new blonde bombshell who Myers and I are promoting."

"And who would that be?"

"You know her and have met her." Bartie paused and winked at him. "My friend, Carroll." He appraised him with a lustful, long pause. "Carroll Madison."

"Good for Carroll! She's a fun gal. Last I heard she was engaged to Bill Mackay? But then I heard he died of a heart attack. Word is she fucked him to death."

"Maybe."

"And why is this of interest to me?"

"Because when you do a fix, you need to confuse the public, and if it ends with one gal…"

"Yes, I'm all ears—and other things." He mustered the energy for a joke.

"It has to begin…with *another*."

Chapter Fifty-Eight

Cora-Lee McCoy
Hollywood
1946

The image of the bum stumbling on the sidewalk with a bottle in a brown paper bag brought Bartie back to years earlier when he lived close by in the boarding house, and being back in the sad, old neighborhood sent shivers down his spine.

The slip of paper Carroll had given led him to a seedy part of town and made him feel like he needed a shower—and pronto. When Bartie knocked on the dilapidated screen door of a creaky, decrepit wooden porch, a swarthy man emerged into the daylight, unshaven, in a sweat-stained wifebeater. He looked like he hadn't showered in days, which, from the smell of him, he hadn't. He could have been cast in a George Raft or Sterling Dumont film as an ex-con or a mafia stooge, which is what some women most likely found attractive.

"Hey, who are you, and why are you here? You're not a cop, are ya?" he asked defensively.

"No, not a cop." Bartie handed him his business card as the man took it and then whistled.

"And to what do I owe the pleasure of SGM Studios? Ya goin' to offer me a directing job?" he laughed.

"This is your lucky day." Bartie took in the dismal surroundings. "Can I come in? I want to make a very generous deal with you for some of your... *work*."

"Really? My work, huh." He nodded his greasy black hair and scratched his thick stubble, opening the door wider, so Bartie could enter. The place was filthy, with camera equipment strewn around bottles of gin and a dirty mattress on the floor that had clearly seen a lot of activity.

"I want to buy some of your photos along with a film. You're gonna be very happy," Bartie enthused.

"Of who?"

"Cora-Lee McCoy. Know her?"

"Boy, do I. That girl has a body that won't quit, but I don't have to tell *you* that." He paused. "All I can say is it's gonna be expensive. The guys drool over her photos. They're some of my best sellers!" he confided.

"I want all the negatives and the film if there is one." Bartie knew he should have taken care of this when he heard Carroll was in her first film, but she didn't have an image or a name yet. Now that the studio and Myers were investing heavily in making her a star, it was time to clean up this earlier mess.

"I'm not sure I want to sell." He looked at him with his dark lidded, forbidding eyes, wanting to drive a harder bargain.

"And why not?" Bartie seemed perplexed.

"See that small room off the kitchen?"

"Yeah."

"Go take a look." He motioned to the area.

Bartie walked in through the kitchen, which was piled high with dirty plates, and into a small back room. Inside, there was a lone recliner chair, a screen, and a projector. A box of tissues and some lotion rested on a small table.

"Wait." Bartie blanched and understood.

"Wanna rent the room? It's ten bucks a flick, but you have to clean up after yourself. The garbage can is over there." He smirked as he saw the clean-cut Bartie take in the small metal can overflowing with used tissue paper.

"Okay, I get it." His stomach roiled.

"I make over a hundred bucks a week here 'cause it ain't a public theater where you have to worry about the vice squad. I also get paid

Chapter Fifty-Nine

Bartie Maddox, Duke Drake, Grace Greystone-de La Faucigny-Drake, and Carroll Madison
West Hollywood
1946

There is a press term in journalism called "on the record," which, for the layman, means something that can be publicly disclosed by the press. Bartie knew that at his lunch with Hedda Hopper, everything would be "on the record," and that was an even riskier part of the fix. That knowledge and responsibility brought a certain dangerous *frisson* to the room, an electricity that one could smell and sense in the air like raging adolescent pheromones in the back seat of a car. That afternoon, the smiles seemed brighter and whiter, the laughs a bit louder, and the theatrics akin to early silent reels when the gestures were a bit more exaggerated—not to mention the nervous sexual energy soon to be on display.

The buzz in the room suddenly became even more electric as Academy Award winner Gorge Lamont strode into the restaurant and as he usually did, flicking some dust off his caricature hanging on the wall. His wife, the ever-so-chic heiress, Letitia St. Clair, and the town's newest social doyenne in her signature black pantsuit, stood by as her movie-star husband stopped to sign leather-bound autograph books for out-of-town fans. Then, the couple chatted with Katherine and Spencer lunching in a nearby booth. Each waved and blew kisses to Hedda and Bartie across the room as Bartie looked at his watch under duress.

After a month of meetings, planning, rehearsing, and even hiring a private eye in Vegas, the ultimate Hollywood fix was now in play—though there were always unexpected wrinkles in any plan that needed to be navigated with aplomb.

"I'm sorry, they both seem to be running late." Bartie looked nervously at his wristwatch again. "Can I order you a cocktail, Hedda?

"No, darling, but I am…on deadline." She seemed miffed at their luncheon guests' apparent tardiness and adjusted the brim of her signature hat. Hedda was a stickler for punctuality and not one to be kept waiting. "They have five more minutes," she said tersely.

"You know LA traffic." He tried to keep a cool exterior, but he was sweating. Then, just as he was about to wave to the waiter to bring more drinks, he saw Hedda light up with her famous press smile and sit up with wonderful posture. They had, indeed, arrived together. "Trust me. It will be worth it."

"If you say so, Bartie." She shrugged.

"Hello, Duke. Grace, so lovely to see you." Hedda extended her gloved hand at the sparkling couple who'd miraculously appeared.

"Hedda. Such a pleasure. I adore your hat, it's divine," Grace said, leaning in for a kiss.

"As is yours! So chic," Hedda effused.

"Yes, from my Paris days," she laughed.

"Hedda, my darling!" Duke said as he walked over to kiss her hand in a gallant fashion. He looked so handsome, tailored, and freshly shaven. "It's lovely to see you. You're looking beautiful as always," Duke offered.

"Well. I think *I know* what you two are going to tell me…." Hedda said in a singsong voice and pulled out her small notepad, fully expecting pregnancy news. She winked from under her towering, black-and-white polka dot hat.

She surveyed Grace's exquisite Cartier crystal, diamond, and aquamarine cuffs with envy as Grace slipped into the banquette.

"Oh, Hedda. It's not *that.* Actually, I think you are going to be quite surprised at our news."

"Really?" Hedda looked a bit deflated, as if she had her column headline already written. Suddenly, a platinum blonde with moist, ruby red lips and a heaving décolletage approached and presented herself at the table with a tentative confidence. Duke rose and kissed her on the lips to Hedda's consternation.

"Have you met Carroll?" Duke introduced the buxom blonde as she thrust herself forward.

"Carroll Madison, Hedda Hopper." He stood, sporting a ravishing and gleaming smile as he kissed Carroll again as she slid into the booth. "I'm not sure I under-*stand*," Hedda scowled. "When did I agree to a *luncheon party* with…*new* people?" she hissed under her breath at Bartie.

"I'm so honored, Missus Hopper," Carroll said in an exaggerated, breathy, seductive tone as Hedda eyed her flashy and boisterous sexuality, furrowing her brow in the process.

"Okay, Duke," Bartie said urgently, sensing Hedda's ire. "Take it away!"

"Well, Hedda." Duke coughed nervously. "I know this is going to sound crazy, but we wanted you to have…the exclusive."

"In this town, nothing's normal! Proceed," she said like a strict schoolmarm as she positioned her pen at the ready. Duke paused to find the words.

"Well, I'm waiting with bated breath!" Hedda shook her head. She knew this was going to be a doozy.

"About a year ago when I was filming *The British Cad*, I was secretly dating Carroll, who, as you know, had a small part in the film as a hat check girl."

"Up until recently, I was always the hat check girl or a girl in a saloon." Carroll shrugged and cracked her gum. "Until I had *lines*."

"Was that before or after that *sweater* movie?" Hedda asked derisively as she raised a sharp brow and rolled her eyes.

"Oh, after, I think." Carroll shrugged. "But now I'm the Atomic Blonde! Opposite Claude Rains," she said with all seriousness.

"So, we were dating, and then when Grace came to town, and we met and went out for dinner and dancing. We had a marvelous time and so much in common, and I really loved spending time with Grace."

"And I loved spending time with Duke after my divorce," Grace added, nodding.

"How many marriages, Grace?" Hedda sighed and wrote in her signature scrawl like a legal stenographer taking court notes.

"Just two. Duke was my second," she said quietly. "Or so I *thought*."

"Thought? *Was?*" Hedda peered at her, steely-eyed.

"Yes, it seems that the wedding chapel in Vegas was not legitimate and never filed the paperwork, so we were never actually married to begin with."

"Yes, you know Vegas—always filled with charlatans." Bartie smiled, knowing it had cost Bartie and the studio $10,000 to destroy the marriage certificate and have it pulled with a call to the town's shady brass.

"Really!" Hedda rolled an eye and shook her head at the news. "Why, this is outrageous!"

"Yes, we thought so too." Duke smiled. "I mean, we *did* elope. It just wasn't legal."

"Yes, I recall the conversation from the marital bed—how convenient," Hedda snarled.

"Then, when I was shooting *Deb-on-air*, and while Grace was away traveling with Mirielle Montaigne, I realized that I missed Carroll."

"And I missed Duke!" Carroll batted her eyelashes.

"Of course, I missed Grace too, but I missed Carroll in a different kind of way. I came to the realization that she was the one I truly loved, and well, when Grace returned from Panama and we found out we were never legally married, we decided that we were better off…as…"

"As what?" Hedda's eyes were popping in disbelief.

"Business partners," Grace answered. "We adore each other, and we spend most of our time talking about his career and the film business, so we will remain as business partners, and we are starting a production company—which I will fund—called Drakestone Productions." Grace smiled. "I have always wanted to be in the film business."

"And then I told Carroll I couldn't live without her." Duke smiled shyly, as if a camera was approaching for a close-up.

"And Grace, how are you feeling about all this?" Hedda looked a bit shocked. "Knowing you were hoodwinked and taken advantage of!"

"Darling Hedda, I'm really thrilled." Grace smiled in a ladylike fashion, thinking of Aunt Rose and how she would comport herself.

"Has Myers heard of this latest *escapade*?" Hedda harumphed and shook her head, the hat following.

"Well, that's just it. Mister Myers actually sent us his blessing and congratulations. And the best news is I'm actually engaged again, Hedda, to the man I am really in love with and should be married to as well," she beamed. "And Mister Myers thoroughly approves."

"Engaged again? Really? To *whom*? The waiter!?" Hedda looked at her like she had more than one head. "This is beyond comprehension, even for Holly-*weird*."

"No, to the other man at this table." She extended her gloved hand.

"This is all very confusing. Duke is now getting engaged to Carroll. How can one man be engaged or married to two women? This isn't..." she paused for comic effect, "*Africa*!"

"No, Hedda, to *Bartie*. I'm engaged to Bartie. We fell in love." Grace reached out and took his hand in hers.

"It's true, Hedda. I'm crazy about Grace." Bartie put his arm around her. "I'm the luckiest man in the world."

"And vice versa."

"Why, you devil, Bartie!" Hedda sighed with a gust of relief and exclaimed, "You know, Grace, I have had a crush on your Bartie from the first time I met him! Why, if I was younger, I would have given you a run for your money...and I know there is a lot of it." She giggled.

Hedda had heard it all but could not get over it. "Are you all sure this is all for real?" she asked, wide-eyed.

"Yes!" both women exclaimed, showing Hedda their glittering diamond rings at exactly the same time.

"Well, now, good for the four of you. I do hope one of these all stick—for all four of you, I mean." She rolled her eyes under her net veil. "I can't keep up with all you young people."

"Oh, it will." Bartie reached over to Grace and they kissed each other passionately in front of Hedda.

"Well, I can't say *that's* not convincing," she offered in a conciliatory tone. After all, Grace Greystone was still Grace Greystone, and norms were different for the richest gals in the world.

"Well, hello everyone." Solly Myers sauntered over as Bartie had signaled.

"Hedda, how is my favorite press gal?" He looked at the table in faux surprise, the best part of the fix. "Well, it seems everyone I know is having lunch here today." He chuckled.

"Hi, Solly. I didn't see you come in. I've been too engrossed in the musical chairs at your studio," Hedda said, with some sarcasm.

"Yeah, well you know how young people are. They can't make up their minds."

"How is Freyda?"

"She's over there talkin' to Joan. I hear ya, Hedda, but you know, when I first came to LA…I was dating Freyda's sister, Bessie. Why, I almost married *her.* And then Freyda came home from college, and I saw her and knew she was the one for me, so I'm the last one to say it can't happen."

"Well, of course." Hedda understood Myer's tacit approval.

"And when I found out that Bartie over here is engaged to Missus Greystone, well, I said he has to have a VP title and a raise for the likes of her. A fat raise too, I can assure ya. He's now a real *macher*!"

"Congrats, Bartie. That's wonderful news."

"And Duke and Carroll will be the new Gable and Lombard. Carroll is our new *it* girl, don'tcha know?" He put his hands suggestively on her shoulder as she giggled and looked at Myers in awe, batting her eyes for effect. "Hedda, we're investing a lot in this goil. *I'm* investing a lot in *her*, do you understand me, Hedda? *In her*!" He paused for effect. "In fact, there hasn't been a blonde in this town who has what she has… since Harlow!" He beamed.

"Clearly, I see." Hedda raised another eyebrow as she saw the lingering touch and the emphasis on Myers's words. And one thing Hedda knew about Hollywood, despite her power and opinions and disapproval, one had to accept and respect the wife *and the mistress* of the studio heads. It was one of the most subtle parts of the studio fix.

And Myers pulled it off like the pro he was; the touch, ever so subtle, gliding over her bare shoulder and then lingering in such a way with his not-so-subtle speech as to make it clear to Hedda that she was being anointed—that being Myers's girl had raised her to another level entirely.

"Well, Carroll." She took a deep breath and played the game. "Then we *must* have a private girls' lunch. Just you and I. I do want to also hear what really happened to your former fiancé, Bill Mackay. Duke, you have to be careful with this beauty!" She laughed in an evil way. "A tête-à-tête! Just the two of us!" Hedda smiled at Carroll and then waved to Freyda across the room, who had stopped by to say hello to Gorge and Letitia. And at that very moment, Bartie knew… the fix was in.

> *HEDDA HOPPER'S HOLLYWOOD*
>
> *Announcing New Hollywood Musical—*
>
> *Chairs, That Is!*
>
> *Only in LA, my friends…only in LA! Duke Drake and Grace Greystone are still going strong as…partners—business partners, that is! While dissolving their quickie Vegas marriage, they are staying together by forming Drakestone Productions, which will produce movies for the handsome British cad.*
>
> *What led to the "altar-cation?"*
>
> *The self-proclaimed Duke of Drake admitted he was still hooked on former girlfriend, Carroll Madison, the "tight-sweater girl" who is taking Hollywood and SGM studios by storm with her new movie* Blondes from Outer Space *as the Atomic Blonde, sure to BLOW up. Word is the blonde's career is now platinum with the sex appeal*

of Harlow and the humor of Lombard—all approved by Solly Myers, himself! Duke and Carroll announced their engagement as his former wife Grace looked on—happily. Happy you say? Yes, because the twice-married heiress is also now engaged to the dashing Barston Maddox, SGM's Vice President, Head of Studio Publicity. Maybe they'll make a musical out of these musical chairs. But suffice to say in LA, multiple wedding bells will be ringing. And love in the air is singing. How Deb-on-air*!*

Chapter Sixty

Mirielle Von Mendelssohn-Montaigne
Paris, Geneva, Vienna
1947

No matter how picture-perfect each day was, Mirielle disregarded the sunlight and actually saw and smelled thunder. She would spend most of her days indoors with the plush drapes pulled and the windows shuttered to block out the harsh light and avoid the imaginary storms. So deep was the pain that there were fragments that would entirely disappear, and then, like a serrated knife, other moments would come stabbing back. Only brief moments of time with Kyla gave her a sense of healing.

The grief and guilt Mirielle felt after Fritz's suicide was so profound, she had immediately broken off her engagement to Michael. He understood and respected her decision but was still devastated at her disturbing emotional state, nonetheless. All she did was weep and lock herself away in her darkened bedroom until Michael collected her and brought her to the studio each day under resignation and silent duress. She had been literally forced by the studio and her director to finish *Immortal* since she only had two major scenes left to do, and the movie was already behind schedule and over budget; the implication being if she ever wanted to work again in Hollywood for a major director or studio, she had to finish the job.

Michael would walk her to and from the set, deposit her, and then pick her up, wrapped in emotional turmoil. Silence was the order of the day, and Michael accepted it without complaint now that she had deemed the relationship platonic. He tried to be stoic and even offered to rehearse lines with her, which she declined.

The last scene of the movie just so happened to be the death of her on-screen Viennese lover, and Mirielle studied her lines in her bath as if in a morbid trance; the two days of shooting were so emotional that real tears flowed as the reality of Fritz's death overpowered the lines of the script. The raw level of despair and loss on the screen for those viewing the dailies prompted talk of an Oscar nomination—not that Mirielle knew or cared.

Given her best friend's deep and unrelenting depression, and Grace's newly-single status, Michael persuaded Grace to temporarily move into Mirielle's Camden Drive estate guest house to keep her company as well as a watchful eye over her and Kyla when she was working. Grace thought it was a smart idea and also convinced her to see a well-known Freudian therapist who she had been working with after her fiasco with Duke. Dr. Ludwig Hauser was a clinical Freudian therapist located in LA and recommended by the émigré community, having fled Vienna, himself. He was also a disciple of Dr. Freud. Grace knew that the issues facing Mirielle were so deep and troubling, she actually feared for her friend's long-term stability. She had found her own sessions with the doctor both helpful and constructive as she had in their earlier days at Breiner's, given her own issues.

With her mental state in disarray, coupled with emotional and physical exhaustion, Mirielle pleaded with Michael and Bartie to speak with Myers to release her from her next film commitment, a Hitchcock thriller opposite Jimmy Stewart, which was to begin shooting only weeks later. Myers reluctantly let her drop out of the film without penalty, the role in *Knife* going to actress Eva Jordaan and rendering Hitch furious and vowing never to work with Mirielle again. Once *Immortal* had wrapped, Bartie crafted another exclusive press story for Hedda, explaining how physically punishing and grueling shooting *Immortal* had been and that Mirielle was taking a well-deserved vacation with her young daughter, which would explain her noted absence.

The therapy sessions she committed to took place twice a week in a small, modest Mexican-style house high in the West Hollywood hills.

Through her intensive work with her doctor, Mirielle started to slowly make progress, which she knew would lead to action. Dr. Hauser, who had also seen the horrors of fascism firsthand, helped Mirielle to understand the deep divide between her public and private personae. He felt those two sides needed to be reconciled, and that, although she was now a glamorous movie star, she was, in fact, like Fritz and himself, a survivor of what was now being termed the Holocaust. She needed to accept that she was not responsible for things out of her control and that they were both *victims* of the Nazis. The therapy also allowed her to accept that her former husband's actions and decisions in the face of the Nazi atrocities, not hers, also helped bring him to a sad and awful end. More than ever, the need to merge her public and private image was now paramount for healing. Mirielle processed this information at first intellectually and then finally, emotionally. Once she accepted the truth, she turned to her best friends for help and advice on the best way to merge her painful past and current status for a better future for her, Kyla, and Michael, whom she still deeply loved.

The plan for this particular, highly-orchestrated fix took place over a month of lunches and dinners at Mirielle's home with Bartie, Grace, and Michael in attendance. The friends all worked together and debated for hours what the right plan was, as they all knew Bartie would have to get Myers's approval before it could be put into action given the impending studio support and financial implications. Of all the fixes he had to deal with over the course of his career, perhaps with the exception of Mavis's and Fritz's deaths and Dumont's demise, Mirielle's emotional transformation would have him going head-to-head with Myers, which put him in a tenuous and uncomfortable position. As everyone knew, Myers was partial to quick fixes—the least complicated and expensive the better—and this was certainly the opposite.

As Mirielle began her healing process, she opened the door a bit for Michael, and there was now a glimmer of hope, finally a path and future for his new family. When the fix was finally mapped out and everyone in agreement, Bartie made an appointment to see Myers as he knew it would be a long and tedious meeting, and he resigned himself to it and imagined the stressful banter and pushback. At first, Myers bristled at the intricate and incredibly expensive proposed studio fix, but in the end, when he saw how unwavering Bartie was, he reluctantly supported the detailed and highly-orchestrated plan, which included an expensive, publicized European concert tour. It was not what Solomon Myers preferred, but he had come to trust Bartie's instincts, and Mirielle was quickly becoming one of SGM's biggest box-office draws and therefore worth the time and investment. Others in the movie industry would face similar, complex challenges that the war had created; even Audrey Hepburn's studio publicist had to deal with the fact that her English father's and Dutch mother's fascist sympathies during the war would have to be covered up, lest it negatively affect their daughter's Hollywood career.

Finally, after much discussion and negotiation, the studio fix was approved and put into motion.

While much of war-torn Europe was still in ruins, within weeks, Bartie gave Hedda Hopper the exclusive in her column and on her radio show that the famous French actress and chanteuse, Mirielle Montaigne, would be returning after the liberation for three European city tour of Paris, Vienna, and Rome. The first stop would be Paris, where she and her best friend, the heiress Grace Greystone and her fiancé, Bartie Maddox, would attend fashion designer Christian Dior's highly-anticipated fashion show. This revolutionary moment would herald in the "new look" tagged by *Harper's Bazaar* editor Carmel Snow, who felt the wasp waist and full skirts offered a lushness and generousness of fabric after wartime rationing highlighted postwar optimism and luxury. The *new look* would also look particularly flattering on Mirielle and Grace, and each ordered many of the best-noted pieces from the collection. The press from the show with the glamorous duo attending created a frenzy for invitations among locals who were in desperate need of entertainment.

Bartie had a booked and promoted a one-night-only, sold-out concert at the acclaimed Olympia in Paris. Posters, press, and ads were created, and a well-known, Parisian-based choreographer and stage designer were engaged to put together a simple yet signature look. The two couples had flown to Europe on the Pan Am Constellation Clipper service and were soon in Paris for rehearsals after a brief stop in London. As their driver drove along the Seine, Mirielle cried tears of sadness and joy. After only a week of staging, grueling choreography, rehearsals, and local press, Mirielle was ready for her opening night. Luckily, she had preferred a cabaret-style approach with a large live orchestra, and it worked perfectly. The opening number had Mirielle singing her signature "J'ai Deux Amours." As the theater was filled to the rafters, the audience broke into spontaneous clapping, whistling, and yelling. This was their moment too.

The director, the famous Rene Goyarde, who had been thrown into a camp by the Nazis for being a homosexual and forced to wear not a yellow star, but a pink triangle in the camps, advised her to delay her entrance and tease the audience. She broke into song at first, offstage, the audience only hearing the arrangement and her unique voice. Then, Rene had a series of spotlights misleading the audience until the dramatic entrance as she stepped into the beam of white light in a French Resistance uniform and jaunty hat. The crowd roared and broke into a spontaneous standing ovation. Next came the French national anthem, "La Marseillaise," which had the audience in tears along with the English version of "Happy Days Are Here Again." It was noted as a triumph in the French press, and the war-weary public viewed Mirielle as Mother France, herself. She took her bow in tears as she held hands with Rene, who decided to wear his infamous Nazi-ordered pink triangle on his tuxedo, to thunderous applause.

Her suite at the Hôtel Plaza Athénée, located on Avenue Montaigne, so overflowed with congratulatory bouquets of flowers that Bartie set up press photos with Mirielle for headlines like "The Avenue Montaigne is Once Again Blooming With Montaigne!." After her Parisian triumph, Mirielle, Grace, Bartie, and Michael would then travel to Bordeaux to privately inspect and start the process of taking back possession of Chateau Von Mendelssohn, which would take years of bureaucratic paperwork and renovation. Upon arrival, they found the grand manor house in great disrepair since the Nazis had stripped the cellars of its historic stock and then let pigs and livestock roam throughout the interior of the mansion. The two couples stayed at a local inn as the house was uninhabitable. Mirielle cried at the overt destruction but was happy that her property was in the process of being returned; they had a child now, and her family legacy was more important than ever.

Before leaving for her next stop in Europe, Grace and Mirielle had paid an important visit to dearest Aunt Marie Bonaparte in her Paris mansion, and the joyous reunion celebrated the triumph over the bleak war years; the princess had successfully helped the Freud family move to London and was now hailed as a bona fide hero after the war. They spent a moving afternoon together, and the hour flew by as minutes.

"Here, my dear." She held Mirielle's hand and kissed it lovingly before Mirielle's departure. "As promised, I have the paperwork you need. I had a good friend in Vienna who, himself, went and got the file." She handed her a large envelope containing her father the baron's official death certificate.

"Now, go to Switzerland and to your inheritance and to hell with those *bâtards*!" She shook her hand in a regal fist, the diamonds sparkling at her wrists.

No one more than Bartie knew the importance of Mirielle's next stop on her tour, and he also knew the value of confusion and surprise, which was a key element to many of the studio fixes he had successfully created. As the head of publicity of SGM studios, he had contacted the heads of the Moritz Bank of Switzerland weeks earlier and had requested a meeting with the eager heads of the bank. He mentioned that his fiancé, the colossally rich heiress Grace Greystone de Faucigny-Drake, would be in Geneva for a family board meeting and requested a time to discuss banking, hinting at opening up an account. She would be bringing with her the SGM's studio's famous international movie star, flame-haired and green-eyed siren Mirielle Montaigne, who was in between concerts in Paris and Vienna. The bank executives who had all profited from the war, of course, were more than surprised and elated at such VIP guests. Upon their arrival at the formidable bank in Geneva, the foursome was greeted by the bank's most senior staff and its President Rudolf Schiad and Vice President Mr. Kristian Bohrman, who looked fit and tan from years of skiing. Bartie had wisely invited members of the press to record the meeting—everything, of course, "on the record."

Upon arrival, much was made; the women's lovely hands were gallantly kissed, speeches were offered with courtly European flourish, and bouquets of flowers procured. It was as if the war had never happened. Everywhere they went throughout Europe, it seemed everyone they met welcomed the Americans as conquering heroes and friends—so happy they had won the war. No one, it seemed, had liked, supported, or mingled with the Nazis or knew of—much less had seen—any atrocities. Yet, now they proclaimed they had all been members of the resistance and made sure to state they risked their lives to save their Jewish friends—as they would be the first to tell you. Geneva and the Moritz Bank of Switzerland would be no different.

"Is there not a person in Europe who saw or stood up for the millions being killed in front of them?" Mirielle shook her head in disbelief after meeting scores of people who claimed to have seen nothing, yet were all now claiming proud membership to the Good Samaritan club.

Once inside the bank's richly appointed headquarters with reporters and photographers in tow, Grace turned over the meeting to Mirielle. They were all entranced by her beauty and glamour, and Mirielle decided on a new, green Dior dress that highlighted her lovely waist and now-famous red tresses, which clearly had thrown them all off. She wore a simple line of good pearls for a ladylike effect.

"It is such a pleasure and an honor to welcome such beauty and talent to our humble offices." Herr Heinz clicked his heels.

"Herr Schiad, I don't believe you remember me," she said slowly, coyly.

"How could anyone forget *you*, Mademoiselle Montaigne?" the bank president said, surveying the beautiful redhead. "We couldn't have met. I am a huge fan and would have remembered it." He shook his head, sensing something was coming.

Mirielle removed her long kid leather glove in a seductive fashion.

"You don't recall our meeting in 1939?" she said sweetly.

He cocked his head. "It's not possible. 1939? There is no way I could not remember you of all people, Mademoiselle Montaigne."

"Yes, I brought the press here as well since I wanted my public to know that my real birth name is not Mirielle Montaigne," she gave a dramatic pause, "but Irene Von Mendelssohn. *Baroness* Irene Von Mendelssohn. If you recall, you all turned me away during the Anschluss, and I fled for my life to America, where I was discovered by this man." She held Michael's hand. "And I became an actress."

They all paled at hearing the story in front of the press's cameras.

"Now, my Aunt Marie," she explained to the press, "I call her Aunt, but she is actually my godmother, Princess Bonaparte—whom you also met, after helping Freud and his family relocate to England—was kind enough to search in Vienna and procure my father's official death certificate, which you said was the one impediment to receiving my funds and access to my safety deposit boxes. I am sure you recall our meeting now." She slid a folder containing the death certificate over to the bank president along with her bankbooks.

"You will see everything is in good Swiss order, including my bankbooks. It seems the Germans and Austrian Nazis were very good at killing Jews, but they were also very good at keeping records. So, I would like immediate access to my accounts and to the deposit boxes that contain my funds and family jewels. Mister Maddox has arranged for an armored car to transfer everything to my new account at Beer und Sohne, you know, one of the few *Jewish-owned* Swiss banks. And I know you will be more than happy to do so since everything is, as I mentioned, completely in order, and you do all so love *rules and order* here in…Geneva." She smiled sweetly.

"Yes, of course, Baroness," they gulped in unison, stupefied with shame.

"And I must say when I heard I was coming to Switzerland and visiting the bank, I was so looking forward to opening up a multi-million-dollar account for the Greystone Railway Line," Grace said, "but when Irene-Mirielle told me of what transpired, I decided that Beer und Sohne is the bank I would also be doing business with as well." Grace flashed her myriad diamond bracelets for effect.

"Yes, of course. We hope that you might change your mind one day. However, Baroness, we will show you to your boxes immediately.

We are so very pleased to see you again and in such good form." Herr Schiad gulped again, opening the bankbook. "I see from the bankbook and accumulated interest, it is such a large amount, it might take us a day or two to arrange for the transfer of funds. However, let us bring you to your safety deposit boxes immediately," he said in a formal tone and frowned, whispering to his associate, Kristian Bohrman.

"That is not acceptable, Herr Schiad. I understand, but I insist on at least half of the money *today*!" Mirielle stood her ground. "Unless, of course, you are the one Swiss bank without any money, which I find hard to believe, but the press would be happy to report that." She batted her eyelashes. "Wouldn't ya, fellas?" she said in an authentic American accent to laughs.

"Yes, of course," he faltered. "I think we would be able to accommodate that request." They looked down sheepishly as a pressman took a photo and tried to avoid the pop of the flashbulb.

"Thank you. Now please lead the way to my safety deposit boxes. I have been missing my mother and grandmother's jewelry, and now that I have a daughter, I know she will want the family heirlooms one day."

"Yes, of course." They looked dead gray and grim-faced as the photographers snapped away.

Within the hour, the safety deposit boxes were all brought out as Mirielle made notations on her father's original list, as they were being emptied of their treasures. The twelve boxes of jewelry and Fabergé and Cartier objects d'art were catalogued and transferred to the Beer boxes. Mirielle oversaw each piece and smiled at certain pieces that brought back tender and loving memories from seeing her grandmother's pearl and diamond earrings, her mother's antique jadeite, onyx, and diamond pendants. However, one deposit box, the thirteenth, seemed to be missing. Herr Schiad urged her to come back the next day due to the waning bank hours.

"I had to wait years, Herr Schiad. I don't mind having you late for your dinner." She raised an eyebrow. "Let's just locate my box please, and we can all leave." There was much discussion and whispering as they tried to locate the missing box.

"I don't understand how a Swiss bank could be missing a safety deposit bank box—do you?" Mirielle asked the two reporters recording the meeting. The remaining box, according to her father's typed records, also contained some of the most important jewels, and Mirielle was concerned it would end up "lost." When they realized the group and the press weren't going anywhere, the bank executives started the "search" themselves. After much hemming and hawing, they procured the box from another safe from the director's personal office and found the missing box as the clock struck 8:00 p.m. It was larger than the rest, and when it was removed with terse looks and opened on the table in the private room, Mirielle smiled at the sight of the priceless jewels: the famed "lace" tiara, which Mirielle tried on for the press, and the multi-strand diamond-and-sapphire choker that Klimt himself had painted in her mother's portrait—now stolen and hanging in the Austrian National Museum with a different title and without attribution. Indeed, the choker would be the one clue in having the famous "national treasure" returned to her after an eventual lengthy legal battle with the Austrian government, who would be loath to give it back and less happy or honest that the painter's subject was a Jewish woman. They would claim they, too, were victims of the invading Nazis, despite the public and many of their head staff welcoming them in as cheering supporters. And then within the box, she found exactly what she was looking for: a stately and opulent diamond-and-emerald Cartier bracelet.

"Grace, this is for you, *ma cherie*." Mirielle smiled with satisfaction.

"Irene, no. I cannot accept that." Grace shook her head vigorously.

"Please, you sold your two bracelets to help me to safety, and I have been waiting for this moment for years. I have only replaced one. It was the last piece my father commissioned for my mother, and I know he would want you to have it." She reached over and unhooked the delicate, hidden safety clasp and placed the shimmering bracelet on Grace's wrist. She slid the platinum tongue into place and snapped the safety catch. It was magnificent, and Grace dabbed her eyes and marveled at the two-inch-wide diamond bracelet with the center fifteen-carat Colombian emerald and repeating geometric baguette pattern.

"Are you sure, Irene?" Grace teared up.

"One hundred percent. Now you have your two emerald-and-diamond bracelets!" Mirielle said happily as she explained the story to the international press.

"It's magnificent, my Irene, and I will treasure it forever, like our friendship." They kissed and hugged.

After the bank transfers and cool apologies from the president of the bank, the foursome had a celebratory lunch of rich and fragrant fondue on the terrace of the Beau Rivage on the lake and toasted the day's events with Champagne before they were driven to the Geneva-Cornavin railway station. Vienna was next on the tour, and Mirielle was both excited yet wracked by nerves.

Vienna, itself, beckoned and felt like returning home to a cheating, abusive spouse. Despite the heartbreak, Mirielle had insisted on booking rooms at the Hotel Imperial since it was widely known that Hitler and Mussolini had stayed there, and her father had been friendly with one of the Jewish owners, Samuel Schallinger, who was forced to sell his interest in 1938 and died in Theresienstadt concentration camp, near Prague. The two couples were given the most impressive suites. The next two days would be comprised of rehearsals for her triumphant return. The city was ablaze with the news that the world-famous movie actress Mirielle Montaigne was staying at the hotel, and hundreds lined the streets for a glimpse of the famous Franco-American star and the impossibly rich American heiress, Grace Greystone, La Marquise de La Faucigny-Drake. The next morning, Mirielle exited through the back entrance, where Mussolini was hustled out to safety in 1943. She darted into waiting cars and was driven to the *palais* where Michael held her as she sobbed for her lost youth and patrimony. She stood in her father's tiered library and was shocked to see it shorn of its books and literary treasures, looking like an ailing, elderly patient only clothed in a paper hospital gown. After walking through the empty and ruined palace, she was now even more determined to make her public appearance in her own way.

The final stage of the fix was now firmly in place, her performance, front and center. Five days later, after grueling rehearsals, she stood in the wings before entering the stage of the relocated Vienna State Opera; she took a deep breath to calm herself.

"I'm so nervous, Michael. Tonight, I have butterflies." Mirielle paced in her shimmering gown, wearing her grandmother's famed old mine diamond "lace" tiara and glittering choker.

"It's very appropriate. Do this for your father and for Fritz." Michael kissed her on the lips as Bartie and Grace cheered her.

"I am the proudest man in Europe right now."

The announcer took to the microphone as the audience hushed, welcoming the well-heeled crowd.

"*Mein dammen und herren*, we are so pleased and honored tonight. I give you the famous international movie star…Mademoiselle…Mirielle Montaigne."

The audience broke into spontaneous applause as she entered stage left. The war and aftermath had left everyone downtrodden and depressed, and they were all so happy to see a bona fide movie star on their soil.

Mirielle walked on a cloud and bowed to the audience and then sang her signature "J'ai Deux Amours." As she stepped into the light, the illumination banished the inner storms.

"I am so happy to be back in my beloved Vienna," she said softly in perfect Viennese German as the audience roared. "Not many people know that I was born here. *Ich bin Wiener*!"

The audience applauded in shock and awe.

"My father was a proud Viennese, nationalistic and cultured. I grew up in the fourth in a palais on the Heugasse. This song is for my father, Baron Friedrich Von Mendelssohn, and my Italian-born mother, Baroness Frieda Margherita Montefiore Mendelssohn."

And as the audience murmured and whispered at the news, the orchestra started, and Mirielle performed Puccini's *Un Bel Di Vedremo* from Madama Butterfly to wild applause.

After three bows and ovations with red roses tossed at Mirielle's feet, a lone light shone on her on the darkened stage.

"Yes, my friends, tonight, you have come to see Mirielle Montaigne, but you are here to see a different person. I am now a proud American, as they took me in during the war. As I said, I was born here, and I want everyone to know, before the war, I was also known as Irene Von Mendelssohn. Henceforth, to honor my name and my Jewish faith, I will be known as Mirielle Von Mendelssohn-Montaigne. This next aria is dedicated to my late husband, the tragic and talented prodigy Fritz Langenheim, who was a victim of Nazi atrocities, forced to lead the death camp orchestra in Auschwitz. I traveled all the way here to sing his bel canto aria, "Mein Engel, Meine Geliebter," from his famous opera, *Die liebesgeschichte Und Die Herzensbrecher*, in his honor," she said to the shocked crowd, many of whom had tears streaming down their faces. Mirielle started slowly and then sang in full force to the stunned audience. As she finished the final anguished and beautiful note, there was a moment of silence before the audience burst into tears and a standing ovation. The conductor, in a black tuxedo, brought out a small object and handed it to Mirielle as he also took a bow. She looked at it intently and held it up, tears flowing.

"This…this is Fritz's baton. It was his only possession from the camp, and it has the numbers of all those killed carved into it." She dabbed her eyes.

"This, and the palais I grew up in, will be donated to the city of Vienna, and henceforth transformed into the Fritz Langenheim School of Classical Music to keep his and the victims' memories alive. *Danke*." She wept during the refrain. And as she exited the stage to thunderous applause and ovation after ovation, she remembered the words of Dr. Hauser and found a unified soul within herself. And Baroness Mirielle Von Mendelssohn-Montaigne, as she would be now known, was reborn and finally happy and set free.

Epilogue

Mr. and Mrs. Barston Maddox
Beverly Hills
1988

It is Tuesday in the City of Angels, and that means breakfast with my best friend, Michael, and a game of doubles tennis afterward with our pros—not a bad way to spend the afternoon. As for the mornings, I always think there's nothing more life-affirming than the smell of percolating black coffee and a western omelet on the griddle, the diced peppers, onions, and mushrooms creating the perfect culinary frisson. As I walk into my favorite destination, The Beverly Hills Hotel Fountain Coffee Room, I nod to a forlorn, retired talk show host noticing his overly-black toupée is slightly askance, wave to my favorite waitress, Diane, and take my usual place at the end of the bar. Michael will be joining me for breakfast, and I save him a seat as I read the paper and scan the news about handsome actor Rob Lowe and a leaked sex tape. I shake my head and think, *If I was his press agent, this would never have seen the light of day*. But that's what you get when things become a free-for-all.

Did I mention we actually live at the Beverly Hills Hotel?

A few years back, when our son, Ben, turned twenty-two, he moved out and to London. Grace and I decided to keep the Malibu beach house and sell the big place on Carolwood Drive. To tell you the truth, although we had many happy years there, I was never one for living in a big mansion with tons of staff, but Grace loved the Italianate palace, and it did have the most enchanting gardens. Once Ben left, and it was just the two of us rattling around, we had dinner at Dan Tana's and, as we usually do, we each came to this conclusion over the Grace Greystone-Maddox chopped salad that we are happiest in hotels. I had loved my time at "The Garden of *Alice*," as Myers had dubbed it, and Grace at the BHH, so we sold the Holmby Hills place to an Arab prince, fully furnished, and moved lock, stock, and barrel into Grace's old bungalow at the Beverly Hills Hotel. Number 5 has a private pool and room service; who could ask for anything more? I play lots of tennis with Michael, and Grace plays cards with old-time stars like Tony Martin and Cyd Charisse at the pool, and the blond Sven who runs the pool area always has our lounge chairs and umbrellas waiting. Mirielle comes over and does her laps in her wide-brimmed hat as Michael and I take in the afternoon sun and reminisce about old times—and we have a lot to reminisce about.

After Myers's retirement, we both left SGM and decided to put out our own shingle. We had a great second chapter running Grace and Duke's production company, Drakestone Productions. What had originally started out as a small shell company that had been part of a PR fix, Drakestone Productions ended up being one of the most respected independent production companies in LA. *The Duchess*, starring Duke and Mirielle and shot in Paris, is considered a '60s classic, and the Oscar-nominated *Shell Game*, starring Duke as a reformed mobster and his wife, Carroll Madison, as his blonde moll, runs on late-night reruns. Then in the late '60s, we wisely ventured into TV production before other movie people did. As you know, *The Carroll Madison Show* was the breakthrough TV talk show/variety format with Carroll's humor and sex appeal setting the tone. Her comedic skits with Reiner and Berle are now considered classic TV comedy. As he aged, Duke mellowed and became a talented producer, himself, optioning novels and Broadway shows for the screen.

We always worked well together, Michael and I, and he was head of production, and I was head of marketing, and it was a joyous golden period for our families. In fact, there was a brief moment where Ben dated Kyla, but as much as we would have been happy in-laws, that would have been too much to ask. Kyla more resembles her father, but she has her mother's remarkable eyes. She eschewed Hollywood despite having the looks and is quite a formidable young woman. She became a trial lawyer, moved to Vienna for a few years, and has specialized in Holocaust reparations with Swiss banks and the return of stolen Jewish art.

I wish I could say we had an easier time with Ben, but during the Woodstock era, he had problems with drugs and alcohol. I am proud he has cleaned up his act and entered the McClean shipping business as the third generation. Grace and I are delighted, although we get to see him less now that he is living in London.

I am also the proud godfather of Duke and Carroll's boy, Duke Jr. While he didn't inherit his father's looks, he does have his mother's wonderful platinum-blonde coloring. The thing is, people whisper, he bears a striking resemblance to a young—shall I write this—Solomon Myers: all wiry, nervous energy with strong beak-like nose and stormy eyes. He is already an up-and-coming agent and just started his own talent agency and is taking the town by storm. As I like to say, it doesn't matter where one starts off, but where one finishes!

After selling the SGM studios to a conglomerate once Freyda died, Sol Myers retired to Palm Springs and spent his remaining years entertaining in style with his new wife; yes, you may have put two and two together...Carroll Madison, after her divorce from Duke. He regularly plays golf and attends the yearly Carroll Madison Championship and enjoys *kibitzing* with the Hillcrest set and raising Duke Jr. In a wonderful turn of events, Gorge Lamont was called in to decorate their glass Neutra house as Carroll had always been a fan of his work. Gorge did a wonderful job and was more than happy to exact revenge with his 30 percent commission and lived out his remaining years as a Hollywood decorator. Until he died a few years back of lung cancer, he and Duke would continue to have dinner five nights a week, holding hands at a remote corner table at the Bel Air Hotel, where they also kept a bungalow. They could be free now, and Duke saw no reason to separate from his growing family.

As for me, one day, I had a group of friends over to our Beverly Hills Hotel cabana at the pool, and I was regaling them with stories from the SGM days and some of my favorite studio fixes under the pink-and-white striped awnings. They all seemed a bit spellbound and wanted to know more. "He should write a book. Shouldn't he?" Grace said out loud to our guests, who all seemed more excited by the prospect than I thought possible.

"Bartie. If you don't, it will all disappear with you, and that would be a shame," one of the great musical stars told me as she ate her tuna salad, crossing her glamorous gams. I briefly gave it some thought, and that was that—or so I thought. One afternoon, I was sitting by the pool, and I was paged over the notorious intercom system. "Mister Barston Maddox, phone call." I picked up the phone, and lo and behold, it was Laura Yorke, the famed literary agent.

"Hey, Bartie. I hear from a few sources you may be writing a book on the publicity department of SGM. I would be interested," she stated.

"Who told you that?"

"A little birdie."

"Okay, Hedda! I know Grace must have spoken to you about it."

"It was Mirielle," she said. "I'm representing her autobiography, and you're in it."

"She's biased," I said.

"Maybe, but I know a bestseller when I see one. Game?"

"Do you think a book like that would sell?" I asked.

"More than you know, and the timing is right. Do you have a working title?"

I decided to go with it and throw all caution to the wind. I was always best on my feet in the moment, and I did have a working title.

"*The Fix*, or... *The Hollywood Fix*," I mumbled.

"I like *The Hollywood Fix*," she said. "Let's have lunch and talk about it."

"Sure, Laura, if you say so," I replied.

When I brought up the idea, Grace clapped her hands in delight. Then, I lowered the boom.

"Only if I can talk about you, Grace?" I teased her. "Are *you* willing to let people know about you and Duke and your first marriage to the Marquis?"

"Of course, darling." She blew smoke rings. "It's not that scandalous anymore, and Zsa Zsa certainly now has a few more marriages on me!" Grace laughed. I was taken aback at her liberal attitude.

So, after getting permission from all the people who matter to me, I decided to move forward with this memoir. I took out my trusty yellow pad and started writing about a time that doesn't exist anymore, and the mere sight of the yellow-lined pad brought back fond memories of the now legendary F. Scott in the bungalow, and that gave me true inspiration.

Reminiscing can produce a variety of emotions. Some of it has been difficult, and some memories are joyous. It was truly a different time; some pages of the Hollywood star system are greatly missed; some things are better put to rest. Perhaps the biggest vacancy is something Grace told me, and she would know. She said, "In Europe, there is a tradition of royalty, and the pomp and circumstance. The Queen, as an example, gives us all something to believe in. It makes things right with the world for the average guy and gal in the pub. The US doesn't have royalty—it's not part of our system, but the stars…well, the stars became our version of royalty, the gowns and the glamour, the romances and the intrigue, the idea of perfection. It gave everyone something to shoot for, to believe in, and to aspire to when the going was tough. There was, after all, something to be said for a white-tie dinner and dancing at Ciro's and Mocambo." I know, I was there, and Grace is right. And the best part, unlike in Europe, is you didn't have to be *born* to the purple. You could be a farm girl or a cockney or a count—it didn't matter. If you were born to be a star, we could make you shine. And we could also fix the broken and the beautiful. And best of all, if it was a good enough fix, everyone would buy it.

My mother once told me that "happiness is fleeting, but if you find something that makes you happy, even if for a moment, grab it." And then, right before my mother died, she held my hand and whispered, "Maybe one day you'll find something or someone, and if you do, even if it's for a short period of time, well…you'll be a lucky guy." Amazing, right? And all from a woman who never found the happiness she deserved, living through the Great Depression as a single mom, her husband having ditched her with a young kid to raise. I only wish she saw the life I have lived and who I lived it with. I am sure she would have gotten a huge kick out of it and, in some way, I am sure she is looking down and does know.

Grace also spent her life looking for love and never finding it, and yours truly, well, I was the opposite. I spent my life running from love until I found it. What I never anticipated was that there would be one studio fix that would end up fixing both Grace and me. Maybe that has to count as my greatest *fix* of all. Not to mention this book. I hope people enjoy the ride; I know I did. And that, my friends, as my old friend Hedda would say, is the *real scoop.*

Barston Maddox
The Beverly Hills Hotel
1988

THE END

Acknowledgments

All my thanks to the smartest and most beautiful muse, Dana. You are my greatest star.

To my children; Georgia, Talia, and Lucas, thank you for inspiring and teaching me every day. Keep shining! Thank you to my sister Susan and my brother-in-law- Rob Perry. I love you both! Susan, keep *bossin'*! To my father-in-law Fred Geier and Marcia Geier, thank you for Dana! And the Joachims! Love you all! Family first! To the late Paulette Kirschenbaum and Cookie Geier, I miss you both dearly.

Laura Yorke, my great friend and editor, I can't thank you enough for paving the way for this literary journey. To my brother Jordan Schur, you always have my back. And to his new bride Kelly Fancher, welcome to the family! Thank you to the legendary Jim Wiatt for your amazing quote, I am honored. Great thanks to the fabulously talented Chris Cereda for the wow cover design and Roman Nevinchanyi for the amazing photo! Adriana Trigiani you continue to be my angel, dear friend and inspiration. Thank you for your quote and support and you, Tim and Lucia are the very best.

Thank you to the amazing Publisher Anthony Ziccardi, Debra Englander and Caitlin Burdette at Post Hill Press. There is no better team. Thank you to Simon and Schuster!

Thank you to Wendy Finerman and Billy Gerber for your ongoing Oscar advice and Eric Rayman, my entertainment attorney.

This novel was started at my favorite cabana at the Beverly Hills Hotel. Sitting poolside and writing is my slice of heaven especially when palm trees are involved.

I have the fondest memories of staying at the BHH hotel when I was young and hearing celebs being paged by the pool, long before cell phones. Was it only yesterday, blonde Sven was welcoming guests and the long legged star Cyd Charisse and Tony Martin and their gang were playing cards by the deep end? It all gave me great fodder and is imprinted in my mind and in this book. Not to mention writing in the Polo Lounge over a chocolate Souffle. To my famiglia; Patty and Danny Stegman, Jay and Amy Kos, Susan Krakower, the Fab Four, Susie and Kevin Davis, Jamie Mitchell, Lois Robbins and Andrew Zaro, Ali and Jason Rosenfeld, Mark E. Pollack, Marc Glimcher and Fairfax Dorn, Chip and Susie Fisher, Muffie Potter Aston and Sherrell Aston, Sharon and Anton Katz, Michelle and Howard Swarzman, Meg Blakey and Glen Pagan, Alexis and Erik Ekstein, Lauran and Charlie Walk, Mark and Karen Hauser, David Mitchell, Stacey and Jimmy Garson, Sarah Foley, Tim and Saffron Case, Harlan Peltz, Helene and Ziel Feldman, Robert and Serena Perlman, Bruce and Maura Brickman, Rosanna Scotto and Louis Ruggerio, Carolyn and Marc Rowan, Katerina and Gunter Frangenberg, Judy and Jerry Della Femina, Ayse and Michael Weinberg, Sachin and Babi Ahluwalia, Scott and Sharon Greenstein, Ilene and Steven Sands, Jennifer Miller and Mark Ehret, Jordan and Debra Teramo, Andrea de Nunzio, Julie Collins, Sheila and David Wiener, Lew and Bobbi Frankfurt, Rabbi Adam and Sharon Mintz, Pam and David Berkman, Lauren and Craig Nossel, Iris and Mark Erenstein, Michael McDonough, David Lauren and Lauren Bush and Zibby Owens. I cannot thank you all enough for being with me through thick and thin.

Thank you to the late, great trailblazer and Miss America, Phyllis George for hiring me and inspiring me when I was right out of the gate. Our shoot for ABC's 20/20 in LA and at the Beverly Hills Hotel was one of my most memorable visits with the talented Marisa Acocella. And also to Michael Ostin and the late Joyce Ostin, we miss you when visiting LA! Joyce, you always brought the fun and the glamor. Thank you to legendary Chris Blackwell and Meg Friedman. One love! Thank you to all my wonderful friends at the Princess Grace Foundation, dedicated to the arts and up and coming talent. To my dear late friend Morgan Spurlock, your sense of humor still makes me laugh. Miss you.

A special toast to my friends and co-founders and board of Amante 1530; Barry and Lizanne Rosenstein, Ana Rosenstein, Len and Fern Tessler, Stuart Ellman, Joe Resha and Sting and Trudie Styler.

Special thanks to the dynamo Nikki and Stephen Field at Sotheby's.

Thank you to Mary Garcia for all you do!

The Hollywood Fix was researched over five years and written at some of my favorite watering holes; the Hotel de Russie in Rome, The Stravinskij Bar, Goldeneye in Jamaica, The Monte -Carlo Beach Cub, the Hotel de Paris, the Perry Lane Hotel in Savannah, The St. Regis in Aspen, The Balmoral Hotel in Edinburgh, Ashford Castle, and the Tivoli Avenida Hotel pool in Lisbon. Thank you to all my favorite restaurants and bars and all the bartenders serving Amante 1530 and Blackwell Rum! I've written chapters at Nobu 57, Planta Queen, Tri-Dim, Wa Jeal, Nicola's, The Whitby, Cipriani on West Broadway, Casa Cipriani, Sen in Sag Harbor and Dan Tana's in West Hollywood. Let's not forget the corner table at Snack taverna, the Manhattan's Grisley Pear or the terrace at The Rams Head Inn on Shelter Island and Call Me Gabby in Miami! In Capri; The Grand Hotel Quisisana, La Fontelina Beach Club and Villa Verde always inspire a good paragraph!!

No matter how many changes I see and experience, I still believe in great stories, stars and page turners. I salute all the pioneers in Hollywood who came before.

About the Author

Richard Kirshenbaum is the author of three #1 Amazon Bestsellers: *Isn't that Rich*, *Rouge*, and *North Bay Road*. An accomplished entrepreneur and author, he has been inducted into the Advertising Hall of Fame and has written comedy for the legendary Joan Rivers and *Us Weekly's* Fashion Police. After selling his eponymous agency Kirshenbaum Bond & Partners, he became the CEO of SWAT by Kirshenbaum, a boutique branding and marketing firm. Kirshenbaum has appeared on ABC's 20/20, the cover of *WIRED* magazine, and *The New York Times* Business section and has also been profiled in *The Wall Street Journal*. Voted one of the "25 Most Stylish New Yorkers!" by *Us Weekly*, he resides in Manhattan with his wife Dana, a former Hollywood publicist and real estate agent, and their three children.